Paris Nocturne

by

Flo Fitzpatrick

Cover Art by *Lisa Dawn MacDonald*

The Wild Rose Press, Inc.
PO Box 708
Adams Basin, NY 14410-0708
Visit us at www.thewildrosepress.com

Publishing History
First Edition, 2025
Trade Paperback ISBN 978-1-5092-6056-0
Digital ISBN 978-1-5092-6057-7

Published in the United States of America

Dedication

To Chuck King, a kind man, a smart man, a superb musician, and a cherished friend: Thank you for letting me bring "Charles Sovereign" to life in these pages!

Chapter 1

Early February 1941, Occupied Paris, France

The sofa was a relic from an era long past, featuring sags, lumps, torn fabric, and a determined metal spring poking out near the left armrest. Given that I was trespassing I wasn't about to complain. The nameplate on the door indicated the room belonged to a Monsieur Jacques Benet. After an extensive search of the entire nightclub, I'd discovered this space was one of three private areas backstage offering more than a rickety chair placed in front of a cracked mirror. Two blessings—the cushions were clean and the sofa long enough to withstand the body of a woman measuring five feet ten inches. It wasn't a silken-sheet-covered bed at a luxury hotel, but I was warm and dry, and hopefully, with a few hours' sleep, I might remember how I got here. Better still…who I was. Not to mention discovering why and how the odd vision of a theater collapsing, followed by a television announcement of a murder, had come knocking into my brain. And who the heck was Ajay Roy?

I shrugged it off as a weird hallucination due to lack of sleep. I needed to rest. I was in the process of mashing down one of the mounds in the center of the sofa when I heard shouts, followed by the sound of chairs crashing. I extinguished the table lamp and opened the door a crack.

The hallway was empty. It appeared I was safe from discovery and questions…at least momentarily.

I slipped out of the room. I should note I was dressed in black trousers, black pullover sweater, and soft ballet slippers, a combination that fortuitously might provide some cover for stealth and action. The angry voices yelling in German convinced me that stealth and action were definitely the order of the day or, more accurately, the night.

They were on the stage now. I could hear the stomping of heavy boots on a wooden floor. From my new position at the bottom of the stairs leading to the stage left wings, I was able to follow strong beams of light swaying from individual torches.

I sensed movement behind me and turned.

A blond man—wearing blue-gray trousers, a short jacket the same color, and a cap with odd-looking badges decorating the front—stood next to a dark-haired man dressed in black trousers and pullover sweater similar to my own outfit. Hatless. Both men appeared to be in their early twenties. They were partially hidden behind an old upright piano in the far corner backstage, only a few feet from where I was standing.

I recognized the man in the black ensemble. About ninety minutes earlier, with not a soul in sight, I'd explored every inch of Café Violette and spotted his photo displayed in the lobby with his name written in easily read letters: *Noel Matheson*. I'd stared at the photo for at least ten minutes, not only because I was drawn to his features but because the name seemed familiar. I hadn't been able to remember why, but I knew it was important. The two men were now looking my direction, their facial expressions conveying both surprise and fear.

It was time to take a chance.

I pointed toward the stage. "They're coming fast," I whispered. "Your best bet is the catwalk."

Matheson whispered. "Who are you?"

If I said, "No idea," he'd think I was a lunatic. I was sure I wasn't, even if my memory currently didn't include my own name. But I sensed folks on the stage were in hunting mode and in no mood for a fun evening's entertainment, so fast action was needed. Based on my earlier, albeit brief, solo tour of this old theater, which had included gazing at photos on walls and checking a calendar I'd found in an open office, I'd determined I was in Paris in 1941 in a city currently under German Occupation, which meant the guys clomping around above us on the stage weren't friendly.

There wasn't time to waste on explanations I couldn't provide.

"Um…look, these guys will be backstage very soon, which is why I suggest the catwalk. There's an exit leading to the roof." I paused, hearing the echo of a male voice inside my head, saying, *Always get the lay of the land when you enter a new building. Escape routes are vital.* I shook it off. Something to ponder later, along with figuring out who I was and what I was doing in the middle of what appeared to be the flight to freedom of a British pilot.

Indecision emanated from the corner. I could feel it. I added, "Hey, I realize this is wacky and you have no reason to trust me, but if they find you, I'm sure life is going to become very unpleasant. If we can find a way to divert their attention for a few minutes, you should be able to get out of the building. I'm kind of assuming you have some help waiting somewhere…"

Matheson hesitated. Well, why shouldn't he? As I'd stated, he had absolutely no reason to trust a strange woman popping up in the middle of some kind of raid. A woman who was brazen enough to suggest a way out he either wasn't aware of or hadn't considered.

But the hesitation was brief, five seconds at most. In English, with a pronounced French accent, he asked, "Mademoiselle, can *you* guide him across the catwalk and outside? There will be a gentleman across the street at the bookstore, dressed in a brown suit and brown fedora, holding a copy of William Faulkner's *The Sound and the Fury*. The password is any sentence with use of the phrase 'Bard of Avon.' You can trust this man."

"What about you? If you stay here, they're liable to find you any minute now. Wouldn't it be better for *me* to try and stall them? I might seem less threatening. At least I'd be something unexpected. You could steer him toward this bookstore. Where, I guess, your, uh, friend knows you?"

"He does, but if you stay, I fear you would be in grave danger. I will be taking the offensive here. I shall go out and meet these Germans. I have a perfect right to be in the club at this hour in the morning. It is where I work and where often I stay to sleep, especially over the last months." He turned to the younger man. "Flight Officer Sam Seymour, meet…this lady. She will take of you." His next word sounded like a combination of prayer and anxiety. "*Oui?*"

I replied, "*Oui.*"

Seymour flashed a cheery smile and, in a broad English accent, stated, "Off we go, then, miss."

I motioned for him to follow me to the spiral staircase a few feet from the piano. Noel Matheson hurried onto the stage as Sam and I hit the middle tier. A second later, I heard Matheson shout, in decent German, "*Was ist hier los?* Why are you here at bloody three in the morning! What in hell do you want?"

****

Sam Seymour and I paused for a moment at the top of the staircase, listening to a mass of voices below blending into a discordant noise. We were surrounded by muddy darkness. The hunters hadn't found the switch which provided a dim light in this part of what must once have been an old opera house before a conversion turned it into a nightclub/cabaret. The lights from the stage provided a small source of illumination but hopefully would not be strong enough to reveal our location, unless some enterprising thug decided to aim his torch upward.

I was about to take a step onto the catwalk when Seymour buckled over, nearly falling down the stairs.

"Are you okay?"

"Just a bit woozy, miss. My balance should be better on the ground, but I can't seem to find my 'sea legs' as it were."

"When did you last eat?"

He tried to smile. "Can't recall."

"Okay. Stay here for a minute. I'll see if anyone's left anything in the lighting booth.'

"But…"

"No buts, Flight Officer. Can't have you tumbling onto a stage full of killers. And I doubt the food where they'd take you would be up to RAF standards. Look, I'll be quick. Stay *exactly* where you are and keep your head down. This is a blind spot for anyone looking up, which helps."

The entrance to the catwalk was also the entrance to

a much narrower walkway leading to the lighting booth about six feet away to the right. *Ridiculous! Sticking a sixteen-inch-wide piece of wood at a height of thirty feet above the stage floor and calling it a passage for grown men to navigate in the dark.*

My balance, in dark or light, is excellent and I made it into the booth without incident, apart from a brief, weird flash of recall. I'd made this kind of trip from catwalk to light booth very recently…just not here. Not in this space. Not even in this country. I remembered the image and hearing myself say, "Chanson Theatre."

I was wasting time probing inside a faint, short, confusing memory. I scrambled around in the dark and quickly found a reason to thank whoever ran the lights at Café Violette. A bag of croissants, still moderately fresh, and several large hunks of wrapped cheese had been abandoned at the end of the show. Any hungry mice must have been sleeping or partying elsewhere around Paris, because they hadn't yet discovered the feast. I grabbed everything and made my way back to Sam.

"Take a couple of bites now before we cross the catwalk. You need as much balance as you can manage," I told him. "Then, we'd best make tracks while the Nazis are still talking and not searching."

"Or shooting."

"Yeah, that too." I thrust away thoughts of a bleeding Noel Matheson sprawled on the stage and motioned Sam to go ahead.

"Miss, shouldn't I be the one to follow? I don't feel very gallant leaving you behind."

"No. Don't worry about chivalry. If you *do* lose your balance I'll be right there to catch you. Plus, if they see me, I'll be in less danger than you. I doubt the Nazis are looking for women tonight. Shush, now. Sound travels."

Our progress halted when we'd reached the middle of the walk and I heard Noel call out in English, "Major Bauer! Are you insane? You are thinking someone to be hiding at the top of the theater? You have quite the imagination. You are to be guessing you will find some British pilot swinging from a rope and preparing to land, like a pirate in a swashbuckling film from America?"

"Sam, get down!"

Sam didn't need to be told twice. We flung ourselves onto the catwalk and flattened our bodies as much as was possible in order to escape the strong beam of light careening from left to right, then back again.

A voice rang out. I'd bet the bag of croissants it was this Bauer person. He spoke excellent English. "This is absurd. We can determine nothing by waving torches into the air. Herr Matheson, how does one attain access to the bridge and whatever dark crevices exist above in this old theater?"

Jeez! The man was spitting out correct grammar at a quarter past three in the morning while conducting a search for a downed pilot of His Majesty's Royal Air Force.

"Sam, hurry."

The flight officer didn't need to be told twice. We reached the other side of the catwalk in record time.

"Follow me." I waved at him.

I ran across the platform leading from the bridge to a large sliding panel. I opened the panel and unveiled a ladder which had probably been installed in the late 1800s.

If this young pilot wondered why some strange young lady knew how to find an exit leading to the roof, he didn't ask. I was his best means to safety.

We made it up the ladder, over the roof, down an outside fire exit, and across the street in about two minutes. It was ironic. Sam was to meet the person guiding him to the next contact at the same bookstore where I'd taken shelter no more than an hour earlier, after I'd toured Café Violette and decided I needed air. The shelter had consisted of staring at the doorway of the nightclub while I attempted to access something in my brain that would trigger a solid memory.

An older man, perhaps in his sixties, dressed in brown, with a wide-brimmed brown fedora atop his head, stood by the door of the bookstore, smoking a cigarette. A copy of Faulkner's *The Sound and the Fury* was tucked under his arm but visible in the light. Quite bold, really, but I supposed, if questioned, he could explain he'd stepped out of the rain for a smoke. Mine was not to reason. Mine was to hand Sam over to him and pray they'd make it to the next stop without incident.

We checked both ends of the street before joining him. The action was all still at Café Violette. Dumb, in my opinion, but I wasn't going to go out of my way to tell Herr Bauer or his buddies their plan to capture this pilot was just lousy stupid. Plus, I had a very weird feeling Bauer didn't really care about tonight's outcome. Something to revisit later.

"Do you speak French?" I asked Sam.

He tried to smile. "Not really. I can ask where to find the W.C. and say 'thank you.' I definitely don't have the skills to come up with a smart Shakespearean reference. We thought…*I* thought…Noel would be handling this part of the escape." He sounded truly scared for the first time since I'd seen him by the piano, backstage.

The contact hadn't said a word. He must be making sure we could be trusted before he found himself in a hole at the 18th Arrondissement waiting for the gendarmes to turn him over to some black-booted officer attached to the Schutzstaffel or Gestapo. I applauded his caution.

"No problem." I winked at Sam and held my hand out to the man in brown, saying, in somewhat fractured French, "*Bon nuit, Monsieur. Intéressant!* I see you have a copy of *The Sound and the Fury*. I love that book. Of course, the title is lifted from one of the Bard of Avon's best works…the tragedy of *Macbeth*."

The older man smiled and responded in French. "Ah, *oui. Merci, Mademoiselle*. An excellent play with its themes of the dominance of power over individuals who were once noble. Sadly, too apropos for our own times." He nodded at Sam and then greeted him in heavily accented English. "We go now, *oui*? Before one of Bauer's soldiers decides to exit the theater and finds a merry little group out in the rain in the middle of the night looking for some culture."

They began to walk away from the bookstore. Sam turned, hurried over to me and hugged me. "Thank you. But what about you? Are you all right to get home?"

I had no idea where home was, so I answered truthfully, "I'm not going home. I'm heading back into Café Violette. I'd say more improvisation is needed to keep our friend safe. And it might also serve as a bit more distraction for your departure."

"You are very brave."

I smiled. "Far less than either of you. And right now? I'm angry. There's no valid reason those Nazis just happen to have arrived at Café Violette at this hour. I'd wager someone in the circle of French conspirators is either an idiot and has a big mouth, or there's an informer. A traitor. Lowest of the low."

Another image, clearer than the one I'd experienced in the light booth, clicked inside my head. I could see myself standing outside a ruined dwelling, crying, as a woman about my age silently mouthed, *"Ajay was betrayed."*

I waved them on. "Take care and be safe."

Chapter 2

I waited in front of the bookstore until Sam and his contact made it to the end of the avenue before crossing the street and returning to the nightclub. We appeared to be the only people taking in the very early morning air. The Nazis hadn't yet called it quits inside Café Violette. I still wasn't sure what flaky story I could come up with to get the focus on me and off both Noel Matheson and any activities that might include a member of Britain's' Royal Air Force once I sauntered back into the café.

Café Violette. The name had popped into my head the instant I awakened from some kind of trance a couple of hours ago and found myself backstage in an old theater. After taking a brief tour, I'd staggered outside to this very bookshop, hoping the fresh air would clear the fog from my mind. From my spot across the street I'd noticed a sign for the club hanging over the entrance door. Seeing it triggered a strange memory. I could see myself reading the liner notes on the back cover of a vinyl recording made at this same club. My name might be a blank, but more than one fact about this club had stuck in my head.

To begin with, Café Violette was one of the nightspots that had been allowed to remain open during the Occupation. "Why" was a mystery. Located in the section of Paris known as Montmartre, the nightclub was frequented by high-ranking officials of the Third Reich, out for a night's entertainment of cabaret and dining, officers with more discerning tastes than the common soldiers who enjoyed watching barely-clad chorines sashaying across tiny, flimsy stages in seedier parts of the city.

Upon first seeing the name of the club, my imagination had supplied a vision of well-fed German men and desperate French women pressing against one another, swaying to the sounds of jazz and blues. I could almost smell the scent of expensive French perfume mingling with cigarettes and strong brandy and hear the musicians and singers who held their views in check in order to pay next month's rent and put whatever food was available on the table.

I also remembered listening to a recording and feeling an intense need to be at Café Violette. I'd been trying for the last couple of hours to regain some sense of where I'd been before, but it seemed I was doomed to grasp at small sparks coming from any direction, while hoping I'd be engulfed in an inferno of answers. Admittedly, I might be phrasing this hope with more than a hint of melodrama, but waking up in a country I instinctively knew wasn't mine and realizing it was occupied by a truly scary military force should give me the right to be emotionally over the top.

I waited until I couldn't see Sam and his friend in the brown suit anywhere in sight, which gave me time to think. Some force outside myself kept insisting I get back inside the cabaret. The same male voice that had teased me with phrases about knowing escape routes now kept piercing through the fog I called my mind, asking, *Are your Cassandra warnings screaming? You need to listen.*

What I needed was less focus on who was in my brain talking nonsense and invent an excuse for bursting into the club in the middle of the night. What was happening inside Café Violette must be clear to anyone passing by that something other than an after-hours party was afoot; signaled by the four vehicles—small trucks of some kind—parked in front of the nightclub. My explanation had to be both plausible yet slightly foolish, while additionally coming across as charming. Somehow the truth about my arrival, "Hell if I know!" wasn't going to work.

I considered entering the same way I'd just exited, via the roof, making my way to the first dressing room I found, and then stumbling out, but too much time had elapsed since the Nazis had entered for me to attempt to convince them I was there for a tryst with Mr. Matheson. Plus, the Germans didn't need to learn about any possible escape routes, so best not to risk being seen anywhere above the stage level.

What the heck. I'd been improvising for hours—or, for all I knew, days—so I might as well brazen it out a few minutes longer.

I flung open the front doors to the club and shouted, "Noel! Noel! Are you there? Is everything okay? Has there been an accident or something? Why are all the lights on and all the trucks outside everywhere?"

Matheson was standing by the stage next to a tall, broad-shouldered, impossibly handsome blond man wearing the sleek black uniform of whatever branch of German military was in charge of hunting down members of the British Royal Air Force. For a long second I considered turning around and going back outside to see if I could catch up to Sam and his French

13

rescuer and head on back to Merrie Olde England with young Mister Seymour. A meaningless phrase, *Just like the Delegates back home,* pounded in my head.

I forced myself to move forward. The big blond Nazi must be the one I'd heard earlier yelling at everyone. Herr Officer Who-the-Hell-Knew-What-Rank Bauer. Very much in command.

I ran toward Noel and Bauer, stumbling over fallen chairs and tables and executing a spectacularly clumsy fall, only to land a few feet from the stage. I stared up at the two men with an assumed expression of embarrassment, and added a wince and an "Ouch!" for emphasis.

Noel Matheson. I'd now seen him twice in person. Once, around two-thirty a.m. when I'd been hiding in the shrubs by the bookstore and watched him as he stepped outside Café Violette to light up a cigarette and pace for a few minutes while he smoked. Then, when we'd made fast plans for Sam Seymour's escape backstage. At three a.m., we'd been in nearly complete darkness. Seeing him now, with strong lighting surrounding him, my fancy took flight.

He's the rebel archangel preparing to do battle and clear the gates of heaven for any sinners he deems worthy of entrance. I wonder if I'll pass?

Noel took my hand in his and helped me to my feet. Those heavenly gates opened. The rest of the world faded, turned mute and opaque, leaving us in a pocket of stillness in time and space where only the two of us connected. Completing each other. Twin souls. Oddly, my own thoughts echoed within me. I'd had them before…sometime.

"Are you okay? Any damage?" He'd seen me earlier

moving like a cat. He must be aware the stumble was meant not only to divert attention but to make the Nazis see me as a less than competent human. A clumsy, very silly girl.

He released his grip and stared into my eyes. "I was very worried about you."

"Thanks. I was too."

We couldn't seem to break the gaze. Didn't want to. We had to. The German was watching.

A cough interrupted the moment.

"Excuse me, but what is going on here?" came from Major Bauer.

I smiled up at him. He stared at me, with a combination of suspicion...and...whoa! Did I sense lust? If so, could I use it to sell my *raison d'être* for arriving at the theater almost two hours after closing?

He barked, "Who are you and what are you doing here?"

No to the lust, then. Merde.

I needed to improvise this scene into a routine worthy of Ajay's favorite tap dancers from the twentieth century. And where that thought came from was another mystery, but one I intended to store away for future use in regaining my memory, starting again with the question of who was Ajay.

I gazed into the blue eyes of the officer and tried to create a nice impression of a girl too daffy to be any kind of threat.

"I'm okay, everybody. Really. No bones broken. And I apologize for barging in and shouting. I was just so happy to be out of the rain. I also must apologize in advance if I suddenly burst into tears, but honestly, things have really not gone well this whole night."

"You have not answered my question, Fräulein. Why are you here?"

"Oh! I didn't say? Well, really, it's such a mess! I was on my way home, but my bicycle went flat and I took a tumble, and then I realized I'd left my bag somewhere at the theater and I figured Noel might still be here, so I decided to just walk back and get my stuff and he could find a way to get me home." I flashed my best disarming and charming smile.

"Where are your papers?"

Papers? What was he talking about? "Well, that's like another whole story. I had them, of course. But I lost them. I'm sure it was somewhere near the theater. Earlier tonight. Last night, I guess it is now. I wasn't really sure where I needed to go for replacements when things open up in the morning." I sighed. "Hasn't been my best week."

I swallowed. This could get tricky. I did have papers. Sheet music. They were in the bag I'd left in Jacques Benet's dressing room about thirty minutes ago when I'd ventured out to greet Noel and Sam. I'd been honest about leaving my bag. I hadn't had a chance to glance at the titles, and it occurred to me now, with the way strange scenes were zipping in and out of my head in bits and pieces, perhaps one of the songs might provide another clue to my identity. But I sure didn't want Bauer to be anywhere nearby when I sorted through them.

After a very long and awkward silence, Bauer turned to Noel. His tone was slightly less threatening, but his words were still pointed. "I did not notice the Fräulein earlier this evening, yet I had a very clear view of the audience. And the Fräulein is very worthy of notice."

Double merde.

Noel's response was quick. "For a reason, Major. She was not in the audience. She was backstage being fitted for a costume. We did not have the time tonight, but she has been slated to perform a number or two at the club. We are hoping for tomorrow, which I suppose is now tonight as it is in actuality early morning."

Nice footwork, Monsieur Matheson.

Bauer began staring at me again, but this time there was something extra. It seemed there was a question he wanted answered that had nothing to do with my bag.

"You seem familiar, Fräulein. Have I seen you perform before?"

Not likely, Mr. Big Nazi Man, but until I know who I am I can't answer.

I smiled. "I'm not sure. Sorry."

He shrugged. "I will try to recall the occasion. But, for now, exactly what kind of 'number' as you call it, is she to perform, Herr Matheson?"

Not to be repetitive, but triple merde. Matheson had no idea if I sang, danced, played the cello, swallowed swords, or trained small dogs to do flips in the air. Come to think of it, neither did I.

Before Noel could respond, some instinct— survival?—set me to belting out the last sixteen bars of the Act One finale from the Broadway musical *Wicked*. Perfect notes and lyrics flowed out of a place in my head, borne by desperation.

The German officer and Noel both looked at me as though I'd turned green and started flying. I couldn't blame them. I didn't remember my name, but I knew that particular musical would not be produced on Broadway until the first decade of the twenty-first century, and I was somewhere in the middle of the twentieth.

Noel recovered first and casually tossed out, "Major Bauer, you should be pleased we have brought in our lovely new addition. The club has been sorely lacking in female singers after Mademoiselle Genevieve is leaving four weeks ago to live with her widowed mother in Provence."

Bauer ignored him. "You have an incredible voice, Fräulein. There must be far better venues for your talent. Why would you waste it on Café Violette?"

More improvisation. "Well, I'm not classically trained, so opera houses are not an option. Broadway musical theater and jazz are more my style, and both are uniquely American, yet here I am in France! And one must eat, and have a place to sleep and one must earn a living."

All three statements were true, if staggeringly incomplete. I was aware I was from America and had traveled to France very recently. *Like last night?* But I sensed my journey had been a very bizarre one. I prayed I could figure out the where and the how and the why of that journey before I got locked up somewhere only crazy people get to go.

Bauer produced a half-smile. "And precisely how will Gaspard Bassett, the master of ceremonies for this establishment, introduce the Fräulein tomorrow night, Herr Matheson? Does she have a name, or do you plan on simply calling her Mademoiselle Genevieve's replacement?"

I could feel Noel's silent pleas for an answer I couldn't give. But he quickly responded with, "Of course she has a name. Although we *have* been discussing using something different as a stage persona here."

I needed to make up something fast. Anything. But my mind, which no more than two minutes ago had so obligingly come up with the lyrics to a show I'd never seen, was blank.

Before I could open my mouth and say Martha Washington or Jane Doe, someone appeared on stage and began to sing—badly. I knew this song. Knew it quite well. It was called "Christopher Robin Is Saying His Prayers." It started life as a poem written by A. A. Milne, creator of Winnie the Pooh, and then became a very sappy song back in the early nineteen-twenties. My dad had sung it to me from the time I was a baby.

I had never tired of hearing him sing about a bear named Winnie the Pooh and the young boy who was his friend. The boy's name was Christopher Robin, and my dad's name was Robin Christopher, which made me very curious—at least when I was a toddler—as to how he'd managed to get himself into the song…but backwards.

I took a breath mingled with an inward sigh of relief. "My name is Cori Christopher. Legally. But I'll also be using it on stage."

The woman who'd jogged my memory with her somewhat out-of-tune singing descended the four steps from the stage and marched right up next to Bauer, who seemed startled and almost intimidated.

She grabbed my hand as she announced, "Enough chatter. Lads, it's nearly four in the mornin' and if either of you were *really* gentlemen, you'd be afta seein' Mademoiselle Christopher is worn out. Exhausted. Has had a bloody long day. And ya'd best be delayin' whatever questions ya got till later. She needs sleep if she's ta be performin' within less than twenty-four hours."

More than a hint of Ireland crept through her words. She was perhaps four-foot-ten, with what could charitably be referred to as a chubby figure, and wearing the solid black shirtwaist and skirt that have made up the unfashionable garb of a wardrobe mistress probably for centuries upon centuries. The black was a match for her hair, dyed a pure ebony and pulled back into a tight bun with—I swear—two knitting needles sticking out of the middle. Her age could have been anywhere between fifty and a hundred. I recalled seeing her before…somewhere…but she'd been dressed far differently and far more flamboyantly.

My dad and my Granny Aubrey had done their best to educate me, teaching me about music, literature, and all the visual arts. Literature had included every one of William Shakespeare's plays and sonnets. A phrase from *A Midsummer Night's Dream* slammed into my mind the instant I saw her: *Though she be but little, she be fierce.*

Bauer started to say something, but the tiny critter straightened her back and wagged her index finger—on the hand not attached to my arm—as she glared upward, way upward, into his face, and firmly stated, "Not tonight. I'm taking Cori to Jacques' dressing room, which has a sofa, and puttin' her on it. I repeat, if she's gonna sing, she needs ta rest. I'll be lookin' after her. Go home, Major Bauer. You too, Noel."

A slight twitch turned up the corners of Noel's mouth at hearing this short imp dictate to the giant Nazi, but he wisely kept silent. Bauer also didn't speak, although his expression was less cheerful. Both men watched as the woman took my hand and led me up the stairs, onto the stage, into the wings, then right back to the room where I'd tried to get comfortable earlier.

She remained silent. She waited until I was safely inside Benet's dressing room and then turned and disappeared. I sat down and opened the bag I'd stored behind the dressing table before I'd gotten involved in getting an R.A.F. pilot out of harm's way. It was crammed with sheet music, including a red-stained copy of "Toujours," printed in 1941, and a water-stained copy of the old spiritual "Joshua Fit the Battle of Jericho," with notes and lyrics written by hand, dated 2061.

A slight scent emanated from the stained paper. Cranberries and citrus, but mixed in with some kind of pastry. I'd bet my life on it. Cranberry-orange scones. I sighed with relief as every piece clicked into place.

I knew the name of the enigmatic witch who'd guided me here. I remembered all the events leading to my journey to Paris—and, most important, why I'd been determined to make it.

I came to try and save Noel Matheson and Café Violette. And myself.

Chapter 3

March 2061, New Manhattan

The implosion and subsequent collapse of the two-hundred-year-old Chanson Theater lasted a total of eight seconds. Mayor (and Morality Now Committee Leader) Erik Brunson's interview, praising the demolition crew for their efficiency in keeping the amount of dust disturbing the tender sensibilities of bystanders to a minimum, consisted of a three-hundred-seconds-long statement broadcast on *Events at Eleven*.

The announcement of Ajay's murder, which had occurred seven minutes after the theater was destroyed, was delivered with undisguised contempt in five seconds by Events Anchor George Walsh...to wit: "Class Five Degenerate Anil Jaichand Kapoor, also known as Ajay Roy, died earlier tonight in an alley off West Forty-Sixth Street."

A wry smile from Mr. Walsh was followed by, "When we return, a look at the week's forecast, including when we can expect Hurricane Thora to hit. Stay tuned. It's going to be another bad one. Back in thirty seconds."

****

I'd warned him. Sitting across from Ajay on a bench near Inwood Hill Park barely a block away from his residence on Payson Avenue, I'd flat-out declared it was too risky to venture to the Square, much less to Center Town on West 48th Street across from the theater. I reminded him about the existence of the new panoramic, high on the Committee's Morality Now building, barely a block from the Chanson Theater, capturing images for everyone in the city to see.

I pointed out the perils of being spotted, either on the panoramic or by some eagle-eyed member of the Delegates. Arrest, a mock trial, internment in the prison formerly called Riker's Island—the name changed to Camp Virtue following the structure's rebuilding in 2043—or more likely, a quick execution to save time and money. I'd asked what, really, was to be gained by watching the destruction of a brick-and-mortar theater in person? The memories were intact. Why not hang on to them instead of wallowing in despair? Ajay was always telling me to live in the moment. Couldn't he do the same when the moment was one of life or death? As in…his?

"I hear you. I do. But I need to see it, Cori," Ajay responded. "The Chanson is the last authentic theater in existence in New Manhattan, even if not a single person has taken the stage there in the last twenty-five years. Architecturally, it's so sound it survived Hurricane Calder intact, and the producers not only continued playing *Les Misérables* but provided free performances, which brought hope to a shattered city during an unimaginable disaster. And now, who in hell has bothered to look inside in all these years? Why should the Committee give a damn about who shows up for its destruction? For me, it's like…like being at the bedside of a dying friend who's been in a coma. *Someone* needs to care."

"Can't you care while sitting on the sofa in the

relative safety of your residence? The whole implosion is sure to be a feature on *Events at Eleven*, doubtless with background cheering, real or dubbed." I brightened. "Hey! Here's an idea. I'll come back up to Inwood when I finish work and we can watch together. You've been hiding bottles of strong spirits for occasions that warrant heavy drinking. This is one of them."

"Not the same." Ajay paused. "What are you not telling me, Cori? Is your inner Cassandra shrieking a warning?"

"Yes. Quite a few warnings, actually, along with some other stuff I can't make sense of."

"Go on. You're holding something back, but it has nothing to do with the Chanson Theater and me."

"Well, the *warnings* all concern you, but—it's weird—I'm having flashes about someone I've never met or seen. And he's speaking French." I shook my head. "Sorry. Tangent. Not important right now. Your safety is."

Silence. Finally, Ajay took my hands in his. "I'm sixty-one years old. Physically, I'm in great shape. But I'm just tired. Tired of fighting. And…I miss Arthur. He's been gone a year now and I'm in the same place emotionally I was the day he died."

He closed his eyes for a moment, stayed silent, then opened them and blinked away tears. "Cori, forty years ago, September ninth of twenty-twenty-one, to be exact, before the storm hit, before anyone imagined a Manhattan like the one we have now, I read a news story in the *Times*, complete with photos showing broken musical instruments, including a gorgeous grand piano and a full set of drums. All the instruments were destroyed in a state-run recording studio in Kabul,

Afghanistan. America was finally leaving the country following the war, and the Taliban wanted the world to see they were very much in power. They brought back their ban on music and I stupidly thought, 'Thank God that can never happen here.' Fast forward to the day the Chanson Theater was boarded up during intermission of *Les Miz,* exactly fifteen years to the day from when I'd seen those photos." He closed his eyes for a moment, remembering, then opened them and stared down the street at his residence. "September ninth, twenty-thirty-six. Our cast was warned that any and all performances throughout the city would not only be shut down but singers and musicians arrested. The bastards forcibly stopped us from finishing the show." He flashed a brief smile. "I was extremely pissed. After all, I was doing such a wonderful job as the first actor of Indian descent to play the role of Marius, playing alongside your brilliantly talented grandmother who, I freely admit, was stealing the show as Eponine."

"Don't. Don't dwell on it. And don't remind me of Granny Aubrey or I'll start crying. I wish she were here. She'd probably handcuff you to the radiator or something to keep you at home. However, she's…well, who knows *where* she is, and I'd rather try and use more gentle means of persuasion, so let me state without reservation every bloody nerve ending in my body is shouting, 'If Ajay Roy makes his presence felt anywhere near the Chanson Theater—hell, anywhere near the Square in Center Town—he's in whopping big danger!' I'd listen if I were you. Cassandra warnings are always spot on, and this one is specific about time and place."

Ajay waved me off. "You're right. I freely admit you're right. But I need to see it. I need to be there." His voice lost its volume and became hoarse. "I've fought and I've fought for twenty-five long years... more than your whole lifetime. But things are just getting worse. I've lost my zeal for the fight. Maybe watching my favorite theater disappear forever will make me so angry I'll be ready to do battle again."

"Assuming you're not promptly imprisoned...or worse," I muttered under my breath.

"What?"

"Nothing. It's clear I can't convince you, and I love you too much to spend another minute arguing. Maybe I'm wrong. I hope I'm wrong. So, change of subject...sort of. Would you like to hear about my *own* trip to the Chanson Theater? Which involved committing more than one minor but definitely felonious act."

****

"You got in? You actually got inside?" Ajay shook his head. "Dammit, Cori! You're worse than I am. You scare the fool out of me. Talk about Aubrey—you're exactly like her. Reckless as a fox shaking its furry tail at the hounds. Impulsive and brash and sassy and far too willing to take chances."

I raised an eyebrow. "So sayeth the man risking punishment and/or death to watch a building collapse."

He sighed. "Yeah, yeah, point taken, but..."

"Well, since the Delegates have been too busy crushing the wave of graffiti popping up all over the old Grand Central Station, I figured they wouldn't be in the area bothering to keep watch over a place scheduled for implosion. Plus, it rained last night, and the Delegates hate the rain. Seriously. Maybe they're afraid they'll melt? One could only hope."

Ajay grimaced. "I heard about the graffiti. Elijah

Terry's daughter, Inez, was being sought for questioning. I smell betrayal of Ostinato, and I'm thoroughly frustrated and angry because there's nothing I can do about it. Onward. Tell me about the theater. I admit to extreme envy at you being able to sneak in. How much of a wreck is it?"

"Ready for this? It's sad because it's not a wreck at all. With some paint on the walls and new upholstery on seats, it could be up and running in a couple of weeks. I hit the catwalk and shimmied across to a light booth, which is still fully equipped. The lobby is kind of a mess, but all the flooring is stable and the stage is amazing. I swear I could sense all the actors who'd ever performed there, starting two hundred-plus years ago, coming to stand beside me. And this blew me away. The giant turntable thing on the stage your cast used for *Les Misérables* can still be seen. Well, the lines leading underneath, anyway. The best part? The set with the barricade is intact."

"Really? How intact?"

I assumed an air of innocence which didn't fool Ajay for a minute before adding, "Um, to be honest, it was a bit *too* intact. This is where Cori Christopher let her rebel spirit shine. Before you ask, I *did* check for escape routes first. It's in my DNA."

"Cori…what did you do?"

"Well, as it so happens, one of your cast members left a flag stuck through a chair on top of the barricade. Perhaps he was careless, but I prefer to call it defiance. I pulled it out and waved it in the air and then I sang a few notes." I paused before adding, "Okay, I lied. It was the entire song."

Ajay groaned. "You're not only impulsive, brash

and sassy, you're completely bonkers…taking risks. Whatever possessed your dad and me to teach you every song from musical theater productions we knew? Along with ancient jazz standards and rock 'n' roll and folksy protest songs…"

"Because you both loved me, and because, according to you, I sound like Granny Aubrey, who'd been teaching me music from the moment I could talk until she went poof into nowhereland. She gets some of the credit…or blame. I miss her so much."

Ajay took a deep breath. "I do, too. But I have this strange feeling you'll have an answer about Aubrey soon, and this is coming through even without your gift of second sight or premonitions." He paused, then added, "Listen, while we're talking about feelings of impending doom, if something *does* happen to me, you need to talk to Jimmy."

I stared at him for a long moment before agreeing. "Okay. Your turn. What are you not telling me?"

"Never mind. Go on. You said you sang." His tone was wistful. "I repeat, I'm envious. To sing inside a theater again with the kind of acoustics built into the Chanson making every note perfect—a dream come true."

"It was. I'm tellin' ya, I completely understand why the Committee banned so much of the arts, especially vocal music that isn't a Gregorian chant or totally devoid of emotion. Way too dangerous. Three seconds on stage and I wanted to go out and break every rule ever imposed. Run down the street waving and smiling and saying 'hello' to my fellow New Manhattanites without fear of being nabbed by some clown in a black uniform who disapproves of happiness in general and me

28

exhibiting it in particular by means of warbling a couple of tunes in public." I took a breath, suppressing the sudden wave of frustration and anger threatening to turn my words into tears.

Ajay patted my hands. "One day, Cori, freedom. With any luck and a ton of work on the part of folks whose names are best left unsaid, it could happen in your lifetime. Sadly, I'm sure it won't be in mine."

He could see I was about to say something and stopped me before I uttered another word. "Back to tonight's demolition. No more arguments or warnings. I'm going. Call it a last act of defiance. Yeah, I'm well aware it will accomplish nothing. But look, if—oh, hell, let's face it, your warnings are never wrong—*when* I'm gone, get to Jimmy's apartment as soon as you can. Check the radiator."

I had no idea what to say to this. He wasn't listening. The more I thought about it, the more I realized I didn't have the right to take him to task for engaging in something that, admittedly with a ton of luck, might end up being less risky than my singing in the same theater. My Cassandra warnings, as Ajay had always called them, hadn't provided details, yet I knew disaster was the likely outcome of his visit to Center Town.

I bit my lower lip but responded with, "If the worst— Okay, fine. I'll check the radiator. And talk to Jimmy."

"Good." He waved his hand as though brushing away all remaining fears. "Enough gloomy talk. I have to ask the big question of the night…what song did you sing high on top of the barricade?"

"I got weird. Standing on the same barricade where Ajay Roy and his valiant castmates stood the night the

Delegates raided the Chanson Theater made me think about wars and battles and revolutions. So I reached into my vast repertoire of songs and grabbed the old ballad 'Johnny Has Gone for a Soldier.' " I paused and grinned at him. "But because of these odd flashes I've been having these past weeks, I sang it in French."

Chapter 4

Twenty-five people crowded into Jimmy Pinder's small living room on the first floor of the four-story house on Payson Avenue, originally built as a single-family home back in the nineteenth century, then split into three apartments sometime in the early twentieth. Ajay Roy's apartment had been on the top floor. Jimmy told me the entire house was searched, then Ajay's apartment boarded up within an hour after he was killed.

For years, Jimmy had been Ajay's best friend as well as his landlord. Once a minister for an Episcopalian church, Jimmy had performed the marriage ceremony for Ajay Roy and Arthur Wright back in 2019. None of the three men—including Jimmy, who was "straight"—had ever quite gotten over the Committee reversing the stand on gay marriage, along with closing nearly every church in the city in favor of the Committee's "government sponsored" religion they'd labeled Morality Now.

Up to this date, no one from the Committee seemed to be aware of the various roles Jimmy had played in Ajay's life, apart from being owner of the house. Consequently, when Jimmy applied for a permit for a small memorial, inviting Mr. Roy's neighbors, he'd been given permission without engaging in a protracted, nasty battle. Jimmy and I both believed the *real* reason for allowing the gathering at the apartment was that the Committee knew very well Jimmy had been Ajay's friend, which meant a friend to other members in Ostinato, and hoped to snag some folks who might show up to pay respects to a beloved comrade.

Out of all the mourners present, I was acquainted with five. Jimmy, of course, and Priya Deshai, who lived in an apartment on W. 204th Street, close to what had been the 200th Street/Dyckman subway stop. Priya was about twenty-four years old, which made her my senior by four years. She'd been classified as Class Three when she turned twenty-one, thanks to her Indian heritage. She'd have been bumped up to a Five had the Committee any inkling of her participation in rebellious activities.

A married couple in their forties, Richard and Jane Warwick, lived next door on Payson Avenue, in a six-floor walkup. It had also originally been a house. They were considered Class One Citizens, which meant white, straight, and deemed safe by the Committee, who did not realize Richard and Jane were top-tier members of the group called Ostinato. The group, made up of people resisting the tyrannies and rules of the Committee, had been started by Jimmy, Ajay and Arthur, my dad Robin Christopher, my grandparents on my mom's side, and three others not currently in attendance at the memorial, the same year I was born…2041.

The other folks gathered at the memorial were neighbors who might have had an inkling that Ajay was more than a fun guy who helped them grow vegetables and herbs inside stuffy apartments, but even if they'd known about Ostinato, they'd never have revealed it, due to their affection for Ajay. Classifications for the others were a mix of about four "white and straight" with the rest being Class Three, which meant "of a different color" but nothing to label as treasonous or "sexually perverse," although I had to inwardly smile, knowing there were six folks in the room who had used Jimmy's services back when same-sex marriages were legal.

It appeared the Committee hadn't bothered to check the living arrangements for some of these people in years. After all, they had more pressing matters to deal with, such as imploding architectural structures that once housed cultural activities, nabbing graffiti artists—including Inez Terry, Ostinato leader Elijah Terry's oldest daughter—and hunting down any and all 'degenerates' they deemed dangerous for not following rules or for being born the wrong color.

I was the only other member of Ostinato present but, because I was under the age of twenty-one, had not yet been classified by the Committee. Thanks to secrets stubbornly held by family and friends for many years, no one knew my grandparents and father had all been involved in theater, bumping me to Class Two. I was also one-quarter Indian (as in South Asian, not Native American) which would have sent me to Class Three.

Not to mention that all my close relatives were rebels who tried every way they could to bring back sanity and the arts to a society that began trampling on both starting in 2035, about five years after the Great Storm, Hurricane Calder, changed the landscape of what had once been five boroughs making up New York City. If the Committee discovered my own involvement in various activities, I'd be fast-tracked to Class Five and facing prison or worse.

Five people, including three of the group's leaders, had opted to stay away from Jimmy's because their safety was prioritized over the shared experience of a memorial. Slight digression here: When I was eight, my dad, Robin, told me Ostinato was a musical term meaning a motif or a phrase continuing a repetition of the same musical voice, often using the same pitch. And, according to an old hardcover dictionary Ajay bought when he was a child, "Ostinato" is the Italian word for "stubborn," which gave great delight to Ajay and everyone else fighting repression.

As noted, there were five members of Ostinato in absentia. For their safety and mine, I only knew the names of three of them…Elijah Terry, Brent Epstein, and Marley Hudson. Jimmy, having been a major player role in the group for years, knew all the rest.

The other reason the five were not in attendance was nasty and grim. Jimmy and I both were certain someone was a traitor. He or she could be one of the leaders involved in planning the most important, most rebellious, most egregious (at least to the Committee) activities. Someone must have told the Delegates they could find Ajay watching the Chanson implosion three days ago. His killers, probably Delegates who were doubtless sanctioned—oh, hell, let's be honest—*ordered* by the Committee to murder, had easily located him, even though Ajay's image had escaped the new panoramic's nearly omniscient eye.

I knew this because I'd been in the Square in Center Town, doing my best to keep track of Ajay's whereabouts without endangering us both. I'd stared at the giant screen, willing it to show only the Committee's handpicked *Events at Eleven*-worthy crowd…which was exactly what I'd seen. I'd been thrilled and hopeful because there hadn't been a glimmer of Ajay's visage. Yet Ajay had been murdered almost immediately after the theater's implosion, and as far as I was aware, neither members of the Committee nor their enforcing bully boys were psychic when it came to pinpointing someone's whereabouts.

I brushed away thoughts of informers. I hated to imagine the possibility someone in this room might be responsible for Ajay Roy's murder. This wasn't the time to worry about things I couldn't control. Jimmy gestured toward the lamps and ceiling lights the minute I arrived at the apartment, so I'd get the hint. I got it. Someone was listening. Part of the reason for the gathering was for my benefit, although only Jimmy, Priya, and the Warwicks knew we planned to try to convince the Committee I was nothing more than an innocent former neighbor come to pay my respects to someone who once babysat for me.

Richard Warwick took the lead in establishing my reason for being at the memorial. "So, Cori? Jimmy says you used to live across the street?"

"I did. My parents and I lived in what is now your apartment until I was ten. I got to know Mr. Pinder and Mr. Roy when I was just a kid. Mr. Roy showed me how to grow anything that could be grown in a garden." I smiled. "I still have more fresh basil and lemongrass than I can handle."

Laughter and smiles all around.

Jimmy added to the story. "Cori's parents died when she was ten. Caught in Hurricane Madison. Twenty-fifty-one. Robin and Celeste Christopher were helping with the crew trying to reinforce the wall down on West Fourteenth Street."

Nods. Jane Warwick sighed. "I lost both friends and family in Madison as well. And, of course, in Hurricane Calder before then. I'm sorry about your folks, Cori."

What Jimmy said about my parents was pure speculation. My father, Robin Christopher, who'd been a set designer before the ban on most theatrical venues, was reportedly working on one of the walls near the old Bowery, but no one actually saw him being swept out to sea. My mother wasn't there. She and I were trying to get out of the city when she was killed by an accident. My maternal grandparents disappeared the same afternoon. Ten years later, I still had no clue who, if any, of my relatives were even alive.

Jimmy stated, "Cori was brought up in one of the city houses for children after she lost her family, but she'd bicycle up here all the time to see me, and usually Ajay was around. He really was a wizard when it came to indoor plants. I've never seen anything like it. Not to mention one fantastic chef."

He wasn't lying. Again, those visits weren't the whole story, but Jimmy's comments carried enough detail to hopefully convince any listeners I was nothing more than a polite former neighbor showing respect.

This was great. Cori Christopher's soon-to-be Class One respectable citizen *bona fides* were established. That Cori Christopher also looked one hundred percent white, thanks to the Irish side of the family, was a plus. Richard proceeded to talk about Ajay's great windowsill gardening skills and how Ajay used to dogsit half the pooches in the neighborhood and walk them through the park when their owners were at work.

All lovely memories. All innocent.

We kept the topics light. No one mentioned the silent anger circulating throughout the room as we all choked down our rage. Our friend had been murdered and there wasn't a blessed thing we could do to bring his killers to justice.

****

Around four p.m. the neighbors began drifting out. At five, the Warwicks left, soon followed by Priya. Jimmy and I stayed behind to do whatever sparse cleaning was needed. I washed dishes and Jimmy dried them. We kept a companionable silence until the last glass had been put away and I decided it was time to ask Jimmy why Ajay had requested I talk with him about more than the sheen on the antique china plates.

"Oh, by the way, Mr. Pinder, uh, Mr. Roy wanted me to…" My voice died away as I tried to come up with an excuse to check the radiator, in case the Delegates were listening.

Jimmy interrupted with, "Ajay wanted you to have the ancient black fedora he used to wear, right?"

I exhaled my relief. "Yes!"

Jimmy smiled and winked at me. "He gave it to me to keep for you months ago. He tended to be forgetful about things. I apologize for holding on to it for so long. I'll get it for you now." He paused, then added, "Meantime, would you mind checking my radiator? I'm not sure if I shut it off. It's been such a warm spring, and I won't need it again until autumn. If we do get a cold snap, I'll just layer clothing on clothing and bring out the portable heaters."

"Sure."

Jimmy turned and headed down the hall toward his bedroom while I walked back into the living room where the radiator stood under the large front windows. I ran my hands underneath until I discovered something taped to the metal. I pulled it away and opened what might best be described as a small pouch, like an old coin purse from about 150 years ago. Inside was a key with a piece of paper wrapped around it. I unfolded it and read a name: *Joshua.*

I straightened up and crossed back to the kitchen where I'd left my carrier bag, opened the large pocket on the bag's left side, and attached the key to the ring currently holding four other keys. Jimmy entered the kitchen and gestured toward the note, silently miming an action of shredding as he handed me a black hat.

"Did you know this hat belonged to Ajay's great-grandfather, Devi Kapoor? He emigrated to America from India in nineteen-forty-six and, according to family legend, bought the hat at one of New York's largest department stores. Told everyone he didn't feel like a 'real' American until he owned a fedora just like actors were wearing in the movie *Casablanca.*"

I coughed loudly as I tore the note to shreds and traded the bits of paper for the hat. I did not mention to Jimmy that Ajay's great-grandfather also happened to be my great-great-grandfather, thanks to the marriage of Ajay's brother, Yash Kapoor, to my grandmother, Aubrey Collier. We'd kept the secret for the twenty years I'd been on this earth, and it was wiser to keep it unstated, although I assumed Jimmy knew. But there was no need to bring it up and interest any listening Delegates.

"I'm grateful Ajay left it for me. I remember him wearing it all the time, and he looked very stylish. Like he was in *Casablanca* himself. It'll keep my ears warm all next winter on bicycle trips to work and back to my residence. I love having a vintage hat!"

Jimmy grinned. "Not to mention it'll look very cute over your bright red hair. Speaking of trips, I guess it's time to get on your bike, Cori. It'll be dark soon." He added, "I'll walk you out, but first I need to use the gentlemen's facility."

Clearly, the note would be flushed into the sewer.

I waited.

Jimmy returned shortly, then asked, "Anything else you need?"

I slapped the hat on my head. "Nope. Ready to go."

He escorted me out the door and, ignoring any possible unfriendly witnesses, gave me a hug, quietly whispering, "You understand?" I nodded. He waited while I arranged my bag over my shoulder before mounting the bicycle that would take me back down to my residence on West 125th Street.

I couldn't help it. I had to stop and stare at the house once I'd reached the corner. Great-Uncle Anil Jaichand Kapoor, who had taken the stage name of Ajay Roy at age sixteen, was dead. I'd seen his body in the street near the newly destroyed Chanson Theater and had been living with the atrocious image in my mind. But today, finally, I was able to envision him as he'd been three days earlier, a different fedora (dark gray, not black) on his head, and a spiffy-looking scarlet ascot around his neck, waving goodbye…both of us knowing we'd never see each other again.

Chapter 5

Two blond-haired men, wearing the sleek, stark black uniform of the Delegates, stood next to the lamp post just outside the old brownstone on West 125th Street where I shared an apartment in the basement with ten other girls. The taller of the two men, about six-foot-four, which was intimidating even to my five-foot-ten, cleared his throat before inquiring gruffly, "Cori Christopher?"

"Yes."

"You need to come with us."

"Why? Is there some problem?" I asked.

Silence, then Delegate Number Two, six-foot-five and sporting cartoonishly broad shoulders, grabbed my arm. "Don't talk back!"

"I wasn't. I was just aski—"

Delegate One held up his hand. "Stop."

I stopped.

He checked his communicator phone, nodded, then summoned an obviously less-than-sincere smile. "Miss Christopher, the Committee is in need of your assistance."

"Assistance" was a weak and fake euphemism for "You're in serious trouble." I waited. From the time I was old enough to talk, Ajay, my dad Robin, and Granny Aubrey had instilled in me the necessity of keeping my mouth shut unless forced to answer a question.

"You were at a private residence on Payson Avenue much of this afternoon. Five hours, to be exact. Correct?"

"Yes. I was attending a private memorial. We were given permission by the Office of Deaths," I stated. "I mean, the owner of the residence got the permit."

"We are aware of this." Slight pause, then he continued. "Miss Christopher, you were acquainted with the deceased Degenerate Class Five, Anil J. Roy?"

No, I always spend half a day cycling another eighty or so blocks uptown to sit around with a bunch of strangers, listening to them talk about someone I've never met. And he was a human being, you bloody robotic A-hole…not some ridiculous degenerate class five thing! *He was also my great-uncle and I adored him…but thankfully you don't seem to be aware of our particular relationship. Yet.*

I did not repeat what was swirling inside my head. I kept my response simple. "Yes."

"You are also acquainted with James Pinder?"

I stiffened. My skin prickled and my inner Cassandra wailed a siren warning. This was about more than someone reporting my presence at the memorial. "I am."

"How do you know him?"

"Well, he owns the house. He's the one who applied for permission to hold a memorial service after the mur…death…of Mr. Roy."

Delegate Two started to say something, but I interrupted after forcing a sickly-sweet smile to my lips. "Excuse me, I don't mean to be rude, but would you care to introduce yourselves? It's very disconcerting answering questions when I don't have a name for who's on the receiving end." This was another trick my dad

41

taught me when I was about six. *Whenever possible, humanize the entire situation. Do your best to make the other guy see you as someone close to them. A wife. A sister. A friend. And then stall for time.* I had no idea if it would help with two goons who spent their days intimidating and terrorizing New Manhattanites, but if nothing else it gave me a chance to get my breathing under control so they might not be able to tell I was as nervous as I really was.

Delegate One, who seemed slightly more willing to be human, raised an eyebrow but actually complied with the request. "I am Delegate Becker. My associate is Delegate Lang."

"Great. Thank you. So, gentlemen, was there a problem with the permit? We finished the memorial about two hours ago, but if I need to sign something else so Mr. Pinder doesn't have to come down to Center Town, I'll be glad to do a proxy or something. He's an elderly man and it's hard for him to get around."

Becker shook his head. "Miss Christopher, please let us ask the questions. When did you first meet Anil J. Roy?"

The day he picked me up out of my mother's arms about an hour after I was born and sang "Amazing Grace" to me. Family legend has it I smiled at him, which is impossible for a newborn, but...

Yeah, best leave details, including the original date, about Ajay and Cori's first meeting out in the ether somewhere. "Um, my parents and I lived in the building across the street, and he was just kind of there, I guess. It was a friendly neighborhood where you chat with folks when you take the trash out, or the power dies in the city and you feel the need to be around other people. He helped me grow a garden on my windowsill. Mainly basil and lemongrass. Basil is amazing. Just shoots up out of the pots all year round." I wondered what other ramblings I could come up with to stall and hope they forgot to get to the point, which I assumed was spilling my guts about members of Ostinato.

"Miss Christopher, please stop. Your plants are not why we're here."

Lang interrupted his partner with a gruff, "You're wasting time, Becker."

Becker sighed. "Yes. You need to understand, Miss Christopher, that the Committee is aware of certain facts regarding Ajay Roy's life. Specifically, he was involved in non-sanctioned acts of treason, along with several of his friends."

I opened my eyes wide, using Dad's, Granny Aubrey's and Ajay's dramatic acting skills, also part of my DNA. My arms and legs felt cold, almost numb, while my stomach threatened to push up the spicy offerings of the Indian vindaloo and veggie korma Priya Deshai had brought to the service.

I waited, choking back the urge to ask how in hell one could commit treason in a city that was supposedly still part of the United States and nowhere in the country's Constitution was it written one city could intimidate its citizens the way the Committee, New Manhattan's harsh governing body, did. Just because a storm had wrecked the city years ago, and the rest of the country decided we weren't worth bailing out and could go our own way, that shouldn't mean Fascist-style dictators could take over.

I took a quiet breath. No question had been asked, and I wasn't volunteering any information.

Then it came.

Lang glared at me. "Miss Christopher, we need the names of Mr. Roy's contacts."

I played ignorant. "I'm sorry, I'm not sure what you mean."

Becker shook his head. "You are not a stupid woman. Don't pretend you don't understand what it is we're asking."

Lang broke into his partner's response with three words, "Not asking. Demanding."

Becker kept his tone calm. "We want the names of the people who've been conspiring with Roy for years in direct action against the Committee. We have three but are aware at least ten more are active around New Manhattan."

I continued my role of innocent acquaintance. "I'm sorry. I can't help you." *Actually, I won't help you, you creep, but it's more polite to go with can't.*

"Perhaps you'd care to hear your options? The majority of which are quite unpleasant." Lang smiled.

"Options?"

Becker shot his partner a look of mild distaste. "Miss Christopher, Delegate Lang has a tendency to rush interrogations in his eagerness to aid the Committee. But, nonetheless, he is correct. There are choices to be made. We would like whatever information you have. Before you decline, please understand we are prepared to compensate you and provide you with a better lifestyle than the one you currently have."

"What do you mean?" Was he offering a bribe for me to betray friends?

"You are currently living with ten other women in one residence. The Committee would move you to a building where you would share an apartment with only two other girls. We can put tokens away for you for certain luxuries. Allow you various other…indulgences. We often grant them to people who work for the Committee."

Yep. Bribery. An attempt to tempt me with the products of wealth.

I tried to appear as disingenuous as I could. "But what if I don't *know* anything about Mr. Roy's friends?"

Shift to Lang and a snarling, "Your options cease to exist and you find yourself sharing space in Camp Virtue with more than thirty women in one room. For an indeterminate length of time."

Well, *that* was succinct.

Ajay began teaching me how to tap dance when I was three and later explained how the phrase "tapping your way out of chaos" was also used for situations in which one frantically tried to verbally improvise an escape from danger. I now tied the bows of my invisible tap shoes to my feet and was about to engage in some fancy footwork with my words when Becker stopped me.

"Miss Christopher. You've had a long day. You are facing a difficult situation. It would be prudent for you to think about the proposition we've given you and consider your decision carefully before you ignore our generosity. Tomorrow evening at seven we would like you to meet with us at the Committee's branch office on Fifth Avenue and Forty-Second Street and have the names and contact information we need."

Lang added, flashing what was basically a leer at me, "Make the correct decision or you *won't* live to regret it."

I assumed he thought he was being witty with the

emphasis on "won't." I didn't find it all that funny.

Lang coughed. "Miss Christopher. One more thing. Extend your left arm."

Oh, hell. They were going to put a tracker on me.

I waited, barely breathing, until Lang snapped the tracking device closed. Becker then stated, "You may take it off to bathe, but keep it in the same room and immediately put it back on."

"Oh. Uh, yeah, got it."

He nodded. The pair then turned in military precision and walked in unison toward the El subway stop at West 125th Street.

I refrained from lifting my right hand and pointing with my middle finger but did mutter a few less-than-ladylike phrases. I took a deep breath, wheeled my bike to the holding pens outside my residence, flipped the kickstand to a secure position, and walked down into the basement apartment, preparing to act, in front of ten women I lived with but didn't trust, as if nothing had happened.

Chapter 6

At precisely seven-thirty of the morning following Ajay's memorial and my confrontation with Lang and Becker, I received a phone call from someone at the Committee's branch office on 42nd Street informing me that, as current forecasts indicated Hurricane Thora was due to hit in less than five hours, it would be best if I came over for my interview at nine a.m. rather than waiting until the evening. I figured I had, at most, twenty minutes to put my plan into operation before a couple of Delegates dropped by my residence to escort me to Center Town to meet with the chosen interrogators for the day.

I dressed in black trousers and a black pullover sweater, topped off with a large, ugly, dark gray raincoat, a truly ugly dark gray, plastic rain hat, and uglier gray rain galoshes over my ankle boots. I tucked some essentials, including Ajay's black (not ugly) fedora, two more sweaters, one more pair of trousers, toiletries, ballet slippers, and some extra undies, into my oversized shoulder carrier, then rode my bicycle down to West 94th Street and the large building that housed Discover Life Studios, my place of employment where we made what were termed educational films.

All things considered, in the repressive world in which I lived, my job was decent. It was surprisingly fun at times. Especially when one considered what my flatmates did. Six of the girls worked in the tech factory on West 72nd Street, creating chips for computers. Two worked in food stores, sorting groceries for the citizens of New Manhattan while making sure fair allotments were given. Two worked as cleaners at the Committee's primary offices on Broadway and 59th Street near Columbus Circle.

I considered myself lucky my job had a spark of creativity in it, albeit a weak spark. I was a "get-it" girl. If the purpose of the film was to explain how to escape from a fire, I was the member of the crew who found the materials to make smoke and wardrobe items for the portrayers who had to roll on the floor in the middle of a fake blaze and emerge relatively clean. Just last week I'd trotted around the city looking for gauze bandages for a film educating people on how to care for a cut on an arm or leg, if the cut was fairly minor and blood wasn't spouting from arteries or something…which was represented in this episode as the time to call for experienced help. The director privately acknowledged the idea was absurd and if one was too stupid to call before then, they probably deserved to expire in a pool of blood.

I parked my bicycle in the outside slots reserved for workers, slung my bag over my shoulder, then hurried inside just as the rain shifted from mild mist to a light drizzle.

Margaret Clark, the organizing manager for Discover Life Films, was seated at her desk in the lobby. She glanced up at me with an expression of surprise. "Miss Christopher? What are you doing here? Didn't you get the message? No one is working today because of Hurricane Thora coming in. You should be home using all the tips from the film we did last year on surviving a storm. I only came in to pick up some items I left last evening and make a few more calls to people whose numbers are only found here."

I smiled. "I *did* get the message, and thanks for sending it, but I wanted to take another look at the script for next week's training film. I remembered it calls for quite a few more properties needed than anything we've done in months, so I figured I'd use the opportunity to find anything currently in storage. This one has some outside shots and it's a sure bet we'll be off schedule due to the weather, so I didn't want to waste time next week searching for stuff. There are some things in the wardrobe room we can use. I hate not having everything ready."

To my own ears, it sounded like a lame excuse, but Margaret Clark was a perfectionist. If anyone approved the concept of preparedness and could understand, she would. Besides, I couldn't exactly say, *I'm hoping to escape a couple of Delegates by sneaking out of this building because they don't trust me to present myself in their stinking Committee branch office at nine to turn informer and they're damned right, because I plan to be hiding in Inwood by two this afternoon, at the latest, if my plan succeeds.*

I added aloud, "Please, don't bother about me. Really."

Miss Clark checked her video caller. "Hurricane Thora does seem to be coming in faster than expected, according to the Storm Safety Office." She glanced at me. "Will you be long?"

"Probably. Some of the properties are tough to find, but…" I shook my head. "Naturally, those are the things most necessary, if the film is going to work." I paused, then added, "Honestly? I'll be fine here. If anything, this building is safer than my residence. My space is in the basement apartment, and it floods every time it rains."

"You might get trapped in the dark, though, if the power goes out."

I smiled at her. "I guess this is why fire escapes are attached to tall buildings. I never take elevators anyway, and I brought a big flashlight. Miss Clark, you live across the city on the east side, right? Well, there's no reason for *you* to stay just for one nutty, over-diligent worker. You need to take care of *yourself*."

She glanced at the window nearest her desk. I could hear rain pelting against the glass. "It does seem to be coming down harder. Um, Miss Christopher?"

"Please, call me Cori."

A faint smile. "Cori. If anyone calls, would you inform them the studio and offices will be shut down for a few days? I think I managed to contact almost everyone, and I did leave messages, so I doubt you'll have to answer, but…"

"Absolutely. I will be happy to spread the word. This assumes the phones don't go out. It's supposed to really get nasty out there. Go on. Please. I've heard the storm will hit the west part of the island first, so you should have time to make it safely home if you leave now. And if I need to hunker down for a few hours…" I took off my carrier bag and laid it on the floor. "Well, I'm prepared with food, and there's always the dispensers in the cafeteria."

Within two minutes I was politely accompanying Margaret, who was covered from neck to ankles in a long water-resistant coat and galoshes uglier than mine, to the front doors. Once she was outside, I watched her walk down two blocks to be sure she wasn't coming back. Which is when I saw them. The rain was falling hard but it was easy to recognize Lang and Becker, who were standing by the bicycle bins staring at the lone bike…mine. I also spotted a plain black sedan on the corner of West 94th Street.

I was right. The Delegates intended to provide Cori Christopher with a ride for the trip to the offices on Fifth Avenue and 42nd Street, ensuring my participation. I wondered when they'd arrived at my residence this morning only to discover I wasn't around. And how long they'd wait for me to exit this building before entering.

I crossed the lobby back to Margaret's desk and found the scissors she kept in the middle sliding drawer. I snapped off the band of the wrist tracker but held on to it and put the scissors back. I then walked toward the "Exit Only" door no one ever used because it led down into what had once been a subway tunnel. Taking the stairs going up to the fifth floor where a railed balcony led to the fire escape would literally be a much cleaner means of escape, but the Delegates would doubtless head there in the hunt for Cori Christopher.

I paused for a second at the entrance to the stairs, opened the door, and left a half-empty water bottle (with my name written on a sticky label slapped on the side) in the corner of the second step as though it had fallen out of my bag, hoping it would reinforce the "leaving by the fire escape" scenario. I then threw the tracker across the room. Didn't matter where it landed. They'd quickly get the message it wasn't on my wrist.

I wasn't sure if anyone in the Committee's employ was even aware there was an old pathway leading from this building to the 96th Street train station. All the underground subway trains had been shut down in 2031 following the catastrophic Hurricane Calder and the astonishing tsunami that destroyed much of three boroughs of New York City—Brooklyn, Staten Island, and Queens—and parts of lower Manhattan. Elevator trains became the primary means of mass transit and all resources were shifted to building them. For the next thirty years, once the sad business of dragging bodies out from underground was completed, the old tunnels were ignored. Even tunnels as far north as this one were considered unsafe and too expensive to reconstruct.

From the time I was a toddler, members of my family had instilled in me the importance of discovering everything about any building I'd be inside of for more than five minutes. According to family legend, my first spoken words were, "Ajay, Daddy, sing!" The next two were "Escape route!" Part of the reason I'd been unafraid to sing to the rafters of the Chanson Theater a few nights ago, as I'd told Ajay, was because I'd scoped out every entrance and exit provided, along with neat hidey-holes under the stage and in the orchestra pit, plus the catwalk above the theater house leading to an upstairs fire escape.

I wasn't enthralled with the idea of descending below ground and dealing with the dirt and the foul stench and the overwhelming feeling of horror left in the empty spaces of air from more than 200 people whose lives ended when they either drowned or suffocated. But, considering what I was facing if caught, I'd brave hell itself to avoid being picked up by the Delegates, interrogated, and ultimately sent to Camp Virtue with its worse dirt, odors, and horror.

The exit leading down to the tunnel had been

blocked only with a trash can. No one apart from me had been insane enough to explore the space since 2031. I took my scarf off, loosely tied it to the can's handle, opened the door, then pulled the can as close as I could to its original position before tugging on the scarf and bringing it back to my hands. If the water bottle didn't convince them I'd gone upstairs, at least it wouldn't appear a real human had gone through this exit. I *did* leave the trash can a few inches from the door to provide a small opening. I needed a way out just in case things were blocked on the other end of the subway tunnel. Getting trapped underground was not part of the plan.

Once the door was closed and the trash can situated, I reached into my bag and pulled out a set of gray coveralls. And if there's a question as to why I happened to have this particular item of clothing with me, I refer any and all interested parties to look at my previous comments regarding escape routes. I knew the day would come when I'd need to flee the Committee's rule, so, in addition to exploring an old subway tunnel, I'd long ago lifted a pair of coveralls from the room where the cleaning crew kept their gear. It wasn't locked. Nothing was ever locked in New Manhattan. Mainly because there usually wasn't anything worth stealing unless you were a member of the Committee or a Delegate.

I put the coveralls over the clothes I'd worn to the studios, shifted my bag so it became more of a backpack than a shoulder carrier, and slowly made my way down the ladder, headed to a place of refuge I knew would be safe, thanks to a note left by Ajay containing one word—the name of "Joshua."

Chapter 7

The long journey through the filthy, bad-smelling, emotionally draining tunnel was not pleasant. I see no reason to provide a play-by-play of my movements. I would have preferred less accompaniment by Manhattan rodents but came to regard them as allies because the Delegates would never imagine a lone girl would brave the aforementioned dirt, nasty odors, emotional horror *and* rats, no matter how determined her desire to escape.

At the entrance to what had once been a subway stop at West 145th Street, I was able to take the crumbling stairs and step back out into the world. This world, which would normally be scary, thanks to Hurricane Thora hitting the west side of the island sooner than expected, was instead reassuring. The wind, rain, and surprising bouts of hail should help deter my pursuers from finding me. They would help provide the means to wash off a bit of the ancient grime clinging to me from various sites in the tunnel. I kept the gray overalls on since they blended nicely with the rain.

The hike to Ajay and Jimmy's residence on Payson Avenue took another hour but was far easier than the first part of the trip, thanks to no longer having to deal with foul air. The rain continued to beat down on me but felt cleansing. My Cassandra warnings weren't announcing, *Delegates nearby!* at me, and I felt confident I could make it to my final destination, a few blocks off of 200th

aka Dyckman, not far from the Dyckman Street Viaduct and the Henry Hudson Parkway. I planned to cut through the park and avoid anyone out for a stroll in the rain. The name of the street where I was headed was Staff, but for years there'd been no street signs so hardly anyone knew of its existence. I was headed to a six-story walk-up in the middle of the block.

I hit the edge of Inwood Hill Park across from Payson Avenue. I stopped. The Pinder house where I'd spent much of yesterday…and my childhood…was gone. Rain flowed gracefully over the charred remains of chairs and tables and beds and dishes and wood and brick and…

About twenty people, all folks who'd been at Ajay's memorial, stood in silence, braving the rain, staring at the ruins.

I stepped out from behind a clump of trees, my emotions swinging from shock to anger to fear that Lang or Becker had figured out I'd be here and driven in a comfortable car to await my arrival.

"Cori?" someone called softly.

I turned as Priya Deshai tapped my right shoulder.

"Priya? What in hell happened?"

"They blew it up. Last night. The cowards are calling it an accident. Claiming there was a gas leak."

"What? Total, complete garbage!" I swallowed. "Was Jimmy…?"

Priya's tears mingled with the rain as she nodded. "Yes. He was inside."

"Oh, God. No. *No!*"

"Cori, they knew he was home and they didn't care. It's been in the back of everyone's mind since Ajay's death, but…but this confirmed it. Betrayal." Priya glanced around at the crowd…at faces we'd known our entire lives. She whispered, "Jimmy isn't the only casualty today. Inez Terry was shot, allegedly trying to escape while being escorted to Camp Virtue. She's dead too. They're coming after all of us. Who can we trust?"

I took a deep breath and forced myself not to imagine Jimmy's last moments on earth. "Priya, two Delegates were waiting for me yesterday at my apartment. I was supposed to go to the Forty-Second Street branch for questioning this morning, and they seemed convinced I could tell them more about Ajay's group. I eluded them, but I'm not sure for how long."

"This is very bad. Look, wherever you're headed, and I don't want to know, in case they find me, but get there *now*. For once, a storm is our friend. This one is totally erratic. Starts and stops and then gets worse the next time it starts again. The biggest winds and rain are due to hit in three hours, tops, but both of us have to get far from here while we have the chance." She tried to smile. "We'll each grieve for Jimmy alone. It's too dangerous to stay here talking. He'd understand. Go."

"What about you? Not asking *where*, but do you have a safe place and some kind of transport?"

"I do. I've already packed some things. Got them hidden around the corner behind a dumpster. I just needed to, well, say goodbye to Jimmy. I hope you and I get to meet again one day."

"Me too." I choked out, "We have to survive, Priya. We can't let them win."

She nodded. I squeezed her hand and quickly turned my back so I wouldn't see which direction she took. I should have vaulted over a bench and hidden again in the trees of the Park in case someone had seen us, but I couldn't seem to move.

Jimmy Pinder, who'd never harmed another person in his entire life, who'd showed me how to cook what few veggies Ajay could grow, who'd taught me chords on a nonexistent piano he'd drawn on the back of a paper bag from the grocery store, who'd bandaged my skinned knees and ankles and arms, who'd taken turns with Ajay softly singing me to sleep after my mom died and my dad and grandparents all went missing, had been murdered. Executed.

Ajay had said I was impulsive, brash, and reckless. He was right. I was in danger worse than I'd ever faced, but for this one moment I didn't care. I opened my mouth and sang Jimmy Pinder's favorite song:

I'm just a poor wayfaring stranger
Travelin' through this world of woe
There is no sickness, no toil or danger
In that bright land to which I go.
I'm going there to see my father
I'm going there no more to roam
I'm only goin' over Jordan
I'm only go...ing over home.

I began the second verse of this beautiful old spiritual, "Wayfaring Stranger":

I know dark clouds will gather 'round me
I know my way is rough and steep
But golden fields lie just before me
Where God's redeemed shall ever sleep...

Suddenly, in complete accord, with total disregard for every ban against music and anything smacking of a belief in a Higher Power, not caring for the moment if fifteen Delegates appeared to haul us all away, about twenty-two neighbors and friends of Jimmy Pinder, of all ages and ethnicities, stood in the rain and joined in the last chorus:

I'm goin' home to see my mother
And all my loved ones who've gone on
I'm only goin' over Jordan
I'm only goin' over home.

I spotted Jane and Richard Warwick among the crowd but did not acknowledge them in case a Delegate was nearby. They were simply part of a group of neighbors paying tribute and they didn't need to be associated further with Cori Christopher, who'd been marked as a member of Ostinato by a traitor.

Jane Warwick was talking to someone I couldn't see, but she caught my eye and nodded almost imperceptibly. She and Richard were probably okay. After all, they'd managed to keep their Class Status One for years, but in any case, I couldn't stay and worry about anyone else who might show up to this makeshift memorial.

It was time to go. Time to find my own Jordan on this earth if I could. Somewhere far from New Manhattan.

****

Joshua. A simple, three-syllable name written on a small piece of paper in Ajay's hand and left in a pouch on a radiator. Wouldn't mean a thing to anyone apart from Ajay and his husband Arthur, my family, and Jimmy. All gone now. But it was a clue to a possible refuge for me. Most likely short-termed, but I had to have faith that if I could rest and plan for a few hours, my brain would snap to and figure out the next step to what would hopefully be freedom.

My best bet might be to try and contact Elijah Terry

and see if he could find a way to get me to Tarrytown. From there? If I could manage to get transportation from Tarrytown, I'd head south to real America. Maybe somewhere inland. Someplace without storms hitting every other month. Someplace without Delegates, Committees, or traitors.

Then it hit me. Elijah had just lost his only child, Inez. He was in more danger than I, and grieving to boot. I was totally on my own. I shoved the thought away. Thanks to Ajay, I had a safe house, albeit a temporary one.

A bit of back history: Ostinato had been founded by people entrenched in the performing arts. Singers, dancers, musicians, along with costume, set, and lighting designers who'd worked for Broadway theaters and opera houses before the various bans. My dad and Ajay had been the ones who came up with the idea for a code based on songs. Robin Christopher and Ajay Roy were not only fans of musical theater, they were rabid devotees of twentieth-century popular music. The Committee had banned almost all music except for a few classical pieces, primarily instrumental ones. Consequently, the members of Ostinato felt confident using these old songs would be a fairly secure way to make contact or convey plans.

For example: The song "Forty-Five Minutes from Broadway." Written by George M. Cohan for a musical of the same name. If an operative in Ostinato received a message with that phrase, it meant, "Meet me at Number 45, at what used to be the New Amsterdam Theater, at 7:06 pm. The time came from the year 1906, which was when Mr. Cohan composed the music. Impossible for someone outside of Ostinato to understand.

My favorite code was the tune "Serenade" from the operetta *The Student Prince*, written by Rudolf Friml and performed at Jolson's 59th Street Theater in 1924. The buildings on Prince Street in lower Manhattan had been demolished in the killer hurricane, but the address sent operatives to the old St. Patrick's Cathedral, which was on the corner of Prince and Mulberry. Time was 5:09 in the evening.

Which leads me to Joshua.

"Joshua" was also a code, but a private one. My grandparents, Yash and Aubrey Kapoor, owned two residences. One was the address on Payson Avenue across the street and about two doors down from Ajay and Jimmy. It was used on all the forms and identity papers required by the Committee for everyone living in New Manhattan.

There was a second house on Staff Street, first purchased by my great-great-grandparents in the 1940s. It passed to my great-grandparents and then, after they died, to my grandparents, who kept it but never bothered to change the names on the address. After 2036, when the Committee became the restrictive governing body of New Manhattan, the house on Staff Street became a place to hide.

I'd been there about twenty times in my life. I even managed to sneak inside, the year I was ten, in the week everyone in my family, apart from Ajay, either died or disappeared. I'd run away from the city-owned residence where the Committee placed me, and I hid and cried. Ajay and Arthur found me, and the three of us spent five days watching movies and trying to figure out if there was any way they could keep me without the Committee finding me. There wasn't.

New zoning hit the city long before Hurricane Calder, yet the house on Staff Street managed to remain a single-family home, with a back yard and a spot where, according to family legend, my great-great-grandfather used to hold prayer meetings that included a lot of loud singing of old spirituals. The majority of the single-family homes were long gone by the time I first visited, but my dad loved the history of the Kapoors' home and meetings, and nicknamed the residence "Jericho" in honor of the hymn "Joshua Fit the Battle."

I'd memorized the tune and the lyrics to the song before I was able to read or write. My dad, grandmother, and Ajay took turns singing it to me from the time I was born. I bugged everyone to buy me a trumpet so I could learn how to blow a gospel horn, a request that was, wisely, ignored.

Yesterday, after the memorial, when I read the note attached to Jimmy's radiator with the name "Joshua" written on it, plus the hidden key, I instantly knew Ajay intended for me to have a place to hide should it become necessary.

It had become necessary.

I was tired, angry, sad, discouraged, and also completely soaked by the time I made it to Staff Street and Jericho. Putting nothing past the reach of the Committee, I half expected to see the Kapoor family home in ruins. When I spotted the house and saw it was intact, I had the feeling that Ajay, Jimmy, and probably Arthur as well had gotten together in whatever passed for an afterlife and, as my own special angels, were guarding the place so it could be my safe house, at least for a while.

Jericho's architecture was quite similar to Jimmy and Ajay's house on Payson. One entered into a hallway on the first floor and immediately was faced with a huge coat rack with a mirror behind it, a seating bench covered with an ancient tapestry, and an antique butter churn doubling as an umbrella stand. Two bone-dry umbrellas, belonging to Aubrey and Yash Kapoor and consequently unused for ten years, still stood upright in the old churn.

A soft left turn led one into the living room to view an eclectic hodgepodge of centuries, colors, and design, made up of furniture taken from theatrical productions no longer allowed. Southern country-style rocking chairs had been placed opposite a twentieth-century sectional sofa and two "assemble-it-yourself" end tables needed to double as bookshelves for the overflow, although there were four gigantic bookcases already taking up an entire wall from floor to ceiling. The Christophers and Kapoors were voracious readers. A rolling ladder stood in the middle of the second bookcase.

I stopped, feeling a wrench in my heart as soon as I noticed the chess set sitting on the small table in the corner of the library. Ajay had taught me the game when I was eight, after he'd played the album from the concept musical version of *Chess* about ten times for me. I'd been intrigued as to why this game had inspired the composers to write such gorgeous music.

I stared at the set with its pieces in place for a game and found myself singing a variety of songs from *Chess,* wishing Ajay had just waited and made this escape (however brief it might be) with me.

I sighed and forcefully thrust away the memory of the last time Ajay and I had been in Jericho. It didn't make me feel more courageous. I just wanted to curl up somewhere and cry.

I also wanted to explore every room, but curiosity

won out over nostalgia. I had to check the shelves to find whatever book the last occupant of the room had been searching for or returning to its place. Every member of the family had partaken in and enjoyed the tradition of leaving a book slightly out of sync with the others on the same row, to suggest an interesting read to the next member of the family to grace the library. Sometimes the book held a clue regarding plans for whatever activity might be upcoming…rebellious or otherwise.

I hadn't forgotten the Cassandra warnings and visions I'd been having for more than a week. I had to find out what they meant. Sadly, those involving Ajay had already come true. The flashing images of France made no sense. Hopefully, someone had left a book for me hinting as to what I needed to do next. Who the someone could be was a mystery. Apart from Ajay, no one had been inside for years. Yet I knew there was a book waiting.

I climbed the ladder and found an oversized coffee-table book sticking out of the second-to-top shelf. The spine showed the title as *A History of Cabarets and Opera Houses in Paris from 1877 to 1955.* Not one's typical relaxing read for an evening. Intriguing.

A large piece of paper was taped to the front piece with the words, "Cori, don't read yet…watch me first!" written in purple ink. I'm no handwriting expert, but the script looked suspiciously like Granny Aubrey's, who used to drive everyone into a frustrated frenzy with her illegible calligraphy-style letters and who, incidentally, loved purple.

Eradicating the somewhat childish urge to slide the ladder from side to side, I held the book in one hand and climbed down the rungs. I had no intention of acting impulsively and crash-landing onto the floor, ending up with a broken arm or leg with no one around to help.

I hadn't eaten all day, so I was about to hit the kitchen for a quick check of the pantry but stopped and gave in to the temptation to sink into a ridiculously comfortable, oversized, faded blue, faux leather lounger chair in the library. I remained paralyzed there for about five minutes, contemplating the various dismal aspects for my future.

I could try staying at Jericho, but until I knew who had betrayed at least two members of Ostinato, I couldn't be sure the Committee wouldn't discover my hiding place and either drag me out or blow up the house. I'd always assumed no one apart from the Kapoor or Christopher families knew of the existence of this particular residence. No one alive, that is. On the other hand, I wasn't privy to all the secrets held by the leading members of our group, so if the traitor was one of them, I might well be out of luck for this particular sanctuary.

I allowed another five minutes of sitting and engaging in a walloping good bout of out-and-out sobbing over the useless deaths of Ajay and Jimmy before delivering an internal smack to the head to stop. There was no point in making myself sick, and nothing would bring back my family and friends. I had to come up with a plan of action for my future.

But I stayed for a few more moments because curling up in the old lounger brought back memories of my dad holding me in his lap and singing to me. Of Granny Aubrey joining us. I smiled as I remembered the time she called to me from high atop the ladder, when, at age fifty-something, she began belting out songs from a show called *Sweet Charity*. She'd been wearing bright purple running shorts and a white sleeveless shirt and cleanly performing high kicks from her precarious perch, to the great delight of the five-year-old Cori Christopher. I remembered Ajay taking over the singing at various times, so my dad could go bake scones in the kitchen. I could almost detect the scent of them…

I sat up straight. I *could* smell them. Cranberry-orange scones.

I jumped up out of the chair and ran to the kitchen. No one was there. I opened the French doors leading to the dining area. Again…no human greeted me, but I immediately spotted a flat machine like an old DVD player sitting on the table and was drawn to it in a way similar to Great-Great Grandpa Kapoor's ancient bees upon scenting a flower.

I felt like Alice in Wonderland seeing the bottle with "drink me" on the label. Like Alice, I had to take a chance. There was a large red power button on the front of the odd contraption, and I decided in this case "drink me" could be the same as "press me."

I pressed it.

Chapter 8

Aubrey Collier Kapoor stared out at me. I was instantly entranced by the big light shining through her midsection.

"Hi, Sweet Cori! Yep...it's me...or I...whichever... I'm a singer, not a grammarian. You found the hologram. Awesome. Or not, because, sadly, if you're seeing this it means you're in big trouble, but at least Ajay found a way to get you the keys to Jericho."

I pressed the pause button and tried to breathe like a normal person instead of a drowned rat coming up for air after staying too long in a deep well. A hologram. Discover Life Studios had done a short film about them not long after I started my job, but I'd never seen a real one in action. I couldn't help it—even with the horrors of the last week, I began to laugh. I was looking at the image of Aubrey Collier Kapoor as I last saw her, when she was sixty-three years old. Which would have been ten years ago on my tenth birthday. She was always demonstrative, but she'd been especially affectionate that day, talking about how fantastic it was we looked and sounded so much alike. She'd told me she was very proud of me. Then she'd stressed how I should be aware and listen to my inner warnings—she'd been the one to label them Cassandra premonitions—as she hinted of dire things to come.

Two days later, Granny Aubrey was gone. For ten

years, when I'd asked Ajay where she was, his response had been, "I'm clueless, Cori. She was picked up by Delegates and they're not exactly forthcoming about what they do with prisoners. You must know she loves you and she's going to try and come back when or if she can. I keep hoping Yash found a way for her to escape with him. But, Cori, I'm absolutely sure if they can get in touch with us, they will."

This appeared to be the day Aubrey Kapoor was getting in touch, albeit as an image I could pass my hand through. She was dressed in an interesting blue coverall set. It reminded me of a paratrooper's jump suit, circa 1940s, but with lace on every edge and hem.

I hit the Play button again, intrigued, sad, confused and, frankly, durned stinkin' angry, feeling betrayed by a family who'd been out of my life for ten years.

"Cori, whatever the reason is for you watching this now, I guess you're grown up enough to understand more about the…oh, let's call them gifts you own, which have been genetically passed to the women in our family for centuries." She stopped and her smile pierced through the light as if she were in the room with me. *"You have the Cassandra sight, and maybe sometimes it seems like a curse, but I swear it's kept me from getting captured by Delegates more than once. The second gift is, of course, perfect pitch and one totally amazing voice."* She paused as she mused, *"Or should I say two other gifts, which then makes it three total? Whatever. Can't tell you how glad I am you inherited The Voice. Your mom didn't, even though she got some of the Cassandra sight. She did have perfect pitch; just not the chops to back it up. Which I guess might have been a blessing because she never had the urge to go down to*

the square following the Committee's big ban and let loose with a variety of tunes from Dear Evan Hansen. *Something I did with Ajay that nearly landed us both in jail when you were a toddler. It was worth it to see the faces of the people brave enough to stay and listen."*

I remembered. Ajay had described the outing to me, and at age four, I'd been miffed because I hadn't been invited to go with them. Heck, I could sing the harmonies for every part required for all the songs in the show. Still could. I pulled my focus back to the holographic visualizer.

"Anyway, back to the reason for this hologram. Are you sitting?" Pause. *"Cori...dammit, sit down."*

I sat.

"Oops! Wait a sec. I spoke too soon. If there's any brandy around, you might pour a glass. I left a couple of bottles in the cabinet nearest to what used to pass as a dining table. Press Pause, Sweetie, and go grab a glass and a bottle. Possibly more than one. You're going to need it."

I did as requested and found four bottles of brandy right where Granny Aubrey had placed them... whenever. The glasses were in the kitchen cabinet and probably hadn't been cleaned in years, but I didn't really care. I grabbed one and poured about four ounces of brandy into it, then wandered back into the living room, sat, took a tiny sip, and pressed Play.

"Are you settled again? Lovely. Be careful, Cori. I have no idea how well you hold your liquor and I don't want you passed out drunk, but go ahead and knock down a few swigs. Big ones."

One small sip had been nice, but this sounded like a better idea. I took a few swigs. Big ones.

"Fine. Now then, do not *jump up calling me a lunatic. Because, the truth is…I have traveled through time."*

I jumped up. "Aubrey Collier Kapoor, you're a lunatic!"

I always knew she'd been a dreamer, with more optimism than any sane person had the right to harbor in a city ruled by a Morality Committee who thought nothing of sending killers out to threaten any human who disagreed with their point of view. Aubrey's idealism (and lunacy) was very evident the morning in 2041 when she somehow persuaded her daughter, my mother Celeste, to name me Terpsichore, in honor of the Greek Muse of the Dance, and added to the wackiness with the middle name, Nira, which is Hindi for "light." Word was Celeste gave birth to me in the middle of one of New Manhattan's frequent blackouts and was too exhausted from puffing and pushing to care if I was alive, much less what anyone called me, including her enthusiastic, possibly deranged mother.

The hologram remained static and silent for about two minutes, allowing me to pace, drink, and pace a bit more. I hadn't bothered to hit Pause. We hadn't seen each other in ten years, but Granny Aubrey knew me way too well.

I sank back down in the oversized recliner and raised my glass to the image. "Okay, Gran. Please continue."

This was just…weird. I was conversing with someone who wasn't physically there, yet a person so in tune with me as to be able to anticipate reactions, including the amount of time necessary to down two ounces of brandy and be ready for the next surprise.

"You're over the whole 'Aubrey is a lunatic' thing,

then, right? Okay, you're wondering where I am. Oops. Should be when *I am."*

"Yeah, kinda top of the list."

"Well, I'm still in New Manhattan but in the year twenty-two-twenty. It's back to being Manhattan, thank heaven, the Committee and all its nastiness long gone. The storms have dissipated. Subways run again and people smile in the streets. Best thing ever…singing is not only allowed but encouraged! Now be quiet and let me explain why I left you when you were ten. And how."

"Fine." I took another large swallow. "Okay, Gran. Can you tell me why I shouldn't have felt abandoned for ten years, believing you'd died?"

"I'm sorry. Really. I didn't want *to leave, Cori. And I had no idea your dad and mom wouldn't be around for you. My own Cassandra warnings just went kaput for a while about anyone but me. Selfish but, let's face it, we can't control what comes through. Anyway, I had to go. I got caught by two Delegates and was sentenced by the Committee to be executed the day after your tenth birthday."*

I took another swig of brandy. Didn't even feel a buzz.

Granny Aubrey continued: *"I'll get to the main action, but first, I want to give you some history of this house your dad named Jericho. It was originally bought in the early nineteen-fifties by your great-great-grandparents, Yash's grandparents, Devi and Gulika Kapoor. Back then the majority of folks in New York City either didn't realize Upper Manhattan existed or didn't care because only poor immigrants lived in the area, mainly Irish or Jewish refugees from Germany and Russia. Still not sure how the Kapoors from New Delhi snuck in. The area was set for rezoning starting around twenty-seventeen, but somehow our house didn't get swept into the whole housing deal. Anyway, both Inwood and Washington Heights were neglected—really, completely ignored—after the Big Storm in twenty-thirty-one, Hurricane Calder, and people were dumb enough to vote into power what became the Morality Committee because the old system fell apart trying to deal with the loss of three boroughs. For some reason, the Committee and the Delegates never realized tons of people do live above Central Park. Strange, because Upper Manhattan is far safer from flooding, and one would imagine safety would be the main issue for the future. I mean, geographically it's on much higher ground, and heck, the Cloisters Museum is one fabulous fortress. I guess all the culture there scared the Delegate goons too much to venture inside, apart from looting the place of every valuable treasure. At any rate, the reluctance of the Committee to move out of Midtown, what they renamed Center Town, was a lucky thing for us."*

She was a bit out of date with the Committee's reluctance to enter this area, considering Jimmy Pinder had been murdered hours ago less than ten blocks away. She was also rambling and it was ticking me off. "Get to the damned point, Gran!"

"I'm getting to the damned point, Cori! Years ago, your grandfather and I arranged with someone trustworthy to look after the place. Keep the power on, the water running. Make sure the pantry was stocked for any visits. And if you're there and watching this hologram, and I guess you are, although I can't tell when it's on, well anyway, it means the Committee and the

Delegates are still unaware of Jericho's existence… at least for a while longer."

"Are you saying I have some time to use this as a refuge?"

"What I'm saying is I'm honestly not sure how much time you've got to hide out. But, for safety's sake, don't take too long to make a decision."

"A decision?"

"Cori, you're not going to believe my story, but you must*. Look, after we celebrated your tenth birthday, Ajay and I went on a mission to rescue a friend of ours, Bernie Goldman, before he was sent to Camp Virtue. He'd been arrested when they found a bag full of leaflets warning people about the Committee being a throwback to the regimes of Hitler and Stalin, not to mention the Taliban in every durn country ending with a 'stan.' Bernie was thrown into jail and was living in positively wretched conditions for about three months as the words 'bail' and 'arraignment' were not in the Committee's vocabulary."*

"Still not," I muttered.

"Still not, I'll bet. Anyway, the three of us—uh, your dad, Ajay, and I—hatched a plan for Bernie's rescue during his transfer. Your grandfather was out of commission from some food poisoning or he'd have gone and things probably wouldn't have been both successful and a failure. Your dad did the planning but couldn't help with the action. He was busy with his own issues trying to keep you and Celeste safe. Point being, I got Bernie out, but I wrenched my ankle trying to climb down a wall and was grabbed. Ajay managed to get away, although I had to force him to leave when he did. I was charged with sedition and treason, and my execution

ordered for the next day. No trial, of course. The Committee had a file on me for what they called 'numerous revolutionary activities' against their New Manhattan. I was quite proud of my record, but it was kind of my undoing. Side note, we were sure someone in Ostinato was informing on us, which means they might still *be alive and could be the reason you're sitting here now listening."*

Chapter 9

I hit Pause. Oh, yeah. A *lot* more brandy was in order. I poured another glass and nearly chugged half of it down my throat in one swallow, which is an insult to good brandy, but my attention was elsewhere so I wasn't exactly savoring the taste.

I punched the Play button again and listened as Granny explained how Grandpa Yash managed to get in touch with an acquaintance he'd met years earlier when this person was working as an usher in some theater. She was not associated with Ostinato or any other resistance group but had told Yash she was a miracle worker when it came to rescues. Yash asked if she could bring Aubrey some clean clothes the morning before she was set to be "exterminated" and also provide one of those miracles.

"The acquaintance turned out to be a very intriguing—and extremely short—uh, witch or angel or deus ex machina or…something…who sent us into the year twenty-two-twenty. Hang in there, Cori. She's about to join us. Her name is Fiona Belle Donovan Winthorp."

A disembodied voice with a pronounced Irish lilt could be heard yelling, *"Don't ya be mentionin' Winthorp. I despised that man!"*

A head popped into view. The rest of the body was invisible…out of sight of the hologram's range. I found myself staring at a mouth stretched into an enormous grin displaying perfect white teeth. They'd do a Louisiana swamp gator proud.

Words issued forth. *"I'll be afta gettin' the scones now."*

"Fiona Belle makes the most marvelous scones on the planet. Her specialty is cranberry-orange, and they're better than mine or your dad's. I wish you were with us."

I didn't have to be. I swore I could smell them. The same scent that had drawn me into the dining room. I wasn't aware a hologram could transmit odors, but apparently this one could. Or was my sensory imagination working overtime? Didn't matter. I was salivating.

Granny Aubrey sighed. *"Dammit. I repeat, I didn't want to leave you, but, if you don't mind me being both trite and somewhat literal here, my head was definitely on the chopping block and I didn't want to die. And suddenly, Fiona Belle appears with an answer for Yash and me. For you and your parents as well, but Celeste didn't want to go with your dad. Not sure why."*

Granny couldn't hear me, but I replied anyway. "I think I do. I heard her and Dad arguing about something but it made no sense at the time. He was saying we all had to escape and some wacky option offered was the best choice. She said she'd had enough of fighting and craziness and just wanted peace and it was too dangerous for her ten-year-old daughter to go jumping into the insanity my father was proposing. I remember my dad talking about the book *Anne of Green Gables* and how an idyllic life in the Canadian wilderness was lovely but ultimately didn't do much to aid the human race. And she said she'd do anything to keep me safe and the human race be hanged."

Fiona Belle's voice could be heard over the viewer. *"Celeste Christopher was as stubborn as clover in a potato field."*

I had to laugh. She was right. My mother could dig her heels in like no one else except for Ajay, and Celeste generally was determined to go the opposite direction from my dad, Robin Christopher. Take Ostinato, for example. If there was a risk to be taken, he was first to volunteer. It was clear from birth I'd not only inherited Robin's red hair, freckles, and temper but his genetic disposition for jumping into danger. I'd gotten perfect pitch and Cassandra warnings from Celeste, but basically, I was Robin's girl.

Celeste died the same time my dad vanished, so I never got to discover what the whole Canada wilderness thing was all about. I was sure of my mom's death because I'd been with her, hiding from Delegates who'd come to our apartment on Payson Avenue looking for my father. Celeste and I made it as far as Fort Tryon Park, but our timing turned deadly. We found ourselves smack in the middle of Hurricane Madison, which produced wind gusts above eighty miles per hour. My mother was killed when one of those gusts knocked down a portion of an awning over an abandoned store. It struck her head as she instinctively used her last moments to throw her arms around me and keep me safe.

I still had no idea if Dad was alive…in any time or place. He went missing the same time as my grandparents. I'd been told he was lost to the waters of the ocean while helping shore up a section of wall—near what had once been the Bowery—in the middle of the storm. Hurricane Madison had robbed me of both parents. I always assumed my grandparents had also been swept into the ocean along with my father. I now questioned whether or not Robin Christopher could also be alive in another time, and why he hadn't tried harder to convince my mother to come with him or to at least let me go too.

I pulled my focus back to the hologram and rewound, having missed a few sentences.

"You back with me? Good. So, Yash and I decided to give twenty-two-twenty a shot. It sounded far enough into the future where the Committee would have long since met its doom, as most tyrannical regimes do at some point, yet not too far in case more storms would have destroyed more of the planet, if things continued the way they were, or technology would have taken over completely and humanity be gone and we'd feel completely lost and out of place. I wish you could be with us now, but Fiona Belle insists it's a 'no.' If you'd come with us originally, it wouldn't have been an issue, but more than two people traveling to the same time and not together is against the rules."

"Rules? Time traveling has rules?"

The hologram of Granny Aubrey ignored my question.

She continued, *"But Cori, Jericho isn't really a viable safe house anymore. And with your twenty-first birthday coming up, I don't want you anywhere near New Manhattan to be married off to someone the Committee deems suitable. When they do a DNA test, and they will, and discover you're one-quarter Indian, well, chained to someone you don't love in marriage could swiftly change to being chained to a wall in Camp Virtue."*

77

I ignored all the comments about dangers I knew quite well were coming and instead focused on the whole idea of time travel. "I'm dreaming this, right? The brandy was laced with hallucinogens? How do I process this stuff about time and believe it?"

My grandmother lapsed into silence for a moment. Then I heard her ask, *"What?"*

"Let me talk to her."

Fiona Belle Donovan Winthorp (oops, scratch Winthorp, the man she despised) entered the viewing screen, holding out a tray piled high with scones. I blinked, then hit Pause to allow the image to freeze so I could take in and appreciate the full effect.

Granny Aubrey had mentioned her rescuer was short. She was right. I remembered Granny once saying she wished she wasn't five-eight—I'd inherited my height of five-ten from the Collier side of the family—as it might be easier to slip in and out of small spaces. This woman appeared to be at least twelve inches shorter than Aubrey Collier Kapoor.

I stared at the image, mesmerized. Fiona Belle's curly pink-and-green hair was trapped by a large band with a huge purple bow attached to the top. She had a round pixie face perfectly suited to her height. Her eyelids were smeared with blue powder and her lips with a blood-red stain. A crimson-and-pink jeweled bra top covered the essentials of her more-than-abundant chest but left an equally considerable midriff bare. Starting around mid-hip were garments I'd seen worn in a Bollywood movie made in India somewhere around 1999—emerald-and-red harem trousers with a variety of silver sparkly beads hanging from a front belt. Six bracelets adorned each wrist. Her feet were bare and the perfectly pedicured toenails were polished with some kind of neon purple paint.

And the fierce little critter was now speaking in a strange dialect, Irish with a twist of who-knew-what. *"Aubrey is afta chowin' down while the scones are hot, so I'll fill ya in and then ya can make your own bluidy decision as to where ya want to go."*

"This is just beyond wacked, but, yeah, sure, what the heck, go ahead. Tell me the next step in this so-called miraculous journey." I downed a few more sips of brandy.

Fiona Belle continued, *"Whatcha first haveta be doin' is findin' sheet music with the time and date relatin' to the 'where.' Can be someone else's cover of the song...doesn't have to be the original artist. Hold the paper, sing a chorus or a bridge or a verse in yer perfect voice while ya concentrate on the where and time...and whammo! There ya be!"*

Granny Aubrey once again appeared on screen.

"It's really rather thrilling. Fiona Belle was kind enough to deliver music from twenty-two-twenty written by a fabulous composer who goes by the name of Venice. She'd already helped your Grandpa Yash travel, a day before me, and I sang a chorus and the next thing I knew...future time! Yash was waiting for me We're talkin' wicked-fab!" She glanced at Fiona Belle. *"But tell her the rules."*

"You get two full trips. So, four times, total, to make up yer mind, in case ya don't like where or when you ended up or you're in real danger. And only one person gets ta find out the truth in whatever time period you are. Ya can take one person with ya if ya choose to go ta some time other than the one you're in. Now, ya can't go

zappin' inta twenty-two-twenty because of the whole problem that can be with too many folks who've traveled showin' up in the same place, and ya got two relatives here already."

Aubrey took over. *"Listen, Cori, it's kind of a jolt when you land, and things are somewhat off for a bit. Heck, they're way off for a bit. I had no memory of who I was for about five or six hours, although I gather its different for each traveler. And why I'm telling you this now is a mystery, because you won't remember when you to get to wherever you're going. For what it's worth, if you do make a second, third, or fourth trip, you should have no memory issues. Anyway, I know this is a* lot *to take in. But, returning one more time to the topic of this area and the house…you* should *be safe here for at least a day or two. Take a few hours to explore and enjoy some music and old movies before you make your choice. Just be sure to* make *a choice. My warnings have never stopped screaming this is the year you're going to be terrorized by Delegates. And as outrageous as it seems, time travel is the best option. Oh! I tried to make sure our caretaker would continue to see the place was always stocked with decent food for at least a month or so, plus Fiona Belle dropped in not long ago to make sure things were in order. Okay. Got it? Hey, I love you. As Fiona Belle said, you can't join us, but she'll get word to Yash and me when you're okay, so we won't worry."*

Fiona Belle waved her off. *"Enough chatter. Sign off, Aubrey. And, Cori? Remember, 'there* is *a balm in Gilead.' Au revoir."*

Chapter 10

As part of my job at Discover Life, I'd learned how to start a fire, escape a fire, ride a bicycle, change a tire on a bicycle, recognize symptoms of a person collapsing from heart failure, perform CPR on a person who'd collapsed from heart failure, and swim using three different stroke styles. Nowhere in the reels of film at the studio had there been any tips on how to traverse temporal highways. But Ajay's favorite movie, which instantly became mine when I first saw it at age ten, was *Somewhere in Time*. Ajay, Arthur, and I had made use of Arthur's house in Riverdale—north of Inwood and Upper Manhattan—where the guys kept a ton of contraband, including movies and books and musical recordings from the early twenty-first century, plus a large load from the twentieth, along with the devices with which to view them. At last count, I'd seen *Somewhere in Time* about forty times.

I wasn't an idiot. I knew the movie was fiction. It had never occurred to me such a thing was really possible, although the romantic side of me always wished I loved someone enough to try and reach them through time, no matter the impossibility.

And now, here I was, head spinning—possibly due to too much brandy without food, as well as the last hour's revelations—sitting in the family safe house. Was this all a trick? Were my grandparents really alive and well in the future? Or had someone forced Aubrey and some deranged actress friend of hers to make the hologram? Perhaps at that very same Camp Virtue where her friend, Bernie, might still be interned?

Nah. Didn't seem likely. Granny Aubrey looked too happy, and I couldn't imagine camp guards allowing Fiona Belle to be dressed as garishly as she was, even if they were trying to fool me. Not to mention…to what end? A practical joke on Cori Christopher? The Committee members, and definitely their Delegates, had no sense of humor, unless they thought sending this hologram would somehow trap me into revealing my whereabouts and spilling my guts about the other members of Ostinato.

I was now ninety-eight percent into believing it was all true and a tiny witch, space alien, or guardian angel was smugly sitting on the ability to send people through time. Which brought up other questions. Who got chosen, and why? My grandparents had traveled separately, but could two folks zip off to another year simultaneously? Neither Granny nor Fiona Belle had explained why Ajay and Arthur hadn't been given a chance to disappear into the corridors of time.

I growled and spoke to the air. "Why in Hades didn't you send Fiona Belle here to rescue Ajay? Granny, you have the same stinkin' premonition or second-sight gift as I do. Didn't you sense Ajay was going to die? Are you so far away in the future you can't access what's happening here? You say you figured out I'm in trouble…why not Ajay? I *know* bloody well he's not in another time, peacefully sipping cognac with Arthur and serenading him with show tunes, because I saw his body seconds before the Examiners from the Offices of Death showed up. And guess what, ladies? Thanks to my job and some fancy CPR and First Aid training, I can spot the differences between a living person and one who is deceased. Giant error, Gran, on not saving Ajay. This goes double for you, Fiona Belle Donovan Winthorp or whatever your *bluidy guid* name is!"

I pushed myself up from the chair and began to wander aimlessly around the house. I was too keyed up to concentrate. I needed music to calm me down. And talk about contraband...the pickings at Jericho made Arthur and Ajay's stash look pitiful. The room Ajay used to refer to as Media Central was filled with stacks and stacks of recordings, a big "boom box" for compact discs, presumably ready to go with fresh batteries placed there by whoever also made certain this house was taken care of. Did Fiona Belle have some elfish handyman on retainer who popped in from other eras and countries? Not important. Anyway, my favorite gadget, gizmo, contraption, whatever, in the room was an antique Victrola machine. It lured me like the Sirens once lured the sailors. I had a strong feeling I'd be using it soon.

I grabbed the giant book about French opera houses and cabarets, and the somewhat diminished bottle of brandy, and made my way into Media Central. Both Granny and Fiona Belle had indicated I had some choice and free rein as to where I was going, assuming I didn't just curl up and try to hide at Jericho for the next twenty years or so, but there were some major hints pointing to, if not the *when*, at least the *where*. Including my own flashes over the last couple of weeks all having to do with something...or someone...in Paris, France. Fiona Belle had ended the holographic conversation with *"Au revoir!"* and a cryptic phrase, "There is a balm in

Gilead," I suspected might be part of a song—a song leading to another place and another time?

Unlike everyone else in our family, my mother, Celeste Kapoor Christopher, had not been an extrovert or a rebel. While Aubrey, Granddad Yash, Ajay, my dad Robin, and other members of Ostinato had been out singing in public and avoiding arrest or hiding friends who might be guilty of a lot more than singing or spraying graffiti on Committee buildings, Celeste had been at Jericho, using her considerable organizational skills to put Media Central in order. She'd brought me here to help, starting from the time I was a precocious three-year-old and could read aloud titles of songs and movies and dates and places.

One of Celeste's proudest achievements was the Book of Songs, which was a misnomer as it was closer to twenty books. Instead of cataloging music by genre, she'd listed songs by name of artist/artists and date of recording. If you had a partial recollection of the name of a song but weren't sure of the date or who sang it, you could look up what you hoped was the title and find the rest, no matter whether the song had been sung in a Broadway show, executed with precision via the London Symphony Orchestra, or performed by an itinerant banjo player meandering through a Southern gospel tent revival. If you were looking for music from a particular time period, you could peruse the book—divided by generations, twenty-five years per book—and find various songs and who sang them or played them on instruments.

I grabbed two of the Song Books, one from 1925 to 1950 and the other from 1950 to 1975, and sank to the floor. I opened the second book, and scanned through the alphabetized listings to see if there was a song called "There Is a Balm in Gilead." A quick search showed a recording from 1975 by folk singer Marcus Kennedy, who, with an album of spirituals, had bucked the trend of the sixties' protest singers who were shifting over to rock or pop. His a cappella version of "Johnny Has Gone for a Soldier" was what I'd sung at the Chanson Theater the night before Ajay was murdered. But Kennedy wasn't French, and my gut was telling me New York City in the nineteen-seventies wasn't the era I was looking for. I picked up the book listing songs from 1925 to 1950, flipped through to the T's, and there it was. "There Is a Balm in Gilead" recorded in 1941 by some collegiate orchestra now disbanded.

I had my year. But I knew this wasn't the right song, given the orchestra had been based in America. My itchy feelings about France were now bashing me over the head. Any other option was wrong.

Another of the books Celeste had organized was made up of all the recordings stored at Jericho. In this index, the music could be found using genre, then date, then singers or musicians or full orchestras.

The next two hours were spent searching. Success came when I discovered a vinyl album recorded in January 1941 in Paris at an old music hall or opera house which had been converted to a cabaret/night club in the 1920s. The name of the club was Café Violette. There were eight tracks on the recording, including the one I was looking for, sung by a Monsieur Jacques Benet.

I took the Café Violette album out of the sleeve and set it on the antique record player. I started to read the liner notes on the back of the recording's jacket to find which track featured "There is a Balm in Gilead," but paused, my attention drawn to the faded black-and-white photo featuring eight people. Four men were pictured holding musical instruments. One man was sitting on the piano bench. Three others…one woman and two men…sat at a table a few feet away from a stage. I couldn't stop staring at a young man who appeared to be gazing directly at me, flashing a very wicked smile at the camera. Black hair curled wildly across his forehead and down his neck. He wore a turtleneck sweater and a jacket over dark trousers and held a cigarette in his right hand.

The liner notes, to my intense frustration, didn't go into detail. There was only one crummy paragraph about Café Violette hosting various famous artists throughout the 1920s and '30s. A list of names was provided as to the regulars who performed at Café Violette, with nothing to identify who was who in the photo apart from Mademoiselle Genevieve, the only female in the bunch. I picked up the book featuring French opera houses and read the sparse information written about this nightclub. When I say sparse, I'm serious. I could find only two small paragraphs on page 278.

Café Violette perished from the records of history sometime late in the spring or early summer of 1941. The owner, Monsieur Pierre Simon, was Jewish and the inference was clear and tragic. Monsieur Simon had ended up at one of the camps earmarked for French Jews. The nightclub was shut down, then destroyed. Apparently burned to the ground, possibly in an explosion. There were rumors the club had been used for various clandestine activities, starting in 1939 right after Paris was occupied by the Nazis, but there was no real confirmation.

I sat and stared at the page for a good ten minutes.

Lunacy. Total wacked-out lunacy. Was I seriously considering trying to go back in time to do…what? Right the wrongs imposed by one of the worst regimes in modern history? I grew instantly depressed, admitting to myself I hadn't been able to make the slightest dent in changing my own time's oppressors.

Thinking about the Nazis made me remember a discussion with my dad, whom I adored, when I was six years old. He'd been my mentor, best friend, and role model. Along with Granny Aubrey and Ajay, he'd introduced me to the forbidden fruit…multiple genres of music, calling jazz especially a "sweet solace for the heart and the soul."

"Daddy, why don't they want us to sing fun stuff?" I'd asked him after he'd sung a cute song called 'Everybody Loves My Baby' for me one night as my bedtime lullaby. Not exactly sweetly nocturnal in tempo (more like ragtime) but I enjoyed every note. "Those mean Committee people."

"Because, Cori, they don't appreciate humanity. They have no desire to nourish hearts and souls," he'd answered. "Music—in fact, all the arts—can lift your spirits. Can make you feel emotions. Make you try to create a better world. So much of life's happiness comes from helping others, and music helps in a unique way. This isn't what the Committee leaders want. It's harder to control people if they're asking questions, or feeling hope, or simply projecting happiness for a moment out of the day. It's happened before, all too often. One of the most recent egregious—um…that means horrible or monstrous or severe—examples was in Europe during the nineteen-thirties and forties. During World War Two, being able to express oneself, to create art and music, was one reason people in occupied countries joined in resisting the Nazis. Sadly, it often got them killed. For example, in Germany itself, once the Nazis came to power, they shut down nightclubs where American swing music was played, and the musicians and the dancers were sent to work camps or simply killed as soon as they were arrested."

"Why were they killed?"

"First, let me tell you about '*La Marseillaise*,' " he responded. "It's a great example of a song used to evoke…to stir up…people to revolt against tyranny. It was written in the late seventeen-hundreds during the French Revolution, which has its own interesting history of both freedom and oppression and right and wrong. Anyway, during World War Two, in Occupied Paris, France, '*La Marseillaise*' gave courage to thousands of French people who wanted their country back. People who wanted the right to sing whatever they desired without interference from the Germans. The Germans knew this, and people brave enough to sing it were sent to concentration camps. Some, as I told you earlier, were executed on the spot."

I'd asked my dad to teach me the song, and he did. But along with a tune and lyrics I found inspiring was the impact of his words when I'd asked why the French people had still sung it knowing they'd be killed if the Nazis heard them.

As always, my dad treated me with respect and total honesty, although the answer wasn't pretty. "We all die, Cori. The leaders, the bullies, the young, the old. The good, the bad. The question becomes what you *do* with your life before your final day. Will you resist hate and fight for a simple right to be allowed to sing or dance or paint a picture or express a feeling? Or will you be the one knocking down the door to murder a brother or a sister because they were the wrong color? Because they dared to love the wrong person? Because they sang the wrong song? It's a choice. You're too young to understand those choices now, but one day they'll be yours to make. You've got boldness and the desire to do right coming down to you from both sides of the family. I don't have your gift of visions, but one day you'll have to make this choice, and I believe you'll go with freedom all the way. To help others find it."

I blinked back tears, recalling our conversation, and then scanned the names on the album cover for artists of Café Violette one more time. A force outside myself told me the young man with the face of a romantic poet was Noel Matheson, the singer for track number five, "Toujours." I counted the grooves and placed the needle on five.

Noel Matheson. This was his voice…a voice I fell in love with the instant I heard the first note. A voice piercing my soul and calling to me through time. The rest of the world faded, turned mute and opaque, leaving me in a pocket of stillness in time and space where only the two of us connected. Completing each other. Twin souls. My breath stopped for a long moment. I'd had the same thought before. Sometime in a past I didn't know existed. I replayed the song at least ten times, although my decision had been made the moment I'd picked up the album. Or perhaps a century and a half before.

It was time for action. I spent the next hour writing the notes and lyrics and placing today's date on sheet music for "Joshua Fit the Battle of Jericho" in case something happened and I needed to come back here.

The paper wasn't totally blank, it was the unused side of "Wayfaring Stranger" and I admit I took more than a few minutes to once again cry out my anguish about Jimmy and Ajay's deaths, and that of Inez Terry as well, although I'd never actually met her. The Delegates had had a very busy week stomping out freedom fighters.

I found a copy of the sheet music to "Toujours" sitting beside a large bag on the table closest to the record player. There was a red stain in the top corner of the music, next to the date, February1941. About a month after the recording had been made. I sniffed the stain. Cranberries with a hint of orange.

I smiled and waved to the air. "Thanks, Fiona Belle. Wherever and whenever you are."

The choice had been made. I was going back in time to Café Violette to try to save the nightclub, the owner, and Noel. Perhaps in doing so, I could even save myself.

Chapter 11

February 1941, Occupied Paris, France

I paused in my recollections of the previous night's events from more than a century in the future, and glared at Fiona Belle Donovan Winthorp, who was reveling in her role as wardrobe mistress for Café Violette. Her attire was right in step with this particular character, from the black dress and black shoes to the hair tied back in a severe bun, but I found myself missing the ridiculous Bollywood belly dancing ensemble I'd seen on the hologram.

"You! Thanks a heap, Mrs. Winthorp," I growled.

"Don't say Winthorp. I despised that man! Ya just be callin' me Fiona Belle. And yer welcome."

"Fine. I *do* remember you yelling about Winthorp across a holographic image of my grandmother. By the way, my 'thanks' was more on the level of major sarcasm for failing to warn me I'd have amnesia for a couple hours after sliding through time. I've been frantically searching in my mind to remember how and when and why I'm in Paris, and who you are, and everything that happened in the last twelve hours or so. Not to mention my own name."

Fiona Belle flashed a set of perfect, white, big teeth at me and slipped back and forth from Irish brogue to standard generic American. "We did warn ya. Aubrey told ya it took her about six hours to get, uh, recouped. Ya just didn't remember the warnin' because ya had temporary amnesia, yet you still recovered faster than she did. Anyway, what are ya griping about? It's all come back to ya, hasn't it? And again, surprisingly fast. Heck, ya recalled yer name in less than three hours. For what it's worth, if ya travel again, ya remember quicker. Sometimes there's no memory loss at all. Aubrey told ya, but ya didn't remember."

I sighed. "Not comforting. And I might have decided to just stay where I was at Jericho if I'd been told I'd be facing large, scary, suspicious, Germanic men within an hour of landing here. Shades of the Delegates, only with bigger, better weaponry. Great."

Fiona Belle shook her head as her tone became somber. She dropped all traces of her Irish dialect. "No, Cori. You needed to do this, and you can accept it if you'll just take a moment to recall how you felt when you first set eyes on young Monsieur Matheson. Take it back farther…when you heard him sing on the old recording."

I could feel my face growing hot but didn't acknowledge the truth of her comment.

She added, bringing back the brogue, "And cheer up, lass! Faith, but ya've already managed to help send a member of Britain's Royal Air Force off to safety. Yer exhausted and hungry. Ya gotta get some sleep. I'll be afta bringin' ya scones and tea in a few hours. Fer now, take a wee bit of brandy. Jacques always keeps a bottle tucked in the corner behind that ugly ash receptacle. For a superb singer, the man has the worst taste in accessories that I've seen in my many years on this earth."

I blinked and grinned. "Which would be how many?"

She winked at me. "Many."

"Well, I'm happy to have the brandy. I'll need it if I'm really expected to perform tonight for an audience of Nazis, not to mention their numerous French lady collaborating companions."

"You'll do a fine job. A superb job. Look at it this way…ya never got a chance to sing in public in the less-than-congenial atmosphere of year twenty-sixty-one on the island of New Manhattan. Plus, if it helps, you'll also be singin' for all the lovely people who make up Café Violette. Musicians and singers and the smart gents who keep the lights on and the stage from falling apart." She batted her eyelashes at me. "And, of course, a certain Monsieur Noel Matheson."

I lapsed into silence for a moment before getting brave enough to ask, "Is there a plan at work? Would you tell me?"

Instead of answering, she said, "You'll be needin' a foin costume for tonight. Now go wash yer face and hands and then make this couch as comfy as ya can. Tomorrow night will be better. Pierre will be findin' ya a place ta live. I've got ta go and whip up a slinky outfit for the new arrival, the American chanteuse Miss Cori Christopher. Then again, it'd be easier to just be stealin' from Val Valentin, the club's female impersonator. He's your height and, while you have real curves, he pads, so the dresses should fit." She squinted at me. "Yep. Royal blue would be great with your red hair and green eyes. Ya got all your coloring from your dad's side of the family. Not surprisin' you were able to pull off the whole white identity thing. You don't look a bit like the

93

Kapoors, although ya do sing like Aubrey, but then, she started out as a Collier before marrying a Kapoor, so she's mainly got Irish in her."

"Ajay used to say the same thing." I stopped. "Dammit!"

"What?"

I couldn't help it. My eyes filled with tears. "Why didn't you save him? Why didn't you get on your time-traveling broomstick or whatever and send him somewhere he'd still be alive? And what about my dad? Is he dead, too? Did the Committee execute him back when I was ten?" My pitch rose higher and the volume louder with each question.

"Cori, listen to me and quit the hysterics. Not to be makin' puns, but there isn't time. Ajay didn't want to go anywhere but into an afterlife with Arthur. And bringin' someone back after death isn't in my line of work. Your father? Well, that's a whole different tale. Now, go to sleep. I'll be back in a few hours."

I wasn't getting any answers. Fine. I took Fiona Belle's advice and plumped up a pillow or two on the lumpy sofa, lay down, and went to sleep. An entire squadron of Nazis or Delegates could have wandered through the dressing room and I wouldn't have known a thing. I wasn't sure what day or time it was, back—or forward—in 2061, but I was exhausted after making up ridiculous stories and I needed to rest.

I slept. At some point, someone entered the dressing room and put a blanket over me. Enough said.

I awoke to the sight of Fiona Belle waving a slinky, spicy, sexy, satin blue dress in my face. She plopped a few pots of cosmetics on Benet's dressing table and turned on the lamp above it.

She squinted at me, impish eyes twinkling with a mix of merriment and sympathy. "So, Chickie, ready to shimmy, shake, and sing your way through 'Hard-Hearted Hannah'?" She stuck several pages of sheet music at me. "Two other songs, all provided by Monsieur Charles Souverain, who leads the band and is even more musically savvy than your Granny Aubrey." She sighed. "Sure, and I was hopin' to sneak in a tune from a certain rockabilly king one night fer ya, but he came to fame too soon after the war and someone might recognize one of his hits in the fifties, about fifteen years from now, and remember they'd heard it before." She thought for a second. "Faith and worse, they might be hearin' the version recorded by one feisty, fabulous, black, female blues singer in fifty-two, and I'd be afta wreckin' a rule or two regardin' time."

I snapped to, now fully awake, took a quick look at the song sheets, and responded, *"Okay. Got it. You love early rock n' roll and old blues. I'm with you. Now then. Let's see. 'Hard-Hearted Hannah.' Yeah, that'll work for shimmying and shaking. 'Nobody.' One of my favorites, but are the Germans aware it was written and originally done by Bert Williams back around nineteen-oh-five and Bert happened to be black?"*

"Yer fine. I doubt any of 'em have heard it, and if they do happen to catch the name Bert Williams, it doesn't sound—and I'm afta quotin' here—'Negro' to these idiots."

"Okay. The other one is 'When Clouds Are Vanished and Skies Are Blue.' Not in my repertoire, but as long as there's sheet music, I can sing it."

Fiona Belle nodded, then added, "I hear tell 'Once in a Blue Moon' has been added to tonight's list. Do ya need music for it?"

"Nah. No problem. It's from some operetta in the early nineteen-hundreds, and easy."

"By the way, Cori, you'll be helpin' out a few folks when ya sing it."

Someone knocked on the door before I had a chance to find out what singing "Once in a Blue Moon" had to do with helping anyone. Fiona Belle opened it and I stared up into the magnetic dark eyes of Noel Matheson.

"Monsieur Matheson."

"Mademoiselle Christopher."

"It's Cori. Please."

He nodded. "Cori. And I am Noel. Ah, I hate to ask this just before you go onstage, but do you *have* any identification papers? Last night was a mess when it came to dealing with Germans and explanations of things so as not to cause suspicion."

I shook my head. "Not really. I have some sheet music and a pass for my workplace in America in my bag, but something tells me neither of those are what your German buddies want to see." *Not to mention, the work pass is dated 2061. They catch the date and I'd not only be on the first train out of Paris but imprisoned in the nearest camp for the insane.*

He scowled. "The German swine are most assuredly not my buddies." He paused, staring at me as if trying to determine how I'd managed to sneak into Paris without papers, then shrugged his shoulders. "I shall take care of getting you some proper identification. Meantime, I am sorry this is being thrown at you very fast, but you are to perform in about twenty minutes." Noel nodded. "I see Fiona Belle has found for you *une jolie* costume. If you would, please, come to the stage, right wing, once you've finished changing. You know your songs? All three of them, including the added 'Once in a Blue Moon'?"

"Perky little tune. From one of those big chorus variety shows from around the turn of the century. Yes, hear me now, I am a walking musical library." I grinned at him. "And, Noel, for future reference, I can sight-sing sheet music and I also have this ridiculous ability to remember melody and lyrics after hearing a song once. I'm up for whatever you need me to do."

"*Très bon!* And *merci beaucoup.* I shall see you backstage."

I headed first to the performers' rest room tucked away in what looked like a storage closet near the kitchen, did what needed doing, then finished changing and adding makeup back in Jacques' dressing room. Ten minutes later I met Noel. He opened the curtain to the wings and whispered my name to the master of ceremonies aka emcee Gaspard Bassett. I had about thirty seconds before I was due to perform.

The full irony of my situation hit me. I'd never gotten to sing in a theater in my own time, apart from my clandestine trip to the Chanson. There I'd belted out a ballad, in French, about the sadness felt by a girl whose lover is heading off to war. The Chanson Theater had been empty, and while I'd put on a brave, reckless face when telling Ajay about my exploits, I admit I was terrified someone would wander into the theater while I was singing. If caught, I'd have been dragged out in handcuffs. Now I was more than a hundred years in the past, wearing one downright sexy dress, getting ready to sing in English the rather saucy tune "Once in a Blue Moon." I related to it in ways no one knew. After all, I'd landed in my own version of lunacy.

I needed this performance to be perfect and to charm the mob of Nazi soldiers in order not to be outed as someone who'd spent part of last night helping a British pilot escape. I had no desire to end up in jail…or worse.

I also must admit I was nervous, very much aware that Noel Matheson would be backstage hearing me sing.

I finished adjusting the shoulder strap just in time to hear Gaspard announce to what clearly was a predominantly German audience, "*Meine Damen und Herren! Das Café Violette präsentiert Fräulein Cori Christopher.*"

I was on.

Chapter 12

I waited for the applause to die down, then hurried offstage and followed Fiona Belle's stubby index finger, which was pointing at what was now my dressing room. Jacques Benet was back and wanted the use of his own space. I couldn't blame him. My new room was about the size of a broom closet, although it did boast a large mirror and a chair set in front of a small, wobbly table, with just enough space for a performer to set out a few pots of makeup. A flimsy clothes rack had been shoved into the corner and held several long gowns suitable for stage and two very cute dresses with peplums clearly meant for day wear. A pair of black shoes—oxfords?— some cotton ankle socks, and my black ballet slippers and black boots lay beneath the rack. A small hat rack stood on the table, with Ajay's fedora neatly topping it. I had no idea where the remainder of my black cat-burglar ensemble was, but I wanted it back.

My bag had also been moved from Benet's room to the new digs. I gave myself a silent reminder to go through it and destroy the work pass for 2061, but figured for the moment I was safe from discovery by any folks in 1941.

I'd barely finished taking off my ankle-strapped high heels when someone knocked on the dressing room door. Time for the masquerade to begin. A masquerade with the very real possibility of ending badly for more than one person at Café Violette…not to mention me. I cleared my throat and called out, "It's open."

I couldn't suppress a shiver when I glanced toward the entrance where Noel stood, politely holding the door open for a trio of German officers. Last night's head Nazi, Major Bauer, followed by a deferential entourage of two, rudely pushed Noel aside and marched into the tiny room as though on parade, filling the air with a stench of, if not total evil, then definitely fearsomeness.

I was surprised he didn't lift his hand in the ridiculous Nazi salute and expect me to reply in kind. Was he a member of the SS, the Luftwaffe, or the Gestapo? Did it really matter?

"You *are* American, Fräulein. Is that correct?"

"Yes." I swallowed hard as I attempted to appear pleasant, innocent, and brave, without any trace of belligerence or terror.

"Your full name?"

"My legal name?"

A brief glimmer of what could be amusement crossed Bauer's face. "Do you have an *illegal* name, Fräulein?"

"Oh! I didn't mean it that way. It's not *illegal*, like a criminal alias or something. It's just that I've always been called Cori but my birth certificate has me down as Terpsichore Nira Christopher."

Bauer's amusement faded. His next words hinted at displeasure sliding right into dislike or worse. "Nira? This sounds like a Jew name. Are you a Jew? And Terpsichore? That is not a name for a person."

"Terpsichore is the muse of dance, so I guess it was originally Greek, although my grandmother, who came up with it, had hopes it would magically turn me into a prima ballerina or a Broadway musical chorus girl. Why didn't Granny just go with Euterpe, who was the muse of music? I mean, the whole durn family is made up of singers. Then again, Euterpe sounds like one has just been sick to one's stomach, so it's really not pleasant to say, is it? She considered Calliope, although she told me once it sounded too much like the pipe organs played at a carousel. *Voila!* Terpsichore it is. Oh. Nira is Hindu. Indian. Means light. Again…all my granny's doing. Rumor has it I was born during a blackout, hours after my mom had eaten really spicy curry from this yummy Indian diner down a few blocks on West Two-Hundred-and-Fourth Street, and the power and lights came on seconds after my birth, which, again according to family legend, required more drugs than my mother originally expected. Granny stayed with her the entire time but clearly took the opportunity to exert some influence in the whole naming process."

I could see Noel out of my peripheral vision, chewing his lower lip in an attempt to contain his delight at this tale. I had to admit, while true, it was still a story with some entertainment value in its absurdity.

As to delighted? Not so Bauer. He frowned. "You spent a lot of time rambling about births and light and did not answer the question. Are you a Jew?"

Visions of being hoisted aboard the next train to Auschwitz filled my head. I wanted to scream, *I'm not, but damn you! If I were Jewish, why would it matter, you stinkin' bigot? What is this whole problem you goons and your sicko leader have with the ancestors of the children of Israel? A world view seared into the souls of the members of the Committee, assuming they have souls—and now I'm rambling in my own head!*

Again...why the hell should it matter?

But in this place and time, it *did* matter, the same way it mattered in 2061. People were classified and given a class designation and number based on race, ethnicity, religion, or the gender of the person they loved. Unreasonable and evil.

Ajay called me brash and sassy with a tendency to leap before looking, and he was right, but I wasn't stupid, and I had great survival instincts. Choose battles wisely. Tonight, I had to save myself if I was going to accomplish anything of value in this time period. Being around gentlemen—and I use the term loosely—who were into stupid stereotypes, I told myself it would be wise to remember a classic and put a damper on my Irish-inherited, redheaded temper.

I choked down the pulsing desire to tell the s.o.b. off, blinked instead, and told the truth. Or at least some of it. I realized revealing the family link to folks in New Delhi would also not be well received. "I'm not Jewish. And, as you can tell, I'm American, which, like most Americans, means my background is mixed. My mom's grandparents were from Denmark and from Ireland. My dad's side was actually a bit of German and Irish and French."

Of course, if the Nazis were rounding up Catholics tonight, I was in trouble. Then again, so were about three-quarters of the folks in France. I badly wanted to rip into this pompous jerk and tell him what I thought of the Nazi attitude, but if I let loose the tirade of fury inside, within minutes I'd be on the train to whatever camp was closest and nastiest. Which would make my screwball temporal journey from the future nothing less than futile. Continuing to hold in my rage was the best course, even if it was making me ill.

I shivered again. The slinky gown I'd shimmied and shaken in onstage while singing "Hard-Hearted Hannah," "Nobody," and the cloudy sky song before the surprise addition of "Once in a Blue Moon," now felt more like a wisp of fabric. Plus, all three German officers were staring at me with expressions I'd bet were regularly seen on the faces of clients waiting for their dates at bordellos.

I'd seen documentaries about the Holocaust on film at Ajay's. Always wondered why no one fought back at the camps. Why, for example, didn't, say, oh, three hundred prisoners join forces and beat the crap out of five or six Nazi guards who'd set their automatic weapons to the side while smoking a cigarette or two? Standing here, facing the pride of the Aryan nation, each and every one of them at least six-three, I realized even someone like me, who's young and physically strong, someone who's not beaten down from traveling for days in an overcrowded train filled with frightened, mostly ill passengers and others already dead, someone without a family to protect, someone who had not seen family and friends slaughtered before her eyes, could still be made to feel as helpless as a mouse staring into the eyes of a king cobra. The black uniforms alone were enough to terrify me into silence.

My answer regarding my family history only led to another question. "Do you have your papers?" Bauer asked.

"Um. I'm not sure. I grabbed stuff because I was late. To be honest, I haven't a clue which bags I brought to the club. I haven't had time to look for them since yesterday after the mishap with the bicycle, and I stayed here last night and I was rather nervous about performing at the club for the first time. Not to mention they might have gotten wet. I sure did!" *Shut up, Cori! You're babbling and it hasn't helped so far. Pretend you're on a witness stand in court. Yes and no answers only.*

The German officer stared at me, nearly stabbing me with his icy blue eyes. The color of the Atlantic Ocean. Not the Caribbean. Huge difference. He stated, "We will find them. If indeed they exist. But I am curious…why is a young American girl here in Paris? Are you some kind of student? Are Americans not aware of what has been happening in France?"

In the year 2061, technology is advanced but, thanks to frequent storms, electric power outages are common. And more than once I've been trapped in an elevator. Thankfully, I've never been claustrophobic, but it's still not a pleasant experience, especially when you don't have a time frame for how long you'll be stuck. Consequently, the lack of control over the situation is maddening. When I found myself facing Major Bauer, searching for an answer to the "why are you in France" inquiry close enough to the truth to keep me from being incarcerated while not annoying the man, I experienced the same unpleasantness and outrage at not being able to control this increasingly scary interrogation.

Apart from the Fiona Belle's Rules of Time Travel forbidding me to tell the truth to more than one person, this was not the moment to gleefully announce *I've come to Paris to meet Noel Matheson, whose voice I fell in love with thanks to a vinyl recording, and to escape a different repressive regime more than a hundred years in your future and hopefully save Café Violette, and a few performers including Monsieur Matheson, although from what exactly, I'm not sure. I'd like to add helping a stray, grounded British airman or two escape a prison camp and possible annihilation to my list.*

It was vital to get this man to soften his attitude. As in immediately. Noel's life and mine could depend on it. I smiled in an attempt to appear as unthreatening as possible. Bauer wasn't some cartoon villain. He was flesh and blood and maybe he'd listen. I decided the best course was to tell as much of the truth as I could without veering into science fiction stories about traveling through time.

"My family is all gone." True. Well, maybe. Jury out as to whether Dad was dead or alive. "I was working for a…a…film company back home, and they wanted to send us to France to get an idea of what changes were happening in Europe." Semi-true. I had worked for a film company. "It was our bad luck, because we arrived in Provence and our plane kind of blew up—I don't want to make this too long, but we weren't able to make the documentary." Big whopping lie. "Anyway, I came to Paris because I've been a performer all my life and wanted to sing at one of the cabarets who might be hiring." Semi-true. "I'd heard this like, wicked-great recording made by the artists at Café Violette and I came here and met Noel and now I get to sing!" Totally true. "So here I am." I took a breath. "Um, did you enjoy the show tonight? I don't mean me, I mean *everyone*. So many good artists at the club, don't you agree? You should listen to the recording they did. I'm not sure when it was made, but I first heard it in America last month."

I'd never spewed out so many run-on, incoherent sentences in my entire twenty years on this earth. I was rewarded with blank stares from Bauer's minions, but another brief flash of amusement from Bauer himself. I couldn't blame them for their reactions. It was a preposterous, nonsensical story, and I wished I'd thought up a better one when I was back in New Manhattan at Jericho getting sloshed on brandy. Mark down "unprepared" on Cori Christopher's grade sheet for her lack of skill in traveling through time.

I inadvertently glanced at Noel, who appeared to be doing his best not to laugh at my lengthy, full-of-holes monologue. He suddenly slipped through the open door and left me to face the inquisitors alone.

My mouth opened again. "Anyway, as you might have guessed, I do love to sing, and Café Violette has awesome acoustics. And Monsieur Du Maurier, who plays piano accompaniment, is fabulous. We didn't get a chance to rehearse, but he was with me the whole way. Of course, Charles Souverain, who leads the band and plays trumpet, is so marvelous in, well, leading the band. Didn't you love his rendition of 'Mack the Knife'? It's from *The Threepenny Opera*, and I'd never heard it in French before. I'm sure you've heard it in German. I mean, Bertolt Brecht wrote the score. Then again, he's not really loved in Germany anymore, is he? I heard he went Marxist at some point."

Mister Head Nazi Bauer raised his hand for silence, and I stopped speaking—with much relief.

"Enough! Stop! Fräulein Christopher, I am Major Johann Bauer," he stated. "This is Captain Kessler to my left and Captain Webber to my right." The two officers, clones of Delegates Lang and Becker who'd dogged me only two days earlier, snapped their heels together, and for a moment, I thought I was about to be saluted. They bowed, and I suppressed a thoroughly inappropriate urge to giggle.

Another silence followed the introductions. This one lasted a full ninety seconds. For once I kept my own mouth shut. I stared at the doorway of my dressing room and wondered where my dark-eyed archangel had run off to during this exchange of ranks and surnames. I silently begged him to return before the interview slid completely off the rails.

Maybe Noel would find Fiona Belle, who seemed one formidable lady when she needed to be, and with her help we could all come up with better reasons for why I'd landed in Paris during a wartime Occupation.

My stomach kept lurching to my throat. I was aware that was anatomically impossible, but it didn't change the reality of the feeling. I had no papers. I was an American with an English last name, a weird first name, a middle name they didn't like, and a quirky sense of humor they considered highly inappropriate for the time and place.

Noel suddenly appeared behind Captain Webber. He coughed to let the Germans know he was in the hallway and politely informed them he had found my papers if they wanted to see them.

Yes! There must be an artistically gifted fairy or pixie inhabiting Café Violette. He or she doubtless spent days and nights hiding in the shadows, waiting patiently for occasions when lost Americans sauntered in to sing Broadway and movie melodies while this maker of documents scratched out the necessary information in a cozy elfin den in the basement.

Noel politely stated, "I am able to be finding Mademoiselle Christopher's papers in the alleyway behind the theater with other items from her purse. It is still damp from last night's rain. It must have spilled over when she was to be having the problem with her bicycle. The papers, they are not crisp and dry, but they are still, what is the word? Uh, legible."

He handed the faked papers to Bauer, then turned and exchanged a very surreptitious wink with me behind all three officers' backs. Again, I felt my heart lurch to my throat, but this time it wasn't from fear. Quite the opposite.

Bauer studied the damp papers as intently as a computer programmer preparing to redo the system for a financial institution, and then handed them back to me. "Keep them safe, Fräulein. You would not find it pleasant spending the night in prison because of absentmindedness or clumsiness in losing your belongings."

He glared at Noel and then swung his gaze back to me. "As to your previous question, I did enjoy *your* performance, Fräulein Christopher. We will return to see you as time permits." He continued staring at me with an odd expression. "Fräulein Christopher, you are an excellent singer, but be aware there are many people at this café who would not be considered proper or fit companions. My advice is to avoid them and concentrate on your songs."

He bowed, clicked his heels together, and then, accompanied by the silent toadies, left the room and, one hoped, Café Violette.

His last words were clearly meant as a warning. I didn't need my Cassandra visions to sense Bauer was going to do everything he could to destroy clandestine activities at Café Violette, and if I was part of them, so be it. Plenty of female singers could be found who were eager to serve the German agenda and, perfect pitch and some nice shimmying aside, I could be replaced in an instant if I posed a threat to Nazi plans.

Noel waited until he was certain the German officers were gone from the backstage area before musing, "It appears, Mademoiselle Cori, you may have an admirer."

"Who? Him? The Nazi assh…uh, creep?"

Noel finished for me. "Asshole. Yes. We might as well call it as it is. And *oui*, Major Bauer is who I mean. This could be almost good but also be bad."

"How good?"

"He might lighten his inspection of activities and people at Café Violette."

"And the bad news?"

"He may be turning his focus on you. What is the old expression from American movies? A 'stage-door Johnny'?"

I winced. "Not my idea of the perfect admirer."

"Nor mine." Noel's eyes held my gaze for a long moment. "I shall do my best to keep you safe, Mademoiselle Christopher."

I stayed silent. I couldn't tell him I'd traveled more than a hundred years through time to do exactly the same for him.

Chapter 13

Two hours after my first performance and the creepy backstage visit from Major Bauer, I stood next to Monsieur Pierre Simon inside the comfortable parlor of a house situated about ten blocks from Café Violette, preparing to meet the ladies with whom I'd soon be sharing an apartment.

"Mademoiselle Cori, may I introduce to you Delys Robinson, Paulette Reeve, and Teresa Dorleac. Your new…what is the word? Roommates, *oui*? You will find this much nicer than sleeping on a cot in Monsieur Benet's musty dressing room at the club. Noel and Fiona Belle are explaining your arrival in Paris to be a bit of a mystery."

The man making introductions raised his hand to stop me before I could respond with another nutty lie. "I am not needing the details, Mademoiselle. Too many people also are…misplaced…these days and need safety. We are so excited to welcome you as *une merveilleuse* addition to our family at Café Violette. I do not remember when I am hearing such a beautiful voice. It makes me happy. I am hoping you will also be happy with the roommates *ici*."

I smiled at Monsieur Simon, or Papa Pierre as I'd been told everyone at the nightclub referred to him, the owner of Café Violette and a fabulous singer—his version of "Old Man River" from the recording I'd heard while still in 2061 made me cry, but in a good way—and my newest friend. He was probably in his early fifties but seemed older.

"Roommates. You're up on the latest lingo, Papa Pierre. And Monsieur Benet's sofa backstage might have been a tad lumpy, but it was still most welcome to me."

I began shaking hands with the girls who'd been kind enough to take in a fourth at this small house about ten blocks from Café Violette. I clicked immediately with Delys Robinson, who reminded me, in an odd way, of Fiona Belle with her impish smile. Delys's eyes, a piercing yet sympathetic green, stood out against her mocha-colored skin. Saucy, bold, and beautiful, Delys seemed to possess the same uncanny ability to see right into my soul. I felt a bond before we'd finished exchanging hellos.

Paulette Reeve was more English than tea in a rose garden with her delicate, pale complexion, small features, soft gray-blue eyes, and ash blonde hair. Both she and Delys were quite petite, at about five-foot-one or so. The third roommate, Teresa Dorleac, had true black hair, hazel eyes, olive skin, a lean, almost curveless figure, and was perhaps two inches taller than the others. I felt like a giant towering over the three of them.

A trim, stunningly beautiful brunette in her early forties stepped around Papa Pierre to introduce herself. "*Je suis…ooh-la-la*! I am so sorry. I will speak the English as I am able. I am Rosemarie Ducote, the owner of *la maison,* uh, how you say, this house. You will call me Rosemarie, *non*? I am *très* pleased to meet you, Mademoiselle Christopher." She smiled. "I love America. And Americans. I was very lucky to be in college in Boston for one year many years past. My

English was better then, as it was more in use. I do admit I was not fond of the winters with too much snow, yet I miss the…*esprit*…the spirit of residents of the city."

"Well, I've lived in New Manha…New York for my whole life, and I'm *still* not used to winters, and I gather we have it a lot milder than Boston." I gave myself a mental note to be sure to refer to my previous home as New York, not New Manhattan. The change to the city's name wouldn't happen until the year 2040. And I also needed to avoid any comments on the *esprit*, given the spirit of my hometown in 2061 was not exactly cordial.

Rosemarie smiled and gestured at all of us. "You come downstairs with me, *oui*? We shall have tea."

Pierre smiled at her. "I have brought a treat from our wardrobe mistress, Fiona Belle, to be having with tea."

He handed Rosemarie a cardboard box. She untied the string around it and opened it, revealing a dozen cranberry-orange scones. The scent was the same as what I'd smelled back at Jericho. Of course, tangible scones hadn't been available, just their odor wafting miraculously through a hologram. I was thrilled I'd finally get to taste the real thing and wondered where or in what decade Fiona Belle had had to whisk into to get the ingredients.

We followed Rosemarie as she escorted us into a small sitting room. I offered to help with the trays and food, but she waved me off. "*Non, non*! Pierre will help. For this day, you are a treasure guest. You get acquainted with the other *demoiselles, oui*?"

The three girls and I each took a seat around a table I could easily imagine taking center stage in an antiques store. It's not my field of expertise, but I'd have placed it as being about three hundred years old. I studied the table for a few seconds while I tried to come up with topics to hide the vast differences between my new roomies and me, including decades of political turmoil and unrest or technological changes.

Three faces stared at me in silence. While there was none of the hostile attitude I'd encountered from Bauer and his men when they'd been staring, I was still becoming uncomfortable. Finally, I turned to Paulette. She understood my English and we might get some conversation started. "It's really nice of Madame Ducote and all of you to take me in."

"We are delighted. We love Americans. And isn't Mademoiselle Ducote a doll?"

"Wait. *Mademoiselle*? Not married?"

Delys answered, "She has the loss of her fiancé in nineteen-seventeen. In the Great War. She was young...*peut-être*...um, perhaps...sixteen at this time. She has no married after. She has been...um... operating? a...how you say? *la* shop for the clothes? We say boutique?"

I nodded. "Boutique. Same in America. Perfect. I'll bet she did a great job with her store. She has a lot of style."

Teresa added, "She has...ran *la boutique...depuis de nombreuses années*...um, during many years...until Germans...um...arrive in Paris."

Delys growled, "Arrive? *Merde!* Teresa, you are make this the sound of normal *pour un événement horrible*. You talk on Germans as if they are walking in and with calm selling the latest in couture the next minute. *Non! Non. Vérité*...the truth is they steal all the clothing to give it to their whores. Rosemarie tell me Nazis burn her accounting books and the, the, um...*les portants*, how you say, racks? the clothing stood on and they begin to set up *le siège social.*"

I wasn't familiar with the term. "*Le siège social*?"

Paulette quietly translated, "Headquarters. But we think it's quite a bit more than some general office for paperwork and schedules. They're determined to root out folks who oppose them." She paused before adding, "*We're* determined to be on the opposing side."

Were my new roommates involved in the *Résistance*? If so, were they connected to what I'd taken part in at Café Violette the night I arrived, helping the British airman? And were these girls also in danger from Nazis like Bauer and his men?

Time to establish my own views. I quickly said, "Well, that stinks. About Rosemarie and her business, I mean. And Delys has it right. Folks in America were shocked the Germans just waltzed in and claimed France as their own. It never should have happened."

The girls all nodded in agreement at my comment about how stunned Americans were when the Germans claimed France, but I thought it might be prudent to change topics. I was speaking from what I'd read in old history books and was bound to make numerous blunders by talking about something that would either happen in the future or was dead wrong. According to Ajay, more than one text about the past was altered once the Committee took over the schools in New Manhattan.

Considering the Committee was mirroring many of the Nazi actions in dealing with people they deemed less than desirable, it was no great stretch to imagine the Committee might have rewritten World War Two history in a manner quite sympathetic to the Axis powers. Some of what I was relying on had been provided by my family, plus a few documentaries on DVDs, and since I'd been ten when everyone but Ajay exited my life, I'd been more entranced with musical theater viewings than the who, what, why, and how of the Second World War.

I turned to Teresa. "You look like a dancer. Am I right?"

She nodded but didn't give me a vocal response. She'd sprinkled only a few words of English in her last statement, so perhaps she wasn't up for casual conversation conducted in anything other than French.

Delys answered for her. "We all are. Dancers. With *le Luc Hebert Théâtre de Danse.* It is why Paulette stay in France. Teresa is prima ballerina. We are to be perform at *le Théâtre de l'Opéra Blanche*...if *le porc* Boche approve the program. We are having...*non*...we are *doing* dances they probably will not be...how you say? Be to their like?"

I smiled. "You're really close. It's 'to their liking.' And I can see where approval for some things could get a bit dicey."

"Dicey?" Delys's eyebrows raised.

"Oops! *Pardon!* Your English is remarkable, but I don't expect you to be up on slang. I'm envious. I'm just limping along with my French. Anyway, 'dicey' means 'tricky.' Perhaps a better word is 'iffy.' 'Dodgy' is another one."

"Dicey and dodgy," Paulette quietly repeated, then beamed at me. "These are fun words. And you're quite right, Miss Christopher. We're currently in preparations for several dances from Tchaikovsky's *Swan Lake,* plus a few other pieces."

Delys jumped in with, "We get ready to be on the agenda...we are to schedule...*oui*? We will be open in next month…unless the Germans will decide to banning Tchaikovsky who is Russian and they hate Russians more than the French."

"That's fantastic. I mean, that you're doing selections from *Swan Lake*, not fantastic to hear the Germans might ban it. Honestly? I wasn't sure which cultural activities were still ongoing. Uh, we'd heard in America the Germans were more interested in 'girlie' shows they can watch in old music halls, and of course, any opera composed by Wagner."

Teresa finally joined the chat using halting English mixed with French. "This is being the true," she said. "Wagner *musique est très populaire.* But *le Ballet de l'Opéra de Paris*…they do works from the old Russian and French composers. Germans are not…uh…*célébré pour leurs oeuvres de ballet.*"

Paulette added, blushing, "The other so-called entertainment you speak of? It appears the rank-and-file soldiers and officers alike don't find it beneath Aryan superiority to drink and watch nearly naked chorines prance about on stage. But these are not *real* dancers. It's rumored some of the girls, um, service the troops. They get better food and often lots of firewood for winter in exchange for their, um, collaboration."

Delys changed the subject. "You are from America, *non*? Where you are having the living in New York? I see maps and I know it is far, but have you the living in New Orleans?"

I shook my head. "Sadly, no. I haven't been able to travel. This is actually my first time away from America. But I've read about New Orleans, and it looks so amazing. My dad taught me great jazz songs from that city when I was just a child."

Delys flashed a huge smile. "This is where Maman is from. New Orleans. My English is from her. She is born in France but is dancer in America and then in France with a very special Negro dancer after she is here. Maman married my papa in New Orleans. I was born there. But Papa died soon after I was born. Maman meets stepfather and move to Paris to dance with Mademoiselle Josephine." The smile dimmed as rapidly as it had appeared.

I didn't want to ask but somehow had to—"Are they both still in Paris?"

She shook her head. "*Non*. Gerard Chappelle, my stepfather, is very much real father to me, and he is with French Army three years ago when they are fighting and destroyed by the Germans. We are having hope he is still alive. My mother is gone from France with the dancers. I stay in Paris with Luc Hebert's company because I am young. I am eighteen. Maman says I am safer *ici*. I have not hearing from her in two years. I have distant cousin who is Irish, and I thought *peut-être*…perhaps…I try to get to her for safety, but the Germans banned travel plans for French, only days after they march into Paris."

"I'm truly sorry about your father. But, Delys, I'm sure your mother is safe. I've heard, uh, this particular dancer your mom is with had…uh…*has* many friends outside of France and they love her, too, and are making sure she's okay, along with the people with her."

I didn't add I knew quite a bit about "this particular dancer," who'd joined the *Résistance* sometime around 1940. Specifically, she'd signed up with the French military counterintelligence agency and been able to snag a ton of information from the Nazis who thought she was nothing but an enchanting performer. But Delys didn't need to hear details about notorious and brave activities, which included sneaking info out of the country by means of sheet music littered with notes written in invisible ink or pinning such notes inside underwear. It was my understanding, garnered from watching a biographic movie back when I was fifteen, that folks working with the entertainer were being extremely careful about security, even more so than my own "cell" of Ostinato in New Manhattan. I didn't want to spill the beans about clandestine operations and put anyone in the *Résistance* in danger or create confusion as to how the newly arrived American girl knew about things that hadn't yet happened.

Teresa inquired, "*Pourquoi* are you in Paris? *Sans bagages? Ce n'est pas habituel.*"

I winced. Inwardly. Bauer seemed to have accepted my impromptu monologue about landing in Provence with a film company and heading to Paris from there, although I had a strong feeling he was going to be requesting further information. But Teresa was right. Flying into France without luggage was unusual.

Neither Pierre Simon nor Noel had asked. They'd accepted my presence at Café Violette as a refugee. Papa Pierre had asked Val Valentin, the female impersonator who performed at Café Violette, if it was okay if a few of his costumes and possibly some everyday clothes were purloined for the American singer. Noel had been very curious about the whole business with my big carryall bag and some of my sheet music, but he hadn't pressed for answers. There was no way I could tell Noel I'd arrived via sheet music and the machinations of the club's short wardrobe mistress. How could I explain I'd jumped quite a few decades backward in order to escape insanity and danger in my city, but primarily to meet him?

I really hated lying to these women I'd already grown to like in the space of one tea party, but I needed to, for everyone's sake. Not to mention Fiona Belle's firm rule about telling only one person about time travel. I decided to repeat much of the same story as I'd given Bauer.

"Well, I'm mainly a singer, but I had this chance to do a story for a film company from the States. I came over on assignment because I speak passable French. Anyway, they wanted an up-close look at what is happening with popular culture in Paris, and Americans can still come in and out of France if we have passports. But we'd barely landed before the plane caught fire and I lost my luggage and equipment, like cameras, and my notebooks and, um, pens. This was what I was wearing on the flight, and when I decided to come to Paris it's all I had left."

I glanced down at the black trousers and sweater I'd originally worn the night I traveled, which I'd found in the dressing room at the nightclub this morning, freshly laundered. Ajay's hat I'd kept on the rack.

"Val Valentin, the café's female impersonator, is providing costumes for my performances at the club and some pieces for day wear. Sometimes it's a blessing to be tall. Thank heaven I can sing, or I'd probably be in jail."

Rosemarie and Pierre entered the sitting room in time to hear my garbled and ridiculous explanation. Pierre winked at me. He seemed aware that much of what I'd said was mostly fabrication, but he also sensed I'd been sent to Café Violette by *someone* to help with their

Résistance activities. From where or how far was the unstated kicker.

The ladies seemed to buy the plane-on-fire story, after Paulette translated about half of the bizarre tale, probably because they were more interested in simply having an American room with them. The six of us sat and drank weak tea and scones prepared by a time-traveling witch from...whenever. They tasted better than anything I'd had in the last five years from New Manhattan bakeries, oddly one of the few luxuries available. I guess the Committee figured if its citizens were happy with sugar highs we wouldn't notice our freedoms disappearing. I felt as though Fiona Belle had baked hope for these girls and Rosemarie within each bite. I stiffened my spine and promised myself I'd do whatever it took to help my new friends here and at Café Violette, no matter how dangerous it became.

Chapter 14

Singing at Café Violette wasn't a full-time job. To be honest, it was barely part-time employment, especially for someone used to workdays of ten or twelve hours, and being the newest hire at the club didn't exactly warrant a pay raise in a country where salaries were dismal or nonexistent. Papa Pierre found a solution for me. I was to help Luc Hebert at *l'Opéra Blanche* as an assistant stage manager and all around go-get-it girl—aka "gofer"—for the upcoming ballet. Rehearsals were held during the day, which worked out for my night gig, which was barely four blocks away.

Papa Pierre and Luc Hebert had been friends from childhood and now were not only "*amis*" but co-conspirators in various *Résistance* activities. My go-get-it-girl duties allowed me to coordinate between theater and nightclub.

I enjoyed the work at *l'Opéra Blanche*. I wasn't a trained dancer, unless one wanted to count Ajay and Granny Aubrey's home lessons, but I was allowed to take classes with the company and learned technique neither my great-uncle nor my grandmother had been able to teach me. Luc Hebert was a perfectionist to the nth degree in rehearsals but also supported his dancers any way possible as long as he knew those dancers were giving their all. And a plus—I could read music, which immediately put me in good standing with Luc and the musical conductor who was in need of someone to turn pages at the proper time for the two far-less-classical numbers Luc planned to sneak into the program.

The *Luc Hebert Théâtre de Danse* company was composed of a total of twelve dancers. Most of them spoke only French and, for the most part, considered me a curiosity but appreciated my efforts in helping to get their next production up and running while meeting Monsieur Hebert's high standards. They were also intrigued with all things American and asked if I'd met famous movie stars or—better still—the ultimate in American dancing, the man who'd perfected the use of the top hat. In less-than-perfect French, I patiently explained I lived in New York City and could only meet celebrities backstage and ask for autographs like all the common folk, and, for the record, most movie stars lived in Hollywood where the movies were made. I was sure they didn't believe a word and, instead, were totally convinced I spent my days sipping champagne with the elite actors, singers, and dancers at slick restaurants around the city.

Delys and I established a close bond within days of my arrival in Paris. Whether it was a personality mesh of two like souls or the indefinable magic of friendships forged in times of stress didn't matter; we had no need to sit down and figure out why we liked each other. We became immediate friends even if I couldn't tell her the truth about much of anything to do with my former life. We discussed fashion and design, our dreams for a future free of tyrants, the big dance companies in the U.S.— which kept me brain-hopping trying to recall information from various theater books I'd read—and spicy Cajun gumbo versus spicier vindaloo from New Delhi. I'd explained I had close relatives originally from India. I did tell her if she was born in New Orleans and her mother was American, she was already an American citizen. She was delighted. She didn't need to hear that blacks in America still suffered from not being provided their full rights. Although, from what I gathered, at least in New Orleans persons of color were treated a helluva lot better than they were in any country occupied by the Nazis.

Delys never asked questions I couldn't answer. We were each aware of a huge distaste for Nazis but kept our chats away from too much German-bashing. We trusted each other but didn't need anyone overhearing.

I also had a warm relationship with Paulette. Not as close as my friendship with Delys, but I always felt calm and secure in Paulette's presence. Maybe it was the whole English "be polite and restrained" thing, but she never displayed bad temper, never put others down, and never waxed too eloquent about what must be emotionally killing her…having a fiancé currently spending his days and nights flying missions with the Royal Air Force. I was amazed the Germans hadn't grabbed her in some sweep of Brits in France, but perhaps keeping a very low profile with the dance company and not venturing out at night had helped keep her safe, at least so far. As long as she wasn't suspected of engaging in other, less cultural pursuits, the Nazis didn't seem interested in one lone English dancer.

Teresa Dorleac, roomie number three, was a bit more distant in terms of friendship, but it was understandable. For one thing, her English was far worse than my French and things got awkward when we tried to talk. Also, she was intensely, fiercely focused on her upcoming performance as the prima ballerina for Luc Hebert's company. Teresa would probably scare the Holy Huey out of audiences when the company did the selections from *Swan Lake*. Her technique was perfect and her acting spot-on in the dual role of Odette (the good swan) and Odile (the evil swan), if a trifle unemotional. Whenever I had the chance I'd just stand in the wings and watch her dance, awed and impressed. She gave a hundred percent in rehearsal and I looked forward to her actual performance.

The fourth occupant of the house, Rosemarie Ducote, had embraced me as a daughter and we instinctively trusted each other. We'd spent my second afternoon after I moved in learning about each other over tea and sugarless bread. Sadly, the scones were long gone.

"Mademoiselle Ducote, I don't want to sound nosy or overly curious, but you look as though you could have been a model. Still could be."

She smiled. "Call me Rosemarie, Cori. Americans are not much enthusiastic about formality in address to one another."

I grinned. "Thanks. You have a beautiful name, so it's a pleasure to use it."

She poured a bit more tea into my cup. "Your question about modeling? I have been the invite…wait…I was invited many years ago to make this my profession, but I loved more the creating of fashion…not the wearing of a garment while someone took photographs or watched me walk down a runway."

"You design?"

"I do. I have been help to Monsieur Hebert with costumes for the ballet. I hope one day again to be able to create beautiful clothes instead of do a repair on garments which are serviceable, or selling them. This war, Cori…it frightens me. I hate seeing my beloved Paris in shreds and my fellow Parisiennes in fear."

"I do as well. But keep your dreams, Rosemarie…I have a feeling in…oh…let's be wild and say in less than ten years…you'll be able to follow those dreams again."

Rosemarie took a sip of tea before responding. "I do not understand how you know this, Cori, but I also see a future where dreams are allowed again."

I took a chance, but my Cassandra visions were telling me this was a sound prediction, so I responded with, "This is going to sound strange, but I'm certain that you're part of my future. Just not in Paris."

A few days after my tea with Rosemarie, as I sat in the wings of *le Théâtre de l'Opéra Blanche* with my back against a giant flat piece depicting a lake, jotting notes for Luc to give to the conductor, Delys plopped down beside me. "You are not really working for a film company when you land here, *non*?"

"No." I waited, holding my breath.

"*Très intéressant*. You come to France *sans* work…no job…in the middle of a war. *Pourquoi*?"

I paused, but I knew I could trust Delys. Well, up to a point. I couldn't reveal the time travel issue or anything about the future destruction of Café Violette, but the rest was absolutely true. "It's just, well, kind of insane. To be honest, I was kind of overly enchanted with voices on a recording of a certain nightclub." *One voice in particular.*

Her left eyebrow rose. "Café Violette?"

"Yep. I say enchanted, but it was really an obsession. I listened so much I got to the point where I had to come and see the people and the place myself."

Delys frowned. "Cori, it is very romantic, but you are to be choosing the horrible time. Did you not care the German Nazis would be here?"

"I did. And I was worried because I wasn't sure how bad things were for ordinary citizens. But I also figured as an American girl I'd be safe, at least for a while. I was determined. I wanted to be here. I really did lose all my family. Delys, I'm not totally nuts. I'm as scared as everybody else, but I feel I need to be here. I need to, uh, be helping at Café Violette." Okay, I was getting close to revelations, but Delys didn't ask what I meant.

Her voice dropped to a whisper. "I have awareness of Papa Pierre and others, included our Monsieur Hebert, are being involved in certain activities and those things are…how you say…?"

The rest of the company was gathering onstage to start rehearsing again and they were noisy, but I kept my volume low. "Frowned on and forbidden by the Germans?"

Delys whispered, "*Exactement*. Will you continue to help them? I would like to help *aussi*. *Toutefois*, the Nazis do not like Negroes, and I feel I am in danger. I do not want to bring danger to others."

"I totally understand."

I was convinced there was a traitor in the *Résistance* group using Café Violette. I knew Delys was loyal to Luc, to Pierre, to Paris. I couldn't provide her any information, though, or at least not yet, although I sensed Papa Pierre and Noel might be in need of her assistance soon. And she'd give it willingly.

But for now, I simply nodded and added, "*Oui.*"

****

While waiting to make my entrance to sing my usual three songs—no coded tunes tonight—I took a moment to sneak a peek at the audience from behind the stage-right curtain.

"Damn," I whispered to myself.

I heard soft laughter and turned. The club's emcee, Gaspard Bassett, stood just behind me. "Is there a problem, Mademoiselle Cori?"

"I'm not sure. Major Bauer is gracing us with his presence again. Third time this week. He doesn't exactly strike me as a huge lover of popular music, so I have to assume he has other reasons for sitting through our performances almost every night."

Gaspard, who was one of the people included in executing extra activities at Café Violette, winked at me. "Perhaps he has what you Americans call a crush on a certain young chanteuse?"

I groaned. "I hope not. Fending off advances from Nazi officers was not in my plan when I came to Paris."

Noel joined us, clearly overhearing my last comments. He teased, "And what *was* the plan, Mademoiselle Cori?"

To meet you. To do what I could to save you, although I'm not sure from what, just yet. Let me repeat…to meet you.

I did not give voice to what was going through my head. Instead, I exclaimed, in a whisper, "To sing at the coolest cabaret in all of Paris!"

"Wise answer, Mademoiselle Cori," Gaspard responded, "It does not sound…how you say… plausible, but it is a wise answer."

Noel simply stared at me with those dark eyes as if he were witnessing every action I'd taken in 2061 that led me here...in real time. If such a thing existed. Finally, he stated, "And I am most happy to have the...how did you say?...the 'coolest' singer in all of Paris here beside me."

Before anyone had a chance to say anything else or inquire as to my *raisons d'être* in Paris, Pierre came toward us. He did not look happy.

"Pierre? Is there a problem?" Noel inquired.

He nodded. "It has been asked by Major Bauer for me to extend his...invitation...to Cori for a drink with him after tonight's show. Café Destin...it is open after hours. It is not far from here."

"What?" I exclaimed. "Bauer is asking me on a friggin' date?"

Pierre turned to me. "We can be trying to make up something to tell the major and keep you away."

Gaspard shook his head. "This would not be wise, Pierre. Bauer is not a man to bring to anger, and refusing an invitation would indeed anger him."

I sighed. "Gaspard is right. Seeing Major Bauer after hours, or any time, if I'm being honest, is not high on my list of things to do, but if it keeps him from poking his nose into Café Violette's business, then I'll...I'll..."

Noel interrupted, "No! We are not letting you do this."

"Noel, I have to. Bauer has to remain reasonably happy, and we don't want to give him any reasons to shut us down." I bit my lower lip. "Maybe I could request a chaperone?" I batted my eyelashes at Pierre. "Such as a kind club owner who does not want to lose an employee thanks to a night on the town? Tell Bauer I'm under age and need a mature person with me?"

Pierre tried to smile. "I will tell the major you would feel more comfortable if I were to be also having a drink at Café' Destin, *peut-être* at another table."

"You suppose there's any way he'll agree?" I asked.

Pierre shrugged in the way only a Frenchman can. It conveyed both "I don't know" and "I'll do my best."

Noel was now muttering under his breath, and I was certain he was using some very nasty words not included in my vocabulary in *any* language. Finally, he stated, "Cori, I mean what I first say. You do not have to do this. We can take care of ourselves. You do not need to be the lamb given to the wolf."

I smiled. "I appreciate the thought, but it's probably the smartest way to go. Maybe a drink and an effort on my part to be civil without being overly nice could make the difference between the next pilot making it to safety or not. I should be able to handle him as long as someone is nearby in case things get ugly or there's pressure to do more than drink and talk. I'm not willing to become a lamb chop at this point."

"I will find a way to be in the kitchen," Noel announced. "We have acquaintances at Café Destin, and I will ask they will hide me there and I will be near." He gently touched my cheek. "I am to be…telling truth and say a lady I am…fond of…is dining with someone else and I am jealous. They are French. They understand romance."

Pierre turned and headed back inside the club to tell Bauer I'd be pleased to join him for a drink and try to persuade him that I was under Pierre's care and needed a guardian.

He came back within minutes to tell me Bauer

would be escorting me to Café Destin after I was through on stage. Bauer didn't see the need for a chaperone and Pierre was not welcome to join us or, in Bauer's words, "spy from a different table."

"Okay. I'll just wing it, then," I said with more bravado than I felt.

Noel grabbed my hands. "I promise I will do everything I can to be somewhere in the café. If I cannot, then I will find another way to rescue you if you need the help. I do not understand if Bauer is liking you as a woman…no…I am sorry, of course, this I *do* understand…but I hate the thought. You are beautiful and smart and kind and strong of spirit, and any man with eyes and even someone with the heart of a German would be liking you. I am not making sense."

"Not completely, but I enjoy hearing you compliment me, although much of it is coming out a bit lopsided."

He relaxed for a moment and smiled; then he grimaced. "I fear also he will try to question you for revelations about Café Violette and perhaps *l'Opéra Blanche*, and I do not want you in a position of being under interrogation. This is not safe for you."

I nodded. "I'm not sure which worries me more, although I can totally keep a secret, and I promise Bauer won't get a single piece of info about the club, the opera house, or anyone involved in anything apart from making fabulous music, unless he decides torture is on the menu. Tell you what. If things go haywire, I'll find a way to spill a drink all over my dress. It could be a signal, plus, if Bauer is any kind of gentleman at all, it should also allow me to put an end to this so-called date."

I paused as something struck me. I tapped Pierre on

the shoulder. "Does Val have any clothes with high necks I could borrow? Something very non-revealing?"

Pierre brightened. "He has *exactement* such an ensemble, from a famous German lady singer who appears in what you call a 'turtleneck' sweater with some men trousers and a suit jacket. Val has not wanted to recreate her image for fear of offending the Boche, so it is never seen or worn."

"Perfect. I'll change as soon as I finish my last number in about...oh, gee...ten minutes now." I paused before adding, "I might also have a swig of brandy on my own before meeting the nosy major. For courage. I need it."

Chapter 15

Café Destin was what I'd call a real restaurant, as opposed to a nightclub. There was no stage and no entertainment. Strike one for the hope Bauer and I could munch on a scrumptious repast of roasted artichoke hearts and peppers and croissants while sipping brandy and listening to the light sounds of various French cabaret singers.

Destin was also much smaller than Café Violette and, consequently, more intimate. Darker, too. Candles were the decor of choice on each table, for a seductive, romantic effect. Several dimly lit, large, overhead lamps kept the place from being pitch black and allowed one to talk to one's companion without squinting.

I silently blessed Val for lending me the soft, cream-colored turtleneck sweater topped by a dark jacket over deep tan, baggy, linen, man-styled pants. They covered me very nicely and helped stave off the chill that had swept over me the moment I'd been given Major Bauer's so-called invitation. I was used to wearing trousers in New Manhattan, so consequently I felt more myself. Val also provided a tan fedora, which reminded me of Ajay's and gave me confidence I could pull off dining and chatting with a German officer without either giving away every secret I knew or throwing up all over him out of sheer anxiety. Bauer had been in such a rush I hadn't had time to take off my stage makeup, which gave the added boost of hiding behind the mask of Cori Christopher, chanteuse. It sounds weird, but I swear I felt more capable of successfully fending off advances with a sweep of a false eyelash and a raised heavily-penciled brow.

Bauer had been politely waiting for me to change after my set was finished. Politely meant pacing in what passed as a hall near my dressing room. Perhaps he was afraid I'd take the opportunity to hoist myself out the window. My room basically had a small porthole, which meant he needn't have worried, although I must admit if I'd been inside one of the larger dressing rooms equipped with a real opening to outside, I'd've considered doing a runner. Then again, those windows were barely large enough to allow a hefty-sized cat to sneak through. And—cute side note—some kitties occasionally did manage to take shelter in Café Violette via Jacques Benet's dressing room, since the word must have gone out years ago among French felines: "Hey, *chats et chattes*, Monsieur Jacques's a total sucker for strays, and we're welcome to a warm space and leftovers from the kitchen."

Side note over. Main action starting.

Bauer hadn't said a word during the five-block walk from Café Violette to Café Destin. The silence did nothing for my nerves. Once we reached the café, we were escorted like royalty to a table on the right side. There wasn't a single patron seated at a table anywhere within ten feet. The only other diners were men wearing German uniforms and ladies who were dressed in satin gowns and appeared a lot more comfortable with their surroundings and companions than I was.

Bauer ordered wine, cheese, bread, and sausages

without asking me if I preferred a different beverage, was lactose intolerant, or vegetarian. I was already ticked about the whole situation, but his attitude upped my anger another notch. I don't like wine, don't eat dairy, and one of the results of the storms isolating New Manhattan from most of America was everyone became vegan whether they wanted to or not, which was fine with me. I love animals and couldn't imagine chewing on anything that once had a face. Bauer did let me finish half of my croissant before beginning any real conversation. I left the cheese untouched.

"Fräulein Christopher, you seem to have settled quite well into your status as the star female performer at Café Violette."

I wasn't sure if he was asking a question, so I went with the Ajay "volunteer nothing" advice from childhood and simply smiled.

"Tell me, though, why did you really come to Paris? People in America are prospering, from what I understand, although I myself have never been there."

Hmmm. He was searching for dirt on me, but could I use this as a way to flip the chat? "You haven't? I'm surprised, Major Bauer. You seem quite cosmopolitan. Where are you from? I mean, yes, of course from Germany, but what city?"

"München. You Americans refer to it as Munich."

"We do. Did you grow up there?"

"I did. I also went to the university there."

"Oh? What did you study?"

His left eyebrow lifted. "Why are you interested, Fräulein?"

"Because I enjoy hearing other people's stories, no matter where they come from. Sadly, I was never able to travel when I was a child."

"Why did you not travel?"

Oops. Mistake in coming out with the pronoun "I" and thus putting the spotlight back on Cori. I shrugged. "Very boring tale. My parents died when I was a child, and I was basically brought up as a ward of the state. Not a lot of money for orphans and definitely not for orphans to go traveling. Like I said, boring. Please, tell me about Munich. I've seen photos and love the architecture, the mix of medieval with modern."

Both eyebrows shot up. Another error on my part, revealing I had a brain and knew words like 'medieval' and 'architecture,' but I couldn't handle the stress of pretending to be a ditz while trying to deflect Bauer from garnering any real information about me or Café Violette.

At least I had Bauer talking. I was given a verbal guided tour of the wonders of Munich, which was kind of fun. As I'd truthfully told the man, I hadn't had the opportunity to travel, and my trip to Paris hadn't exactly included a nice train ride from Marseilles. Although it was now a Nazi stronghold less than twenty miles from the gruesome site of Dachau, Munich sounded like it had once been a gorgeous city with exotic medieval palaces and castles and museums and several universities. I didn't let on that I knew quite a bit about Munich. I knew much of the city would be destroyed by Allied bombings during the war. I knew one of the universities was the birthplace of the student resistance movement called The White Rose. And if anyone is questioning how I had these facts at my disposal, I simply point out that Robin Christopher loved history and I managed to inherit his curiosity about times and places and how regimes began and ended and why and how some people got suckered into the desire to rule the world over and over again.

Back to Bauer. Once he was on a roll, he opened up with some goodies about how he'd joined the Hitler Youth at age fourteen. He was now twenty-four. Same age as Noel. He'd loved his time with the group and realized he was fully on board with the idea of the superiority of the Aryan "race" as exemplified by the Germans. I decided not to argue the point that Aryan wasn't technically a race and letting one's brain get washed in the principles of Hitler's master plan was one stinking bad way to spend one's teen years.

"And you studied at which university?" I asked when Bauer took a breath to drink a glass of wine and order another bottle. For the record, I was doing a stellar job of avoiding the fermented grapes. A dish of artichokes and peppers had arrived at our table during the Munich tour, and I have to admit I dived in with much enjoyment to eat fresh veggies along with the croissants.

"Ludwig-Maximilians-Universität München. The oldest in Bavaria."

"I've definitely heard of it. Fabulous reputation. Were you able to get a degree before…uh…you joined the service?"

He nodded. "I studied sciences. And art. I played violin with the orchestra. I considered going into medicine. But, as you have seen, I have a gift for languages, and this talent alerted various ranking members of the Nazi party to my usefulness as an officer who could be best served in something other than combat. I was able to transition from Hitler Youth to the Army upon graduation from the university. And from there I was promoted to serve with the Abwehr. Military

Intelligence."

"I see."

The waiter poured more wine into Bauer's glass. Mine was still full. I wished whoever had arranged the decor at Café Destin had provided a few potted plants for young ladies to discreetly dispose of a few shots of whatever booze their escorts happened to be providing.

And I was experiencing a moment of sad insight. Bauer was an extremely intelligent man. Cultured. Handsome if one were into the blond-Aryan thing. If Hitler hadn't started a movement designed to turn normal people into supermen, commit mass murder, and start a world war in the process, Bauer would have been a neat catch for some nice, sweet German girl who would have baked nice, sweet kugels and schnitzels for him, listened as he played nice, sweet tunes on his superbly crafted violin, praised his nice, sweet watercolors, and provided him with a nice, sweet family to come home to after saving lives as a nice, sweet doctor. Or maybe he'd have rebelled by going Bohemian and painting brilliant Impressionist pieces or moving to Ireland to find a Celtic folk band in need of a fiddle player. Either way, he would have been a decent person. Someone who would have been shocked at the idea of killing another human being. It was a shame Fiona Belle hadn't popped into Johann's life when he was fourteen and encouraged him to travel back to *La Belle Époque* where he could apprentice with Degas or Renoir or Monet.

Bauer was staring at me. "You have learned about me. I still haven't heard what brought you to Paris. Why did you really arrive here at such a time of turmoil? Why at Café Violette?" He paused. "You are not drinking your wine. Is there a problem?"

"I'm not a drinker. Especially wine. It doesn't really agree with me. Brandy on occasion, for medicinal purposes or stress. I'm fine, though. Enjoying the bread and veggies very much. But you asked about Café Violette? I was very impulsive, Major. A genetic trait, according to the one living relative I had up until a few months ago. I worked for a film company. But I've always wanted to be a singer. They weren't exactly providing voice lessons at the…orphanage. But I sang any time I could. Before I decided to take the risk and come to Paris, I heard a recording made at Café Violette. The musicians were amazing. So, when I had the opportunity to travel here, I took it in hopes what happened *would* happen. I was given the chance to sing with those same musicians. It's obvious how much I love performing. End of story."

"No. That was not the end of the story. But perhaps you will be more forthcoming with your past…and present…if we leave and find a place less crowded."

Oh, crap. Here it was. Bauer couldn't get me sloshed on the wine, so he'd decided it was time to get me alone. Whether the intent was to make some sexual advances or try to dig out info about activities at my place of employment, I needed to find a way to bring this night to an end. Saying I was tired after performing wasn't going to cut it.

My improv skills had evaporated. I'd never actually been on what is termed a "date" and had no clue how to resist the attempts of any man, much less a member of the Nazi intelligence service, trying to seduce me into a cozy one-on-one at some seamy hotel. Did I tell Bauer I'd prefer a night in Camp Virtue, being interrogated by Delegates about the resistance group, to being anywhere alone with him? Did I admit the closest thing to a sexual encounter with anyone in my life had been the touch of Noel's hand helping me up from a fake tumble the night I arrived at Café Violette? Did I flatly state I'd prefer any and all future romantic encounters be with Noel and Noel only?

I almost smiled, thinking about the night I met Noel, when I hadn't a clue who I was. Somehow I had divined he was the reason I was at the Café Violette hours before Fiona Belle appeared and saved me by singing the song about Christopher Robin. The moment I set eyes on Noel, as he hid backstage with a scared English pilot, I understood that love at first sight was real, even if in actuality it had been love at first hearing a hundred years in the future and thousands of miles away.

I came out of my musings with a visible start. The same Irish voice who'd massacred the song about Christopher Robin a couple of weeks ago was warbling the intro to a funny tune from the Broadway musical *Guys and Dolls*. The number is about a young woman coming to the realization her wheezing, sneezing, and coughing is due to a never-ending cold brought on by her lover's inability to commit. I had no idea how Fiona Belle had managed to sneak into the café and find a table for one in the corner, but there she sat.

Her broad hint worked. I began to cough, and quickly added some loud wheezing and choking sounds, although I couldn't quite figure out how to fake a sneeze.

"What is happening?" Bauer demanded.

"Sorry! It's the wine. I must be allergic. I told you I generally don't drink the stuff." Cough, cough. Wheeze, wheeze. "I need water. A lot of water."

Bauer called the waiter, who brought me a ton of

water. The waiter was accompanied by Fiona Belle, who'd come running over to our table the instant I got the first hacking noise out of my throat. "I'll be afta takin' ya home, Miss Cori, now. I've got a smashin' remedy fer this kind of bad reaction to wine, although we're not drinkin' much of the stuff in the old country. Whiskey is much better fer the throat."

Bauer stood and, for a moment, as I peeked up at him in between bending over to deliver more coughs, I thought he was going to command Fiona Belle to release me into his care. He thought better of engaging in a battle with one pugnacious Irish gremlin and bowed. "Please feel better, Fräulein Christopher. I would not want you so ill you cannot perform."

I nodded as Fiona Belle and I exited the Café Destin. I continued the coughing and wheezing for the next five blocks to Rosemarie's house, in case Bauer decided to follow us.

Once we hit the front door, I stopped the act. "You boggle the mind, Fiona Belle! Thanks for the song."

"You'd a thought of it sooner or later. But sooner was better. Noel made it into the kitchen and was hidin', and I was afraid he was about to come out and begin a battle royal with Bauer. It's not the right time fer either of ya."

"Ah. So there *is* a plan? A time and place for action?" I asked.

"Night, Cori."

I watched her walk back down the block…to where—or when—I had no idea.

Chapter 16

Delys, Paulette, Teresa, Rosemarie, and I had been given fabulous seats in Café Violette for tonight's performance. Papa Pierre had arranged for my roommates to come see the show and included Rosemarie Ducote in the invitation. For the first time in two weeks I wasn't slated to perform, and I had to admit I was excited to get to watch the other acts, although how long my role as a member of the audience lasted would be determined during the first act. Noel had intimated earlier I might need to sing a number as a signal for someone in the crowd, who would then pass along a "yes" or "no" regarding a recent British arrival who was waiting to hear whether or not he had to stay hidden at his current location.

I glanced around the nightclub, savoring a few moments free of anxiety. We—the artists who performed at Café Violette—had, up to this time, managed to get away with providing entertainment long past curfews, perhaps because the Nazis who frequented the club needed some respite from being overbearing bullies all hours of the day and night. It was restful tonight to be nothing more than a girl enjoying a show. I didn't see Bauer anywhere in attendance.

He hadn't paid any visits to Café Violette for at least five days. Hadn't tried to contact me following the supper date I somewhat rudely ended with my fake coughing spell. The team of Kessler and Webber hadn't been around either. Good news for all of us at the nightclub, but doubtless bad for various French men or women who'd incurred the displeasure of the German officers at some innocuous *patisserie* in Montmartre by voicing an opinion about the "Boche."

However, there were other Nazi soldiers in attendance this evening. They'd tried to chat up Teresa and Paulette and me at the entrance to the club about ten minutes earlier. A few attempted to converse with Rosemarie, but she produced one very icy glare and they left her alone. They were less interested in Delys…I assumed because no matter how beautiful she was, their commanders would frown on fraternization with a black girl. I vowed to stick close to her side in case the feigned disinterest shifted into active aggression.

Neither Paulette nor Teresa seemed pleased with the attention. Apart from her distaste for anyone in the employ of the Third Reich, our English rose was engaged and very faithful to her pilot. And our French prima ballerina not only had a ridiculous cadre of admirers who lingered outside the stage door after rehearsals—and, one assumed, would be there for future performances—but it was rumored she was steadily dating William Gale, an American clarinet player who worked at both Café Violette and *l'Opéra Blanche*.

Papa Pierre took notice of the crowd of eager German suitors as our party entered, and quickly but politely escorted us inside and seated us before their attentions became something darker than a nuisance.

As Pierre was leaving our table, he nodded at me. "You will especially enjoy Monsieur Donald Joseph's selections tonight, Cori. From the musical show *George*

White's Scandals."

"Oh?"

"*Oui.* Monsieur Joseph gives *'I'll Build a Stairway to Paradise'* a, how you say…mischievous…quality you will appreciate, and he would be appreciating to hear your evaluation of how he does this song."

"I'm sure I'll love it." It appeared I'd be performing this night after all.

Built as a small opera house more than a hundred years earlier, Café Violette still retained a large stage, a section in front of the orchestra used for patrons who wanted to dance, and a tiered audience section. Each tier held at least six small round tables. Café Violette's maître d' and sommelier, Monsieur Michel LaFontaine, had ushered the German soldiers to a table dead center on the third tier, which was, for any audience member without a hidden agenda, like the need to be close to an exit, the ultimate in perfect seating. The soldiers had no reason to complain they'd ended up a bit farther from a group of young ladies—us—than they wanted to be.

My roommates and I were escorted to what might be referred to as the cheap seats about two tiers above, near the east side exit. Although it wasn't quite as desirable in terms of viewing the stage, it was far enough from the officers to forestall any conversation, yet close enough not to appear we were deliberately trying to avoid them.

We ordered wine and cheese and bread, and refrained from guzzling the wine while waiting for the show to start, about twelve minutes after our food and drink arrived. I made sure I didn't drink a single sip, in case someone was watching any reactions on my part and reported back to Bauer. Pierre brought me a glass of brandy, and I felt almost relaxed enough to completely enjoy the evening.

The first performer, Donald Joseph, was well worth a twenty-minute wait. He was one of those singers who has an innate magical connection to the audience—a warmth that translates in a small cabaret or a 5000-seat house. He sang a medley of old Celtic folk songs, and I could literally feel the energy rise from every listener. Well, every non-German listener. A lot of the boys from Berlin appeared bored. Perhaps they needed more beer. Or perhaps they'd have preferred to go back to Germany and sing along with a marching band playing "*Deutschlandlied*" or find a huge opera house where they could cheer along with the strains of Wagner and his Ring cycle.

Although Monsieur Joseph's "I'll Build a Stairway to Paradise" was a signal to *me*, Papa Pierre had nailed it with his praise of Donald's interpretation. It had just the right amount of what the British might call "cheekiness" and most of the Nazi boys suffering from musical ennui perked up.

Donald Joseph's clear, rich baritone gave way to my friend, our comic female impersonator Valentin Valentin, who wisely steered clear of any political figures and instead provided impressions of American film stars, including famous pin-up girls and vaudeville era comedians. Val was followed by a trio of female singers Pierre knew from "around" who occasionally were able to drop in at the club on request. These ladies took advantage of Café Violette's small but energetic band, led by trumpet player Charles Souverain, to belt out tunes from America. It was impossible not to let one's feet start tapping to the sounds of "Give My

Regards to Broadway" and "Bill Bailey, Won't You Please Come Home" and I glanced around at an audience enthralled and happy for the moments the trio was onstage.

I half expected the Germans to shut the place down after this bombardment of American music, but perhaps seeing attractive women perform with such enthusiasm softened their hearts enough to allow them to enjoy what bordered on "jazz." Also, the ladies were smart in their choice of songs, which were primarily from early Broadway shows and not recorded by any Jewish or black musicians.

The next act was Jacques Benet's lovely version of Irving Berlin's "Because I Love You" sung in French. His performance was to be followed by a fifteen-minute intermission and an encore by Val Valentin.

The instant Benet left the stage, the sommelier Michel (who was also Val's romantic partner) arrived with more wine and brandy, another basket of bread, and a note written in Noel's hand for me. It simply read, *Did you enjoy Donald's rendition of "I'll Build a Stairway to Paradise"? Or would you have preferred "Always"? You could sing both, Mademoiselle Cori, and as the expression goes, knock them out of any American park. But Monsieur Joseph would appreciate your critique. Perhaps he will suggest which one would sound better for you?*

Delys glanced at me. "Cori, *est-ce tout va bien*? Everything is okay?" She flashed a grin remarkably similar to the one I'd first seen on Fiona Belle's face in a hologram. "*Qu'est-ce que c'est?* A *billet-doux* from Monsieur Noel?"

"He says?" asked Teresa.

I passed the note to her, silently wishing it really was a "love letter" from Noel instead of a cryptic message about songs from American musicals.

Teresa read it, then gave it to Delys. Within seconds all my roommates and landlady knew what had been written and all four were smiling. Which was fine with me. Anyone watching would see a young lady enjoying a note from someone with romantic intentions.

"You are...how you say...flushing, Cori. Are you feeling well?" Delys winked at me.

I stood and responded, "I'm fine. Just need some air. Anyone care to join me?" I crossed my fingers no one would.

Delys shook her head and teased. "I am drinking more wine. We will try to keep *une peu* drinks for you, although you are being *très* more impressed with someone *outside* than with wine."

Paulette chewed her lower lip. "I've had a rough week, so that decanter may be empty by the time you get back."

I laughed. "I've heard rumors, Miss Reeve, you are completely incapable of holding your liquor, regardless of what happened during the week, so no more than two glasses for you. None of us want to carry you fireman-style all the way back to our apartment."

She giggled. "I'll just eat a bit more cheese and bread to soak up the wine." She sighed." I've missed these treats."

"I understand. Feel free to order a ton more bread. Papa Pierre's orders."

Teresa shook her head. "*Rien pour moi*." She'd found a German soldier she obviously thought was attractive. I couldn't help but notice they'd been winking

146

and smiling at each other after the lights came back up following Benet's performance. I hoped William Gale wasn't watching when Teresa rose with me and headed toward the German's table one tier down.

I'd just started to open the exit door leading to the garden when Teresa grabbed my arm. "*Il ne m'est pas étranger*," Teresa said, although I hadn't asked her if she knew him, or passed judgment with any expression of surprise or disgust. She continued in French, which I loosely translated. "I grew up in Alsace-Lorraine, and it is an area that goes from under the government of France to Germany and back again. Frederick and I are *amis* in childhood."

"Ah. Well, how nice you can remain friends. I'm sure it's rough during wartime," I said.

Her expression brightened. "*Oui*! *C'est très bon!* We can be help of each other in this bad time."

Teresa and the young soldier embraced. I headed through the exit to find out whether I was needed to sing on my night off and whether the tune I sang meant a soldier was on his way to freedom…or forced to remain where he was so as not to get captured.

Chapter 17

As soon as I stepped outside into the small walled garden, used by performers during breaks and the occasional couple looking for a semi-private space to engage in a quiet flirtation, I spotted Donald Joseph standing with his back against the flimsy latticework, smoking a cigarette. Seeing him up close helped ease any fears about any assignment I might be given. A man well into his fifties, he reminded me a lot of my grandfather, Yash Kapoor, who had the same professorial air of absentminded brilliance mixed with sheer kindness.

I approached Donald, smiling but unsure what I was supposed to say. "*Bon nuit*, Monsieur Joseph. I enjoyed your performance very much," I told him.

He bowed, then kissed the hand I offered. "*Merci*. You are the American who has been singing for several weeks earlier, *oui*? I 'ave heard wonderful things about you, but not yet had opportunity to listen."

"*Oui. Je suis* Cori Christopher. Please, call me Cori. And *merci* for the compliment."

He smiled and got down to business. "May I ask which song you liked the best from my repertoire tonight, Mademoiselle Cori?"

"Definitely 'Stairway to Paradise.' From one of the *George White's Scandals*, right?"

He nodded. "*Oui*. It has what you Americans call 'catchy' in both melody and lyrics."

"It *is* catchy!" I paused, then added as though a thought had just crossed my mind. "I have to admit, much as I love the up-tempo songs one of my favorite old tunes is the ballad 'Always.' It's very poignant and sometimes makes me cry, but it's a beautiful song."

"Ah. *C'est une belle melodie*. Irving Berlin wrote the song for his wife. *C'est très romantique*! You should sing it for our audiences. Noel has said this is your night *not* to perform, but perhaps you could make an exception, *pour moi*?"

I relaxed, then stiffened when I noticed Teresa and her German friend standing by the door. He lit a cigarette for her and I couldn't tell if they'd overheard, although our discussion should appear to be nothing more than musical artists conversing about song choices, and Teresa might have trouble keeping up with some of the English terminology.

I was so intent on Teresa and Frederick I failed for a few seconds to notice the third person who'd quietly joined Donald and me. "Snuck up behind us" might be the better phrase.

"Fräulein Christopher. How odd to find you here. Is it not a bit cold to be outside with only a light jacket?"

Bauer. *Merde*! He must have spotted me leaving my table and followed. I hadn't seen him in the audience. Perhaps he'd slithered in when I was focusing on one of the performances on stage.

I responded to his concern about my well-being, attempting to be upbeat. "Major Bauer. *Guten abend*. Um, thanks for asking, but really, the temperature isn't bad at all. Could be due to the two large brandies I imbibed, which are keeping me warm for the moment."

Joseph bowed. "And I am more than willing to lend

Mademoiselle Christopher my jacket, should the need be required."

Bauer ignored Joseph and continued to train his gaze on me. "But I fear you might catch a chill out here, Fräulein, and become ill. I shall escort you back inside. Now."

Could I ask Donald what I needed to do? How could I phrase a question without it sounding awkward?

Monsieur Joseph was smarter and quicker in improvisation than I. "The officer may be correct in his worry over your health, especially if you decide you are willing to honor us with a song in the next set, Mademoiselle Christopher." He quickly glanced at Bauer. "Mademoiselle Christopher is such an accomplished singer. We are hoping she will sing tonight. Many, uh, how you say…repeat patrons…have been requesting a performance."

My muscles unclenched and I almost audibly sighed with relief. "Thank you. I *always* appreciate the opportunity to belt out a tune or two." I grinned. "Stage hound. *C'est moi.*"

Joseph flashed a charming smile and asked, "What *would* you like to sing this night? I will inform our bandleader, Monsieur Souverain, while you go backstage and change. But first I would like to finish my cigarette. I have not the care if the garden is chilly." He inhaled and I sensed him choking back a desire to exhale smoke into Bauer's smug face.

I casually stated, "Well, we were just discussing romantic ballads, so maybe you could ask Monsieur Souverain if he'd play 'Always'? If possible, I'd prefer the key of A-flat."

Bauer visibly stiffened. He stared at Donald, then at

me, before saying, " 'Always' is not a favorite of mine, Fräulein. I would rather hear, 'Once in a Blue Moon,' which you sing so beautifully."

I made an effort not to faint, breathe at a rapid pace, or run screaming from the garden. It didn't take a Cassandra warning to tell me there was danger. He knew! Bauer knew. What I wasn't yet able to determine was whether he knew I knew it was a signal, or still thought I was just an innocent performer who sang whatever management or admirers told me to sing. Too many "knews" and too few answers.

I also had no idea if he was aware that my coughing spell at Café Destin had been one giant fake to keep from being alone with him and he was upset he'd been unable to do more research into the life and times of Cori Christopher. But the man was in military intelligence, and I imagined that even without benefit of an Internet the Abwehr had a great network unearthing everything about everyone who interested them. Which would be one big surprise when they discovered Cori Christopher didn't exist. Thank heaven my last name was fairly common and it might be difficult to figure out who my relatives were.

Back to the matter at hand.

Donald showed no visible signs of stress, although I sensed his heart was racing along at the same tempo as mine—*allegro*. "Herr Bauer is correct. It is rumored Mademoiselle Cori sings 'Once in a Blue Moon' with such feeling and perfect notes one cries in happiness. However, my understanding is she has sung the number many times, and there is a large repeat crowd tonight." He winked at me. "It is also more enjoyable for a performer themselves to be able to sing a new song,

151

n'est-ce pas?"

I nodded and managed a smile. "Absolutely. I'm totally up for something new, and I've been dying to sing 'Always.' "

Bauer bent his elbow and forcibly put my arm though the crook to top his. "No, Herr Joseph, it is *my* request, and I would like to hear what I want. Please, you will accompany Fräulein Christopher and me backstage now."

Sunk. We were sunk. If I sang "Once in a Blue Moon," the R.A.F. pilot who'd been hiding in a basement dressing room at *l'Opéra Blanche* for the last two days would be worse than sunk—the message "all clear" would be given and he and whoever guided him to his next contact would be captured.

"Always" was our warning tune. It meant "too dangerous to travel. Remain in place." Bauer probably had a goon watching the "safe" location where the contact would be waiting if the "all clear" message was received, but I'd bet he was clueless as to where the pilot was currently taking shelter.

The major had boxed me in. No matter what I decided to sing, someone was going to be hurt. Bauer escorted Donald and me back inside and over to the right wings. I desperately tried to come up with a way to keep a pilot and our *Résistance* contacts safe without me ending up in a camp or shot by Bauer for noncompliance with his song request. Not to mention trying not to endanger Noel, Pierre, Joseph, and about half the musicians and staff at the club. It took more than one person to pull off the escapes managed at Café Violette, and no one needed to end up in a camp because of my choices.

Our trio ended up standing close to the piano which had provided a brief hiding place for Noel and Sam Seymour my first night in Paris. Noel himself suddenly joined us and asked why we were there.

Bauer answered him with a tone of extreme self-satisfaction. "Fräulein Christopher is going to sing. I have personally specified the song. It is one of her best, 'Once in a Blue Moon.' She can tell your band leader once she is on the stage. Please, Herr Matheson, stay with Herr Joseph and myself. There is no time for you to return to the audience without interrupting the Fräulein's entrance."

Noel was as accomplished an actor as Donald. Not a hint of emotion other than surprise Bauer had made a request. He smiled at me, but I could see the anguish in his eyes. No way to warn our contact in the audience that he or she was about to be given the wrong information. And, I hate to be repetitive but I will because it was a huge concern, a pilot would be captured.

We were joined within seconds by our Master of Ceremonies, Gaspard Bassett. Could I get him to make an announcement about Cori singing "Once in a Blue Moon" with a coded message to our contact that we were sending a false signal? How could I convey this information with Bauer standing next to me?

"Oh! I need to change into one of my costumes," I exclaimed. "Where is Fiona Belle?" She'd be able to get the word out if I could just get back to her.

Bauer shook his head. "You are fine in your dress." He nodded at our emcee. "Gaspard, Fräulein Cori will be singing 'Once in a Blue Moon' for her surprise performance tonight."

Gaspard flashed a glance at me, then at Noel. I

couldn't tell if he knew this was the wrong choice or not.

On the stage, Val Valentin finished his impersonation of the comical American singer who generally included a tall, fruit-laden hat and samba movements in her act. He paused at the stairs leading down into the space where Bauer, Joseph, Noel, and I stood, bodies motionless as each of us imagined the scenario that would be played out thanks to one song.

"Is there a problem?" Val asked. "Is everyone feeling well?"

"There is no problem. Fräulein Christopher is about to honor my request for a song tonight. You will be unable to do an encore," Bauer stated with satisfaction.

"Of course." Val bowed. "We love having Cori sing. She has a way of making an audience feel as if they are part of her family…her home, for when soldiers are so sadly away from their loved ones." The bananas on his hat bobbed and swayed and the absurdity of this situation flooded into my brain.

I wasn't sure which was spinning more…my stomach or my brain. I had to step up. I had to find a solution. And then I spotted Fiona Belle crossing behind the stage, headed back to the dressing rooms. She was wearing a red dress such as had doubtless been all the rage during American Colonial days. Speaking of spinning, she was actually carrying a spinning wheel in one hand. Yes. A spinning wheel. The other hand held a fake sword. And I knew what to do.

I could hear Ajay's voice in my head warning me about being impulsive and brash but having the courage to use those traits when the occasion called for them. If there was a time for boldness mixed with a dash of insanity, this was it. I felt moderately sure no one else could be held culpable.

Bauer pointed at Gaspard. "You are on. The patrons do not like an empty stage for long."

I grabbed Gaspard's arm. "Let me be my own emcee tonight, *s'il vous plaît?*"

I didn't give him time to respond, or Bauer time to grab me and pull me back. I ran up the stairs leading to the stage as though it were any other night, watched by four men who stood silently in the wings.

Once onstage, I waved my hand for silence.

"*Guten Abend and bonsoir, meine Damen und Herren et mesdames et messieurs* and ladies and gentlemen," I called out. "For those who haven't been to Café Violette before, my name is Cori Christopher and I normally do a set of three or four tunes. I was supposed to be off tonight, and I've taken advantage by drinking a few brandies..." Laughter arose from those in the audience who understood me. "...but it turns out I've been asked to sing. The song requested by your own Major Bauer is a lovely tune, but I'm going to sing something different because, much as I love Paris, for some reason I became *very* homesick for America tonight. And I'm sure most of you soldiers in our audience miss your own homes. So I dug into my repertoire of unusual songs and came up with a ballad I happen to love."

Less than a month ago, in another century, I'd stood on the stage of a theater slated for destruction in New Manhattan. I'd sung in French, to an empty house, a stirring number about a woman's sadness in seeing her lover go off to war. I now faced a sold-out group of primarily enemy soldiers and prepared to sing the same stirring number, which could well get me killed. I was counting on half the audience not translating English well enough to understand all the lyrics, and/or becoming so entranced by the melody and my marvelous voice they wouldn't catch the nuances about the pain caused by wars and killing.

I smiled. "It's an ancient Irish folk ballad, but it was popular during the American Revolution and America's Civil War. It's called 'Johnny Has Gone for a Soldier." I waved at Charles Souverain and our pianist. "If Monsieur DuMaurier would please hit an opening chord in the key of B-flat, I can do the rest a cappella." Charles nodded, concealing any surprise at this request. I turned back to the audience. "I hope you love this song as much as I do."

Chapter 18

Teresa Dorleac had not accompanied us back to Rosemarie's. She'd told Paulette she was meeting a friend after Café Violette closed for the night and to go on without her. Curfew would not be an issue as the man was a German soldier who could see her home safely. She didn't go into detail, but I assumed she was going to have a cozy reunion with Frederick from Alsace-Lorraine, who seemed, at least to me, interested in upgrading from old childhood buddy to new romantic partner.

My roommates and Rosemarie weren't always thrilled with Teresa's lack of taste in men. She often seemed not to care who she went out with as long as he could supply a bottle of decent champagne and send her red roses the next day. She was kind enough to share the champagne and use the roses to brighten up the apartment, which might have been why no one chided her about her questionable dating habits. Supposedly, her steady boyfriend the last few weeks had been William Gale, but musicians aren't generally wealthy and Teresa liked nice things. She was also diva enough to enjoy attention, no matter from what source.

I'm ashamed to admit I didn't much care what Teresa was doing with her German "friend" once everyone left Café Violette because I was relieved I hadn't been shot or gotten Noel, Donald, Papa Pierre,

Gaspard, or Val Valentin shot.

Noel had been brilliant. Following the standing ovation for my Irish ballad, he, Donald, and Val immediately joined me onstage. Noel waved at Monsieur Souverain to play the traditional closer at Café Violette, "Bye, Bye, Blackbird" in its entirety, including all the verses. The audience was asked to chime in just like any other night, and it was a great way to send everyone out in a good mood, regardless of how hellacious life was beyond the club. Noel knew it would be near impossible for one or more German officers to start arresting people—beginning with me—in the middle of a chorus. Heck, the majority of folks singing were members of the same army and fairly drunk to boot.

Bauer apparently realized he couldn't provide proof about any clandestine messages being sent, or any wrongdoing, apart from one female singer going rogue with her choice of music or Noel Matheson choosing to barge on stage to get the audience primed for a sing-along. He must have decided there was no point in hauling in either Noel or me with nothing else to show for his efforts. I stayed free of bullet holes and handcuffs. As did Noel.

Which leads to the morning after. All the excitement generated by defying Bauer and waiting for a proverbial head chop left me barely noticing my wayward roommate's absence. But when Delys saw that Teresa's bed had not been slept in, she, Paulette, Rosemarie, and I became united in our anxiety regarding Teresa's safety. Spending a full night away from home was totally unlike our prima ballerina. She might be a party girl when given the chance, but she was first and foremost a professional. Her sleep schedule was rigid and kept her healthy for practice and performance.

Delys and Paulette called the Paris police, using the public phone at *l'Opéra Blanche*. The prefect at the police station had not been overly worried when he heard a twenty-year-old dancer hadn't come home last night or today. His tone and words were more on the lines of "couldn't care less." Delys translated for my benefit: "Perhaps she has gone home to her village? Or is staying with a lover?"

Delys told me she and Paulette tried, in vain, to make the policeman understand that Teresa had no family left in Alsace-Lorraine and she did not engage in overnights with gentlemen. Teresa not showing up to a rehearsal was unthinkable. All of us shifted from feeling mildly uneasy to becoming very disturbed.

Delys explained to the policeman, despite his attitude, that Mademoiselle Dorleac was playing the dual role of Odette/Odile in the portion of *Swan Lake* Luc Hebert's *Théâtre de Danse* would be offering in about a week and that this was more important to her than anything else in the world. She told him Teresa had confided to her one night following a grueling rehearsal that she'd dreamed about executing those thirty-two *fouettes* as the Black Swan in the Coda *pas de deux* for Act III from the time she was four years old and she and her mother had traveled by bus from their village just so the entranced child could attend a performance of the company Ballets Russes doing the full *Swan Lake* at *l'Opéra de Paris*.

One could almost see the shrug on the part of the policeman. There were pockets of resistance to German authority cropping up all over the city, and the local gendarme, clearly wishing to curry favor with the occupiers of Paris, decided that for the time being rebellion took priority over the disappearance of a silly girl who would doubtless return when she and her lover grew bored with one another.

I didn't buy it. I'd seen the look in Teresa's eyes during rehearsal after she'd hit the final pose following those thirty-two *fouettes*. For her, dance was a love no soldier boy could match, childhood friend or not.

In Teresa's absence today, the company was rehearsing *Swan Lake* with its understudy, my friend Delys Robinson. Delys was amazing. As previously noted, Teresa was technically perfect. Her dancing rivaled ballerinas I'd seen on film from American Ballet Theater, New York City Ballet, the Kirov, and the Bolshoi. The one caveat to Teresa's perfection was a warmth missing from her performance, even when portraying Odette, the sweet and gentle swan.

Delys didn't have Teresa's exceptional technique, but from her first entrance, dressed in sloppy old rehearsal clothes, it was clear she had the extra charisma necessary to make an audience love her. Her *fouettes* might not match Teresa's jaw-dropping expertise, but her emotional involvement and energy kept me mesmerized. Watching Delys, I found it difficult to remember my duties as assistant stage manager. This was not some wannabe understudy filling in during rehearsal. This was Odette/Odile ready to perform.

Following five hours of nonstop movement, Luc finally gave everyone a late afternoon stretch class before calling it quits for the day, recommending as much rest as possible before the next day's rehearsal. I took the class with them. I was physically and emotionally spent and glad Café Violette was dark tonight, as I wasn't quite up to giving a stellar performance. Last night's performance had wiped me out. Not the singing…but the fear of being hauled off in handcuffs once I was offstage.

After class I lay down close to the stage and closed my eyes and tried to let my thoughts drift into nothing, although Noel's face did keep drifting into my mind's eye, which was marvelous, albeit not relaxing.

Not long after I'd started my break, I was interrupted by a pleasant baritone voice. "*Pardon, Mademoiselle* Christopher, but I cannot help but notice the quite extraordinary position you have placed yourself in. How are you possibly comfortable?"

I opened my eyes and stared up into the amused, cocoa-brown eyes of Noel Matheson. Next to him, wearing a similar expression, stood Monsieur Pierre Simon. I could feel my face flush as I unwrapped the blanket from my feet and swung my legs off the wall of the orchestra pit where I'd been resting them in a partially successful attempt to ignore the spikes of pain from toes to hip.

I hoisted myself into a sitting position, back up onto the stage, but kept the blanket over my legs. March in Paris sounds very romantic but, in an old theater, the temperature is not conducive to keeping a person warm.

"Gentlemen, take my word for it, it's quite comfortable. Helps keep one's feet from swelling after one has experienced the torture of a ballet class with Monsieur Luc Hebert and company. The only thing better would be a hot tub filled with Epsom salts and several large glasses of brandy within easy reach. Let me explain the results of his ballet classes in a word, albeit not an impressively high-sounding one, *Ow!*"

Noel and Pierre laughed, then lowered themselves to sit, one on either side of me, on the edge of the stage. Noel mused, "With this talk of maintaining healthy feet and legs, I must admit I never considered placing mine on a wall to be advantageous after a long day. I may try it. I wish I could do something similar for the throat."

"Ah, Monsieur Matheson, this is where the brandy comes in handy. Excellent for the legs and circulation, excellent for the throat, although perhaps not medicinally approved, excellent for the psyche, especially when one has imbibed an even more excellent French cognac from the region of Gers, as suggested by the sommelier at Café Violette. Michel truly has a knack for finding the right booze for the right person. I gotta tell ya, I wouldn't have made it through last night without more than one glass."

Noel nodded. "I agree on all counts."

A long moment of silence ensued. I grew increasingly anxious. "Uh…is there a problem? Did something bad happen because of my impromptu performance of 'Johnny Has Gone for a Soldier'? Please tell me Major Bauer isn't lurking in the wings with ropes and chains waiting to arrest me for singing something he didn't like. Tell me you're just here to see Monsieur Luc?"

I glanced around the theater but didn't see the director/choreographer. Luc Hebert and I had engaged in an interesting conversation a few days earlier, where he revealed le Théâtre de l'Opéra Blanche was one of the way stations for certain people trying to leave France undetected. Luc, his stage manager, and two of the musicians who played at Café Violette and l'Opera Blanche—Teresa's friend William being one—were also part of the small network. Luc thanked me for my part in providing information needed by contacts at the nightclub by means of singing particular songs, and warned me the majority of the dancers and musicians were clueless when it came to knowledge of extracurricular activities and to be wary of any inquisitions I felt to be a bit too nosy.

I lowered my volume as I told Noel and Pierre, "I have to admit I've been terrified. I kept expecting Bauer and his minions to roust me out of bed early this morning and march me off to a prison cell accompanied very closely by Gestapo officers. With his near-perfect English, I'm sure he caught the pointed darts thrown throughout the Irish ballad regarding the misery of soldiering."

Pierre shook his head. "Bauer has not the interest in any of the *petit poisson*…how you say, little fish. And, if you are not insulted, you are…to him…a little fish. He would also like to make the catch last night, but he is more interested in hooking larger prey. Cori, you were quite wonderful, as you have been each time you have graced the stages of Café Violette. Our patrons deluged me with requests for you to sing again, and there was no mention made of the anti-war sentiment in your song. A German officer sitting at a table near the stage asked me to inform him when you would next be singing because he was *enchanté* by your performance." Pierre smiled. "Like many of our patrons, I find I focus on the notes stirring emotions instead of lyrics, and you hit with the perfection in every song, but in your ballad you sailed to *le grande* heights."

Noel nodded, then leaned closer and whispered, "But you are needed for your help. This is why Pierre and I came to see you today, although we will be talking to Luc as well."

"I'm ready. Whatever you want."

"*Bon.*" Noel continued, "Cori, if you can go on being brave and you have the energy after you do what Monsieur Hebert requires here, Pierre does not lie when he says you are needed. But you must realize all our efforts are growing more dangerous because Major Bauer is determined to destroy the work at Café Violette." He paused. "This is very secret, but a very large fish is swimming toward France very soon, and we cannot allow a catch."

"I understand. And I'm willing to help out any way I can."

Noel gave me a 'melt my bones' look. "I…I mean, *we* at the Café would want you there no matter if circumstances were normal. I…we…love seeing you on stage and off stage. And, of course, your singing *c'est très beau* and we have been receiving many compliments."

"*Merci,*" I whispered. "I also love seeing you, um, on and off stage." My cheeks began to burn and I quickly added, "I have to tell you, I haven't said much, but back home in New Man—York, well, it's not always safe. I've seen things happen which are just scary and, to be honest, I've lost trust in the people who should be on the side of the angels…but aren't. Folks you'd never imagine would betray you are the very ones turning against you, usually for their profit rather than any ideals."

Pierre quietly stated, "Cori, you are wise to fear and also not to completely trust those around you. We worry over who might be informing to Germans. We have the certainty someone is a betrayer but we cannot, how you say, ferret them out? But if Bauer had succeeded in his plan last night? *Mon Dieu*! I prefer not to imagine the consequences."

I shuddered. "Same here. I wish I was simply too stupid to envision some truly horrific outcomes."

Pierre asked, "What did your young lady roommates and Rosemarie think about the evening? Did they suspect your singing was for something other than simple pleasure?"

"Well, Teresa never came home last night, so her reaction is anyone's guess. I'm sure Delys is aware something more than entertainment is happening at Café Violette, but I totally trust her. And she, Paulette, and Rosemarie were lovely in their compliments to me when we returned to our flat. If Paulette suspected something, she'd be more than happy to help in any way she could. Her fiancé is in the RAF and she's terribly concerned about him. There's not a lot of news coming from Britain. Or anywhere else." I paused. "Um, I haven't wanted to bring this up, with all the stuff going on at the club, but two days ago several German soldiers did a sweep of our apartment while we were gone. They took our radio and made a mess of the furniture."

Noel exclaimed, "What? This is, what is the word? Alarming? We have been thinking Rosemarie has a safe place."

"Well, she's convinced it's nothing more than sheer annoyance because she's been trying to get her clothing boutique back from the Nazis and has been dropping by what's now their headquarters to make her feelings plain. Gutsy."

Pierre nodded and told Noel, "I hear of this sweep. Rosemarie came by the club the morning after the Germans are at her house. She told me she is *épuisée*."

He turned to me. " 'Exhausted' is, I think, the English word. She is exhausted of being passive and she wants a going back to her boutique. She tells whoever was in charge they do not need the headquarters but both French *and* German ladies can badly use clothes which haven't turned to rags."

"Rosemarie is one tough, courageous lady," I stated with admiration. "As for the sweep, at least the goons left Paulette's record player intact, so we can listen to all her albums. And the only news today has been from company members here at *l'Opéra Blanche* with working radios, and most of them are too focused on the upcoming production." I took a deep breath and then added, "I hate to say this as well, but it's important— Delys is terrified she'll soon be sent to a camp. When they did the sweep they also left two words splashed in paint in the room she and I share." I winced. "*Schwarz Hundin*. And they were not referring to a black female Labrador retriever. Anyway, she and I talked about the Germans and their whole white supremacy garbage. She's in danger. I get, um, premonitions, and I feel this in every bone in my body."

Pierre and Noel exchanged a quick glance with each other.

Papa Pierre then spotted Luc in the left wing. "I will excuse myself now. I need to speak with Monsieur Hebert."

Noel lapsed into silence for a moment, then referred to my comment about my roommate. "Your worries are correct, Cori. We have heard from some of our friends about different people in this city who are soon to be put on a train to a camp. The same Gestapo pigs who used to cheer for American black performers now are calling our black sisters and brothers vile names and claiming they're not human. And they are not the only ones who could be sent away. I am frightened because…"

"What?"

"There are performers at Café Violette who are considered less-than-desirable by the Nazis. *Je suis très concerné* about Val Valentin and Michel La Fontaine, who are a…couple. And of course, we all fear for Pierre when the Germans decide they are not wanting him to run the club. They will send him to join other Jewish people at some relocation camp." He gave a wry smile. "If I am being honest and selfish, I also worry about me."

Chapter 19

I stared at Noel. "You? Why? I mean, is there something other than your activities at Café Violette?"

"Yes. My mother was a full-blooded Romany gypsy. Why the tribes became one of the groups the Nazis love to hate is a mystery, but…there it is." He shrugged. "You say you trust your roommates?"

"I do. Well, Delys and Paulette. And definitely Rosemarie. As for Teresa? Hard to say, because I don't feel as close to her and haven't talked to her as much." I smiled. "Her English is worse than my French, which makes conversing a bit difficult. Anyway, if you're considering asking any of the girls for help with stuff at Café Violette, well, you don't want them trying to lie to Nazi soldiers. Paulette tends to be very nervous and look guilty even when she's done nothing wrong. Plus, as we've already discussed, Delys is going to need to escape soon." I chuckled. "It's not funny, but I have to laugh at some of the most delicious curse words I've heard pouring out of her mouth for days following the sweep of the apartment, once she realized just how much danger she's in. Delys is quite expressive and creative and just…awesome. It's like we've been close friends all our lives."

Noel flashed a brief smile, but then his tone turned grim. "Delys is not the only one who has added to his or her vocabulary lately, although some of us began the storing up of epithets much earlier than six months ago. *Salauds de connards!* Ah. I am sorry."

"Don't be. Nothing I haven't thought many times since arriving in Paris."

We fell silent for a long moment. Finally, I nudged Noel's arm. "By the way, on a lighter topic, and if this isn't too nosy, I can't help but notice *your* English is amazing. Are French schools so much more ahead of the States in teaching other languages?"

"I learned much in America. My father is French, and as I say before, my mother Romany, but she is born in America. I was born here in France but my parents divorced when I was nine. I was sent to the States to live with my grandparents from my mother's side. They emigrated there during the Great War. I gather Romany peoples were also not in favor in Europe back then. And so, I spent five years in American schools. In New York. I would say I was surprised I didn't run into you, but it is a very large city."

Not to mention, I wasn't born until more than a hundred years later, so I wasn't exactly wandering around what used to be Times Square while you were living there.

I glimpsed the sadness in his eyes and forgot about the time travel issue. I quietly asked, "What happened after those five years?"

Noel's voice caught for a moment. "*Maman* died the year I turned fourteen. Ten years ago. I returned to France to live with my father and his new wife." He wryly stated, "In some ways the phrase 'lived with' might be a bit of a…what you call a misnomer. I was sent to a boys' school in Lyon. My stepmother was not interested in having a teenager around. I remained at St.

Jerome through my years in high school. But I am, how you say it, rambling on. To answer your question, I learned most of my English in New York." He shrugged. "I was quite highly sought after as an English tutor at my school in Lyon, although I forget much when there is no need to use it. But let me return the compliment, Mademoiselle Cori. I have overheard several of your conversations backstage with other performers at Café Violette, and your French is quite good."

"*Merci.* I have a very eclectic background with relatives from India, Ireland, England, France, and Denmark." I paused. "Of course, the India part is not for public consumption because Indians are up there with your Romany tribes in the minds of Germans. Anyway, all my formal schooling was in New…uh, York, but my family was determined I learn as much *out* of school as possible, including languages. When pressed I can come up with a few phrases in Gujarat. Courtesy of my grandfather, Yash Kapoor. There are actually a lot of Indians in Manhattan."

Pierre had returned from speaking with Luc and now beamed at me as he jumped back into the conversation. "I love Manhattan! I am visiting the city over and over for twenty years. There is such a, how you say, eclectic mix of cuisine and music, and most of it is superb. Coming from a native Frenchman I have the high praise. But my favorite place in America is New Orleans. Better are the restaurants, and I love the bands in the streets from the funerals. One envisions the dead person is dancing into heaven with the music." He assumed an air of innocence. "I have stolen more than one member of a band in the Quarter with persuasion to come to Paris, including our leader, Charles Souverain, who is

American and part Cajun. I only wish we could play more of the jazz music without fear of being shut down."

Our discussion was interrupted by the sound of heavy footsteps marching down the theater aisle toward the stage. Noel immediately turned and slid off his position on the stage.

A small, grim parade approached us. Major Bauer, fresh from last night's encounter at Café Violette, plus Officers Webber and Kessler, and a much shorter fourth man, dressed in the obligatory, stereotypical long trench coat common among the detectives of the French police.

I held my breath, but Pierre Simon hailed a friendly greeting. "Major Bauer. *Bon soir!* I hope you enjoyed the show last night? We are filled with delight because Monsieur Joseph is back with us following an illness."

Bauer's blue eyes bore holes through the owner of the café. "There were portions of the program that were enjoyable, although Fräulein Christopher's unexpected performance was not as I'd planned. But I did not come to *l'Opéra Blanche* to discuss music."

Pierre fell silent. Wise move. Let Bauer take the lead. Which he did. "We are here to question the members of this dance company."

"*Pourquoi?*" Noel asked.

"*Our* business, Herr Matheson. Not yours. But, as you will soon learn, there has been a death of a dancer who was a member of this company. We are convinced her death is linked to someone at *l'Opéra Blanche*, and at Café Violette, which is where we go next."

"Oh, my God!" I jumped up. "Teresa?"

Bauer glared at me. "How did you know this?"

"She didn't come home last night. I was worried."

Bauer growled, "Mademoiselle Teresa Dorleac was

found dead ninety minutes ago."

I flinched. "Oh, my God!" I repeated. "What happened? Was there an accident?"

Before Bauer had a chance to respond, the fourth man, middle-aged, the one dressed in black slacks, white shirt, and a black trench coat, answered for him. In barely accented English, he stated, "Accident? *Non, Mademoiselle.* We 'ave the determination of Teresa Dorleac being murdered late last night or early this morning."

Chapter 20

The man in the trench coat, who'd delivered the horrible bombshell about Teresa, introduced himself. "I am *Capitaine* Albert Paquette with the *Paris Police Nationale, Arrondissement dix-huit.* I will speak the English for all so this American girl will understand. We are here to uncover the whereabouts of members of this company for last night and early this morning."

I was fairly certain *Paquette's* mission was to find a killer. Bauer's intent was more global. Interrogating suspects possibly connected to Teresa's death gave him a great opportunity to uncover any collaborators outside of Café Violette who were continuously involved in a joint effort to help British fighter pilots flee the country...not to mention French citizens slated for journeys to various camps.

Bauer stated, "I have informed Monsieur Paquette that Fräulein Christopher, her housemates who are members of Luc Hebert's dance troupe, and their landlady were in attendance at the Café Violette last night. Included also was Teresa Dorleac." His tone changed to one of sheer malice and I was shocked at his words, praying they weren't true. "I received information from a person Teresa Dorleac trusted regarding clandestine activities resulting in the escape of an enemy of the Third Reich. These were planned for last night. Activities centering on Café Violette but additionally involving someone at *l'Opéra Blanche*."

Noel turned and faced the major. He spat out, "And did any of these so-called clandestine activities actually take place? Or are rumors abounding perhaps to deflect suspicion from the real killer of an innocent girl?"

I stopped myself from grabbing his arm and warning him not to antagonize Bauer. Noel's temper was rising and I was afraid he'd say something to make the German officer so angry Noel would find himself marched out the door under arrest for asking a question in a tone not to Bauer's liking. But my Cassandra prophetess was telling me to stay out of the fight and remain calm. It was the best way to keep the lava staying inside the volcano of Monsieur Matheson. I casually rested my hand on his arm, as if I were supporting myself after hearing the news about my roommate. I could feel a bit of Noel's tension release.

Bauer stiffened and responded to Noel's taunt. "Unfortunately, nothing of value was discovered last night, apart from learning Fräulein Christopher possesses an incredible vocal range and can pull songs no one has ever heard before seemingly out of the air."

I sighed. "Thank you. Nice of you to say."

He stared at me. "Sadly, the Fräulein does not seem to understand there could be consequences for failing to comply with the song request of a patron who also happens to be an officer with the Third Reich."

I couldn't help it. Cocky, impertinent, rash Cori had to put in her two cents and try to steer the conversation away from murder and clandestine activities. "Hey! I was homesick. And two brandies in, the song just felt right for everyone who's had to say goodbye to someone going off to war. You've got to admit it's one fabulous piece of music. I love heading for that awesome high note at the end and nailing the sucker."

He stared at me, then shifted his gaze back to Noel. My attempt at lightening the conversation was a bust.

"Teresa Dorleac had information regarding more than one person involved in secretive operations and how those activities are handled through the nightclub and here at *l'Opéra Blanche*. Which means someone from Café Violette or Luc Hebert's company killed her to keep her silent."

I'd been dead-on right last night. Bauer knew. About the songs and probably also who at Café Violette was involved in "operations" and "activities." If true, it meant one of his informants was my roommate, which was like a punch to the stomach. Had her meeting with her old German friend from Alsace-Lorraine been more than a sweet reunion? Or was Bauer bluffing, trying to get a rise out of one of us to inadvertently reveal what the next "activity" would be? I honestly couldn't buy that Teresa had had enough time to listen to conversations, translate, and then pass them on to Germans.

Noel's next words were spoken in a monotone. "Major Bauer, you say things based on rumors with no substance. What you allege regarding Mademoiselle Dorleac lacks the evidence to be tainting anyone about anything. In my opinion, it is never smart to rush to judgment. Perhaps you and Paquette should dig elsewhere for motives for who would want to hurt this lady. My friends from Café Violette and *l'Opéra Blanche* are not killers…unlike others."

For a second I really thought Bauer was going to take his nasty-looking gun out of its holster by the man's hip and shoot Noel Matheson dead where he stood.

I quickly jumped in. "Major Bauer, my other roommates, who are part of Monsieur Hebert's company, actually phoned the police this morning because Teresa did not come home last night. And the police ignored them." I swallowed. "Delys told the police Teresa had a date with a German soldier, Frederick Müller. An old friend of hers. I saw her with him at the club…you probably saw them yourself in the garden…they were there when you joined Monsieur Joseph and me…and they left together at closing time."

Noel interjected, "So, *peut-être*, Major, you would be wise to question persons in *your* troop who were last seen with Mademoiselle Dorleac?"

Bauer narrowed his eyes and grimly announced, "There is no need. I am certain Obersoldat Müller did not kill Teresa Dorleac." He narrowed his eyes to snakelike slits. "Where were *you* last night, Herr Matheson? After Café Violette closed?"

"At the club. I stayed the night as I do many nights since we have no security there and break-ins have occurred by people looking for food or drink." He gestured toward Pierre. "Monsieur Simon also stayed, as did Monsieur Valentin. Our wardrobe mistress, Madame Fiona Belle, was there *aussi.* And Chef Henri."

Bauer asked, "Why? For security, as well?"

Pierre nodded. "In part, *oui.* Also, I am having the check of inventory in the kitchen and wine cellar. This I do once a week. It is peaceful after crowds. And Monsieur Valentin has been searching for costumes for a new act he is preparing."

Bauer snorted, then turned back to me. "And you, Fräulein? Where were you?"

I doubted he suspected me of Teresa's murder. He

was being nosy and officious and showing his power. I answered truthfully, "You were there. I sang and then I went home with my other flat mates and landlady. Last I saw Teresa, she was talking with Müller and telling us to go on without her. Her English isn't great, so I didn't catch what her plans were."

Bauer wasn't happy about our responses, but he seemed willing to let things stand. "Enough. We will now go backstage and talk to Herr Hebert and company members and anyone who might have caused harm to Fräulein Dorleac...or been in league with anyone involved in aiding in illegal activities." He whirled around and took what I was inwardly calling his toadying punks, which now included the prefect, Paquette, with him.

Pierre Simon quickly leaned down and kissed my cheek, then whispered, "I must be going back to the café. I need to be in the present when Bauer and his associates come to interview *my* staff as well. I am 'aving the concerns. There will be reprisals." He added, "Cori, I am so sorry for your roommate's death, even if it is determined true she is talking to the Boche. I hope one of our own did not discover such thing and have taken such a rash step, believing he was guarding us. Mademoiselle Dorleac may simply be sharing words she has heard or she may be confused over who to give her loyalties since the Germans have allowed her many latitudes and she is young and wants what she had before this occupation." He shook his head. "Too many young lives lost. Too many. Confusion should not be a reason for death."

We hugged each other. He added, "We are seeing you tomorrow night to sing, *non?*"

I nodded, then casually tossed out, "Any song in particular?"

Pierre smiled. "Non. Your standards of 'Nobody' and 'Hard-Hearted Hannah' will be enough. We shall let other songs be at rest for a night or two while this investigation is happening. There is no urgency... *maintenant*."

I watched him stroll down the now-empty aisle toward the front of the theater as though he wasn't carrying a ten-ton load of worry about last night's activities coming out. Was Bauer telling the truth about Teresa? Was she some kind of agent? Had she been faking her grasp of English? Could Pierre's fears be true? Could a member of the *Résistance* network at the club have killed her? Or was her death the result of a romance gone wrong? I'd seen the look on William Gale's face when she went off with her German friend. Had he tracked her down after the café closed for the night and just gone with the classic "If I can't have her, no one can" motive for murder?

Chapter 21

Pierre Simon headed out of the theater via the front entrance. Noel Matheson remained. We sat side by side on the stage in silence, as the harsh voices of Bauer and his men questioning Luc's dancers faded into background noise. We couldn't stop them and didn't need to discuss agreeing to ignore them.

I snuck a glance at Noel as he focused on the ceiling of the theater. He wasn't classically handsome. His face was on the thin side, with a tiny cleft in his chin and a nose hinting of someone's fist smashing into it and breaking it once upon a time…intentionally or accidentally. His hair was thick and so dark one couldn't state if it were black or brown. He kept it longer than the current fashion here in Paris. His eyes were an unusual chocolate brown with hints of green and an intensity piercing right through my soul. His smile, glimpsed rarely in these serious times, could warm the heart on the coldest day. His voice was like hot buttered rum poured over whipped cream—a treat I'd experienced at Café Violette about a week ago when a German officer had requested the drink and there'd been leftovers snuck back to any performer interested. A voice both rich and decadent with an ability to shift from aspects of humor to gut-wrenching emotion, depending on the song. A voice that had drawn me more than a hundred years into the past.

Noel and I hadn't been completely alone for longer than five minutes since the moment I'd met him the night we helped the young pilot, Sam Seymour, escape the Germans storming Café Violette. Those very few times no one else had been within hearing distance, he'd kept the conversation light, mainly focusing on the topic of music.

I honestly wasn't sure what he thought of me. Did he view me as some flighty, silly American out for the adventure of living in a dangerous place? Would I ever be able to tell him the truth about "when" I was from? Would he believe me? Would he be willing to make a leap of faith if the time came to trust? I'd helped him with Sam, but for all he knew I might have been trying to get into his good graces simply to install myself at the club. After the first night, yeah, I'd sung what was asked, sending out songs as coded messages, but singing wasn't the most treacherous gig out there. To be honest, until "Johnny Has Gone for a Soldier" there'd been almost no danger to me at all.

I'd traveled more than a hundred years into the past because I was sure I was needed. But, more than that, because I'd heard his voice and fallen in love with a man I'd never met. Was there any hope of any kind of real future for the two of us together? Would he even want a future with me?

We sat side by side, watching dancers who appeared dazed as well as upset because the prima ballerina they'd worked with the day before was dead. We weren't alone, but for once no one was near enough to hear our conversation.

I finally asked a question I wasn't certain he could answer, thanks to the whole "what does he really think of me?" issue. "Noel, how has Café Violette managed to remain open since the Nazis took over Paris? I mean, the wine and brandy is abundant, somehow the food is fresh and there are amazing treats now and then, the performers are incredible, but we're talking about Nazis who are very suspicious, very curious, and very certain a heckuva lot more is going on than just great entertainment. It's rather bizarre how much everyone has been able to get away with."

He kept silent for a long moment, then started to speak.

I raised my hand, motioning him to stop. "Wait. Before you say anything, I'm not asking for vital information. You only met me a few weeks ago. Singing songs in an effort to signal who should stay and who should go isn't enough for real trust, and I understand. You don't have to tell me anything that isn't already common knowledge or simple speculation. Really. Sometimes I just let my curiosity take over."

Noel shook his head. "It is fine. And, Cori, you have done so much more than simply sing, no matter how perfect your singing is. I do trust you. Partly on instinct. And my feelings... The truth of it? If you were working for the Germans, you would not have risked your life to help Sam Seymour the first night you arrived at Café Violette. Or to save another flight officer by singing a strange Irish song in defiance of Herr Bauer. I was terrified for you. I am amazed he did not...how you say...yank...you off the stage and march you away."

I smiled at him. "I hate to admit it, but it was kind of fun. Both helping Sam escape and coming up with an unusual choice of music to keep someone else I'd never met...never *will* meet...from being scooped up by the

Nazis. Scary, yes, but being able to help while also shoving failure into Bauer's face was *so* worth it."

Noel chuckled. "Has anyone ever told you, you are quite rash? Audacious? Impulsive? Are the right words?"

"Yep. And the answer is 'now and again.' My great-uncle used to toss in 'sassy' as well. I'm not sure, though, how many of those traits are considered desirable."

"Well, they are all delightful in many ways, but from the first night your impulses could have proved disastrous. You could have fallen from the catwalk or been shot by one of the Germans. I...care...about you. I do not want to see you hurt. It is...it is the why I have tried to stay away from you at the club when the Germans are near...which is too often. I am afraid for you if Bauer is seeing we have feelings more than friends."

I wanted to ask Noel if he himself saw us as more than friends, but this wasn't the time. "Would it make a difference in what he does?"

"It would. Cori, the Nazis find means to use relationships between people as weapons against those people. Again, I *do* trust you. I have from the moment I saw you beckon to Seymour and me when we were hiding behind the piano."

I stared into those dark eyes. "I feel the same about you."

"I am very pleased to be hearing this."

We smiled at each other, and then Noel added, "Your question about the club and Bauer...all the Germans in charge yet they do nothing to close us? We have our theories and suspicions. Café Violette *was* shut down during the first month of the Occupation, but one of the German commanders, General Gunter

Hauptmann, who is very high ranked and had been in Paris many times before other troops marched in, has a large fondness for the more popular forms of music. He is the one who lets *l'Opéra Blanche* to perform dance. Once cabarets and theaters reopened in the city, he let us reopen also. Pierre Simon is a Jew and the Nazis have systematically clamped down on anything Jewish, yet Café Violette continues."

My eyes widened. "Interesting. What's *really* behind the general's reasoning in allowing the club to remain open? Any ideas?"

"A few. Pierre surmises several reasons. It is true Hauptmann loves music and has allowed us to continue to offer entertainment." He dropped his volume. "He also has a…weakness…for our *sommelier*…Michel. Michel in turn is very frightened, because he would prefer not to be involved with anyone other than Valentin. Hauptmann has been friends with Hitler's close ally Hermann Goering from when they were children, and so the general holds more power than most officers of his rank."

"Makes sense, I guess. I mean, as to how the club has still in business." I paused, then added, "Speaking of fondness, I'd say Bauer is not exactly planning to become your best buddy any time soon."

Noel shrugged, then laughed. "There is no love lost there, *chérie*! But we try to keep out of each other's way. We are both aware of the, how you say, uh, sexual peccadillos? of his commanding officer, and we both have reasons for keeping them quiet. I do not have a certainty how long this particular truce will last. Bauer wants very badly to flush out any clandestine operations to the Germans. He is to be promoted much faster if he can bring in an important cell operating in or near Paris than he would by simply protecting his commander. It all depends upon just how close General Gunter Hauptmann is to Goering these days so he is assured of keeping power. Hauptmann is willing to let a few pilots slip through so he can indulge his…pleasures …and…" He paused. "There is one more thing."

"Which is?"

"As Pierre said, he is waiting for the big fish to catch. And the word is that a big fish is coming soon." He shook his head. "Could Mademoiselle Dorleac in truth have discovered something of interest to the Germans and she told them?"

I gazed down at the stage floor for a long moment, then took a deep breath. "It's truly frightening. What a web of nasty emotions and ambitions. Teresa kept a lot to herself, and I sensed she might have been lonelier than she ever let on. She seemed to enjoy keeping more than one man on a string, but I often thought she was masking some kind of insecurity. Did her murder have anything to do with information about rebellious activities or was it more about the company she kept? Jealousy is a powerful motive, and I saw how William looked at her when she left with her soldier friend."

"This could be important to us. If her killing *was* the result of a jealous lover, then Bauer and Paquette might be relaxing their surveillance of Café Violette, at least for the time we need for the next round of certain songs. And for the important person I spoke of who is to be coming—later. But tell me the why you feel the murder of Teresa might have nothing to do with our actions?"

"Her English wasn't the best, which could be one reason she and I didn't exactly exchange confidences.

But she didn't go out of her way to become part of any company camaraderie. She was nice but kind of distant, and I'm not sure anyone *really* knew her. She was very smart and very beautiful and she received gifts from more than one man, but her primary focus was on dance. I refuse to buy she was some kind of double agent. She was so involved with her dancing it did not matter to her who was in charge in France as long as she could be on stage. She never came across as very political."

"This is horrible to ask because it is intrusive, but was she having a serious liaison with anyone other than William?"

I shook my head. "If so, she was very discreet. Casual dating was what I saw, including William. And, Noel, I have to say, while logically jealousy could be motive for murder, my instincts don't scream 'killer' when I hear his name. What do you know about him?"

"He is like me. Dual citizenship. He is originally from Austria but spent some years in America." Noel shook his head. "It is all very confusing. Bauer and Paquette didn't tell us how she was killed. Or where. Or when."

"Taking the opposite side, if Bauer *is* telling the truth, which is a big if, maybe she really *did* discover why I was meeting with Donald in the garden. I saw her by the door with the German soldier, Müller, just before Bauer arrived. And I'm sure Bauer knew exactly which song I was supposed to sing as a signal, which was why he was determined I sing the wrong one. But how Teresa could have learned about those songs is a mystery, and who would kill her for informing is another whole big question."

Noel thought for a moment. "I doubt she would

understand all the talk of songs to sing, yet she might have heard from someone on our side about something was being planned for the night." He frowned. "William is aware of the importance of certain music. And he was told about our big fish, although only Pierre and myself have his identity."

I winced. "Is it at *all* possible William could be the one spilling the beans about activities at the club? And *l'Opéra Blanche* as well?"

"In collusion with Bauer? Perhaps, like General Hauptmann, our traitor at Café Violette will let a pilot or two slip by, waiting for the day when he can provide someone far more important to the Gestapo…and destroy us all in the process."

"It's all just so much speculation."

Noel smiled wryly. "Herr Bauer has achieved one thing with his talk about Mademoiselle Dorleac's possible betrayal…there will be an atmosphere of distrust at Café Violette from this day on. Sadly, this is something we must have for our safety."

Chapter 22

Noel and I listened from our perch on the edge of the stage for another five minutes or so while Bauer and Paquette harassed the dancers and stagehands of Luc Hebert's company.

Finally, Noel said, "Enough of this sour talk of betrayal. Bauer has brought with him a foul stench, do you agree? I must to go back to Café Violette and be present when he comes to interrogate wait staff and musicians and anyone who is to aid his true mission…to destroy us. He has no care about Mademoiselle Dorleac, no matter which side she was with." He hesitated for a moment, then asked, "Will you come back with me? Please? I would like you with me."

To Hades and back, I thought, but I simply nodded. We'd started to walk toward the front of the theater when we heard Bauer shout the name "Delys" in anger, followed in German by *"Nein! Nicht danach Dorleac! Nein. Nicht der schwartz! Untermensch! Sie darf nicht tanzen!"*

Noel froze.

"What is he saying? Or rather, what is he screaming?" I asked. "My German is not quite up to my French, especially when it's spoken so fast."

"He has called Delys a derogatory name and is saying she cannot be allowed to dance…not following the perfection of Teresa Dorleac. But it is nothing to do

187

with Teresa. Bauer wants only a white girl playing swans. No black person in the ballet."

"What?" I whirled around. "Bloody, stinkin', racist pig—I'll scratch his damned eyes out!"

Noel and I stood in silence for a moment.

Then he winked at me. "Cori, are you up for a fight?"

"Always."

"*Bon!* You and I might end up in the jail tonight, but we will go down in defiance for Mademoiselle Delys's right to dance the role of her lifetime. Come. Let us interfere and cause much trouble."

He grabbed my hand and we raced up the stairs leading to the stage and joined the tense grouping of Bauer, Paquette, Luc Hebert, Delys, and Bauer's attached-to-the-hip underlings Webber and Kessler. A true match for the Delegates Becker and Lang of 2061.

Bauer spotted us immediately. "Go away. Go back to the nightclub. I will be there soon, as I have people to question. This is another matter and it does not concern you."

My mind screamed *"Like hell it doesn't!"* but I managed to keep my voice level as I addressed Bauer. "You're wrong. It concerns me very much. To begin with, Delys is my friend. But more important to the discussion at hand, she is a fabulous dancer and the *only* one able to do justice to the role of Odette/Odile."

Webber dared to speak for Bauer. His voice dripping with disdain, he declared, "She is *schwartz*. An inferior. She is garbage."

Delys bit her lower lip, clearly trying not to cry.

Luc glared at Webber. "Mademoiselle Robinson is beautiful and she is also the most talented dancer in my company. She *will* do the role."

Bauer inhaled. I waited for fire to come flowing from the dragon's mouth. He remained mildly civil but determined. "She will not dance. We will shut down the entire performance rather than allow this."

Luc suddenly began yelling at Bauer. His French was so rapid I couldn't understand a word, but Noel hid a smile before murmuring to me, "He is uttering many brilliant curses a lady should never hear."

Noel raised his hand to stop the flood of vitriol before Bauer lost patience and shot the man. "Luc...*attendez.* One moment. Major Bauer, perhaps you are unaware of a certain patronage to *le Luc Hebert Théâtre de Danse*?"

"What are you talking of?" Bauer spat.

"General Gunter Hauptmann himself gave permission months ago for this company to perform these pieces and specifically requested a prima ballerina take on the dual role of the white and black swan. I have heard it is his favorite work. He has spoken many times of this when he has enjoyed entertainment at Café Violette. I am very positive he would be bitterly disappointed if he were not able to see Mademoiselle Robinson's performance."

Bauer snarled at him. "That was before Fräulein Dorleac ended up dead in a ditch this morning. We can't allow this...trash...to be onstage."

My stomach turned to acid, both at the cruel, cavalier, inhumane way he referenced Teresa's death and his 'toe the Nazi racist party line' when it came to Delys, who now appeared to be experiencing the tragedy of a dying swan rather than the excitement of getting to display those thirty-two *fouettes*.

I recalled Ajay telling me how proud he'd been when he was cast as the first actor of Indian descent to play the role of Marius in *Les Misérables* on Broadway. I'd seen the look in Delys's eyes when she realized she had the chance to perform Odette/Odile. That look had been replaced moments ago with a combination of sadness, defeat, humiliation, anger, and fear. Removing Ajay from the stage in the year 2036 had been unfair and wrong. But at least he'd been able to perform for more than a year before the theater was shut down. This was worse, because it was Delys herself, not a theater, being rejected for the stupidity of possessing a heritage which happened to include darker skin than the Germans cared for.

Oddly, the next face in my mind's eye was Fiona Belle's as I'd first seen her on the hologram, dressed in her outlandish harem costume and the garish makeup she'd smeared on her lips and eyes and cheeks. It was as if she was giving me a hint as to a way to let Delys dance.

Luc and Bauer continued to shout at each other, with neither listening to a word the other said.

I raised my hand and made myself loud enough to be heard over the chaos. "Excuse me, but I might have a solution if anyone cares to hear it."

Silence. All heads turned to me. The expressions on the faces varied from rage in Bauer and Webber, to indifference in Paquette and Kessler, to hope in Delys and Luc, to what seemed to be admiration in Noel.

"Go on," Noel urged me. "What do you propose?"

"It's very simple. Delys goes on as planned, but with a slight change in costume…she wears a full mask and gloves. Her identity stays secret. Her skin *(the color of which so absurdly disturbs you pigs)* is invisible.

190

Hauptmann will be happy because he is quite the fan of ballet, and if everyone standing here now just keeps quiet, *no one* will be in trouble. It's kind of a boost dramatically for the dance, because the performance has to be all through the *body* instead of the face. Which Delys does to perfection."

Bauer glared at me, then glanced at Webber and Kessler to gauge their reactions.

I took the opportunity to catch Delys's eye and silently mouth, "I'm sorry. You deserve better."

She whispered, "Non. *Merci*. It is brilliant."

Luc was grinning. He began to applaud. "*Très bien. Très bon* is this *idée*. You have found a unique way to portray Odette/Odile so the audience focuses on the dancing and not the features of the ballerina." He turned to Delys. "*Qu'est-ce que tu penses?*"

"I love it!" she said.

Everyone turned to Bauer, who was caught between his loyalty to the racist policies of Hitler and the desire to keep sucking up to his superior officer, General Hauptmann. "I will allow this on one condition."

Luc raised an eyebrow, "*Oui?*"

"Delys Robinson does not tell a soul she is the one doing the role. Ever."

Noel stated, dryly, "We assume you are not excluding company members."

Bauer narrowed his eyes. "Yes, yes. Anyone connected to this show, of course they will know. But no one else. And if Hauptmann wishes to *meet* the dancer who creates this role, Herr Hebert will find another ballerina who will take the final bows unmasked as if she were the performer. Does everyone understand?"

I was devastated that Delys would be robbed of the

recognition she deserved, but I figured we could eventually manage, quietly, to get the word out regarding the truth behind the mask, if not in the near future, then when these creeps left France, which would be late summer of 1944. Who in this group would still be alive? I shivered.

Bauer motioned to Paquette, Webber, and Kessler. "Come. We need to interrogate the entertainers at Café Violette. There is a murder to solve. We have wasted enough time on fluff and stupidity."

Luc, Delys, Noel and I remained silent and watched the quartet leave. It was safer to stop the conversation before Bauer changed his mind.

Delys and I hugged each other. "We need to talk to the wardrobe mistress at Café Violette to see what kind of mask she can create. Just not tonight. None of us want to meet up with Bauer while he's there."

Noel sighed. "Unfortunately, I have no choice. I must go to the club. I must attempt to stop Bauer and Paquette from arresting one of our people simply to be making an arrest."

"Do you still want company?" I asked.

"Very much. But you might have reached your limit of how much you can push Bauer…at least for today. Go home with Delys and rest. I shall speak to Fiona Belle and tell her what's been happening here." He flashed a quick smile. "She will enjoy the intrigue although hate the reason."

I had a strong feeling Fiona Belle already knew. And approved. My Cassandra senses were hinting there would be more to our Odile/Odette masking than I could ever imagine.

Chapter 23

Late March 1941, Paris

Following Bauer's grudging approval for Delys to perform as long as she was masked, my job description changed. Instead of attending to errands as the assistant stage manager at *l'Opéra Blanche*, I would act as dresser for one particular ballerina. My task was to help Delys into costume and masks for the grand opening of *Selections from Swan Lake and Other Pieces*, first as Odette, the "good" swan in white, then as Odile, the "evil" swan in black, and finally to help Delys switch costumes with Paulette before final bows to ensure no one could identify her.

I was pleased to be with my friend to provide moral support just before she took the stage. Watching from the wings as Delys took on the dual roles, I was also thrilled to witness her take possession of both "swans." Luc and I had been right—with a mask in place, the focus was on Delys's entire body. Her technique and lines were softer as Odette, sharper and rougher as Odile. The dances lit the theater with Delys's natural warmth and presence.

Luc had also been brilliant in his casting of French *danseur* Georges Valmont as the prince who guides Odile in the *pas de deux* sequence. Georges captured the audience's attention before Odile's appearance, giving Delys enough time for the costume change from white to black, but Luc had also choreographed a brief solo for him, to follow those fabulous *fouettes* which allowed Paulette to don Delys's costume and then head back onstage to remove the mask during the final bows.

The standing ovation lasted almost as long as the dance. And, as we'd foreseen, word was sent by General Hauptmann requesting a meeting with the prima ballerina who had brought him to tears with her portrayal of Odile/Odette.

The decision to use Paulette as the substitute dancer and "unmask" her before the final bows had been made by Luc the same night we'd fought with Bauer to allow Delys to perform. Paulette and Delys were the same height and weight and, although not technically or emotionally as powerful as Delys, Paulette knew the choreography perfectly, so could discuss nuances if Hauptmann so desired.

I hugged each girl in turn as I explained I couldn't stay for the patrons' "meet and greet" Luc was holding at the theater in honor of opening night. "I'm so sorry, but I'm already late. Papa Pierre sent word earlier they wanted me at Café Violette tonight to do a couple of songs. But, Delys, you were so incredible! I only wish…well, one day. So many things need to change."

"Go on, Cori," Paulette said. "And don't worry about anything here. I will make certain everyone believes I am the dancer they saw onstage. I hate this deception but agree it is safer for Delys."

Delys grinned at her. "I am floating in the air after I am doing the dances. Cori, do not have a heartbreak for me. It is enough to be on stage as the two swans and with people I care about and admire having pleasure with what is being done." Her grin faded. "I hope I am able to keep going a charade of one of the hired wait staff for the party."

"You showed everyone you can take on two incredible roles behind a mask, so I'd wager you can manage to fool people as you pour champagne," I told her.

I waved goodbye and headed out the backstage exit, then ran to the club, grateful it was only a few blocks away. Pierre had specifically requested I sing tonight. Something was afoot.

I crashed into a German in uniform who was standing guard outside the backstage door, appearing bored and angry.

"Ouch!"

"Fräulein, why do you run?"

"Late! I'm onstage in fifteen minutes. Have to change into my costume." I bit my tongue before asking, *And why in hell are you in my way, you big dumb jerk*? The Nazis had presented a decent force of men in front of the club for the last week, following Teresa's death, but this was the first time I'd seen anyone hanging out in what was essentially the alley. Germans in so many different areas signaled trouble for anyone inside Café Violette.

The guard politely opened the door for me.

For the second time in less than three minutes I plowed into another man…this time it was Val Valentin. Val had become a close friend during the last couple of weeks. He was fascinated with American show business and we'd spent many hours sipping *café*, eating croissants, and discussing the best way to impersonate American film stars while avoiding caricature. He'd also been kind enough to give me clothes he wasn't using for his acts as well as lend me costumes for my own performances. We were the same height and nearly the same weight and the man had great taste. He reminded me of Ajay with his humor and immediate willingness to lend a generous hand to anyone who needed it.

"Ah! I am so sorry, Mademoiselle Cori! I am not looking where I am walking." Valentin's voice was shaky and hoarse.

"No problem. Probably more my fault anyway, and no toes injured," I told him. I stared at him. He looked as if he'd been crying. "Val? Is everything okay? You seem very distracted."

He inhaled, then whispered, ""*Je suis*...I am... afraid."

"Of?"

"Is the young German out of the door?"

"Out of the...oh...*outside*. Yes. Something new and ugly added to the alley's décor." I paused, then shot a sharp glance at Val. "Is he here to cause trouble for you and Michel?"

Val swallowed. "How do you...?"

I placed my hand over his arm and smiled. "You two remind me very much of some folks I dearly loved back in New York, one of whom was my great-uncle. It's hard to disguise the care and love you obviously share."

"Ah. You are kind. But this is why I am afraid."

"But, Val...look...Noel told me about Hauptmann, and he's sure it's one reason the Nazis have left the club pretty much alone. Hauptmann's actually over at *l'Opéra Blanche* this evening."

Val's eyes filled with tears. "You do not hear?"

"What?"

"It was terrible! Monsieur Gaspard Bassett, our

emcee, he was dragged out of backstage during a rehearsal early this past day. I heard the word 'Drancy' from the soldiers who took him. He told me yesterday Hauptmann had—how do you say? propositioned him? He was polite but he say, *'Non*!' I am afraid Michel and I are next." He tried to smile. "Michel will do more than say 'Non.' He will possibly slap the officer in the face and will cause much trouble. *J'adore* Michel, but his temper can be not in control. The both of us may next be on a train to a camp."

"*Merde!*" I stared at him in horror. "We can't let that happen. Where is Noel right now?"

He shook his head. "He was last in the kitchen."

"Listen. Go to my dressing room. I'll find Noel, and we'll come up with something. Where's Michel?"

"He is at our apartment, hiding." Val began to shake. "We have no telephone, and I worry if the Germans notice he is not the one pouring wine this night… *Mon Dieu*! I must get to him. I have been inside here being afraid, but this must change."

"Let Noel and Pierre handle this. And you're right. If *you* try to walk out the door you'll be snatched up by one or more big goons before you ever get close to your apartment. Does Noel have your address?"

"*Oui*." He grabbed my hand and squeezed. "You will help us? For the real?"

"Of course. Quick…head to my dressing room. I'll be there as soon as I track down Noel."

Finding Noel took all of two steps. He was coming to find me.

I gasped. Noel had bruising on his chin and one eye was swollen, well on its way to becoming a nice shade of black or purple.

"Noel!"

"I know."

"What do you know?" I asked. "And what the hell happened to you?"

"What I know is about Val and Michel. They are to be sent to one of the camps. We must get them out of the city. It's why Pierre is sending word for you to be performing tonight."

"How did you find out?"

"After Gaspard was escorted out of the club this afternoon, I am assuming Val and Michel are to be next." Noel's tone was grim. "Damn and damn! Nothing I could do to save Gaspard. Five Germans holding very large guns, against me holding sheet music. Not of much help as a weapon. I tried to intervene, received the butt of a gun in my stomach—followed by a boot heel, a punch to the jaw and my eye, and a fierce warning I would be dragged out, *aussi*, if I tried to stop the action. I am sure Gaspard is currently on his way to Drancy."

"Oh, no! I'm so sorry about Gaspard. And about your injuries."

Noel was lucky they hadn't just gone ahead and shot him.

"Noel, I told Val to head for my dressing room. Last anyone heard, Michel is at their apartment. We need a quick meeting to strategize how to save them both."

Noel nodded. "I agree. Let us get this done."

Chapter 24

Five minutes later Noel, Val, Pierre, and I were standing in front of the mirror in my tiny dressing room.

"Does anyone have the idea for how we can be accomplishing the escape for Val?" Pierre asked. "Out of the club he can go to a place of safety, but it is the getting him free of *here* I cannot plan."

"We can't sneak him out the back, thanks to the giant, nasty, scary Nazi guarding the door," I said. "I could try and distract him, but he seems a bit too responsible in his job. I wasn't sure he was going to let me *in* earlier."

"We cannot be allowing you to do such a dangerous thing, Cori. Distraction could land you in a very bad place," Pierre exclaimed. "Bauer is still not pleased over your song choice the night Teresa was murdered."

Noel quickly agreed. "Pierre is right. Cori needs to stay out of this. But Val also cannot simply walk out the front door. Bauer or one of his thugs will escort him to the nearest train station."

"Could I go in costume…disguise as *une femme* from audience?" Val questioned.

Noel grimaced. "They will know it is you. They have seen you dressed as a woman on stage for weeks."

"What about as a *man*?" I suggested. "Put him in a suit with a fedora?"

Papa Pierre discarded the plan. "I have thought the

same, but the Boche has memorized all in attendance in the audience. They have the posting of a guard outside the lavatory."

Val bent his head and stared at the floor. "Perhaps I should give myself up. If only I could have certainty Michel is gotten away. I could try to convince the Germans the *raison d'être* for my dress in the clothes of women and sing like the female movie stars because it is the earning of my living?"

Pierre shook his head. "They do not care. They have made up their minds and are acting on their worst impulses. *Aussi*, I heard someone shouting about you and Michel and 'pink triangle' this afternoon as Gaspard was being dragged away. They are aware of your closeness to each other."

He took Val's hand in his. "Valentin, *Je m'excuse*! I should have said *immediatement*— You will be glad to hear Michel has gone from the city. Fiona Belle offered to go to your apartment as soon as we saw what is happening with Gaspard. I am waiting word from my cousin in Saint-Denis when Michel reaches his house. This is where you go and from there to England. My cousin has many friends. You must keep courage, *mon ami.*"

Val was visibly relieved to hear Michel had gotten away, but terrified he wouldn't be as lucky.

Noel suddenly snapped his fingers. "Tunnels," he said.

"What?"

"Tunnels. *Oui*…I have it. *Phantom of the Opera*."

"Fabulous show! My dad owned the DVD."

Silence and open-eyed surprise. Ouch. Too late to take it back. How did I explain a video disk and the player one used to access it?

"Pardon, but what is a DVD?"

I thought fast. "There was an original musical based on *Phantom of the Opera* composed...um...a few years ago and performed in Manhattan. Beautiful music. A DVD is the...program...they were selling at the theater with all the story and photos and my dad bought a copy. It's uh...like a souvenir of the show but I can't recall what the initials actually stand for. Something like uh, direct visual document. I think." I smiled.

Three men stared at me like I'd grown Viking horns and was about to bellow out half the Wagner Ring cycle as a baritone.

Papa Pierre finally shrugged his shoulders in the classic "saying everything without saying a word" French gesture, then smiled at me.

"*Interessant*. I should like to hear more later. For now, Cori, Noel has the idea perfect. You see, Café Violette was once a small opera house built on top of tunnels like those described in the Lon Chaney cinema. There are being no lakes below, but the tunnels are deep and long and—how you say, intertwine?"

"Intersect," Noel prompted.

"*Oui*. Intersect. They intersect with a tunnel under a church built centuries back. Middle Ages." He paused. "I take too long to describe. But the Nazis are as yet unaware of these tunnels and we have not used them for anyone else coming through the café."

Val visibly brightened. "*C'est formidable. C'est parfait.*"

Pierre held up his hand. "There is a problem."

Silence.

Pierre stated, "There are only two entrances to the

tunnels. One is backstage and it has been boarded for many years and many hours are needed to undo the rubble of, um, impediments. The other is clear of the obstacles, but it leads from the kitchen."

Noel winced. "Which is only accessible from the house of the club or from outside. Val would be seen."

I thought back to *Phantom of the Opera* and the "make-you-jump" scene, the one when the giant chandelier swings down over the audience, astonishing watchers and performers alike. "Diversion," I muttered.

The three gentlemen turned as one to look at me. Noel quickly asked, "Anything in mind?"

"Nothing definite. I was just thinking if something happened…outside the café is best…the Nazis would leave the club and Val could haul it—um, could run to the kitchen and zip down into the tunnels with no one the wiser."

Pierre nodded. "I will take care of it."

"How?" Noel asked.

"Our friends who have been waiting for something to strike back will help. Most are impatient and they are angry. They have been looking for an excuse to…what Americans say…'raise a ruckus.' " He raised his hand. "This is all I can be saying. I want all in this room to be safe."

"So what do *we* need to do? I mean, Noel, Val and me?"

Pierre was quick with the next idea. "Cori, a second diversion is to be necessary. You and Noel will take the stage and perform a very long duet. You will be clearly visible to everyone in the audience. I shall be having the stand in the wings. Val, you will make your way to the kitchen at the right time. I go tell Chef Henri our plan and he will direct you and open the trap." He shook his head. "We need a telephone line back of the stage for these times. But I will tell Charles first about the duet. I go next to the front and make a call to set these events in motion. We can bring all this to… uh…boil the pot…in the next twenty minutes. Val, you stay in the dressing room until you hear Cori and Noel sing and…whatever chaos happens after."

All signs of the sweet Papa Pierre were gone. He was the very image of the older *Résistance* leader, the soldier leading his troops, or the quiet man standing up for what's right…the heroes in *Guns of Navarone* or *The Great Escape*, or the character of Rick Blaine in *Casablanca*. Yes, in case it hasn't been obvious, Ajay had had very eclectic tastes in his movie viewing and passed them right on to me.

Pierre left first. I gave Val one more quick hug and kiss on the cheek for luck, and then Noel grabbed my hand and led me out of the dressing room toward the wings of stage right. He signaled to Charles Souverain, who took over Gaspard's task as emcee by announcing to the audience that they were in for a treat…a new duet of song and dance performed by Noel Matheson and Cori Christopher.

Chapter 25

Noel held out his hand to me. I took it, curtseyed, stood up straight again, and couldn't stop the smile radiating happiness as he swept me into a closed partnering dance position and we whirled around the stage, improvising each move, yet making it appear we'd rehearsed for months.

I whispered, "You do one mean, clean foxtrot, Monsieur Matheson. I'm impressed. I'm also glad my uncle taught me how to follow when I was a child."

He whispered back, "I have the hidden talents, Mademoiselle Christopher. Hopefully more are to be revealed one day under better circumstances. And we have the luck of being… What is the word? In the sync with each other? As opposed to leading or following."

The warmth enveloping my body had nothing to do with the activity of our dance and everything to do with Noel's words. We'd been singing a medley of tunes from old Broadway shows and were now midway through a kicky foxtrot to the instrumental piece "Afghanistan." We were dancing in front of a full house made up of German soldiers and their mostly French companions, but for a moment I imagined we were alone, sharing secrets and touching bodies in far more intimate ways than the feel of a dance partner's hand on one's waist or back.

The Charles Souverain band's volume grew as our

dance became a bit more energetic. Noel lifted me in the air and twirled me once, then twice as the music swelled to a crescendo using trumpets and percussion cymbals. Which was when we caught the flashing light of the explosion outside and heard the blast. The music stopped as horrified patrons began to scream and… better…every man in uniform hurried outside. Tables and chairs toppled in the haste to be first on the scene.

Noel and I jumped down from the stage to stand alongside Charles and the drummer, Nicolas Reno. We all rose on our tiptoes to see the action at the front of the club—and provide cover for Val Valentin. Behind where we stood I could feel a very gentle breeze as Val half crawled and half ran—surprisingly well hidden by our bodies—toward the kitchen. Once Val made it inside, it was up to Chef Henri to open the trap door leading to the tunnels and assist in guiding our friend on his way to freedom.

In my peripheral vision, I could see exactly when Val slipped into the kitchen. I squeezed Noel's hand and nodded. He nodded back. We ran to the entrance of the club to join all the other spectators. It seemed like the natural thing to do when one hears a blast.

"What happened?" Noel shouted. "Is everyone safe?"

An anonymous voice yelled back in French, "Major Bauer's car exploded!"

Other voices chimed in, "A bomb! It must be a bomb!"

Noel again asked if anyone was hurt. The response came from one furious Major Bauer himself, who came striding through the packed crowd watching at the doorway, pushing folks aside as he headed directly for

Noel and me.

"No one is injured." He paused. "Which will *not* be the result when I catch who did this."

Bauer snapped his fingers and all his German minions not currently outdoors tossing buckets of water over a black limo with a big swastika emblazoned on the front hood hurried to his side.

Bauer glared in fury at Noel and me but addressed his buddies. "We have just witnessed a diversion. One designed to provide cover for Monsieur Valentin to attempt to leave Café Violette. An attempt which has failed."

My stomach lurched. Had they found him? They'd been outside in the front, and even if the guard in back had stood his post, Val was underground. No. There was no way he'd been caught. Bauer was clueless about any tunnels. He had to be bluffing.

Noel, risking further bruises, boldly inquired, "But Major Bauer, why should Valentin need to leave the club? Is there a problem?"

Eyes narrowed. "Do not pretend ignorance, Herr Matheson. It does not become you. As you are well aware, your degenerate performer was to be escorted to headquarters this very night to answer certain questions."

"Regarding?"

Bauer glared at him. "Regarding things which are no concern of yours, Herr Matheson, unless you care to join him?"

Noel and I were still holding hands. I didn't consciously exert pressure on his fingers, but I suddenly felt a squeeze back. He didn't really need the reminder to stay civil, not after receiving the toe end of a boot when he'd tried to help Gaspard earlier, and he heeded the gentle warning.

Apart from giving Val more time to escape and keeping himself out of jail, Noel had more to do at Café Violette. Stranded pilots from the Royal Air Force and, apparently, some legendary leader, would be in serious danger in the coming days and weeks and months if Noel ended up beaten to a pulp and tossed into a Nazi dungeon somewhere. Or worse. He lapsed into silence.

As the German soldiers began herding patrons, performers, backstage crew, and wait and kitchen staff into the theater house, Bauer didn't bother to shout an order for silence. He barely raised his hand. No one spoke. No one sneezed or coughed or twitched, although, surprisingly, everyone, Germans and non-Germans alike, looked guilty.

It was interrogation time.

Chapter 26

Bauer dispensed with the majority of the people who'd made up the audience within about ten minutes. He could have achieved this winnowing down of suspects in even less time given that half the crowd were rank-and-file German soldiers and their dates, a quarter were German officers and their dates, and one or two couples of questionable nationalities were obviously too sloshed on wine to have engineered a diversionary tactic aimed at helping a homosexual song-and-dance man to flee his own country. But I guess Bauer wanted to appear tough and efficient. He succeeded.

After Bauer sent away the officers and their dates, the soldiers and their dates, and the drunks with or without dates, the parasitical Webber and Kessler stayed. As did all of us connected in any way to Café Violette.

Visions of campy B-grade World War Two movies, seen courtesy of Ajay's DVD player, kept pounding through my head, especially the ones featuring creepy German actors eyeing prisoners through their monocles, managing to hiss without the use of more than one 's' word while repeating bad lines like, "We haf waysss of making you talk!" I suppressed an urge to let loose with hysterical laughter. Not the time or place. I needed all the control I could hang on to and all the acting skills I possessed to play innocent once it was my turn for the Q and A.

Bauer motioned for everyone to line up on the stage. Five musicians, one stagehand, two waiters, two kitchen staff, and only four additional performers were present. Then there was a certain short, fierce, wardrobe mistress—who'd made it back from Val and Michel's place in record time, possibly doing a spot of temporal traveling to avoid the Metro—and lastly, Papa Pierre.

We stood, silently waiting for the hammer to drop. The major began a slow stroll down the line without saying a word. I had to admit, I was impressed with his expertise in intimidation tactics. The man had style. He hadn't laid a hand on anyone, yet I was sure I wasn't the only person ready to throw myself on the ground and confess to the kidnapping of the baby of one very famous airman, the serial killings of prostitutes in Victorian London, and the sinking of the *Titanic*. The Delegates in 2061 could learn a thing or two from Herr Bauer.

Bauer paused in front of Fiona Belle.

The muscles in my arms and legs—and heart— tightened. I alone knew she was capable of escaping by means the Nazis would never imagine, but there was no way she'd go popping into another time in plain sight of, well, everyone. For a moment, though, I was tempted to toss her any sheet music left lying on a stand. By saving Valentin had we inadvertently exposed another of the Café Violette family who until now had been out of view of Bauer and his men? Did they realize she'd helped Michel escape?

Major Bauer wanted to see her papers. For once, Fiona Belle remained silent as she reached into a deep pocket in her apron and handed over what looked like an ID card and passport. I continued holding my breath and tried not to faint.

The minx caught me staring at her and gave me a surreptitious wink just as Bauer read aloud, "Fiona Belle Donovan Winthorp. Boston, Massachusetts, United States."

"Don't call me Winthorp. I despised that man."

I nearly choked on the hysterical laughter threatening to bubble up out of me.

Bauer frowned but handed the papers back to her. I began to breathe again. The elf or pixie who'd given me a birthdate more in line with the norm, the night I first performed at Café Violette, had been sharp enough at some point to turn an ageless witch into the equivalent of an Irish housemaid from Beantown. Whoever he or she was, they were top notch in forgery.

Bauer continued demanding to see papers, allowing performers in costume to go backstage to dig through belongings to retrieve documents as long as they were accompanied by Webber or Kessler. When Bauer got to Noel, my oxygen level dropped again.

"Herr Matheson."

"Major Bauer."

Their mutual dislike was more than evident, it was electrical in its intensity.

"I am curious. For several months, I have seen you on stage, but it is a mystery. Are you American? Or French? Or something else perhaps more...*tribal*?"

Noel stared into Bauer's emotionless eyes. "Dual citizenship, Major. France and America."

"And your loyalties?"

Noel flashed a lovely smile. "To my Creator. To my family here at Café Violette."

"Including those engaging in unnatural acts?"

Noel stiffened. "Define unnatural, Major."

"Do not say asinine things." Bauer waved his hand in dismissal of this pointless chat. "But I tire of engaging in cat-and-mouse word games." He turned, walked down the few steps off the stage, headed toward a table, sat, pushed aside the dishes waiting to be bussed to the kitchen, then casually plopped his feet on top of the table and announced, "Someone in this club is responsible for setting off a bomb to destroy an official vehicle of the Third Reich in order to aid in the escape of a person of questionable morals." He pointed at Noel. "I will begin with you. Let us talk in private."

A very muscular Nazi grabbed Noel's arms and began to march him toward the kitchen. An area filled with heavy pans and large, sharp knives. I took a step forward, but Noel shook his head at me.

Bauer noticed, frowned, and signaled his goon to stop. "Are you feeling protective, may I ask, Fräulein Christopher?"

My knees shook, but a voice in my head sounding remarkably like my dad kept whispering, *"You are strong and you are brave, Cori Christopher. And smarter than this low-life Nazi can ever imagine."*

I swallowed hard and looked directly into Bauer's eyes. "Major, questioning Monsieur Matheson is a waste of your time. If you'll recall, he and I were in the middle of a performance of a very fine foxtrot when we heard an explosion outside. We sing and we dance. We do not perform magic by managing to be in two places at once. Neither of us knew what had happened until this roundup, when we finally heard an explanation for the sound of a blast. Protective? Yes. Monsieur Matheson told you he is loyal to his family at Café Violette…as am I. Family which includes Noel Matheson."

I waited for cuffs to come slapping over my wrists or for a bullet to pierce my heart. An end to my crusade to save Noel and Café Violette and possibly a few others, like my friend Delys. Chalk up another failure on Cori Christopher's part to do one bit of good on this earth in *any* time period.

Bauer sighed. "Do you think me a fool, *Mademoiselle*? Or perhaps stuck in a bygone era long past, before bombs could be put in place and set off—what is the word? Ah, yes—remotely?"

Oh, crap. Bauer had me there. This wasn't 1841. It was 1941. Heck, I'd spent several weeks watching and thoroughly enjoying three seasons of a satiric comedy show called *Hogan's Heroes* about a band of prisoner-of-war saboteurs causing havoc in Nazi Germany. Ajay taped the show from some kind of nostalgia TV channel back when television included more than *Events at Eleven* and propaganda created by the Committee. Anyway, Hogan's merry band of resisters had blown up more bridges than existed in Germany and used timers or remotes to detonate each device.

Bluffing time. I managed to produce a weak laugh. "Well, clearly, Major Bauer, I myself am stuck in one of those other eras, because it never occurred to me there was a way to blow up a car without being in its vicinity at the time. As noted, I sing and I dance. I have no idea how to make a bomb, much less a remote device. I'm always amazed when I can flick a switch and watch lights go on."

This ridiculous game might have continued for at least another ten minutes or more—Bauer seemed to actually be enjoying the discussion—but before he could respond to my last statement, Captain Webber came racing in, looking far too cheery, and marching up to his commanding officer he whispered something in his ear.

Bauer smiled, slapped Webber on the back, and barked out something in German I didn't understand.

Noel did. His expression froze and he closed his eyes, obviously to shut out the pain of what he knew was about to happen.

The two soldiers holding Noel pushed him back into what I was calling the usual suspects line-up. We exchanged glances and the look in his eyes told me the emotional anguish I'd witnessed was real. Something was very wrong. Had Val been caught as he escaped the tunnel? Was Michel arrested in Saint-Denis?

Two other soldiers thrust open the front doors of Café Violette and dragged a very young man inside and all the way to the front to dump him at Bauer's feet. He couldn't have been more than fourteen. The expressions flitting across his face ranged from bravado and terror to, oddly, resignation.

Pierre gasped. "*Non!*"

I couldn't stop myself. I ran to Noel's side and grabbed his arm, whispering, "What's happening? Who is he? Do you know him?"

Bauer proudly announced, "Our fine soldiers have found the criminal who destroyed my automobile. His attempt to escape by the Metro was in vain, as loyal citizens saw and smelled his sooty clothes, filled with the smoke of the bomb he so recently discharged, and held him until Captain Webber arrived. You are well acquainted, are you not, Herr Simon? Is this not your nephew, Gabriel Driesen? The son of your late sister?"

Pierre's voice shook. "Major Bauer. Please. He is a boy. A child. No one was hurt. Only a vehicle. A machine replaceable within hours. I myself will be a provider of funds for another car."

Bauer's handsome features hardened. "Do not make a mockery of these actions. It is an act of violence against Germany." He nodded toward Webber and the two exchanged a long look. "Escort the prisoner, Captain Webber."

Webber pushed the boy toward the entrance of the club. There was absolute silence inside.

Which made it easier, and more appalling, to hear the sound of a shot firing only seconds after the German closed the entrance door.

Pierre fell to his knees on the ground, sobbing. Noel hurried to his side and put his arm around him to help him up.

Webber came back inside, holding a literally smoking gun. He approached Bauer, put his gun back in its holster, and announced, "There was nothing to be done. The prisoner attempted to escape."

Noel turned to the two German officers. For a moment, I was afraid he was going to slug one or both and be killed in front of my eyes. Instead, he quietly asked, "And how badly injured is Gabriel Driesen?"

A smile flashed across Webber's face, displaying the cruelty behind the civilized mask. "Badly."

Chapter 27

April 1941, Paris

The Sacré-Coeur Carousel stood vacant, silent, and isolated. There was no twentieth-century amusement park anywhere nearby with various booths and rides to keep the carousel company. Perhaps the Nazis didn't like to be amused. I climbed onto the base of the antique merry-go-round and sat on one of the garishly painted horses, willing it to move. Willing the sound of polkas and waltzes pumped out on a pipe organ to begin to play. Willing the era of *La Belle Époque* to suddenly come back to life.

But the only things in motion were my thoughts, and they weren't pleasant. Major Bauer had shut down Café Violette for two weeks following what he called "egregious activities." He'd also informed Luc Hebert the dance company would cease performances for the same amount of time. If dancers wanted to stay in shape, they did so at home, holding on to a chair instead of a ballet *barre*. It was clear Bauer and his group of Nazis were speeding up their plans to remove "undesirables" from both Café Violette and *l'Opéra Blanche*, and Delys was frightened. She was disappointed she wouldn't get to perform, masked or not, for the next couple of weeks, but more concerned and terrified she'd be in a camp far from Paris very soon. The loss of playing Odette/Odile would be trifling in the face of possible torture or death.

I didn't care about not singing at the club or the delight I'd taken in watching Delys dance.

I *did* care about the murder of a boy who'd given his life so someone else could flee to safer spaces. I was in shock. I kept hearing Webber saying, "Badly," when Noel questioned him as to how much Gabriel had been "injured." This wasn't an act carried out in the middle of a battlefield. It was a deliberate execution. Murder. It had nothing to do with how ticked off Bauer was about a stupid vehicle. It was a message. We all knew it. We might heed some of it, as in no explosive devices tossed into cars or onto motorcycles or tanks rolling through the streets of Paris. But the other message—desist with the escapes of pilots and "degenerates"—well, those *had* to continue. Too many lives were at stake.

Thankfully, Val Valentin had gotten away clean. I was right about my hunch. Bauer had been bluffing about Val's capture, trying to intimidate folks by prematurely announcing the failure of the escape. Papa Pierre was able to get word to those of us wandering around Café Violette who were somewhat lost without performances to look forward to. We'd all been involved in getting Val to safety and were thrilled to learn he'd reached the residence of Pierre's cousin and been reunited with Michel. By blowing up an empty limousine marked with a large swastika, a brave young man saved two people from certain horrible death in a Nazi prison camp.

It was a mystery why Bauer hadn't rounded up the performers and musicians and the wait and kitchen staff at Café Violette, all those in attendance during the explosion. He could have sent us all to Drancy or worse. A puzzle I was too exhausted to solve. A better choice of words might be "too numb."

I'd known, back when I was sitting in Jericho in 2061, that traveling to Occupied France in 1941 meant I could be connecting with some pockets of French *Résistance*. Joining whatever group centered around Café Violette was, after all, part of my plan. I'd get to be one of the gang who stuck it to the Nazis. Very exciting. Like being an extra in a movie spy thriller. The operative word was "extra." I'd loved being able to help RAF pilot Sam Seymour and others whose names I'd never learn get smuggled out of the country thanks to a collaborative effort between Café Violette and *l'Opéra Blanche*. My involvement was very cool. Very clean. Very…peripheral. Yes, I'd managed to sneak across a catwalk with Seymour, which could have proved dangerous, but other than serving as an escort to a bookshop, my role had merely been to sing. The most dangerous act I'd undertaken had been to sing "Johnny Has Gone for a Soldier" in defiance of Major Bauer's request.

Last night I'd become part of the main action. Been involved in the planning, provided a farewell hug, been part of the group hiding a man as he made his way toward a tunnel to freedom, inwardly cheered at the sound of an explosion. But when the shot came and Major Webber swaggered back inside the club waving his gun like a trophy, and when Papa Pierre fell to the ground unable to process the outright murder of his nephew, "peripheral" ended.

I leaned over, threw my arms around the blue neck of the silent, solid, carousel horse, let my head sink down, and sobbed.

A hand touched my shoulder and a quiet voice said,

"It will be all right. Cry now, Cori. Tomorrow, you will dry the tears and prepare to resume battle. We need you. *I* need you."

I kept my head in the carousel horse's mane. Before I had a chance to say anything, he continued, "This is not a consolation, but Pierre's nephew, Gabriel, had received word his sisters had been sent to Drancy. Because they are Jews. Gabriel was about to be arrested and join them, and he made the decision to go down fighting. In doing so, he did the saving of two innocent people."

"He was a hero."

"He was."

Noel put his hand under my chin and lifted my head to look at him.

I gasped. "Noel! What happened to your face! I mean, you had a bruise or two from when you went up against the soldiers grabbing Gaspard, but it's worse now."

"Not so pretty, *non*?"

Understatement. The crooked nose was swollen and bruises covered his cheeks and his chin. He sported not one but two black eyes.

"Bauer?"

"*Non, non.* He does not do the dirty work. He has others do it for him. He is less than a man."

"They all are."

Noel nodded, then winced. "My head is not in right feeling today."

I had to smile. "It's muddling your English a bit, too. But I can see why." My smile dimmed completely as I asked, "Noel, how old was Gabriel?"

"Thirteen."

I couldn't breathe for a long moment.

"Those…bastards." I began to shake. "How does anyone go on after this? I just want to stay here curled underneath this blue horse and hide."

"I understand. I do. But we all go on because the Nazis cannot be allowed to win. Because Gabriel would despise us all as cowards if we let his death stop our work. Because there are thousands, possibly millions, of people we must try to save if we can. Cori, a few years ago I was in the French Army helping with injured soldiers. What Americans call a medic. I helped to stitch up brave men, many my age, who fought enormous physical pain and came close to dying, and through the pain they asked me when they could return to battle because they did not want Germans to take over our country to destroy people who are different. We must now do the same, for all the 'Gabriels' who should be allowed to grow up in freedom."

"You're braver than I."

Noel took my hand in his and helped me down off the carousel horse. "No. This is not true." He managed a smile. "Remember you are the bold, brash, sassy Cori Christopher. You have it within you, and I have witnessed it. It seems like it is not a big thing to you, perhaps, but standing in front of an audience of… pigs…and singing to distract them? To sing a song about losing one's lover to stupid wars instead of singing a song to save oneself but put a pilot into danger? Defying Bauer to his face so a new friend has the chance to dance her dreams? These acts are also bravery."

"Thanks for saying that, but I swear I'd turn into a quaking mass of goo if someone slapped me or worse."

"Goo?"

"Goo."

Noel laughed, then winced with the pain to his face. "If 'goo' is as bad as the word, I am not sure I want to hear the meaning."

"Well, picture a bean soup boiled down to total slop with not a bean remaining whole."

"Ah. Goo. I shall avoid eating it or becoming it." He paused, then continued. "None of us know how far we will bend before breaking. But I heard you argue with Bauer as his men were trying to force me into the kitchen after the explosion. Cori, this is very, very courageous. And…I believe God above gives us a strength when we need it most. When we are faced with a choice of betraying friends or feeling a fist on your face."

I touched his cheek as gently as I could. "I can see which choice you made."

"*Oui.* But I admit I am confused because they did not go further."

"Not to mention, why didn't they completely shut down Café Violette and take every one of us who was there during Bauer's big interrogation to the nearest train station, with the next destination being Drancy? They really are onto something else, aren't they? Something they see as more important than a haul of performers who help with an occasional British pilot."

"I agree. So does Papa Pierre. And the only explanation with any sense about this knowledge of the Germans is there is definitely a traitor in our midst. One who, blessedly, was not aware of the tunnels."

"True. But I'm confused. You told me Hauptmann has allowed Café Violette to stay open partially because he enjoys the entertainment and because he had an interest in certain men there. But now that's all gone. I heard Gaspard was sent to a camp. Michel and Val managed to escape. Pierre is Jewish and you have gypsy in your background, yet neither of you has been hauled away…thank God. There's some cat-and-mouse game being played because you're all, I mean *we're* all, basically small fish. And I'm mixing my animal metaphors. Does this just come down to grabbing one supposedly big *Résistance* leader?"

Noel took my hand in his.

We sat in silence for a few minutes, then. I lightly touched his hand. "I'm so sorry. In so many ways I'm an outsider. I have no business asking you these questions, and I promise I'll just shut up now."

"You are *not* an outsider. Never. I hesitate because with all my fine words about bravery I am terrified for you. I do not want you in any more danger."

"Me?"

"Cori, it is obvious Major Bauer is interested in you as a *woman*. This is why he has not interrogated you with brutal force or imprisoned you. He hates me. I see the personal in this hatred. He is not a stupid man and he sees how I feel about you. He is torn between his desire to catch this leader and his attraction to you. I fear if it should be he will turn his obsessions against me or against you or us both. And…I can't…lose you. Am I making sense?"

"Noel…"

He leaned forward, a question in his eyes. I nodded.

His lips met mine for a brief moment, and then he drew back. "I'm sorry. The Germans did not leave a lot of skin untouched on my face. This may not be pleasant for you."

I couldn't help but laugh. "Pleasant doesn't begin to cover how marvelous I feel! But you? Wait. Does your mouth hurt?" I asked.

"A bit, but I'm willing to bear any amount of pain to kiss you again."

Our kiss didn't last long. The carousel was in a fairly isolated area, but it was part of a public space in a city where affection was currently frowned on. And Noel was trying to extinguish more than "any amount of" pain from his beating. But it was definitely quality over quantity of time. Feeling his arms around me and his lips searching mine was sheer vindication I'd made the right decision in leaving New Manhattan, even if it meant losing my life in this time period.

A giggle from about six feet away put a stop to our activities. Two kids, about six years old, were clearly delighted to see the *"fou"* adults kissing in broad daylight. For a moment, everything was normal. Children laughing at adults. Birds overhead singing and butterflies flying in the breeze. The Nazis hadn't killed the spirits of any of us.

We drew apart, then sat in silence, simply holding hands, savoring this brief moment of happiness.

Chapter 28

A siren sounded from a distance of maybe six blocks away from our spot at the carousel. The noise could be indicating a fire. It could be a police action against a pickpocket. Or it could be Nazis rounding up people for reasons as stupid and as old as hatred of "the other." The mood of contentment shattered.

Noel and I waved at the kids, who scampered off, hopefully to enjoy a beautiful spring day in the sunshine. Would they ever get the chance to ride on a carousel? To experience being children? According to history, which I assumed wouldn't be changed in the big picture no matter what happened with my friends at Café Violette and *l'Opéra Blanche*, the war would end in September of 1945. The Nazis would be gone from France and Paris would get back to rebuilding and trying to forget. I sent out a prayer these children would survive through these next years.

Noel kept his arm around me and I snuggled next to him.

"By the way, Cori, you were wrong."

"Not surprised," I said. "I'm probably wrong more times than I'm right. But about what, specifically?"

"When you said it wasn't your business about what happens at the café. It *is* very much your business. I trust you. Pierre trusts you. You care about justice and freedom and most of all about other people. And, selfishly, we need your help more than we have over these last few weeks. However, I will not be telling you everything because it will be safer for you."

"Go on."

"Pierre and I have been aware for months someone connected to Café Violette or *l'Opéra Blanche* is collaborating with the Nazis. But we do not want to be shutting down our activities, although we have tried to avoid bringing our British friends inside the club unless there is absolutely no other way to help them on their journey. As you pointed out to me, pilots are escaping, yet we remain open. While Hauptmann has his… peculiar…interests, there must be more reasons he is allowing Café Violette to stay in business so he can flirt with Gaspard or Michel. I do not understand why Gaspard was taken this particular day and Bauer then came for Michel and for Val, but had it not been for the explosion, the Germans might have let Val's escape go by without punishment. Bauer does not really care about the sexual habits of these men nor about a few RAF pilots slipping through his grasp. Because he does not want to close the club. He is waiting."

I nodded. "He's sucking down both his moral outrage and his wounded pride, yet apart from this whole stupid two-week hiatus, he's leaving Café Violette open for business and you and Pierre and others free. What are the odds he's discovered when this *Résistance* guy is coming? And can you tell me who he is?"

Noel glanced around the park. Not a soul in sight, including the children we'd entertained with our kiss. He whispered, "Have you heard the name *L'Audace*?"

I shook my head. "No. Means 'bold,' right?"

"The bold or daring one. For nearly ten years,

throughout Europe, he is…what is the word? Um…he is almost synonymous—*oui*, synonymous—with *la Résistance*. He helped young people in Hamburg flee Germany during the arrests made at various dance clubs. He was responsible for leading missions resulting in the rescue of more than one hundred Jews in Poland as they were headed for concentration camps in Germany. He and his people are blowing up more Nazi headquarters in the last year than I am singing songs. *L'Audace* is legendary and also he is inspirational. His whereabouts are always secret, and so is his real name."

"Oh, wow! Like Viktor Laszlo in *Casablanca*!"

"*Quoi*?"

Uh-oh. Had *Casablanca* yet been released? How did I lie my way out of this one? I thought fast and told a version of the truth.

"*Casablanca*. It's a film. About an American expatriate who owns a café in Casablanca and is reunited with his love, who turns out to be married to a very important leader of the Czech *Résistance*…Viktor Laszlo."

"I have not seen this film."

"Well, it's, um, it's only been recently released in America. And something tells me it's not going to be showing in cinemas around Paris anytime soon. The Germans aren't going to allow anything which might stir folks up to resist…and this could do some major stirring. There's a scene where the Nazis in the American's café are singing some stupid German song and Laszlo gets the house band to play 'La Marseillaise' and everyone stands up and sings with them." I paused before adding, "I cried."

Noel grinned at me. "Ah, my sentimental

American."

"Yeah, yeah. Sue me. And remember, you've got dual citizenship, Monsieur Matheson. You'd've been wiping tears away too!" I grinned back, then sobered. "I'm sorry. I interrupted you, and this is serious."

He leaned over and lightly kissed my cheek. "*Oui.* But I would like to see this film one day if it is ever allowed in France." He inhaled. "*Résistance.* Your Laszlo in the movie was Czechoslovakian? Well, the nationality of *L'Audace* is secret. He is like…like the Scarlet Pimpernel. Or perhaps a modern Robin Hood because he has led break-ins at German banks and homes of wealthy Nazis and distributed monies to refugees. And retrieved artwork stolen by those Nazis."

"Okay. I'm impressed. So what do the Germans call him?"

"Many more descriptive and less elegant names." Noel smiled.

"I'll bet they do. But we got off track again. I'm assuming *L'Audace* is the one coming to Paris? To Café Violette?"

Noel nodded. "*Oui.* We have not been told the exact day when he arrives, but rumors have been spreading for the last three months. He is planning a large commotion in the city to disturb our German occupiers. It is a mystery. But he has asked for refuge for a short while at Café Violette, and it is very soon now."

"And the Germans have suspicions he's headed to Paris?"

"They must. Otherwise why would we be allowed to continue small activities? Keep Café Violette open? *L'Audace* is like a shark, a lethal one, to the Germans. They want badly to catch this very big fish."

"And if they do…"
"More than Café Violette will be destroyed."

Chapter 29

If Bauer and his men had concluded that a two-week break from performing at Café Violette or *l'Opéra Blanche* would result in squelching spirits and ensure tame submission to Nazi rule, this assumption was what Ajay would have referred to as "whacked."

True, there were inconveniences and annoyances resulting from the temporary closings of the club and the theater, primarily for the dancers who needed to practice daily and, of course, financially for all concerned. But the dancers found places throughout Paris where they could take class, and the owners of a variety of venues were happy to allow their space to be used for an hour or more of rehearsal time. Delys and Paulette took me with them to the studio where the Paris Opera Ballet held class and, following the barre and center floor combinations, they rehearsed each of the dances for Luc's selections from *Swan Lake*. The principal male dancer, Georges, accompanied us, and I watched, with delight, as he guided both Delys and Paulette through the movements of the Odile *pas de deux*. Paulette grew stronger in both technique and confidence. She was determined to be ready to assume the role in case Delys needed to escape the theater…and we all knew the time was coming soon.

I could practice singing almost anywhere, although I never tried to do any street entertaining, convinced I'd end up in the closest jail, but part of the daily ritual for ballet and rehearsal generally ended with me singing for the dancers. It was fun for everyone because I didn't bother to censor my tunes. Everyone thought the American girl simply knew the hottest contemporary American music.

I did try to temper my choices of songs to hide the "when" of the time I was really from. Consequently, I left out tunes I knew would be composed within the next fifty years or so. I had to clamp down my somewhat impish desire to teach the companies of Luc Hebert and the Paris Opera Ballet the words and music to just about every song from *Les Misérables*, because it could cause trouble if some aging ballerina in the nineteen-eighties proclaimed she'd heard this music back in 1941. Fiona Belle would not be pleased if questions arose, and I had no desire to make the woman mad or break her rules, including those unspoken.

I did sing a stirring piece from *Dear Evan Hansen* for the dancers nearly every day. While not as defiant as those from *Les Misérables*, the song oozed hope, which was something every Parisian could use. The show hadn't been produced until 2017 and I figured it was a decent enough space not to raise eyebrows about future tunes being sung in the past. One afternoon, about a week into the shutdown of both Café Violette and *l'Opéra Blanche*, when the rain was beating down outside so hard no one wanted to leave, I sang the entire score of *Hamilton*, calling it an experimental work from a composer in Washington Heights, Manhattan. Which was true. The dancers especially loved the songs sung by the character of the Marquis de Lafayette. And really, why wouldn't they? A French fighting genius!

Three days into taking class with professional

ballerinas, I decided I wasn't up to being sociable or lifting my leg in a straight line by the side of my body in an insane attempt to match the dancers I worked with. It wasn't just the physical stress of going beyond my capabilities. Too many emotions were descending on my psyche. Images of the frightened expression on Val Valentin's face as he waited for word about Michel morphed into the angry yet terrified countenance of Delys when she was told she wasn't allowed to dance. I kept seeing the anguish and despair I'd witnessed in Papa Pierre's eyes as he heard the sounds of shots transmitting the very instant of his nephew's murder. Behind each of those faces was Bauer's—wielding the power literally over life and death, and the cunning behind his penetrating gray-blue eyes as he played his waiting game in an effort to catch *L'Audace* and make his bosses proud.

Oddly, what also haunted me was the smile Teresa Dorleac had flashed at my roommates and me as she went off with her friend, the German soldier Frederick Müller. There'd been nothing sly about it. No malice or hidden meaning. It was the smile of a girl doing exactly what she claimed…enjoying some time alone with a childhood friend. I couldn't reconcile her smile with Bauer's claim that Teresa had been a spy. If someone at Café Violette, like William Gale, her on again/off again boyfriend, had told her about the code songs we used for "all clear" or "stay in place," the only way I could imagine her mentioning it to Müller would be in passing, as something intriguing. But I refused to label Teresa as some dancing double agent. There was something off about the whole business, and I was determined to find out the truth behind her death. If I could also discover who really was acting as a traitor at Café Violette, well, we're talkin' major bonus…the information might save a life or two.

Conducting an investigation into a murder wasn't in my skill set. The job I'd held at Discover Films from 2057 to the day I escaped the Delegates in the spring of 2061 hadn't exactly covered police work. But I remembered an episode we'd filmed about workers building an annex or warehouse for the Committee to store files and records. Not the most exciting thing to watch, with various workers sweeping out debris and creating a new foundation, but those were the very activities I now needed to perform. Sweeping out the debris. Which meant tossing out information, innuendo, and outright lies spread by more than one German official.

So, apart from aching limbs, I'd blown off class today after deciding it was time to have a visit with Rosemarie. She'd been Teresa's landlady for the two years Teresa was with Luc Hebert's company. She was easy to talk to, and it wasn't a big stretch to imagine Teresa might have confided secrets about her romances to a sympathetic ear.

From the kitchen, I could hear the kettle whistling, and within a few seconds Rosemarie entered the parlor where I'd been sitting staring at a photo of Teresa, Delys, Paulette, and Luc Hebert.

"Cori. Please, share tea with me. I have been able to make some croissants, thanks to Chef Henri at Café Violette. There are foodstuffs going to waste because of this idiocy about closing the club these last weeks."

"I will definitely take you up on the offer."

I helped her bring the tea and rolls to the table, and

we sat and sipped and ate, just enjoying the peace for a moment.

Rosemarie suddenly put her cup down. "Cori. You are troubled about Teresa, are you not?"

I nodded. "I am. The German major, Bauer, more than hinted she was acting as an agent for the Nazis and therefore someone who, uh, didn't like her informing killed her on behalf of the resisters."

"Someone in Café Violette. There are more than one or two," Rosemarie responded with a smile. "I am aware. I have been a close friend to Pierre Simon for many years."

"I had a feeling. I didn't want to say anything. I mean, we're all so…"

"Frightened and distrustful?"

"Oh, yeah. You nailed it."

She took a small bite of croissant and swallowed, then just came out with it. "Cori, I have the certainty Teresa Dorleac did not betray anyone. I have been well acquainted with Teresa for more than two years. She has live here in this house. We have many talks over tea, like you and me today, and she told me how much she has been of sadness because of Paris being taken by the Germans." Rosemarie smiled. "Teresa is beautiful dancer, but Teresa is not the actress. You have seen this in her dance. What is the word? Too precise with not enough of the emotion?"

"Technically perfect."

"Yes. Teresa could not pretend feelings she does not have. And her feelings for France are clear and with love. Pierre and I discuss this. If talk about songs or escaped pilots was discussed, it is Teresa herself who was betrayed. She never provided any information to her young soldier friend…at least not in any intended way of harm."

"I can't stop wondering if the whole double agent idea is just one sick charade on Bauer's part."

"I agree. What is the term? 'Gaslight'? To make games with one's mind until one confuses truth and lies?"

"Rosemarie, I can't prove anything, and Bauer and Paquette seem not to care much about who killed her, but I have this odd feeling they know. They've been sitting on the knowledge since the night she failed to come home. Honestly? It wouldn't surprise me to learn they set up or at least sanctioned her murder. They want more suspicion and distrust sown among the *Résistance* at the club…and at *l'Opéra Blanche*."

Rosemarie nodded. "Sadly, Bauer and Paquette will arrest someone only if they feel it works to what you call an advantage."

"So there's nothing for us to do, apart from grieve for a friend."

Chapter 30

I peeked out at the audience from behind the side curtain and immediately spotted Noel, sitting at the table I'd shared with Delys, Paulette, Rosemarie, and Teresa the night I'd met Donald in the garden to exchange song ideas. The night I'd sung an unauthorized, anti-war ballad. The night of Teresa's murder. It was *déjà vu* with a twist. Tonight, Noel sat with Delys and Paulette.

My gaze shifted to another table not far from my friends. This one was occupied by Bauer, Webber, and Kessler. With them sat the police detective, Paquette. Unless the unholy trio of Germans and their gendarme buddy had developed a huge liking for the music of big band American jazz, I was afraid they'd completely penetrated our wall of secrecy and had a very organized bullet-point list of every move we were about to make. This was the first night of the club's reopening following the arrest of the master of ceremonies Gaspard Bassett, the escape of Michel and Val, the bombing of Bauer's car, and the murder of Pierre's nephew Gabriel, just over two weeks ago.

L'Opéra Blanche had resumed performances of *Selections from Tchaikovsky* last night. I'd been accompanied backstage by Fiona Belle Donovan Winthorp—oops! I keep forgetting, must cut the Winthorp since she "despised that man," and someday I hope to hear the story behind the sentiment... But I digress. Fiona Belle helped me with the quick costume changes for Delys and Paulette, and had taken great delight in ensuring the success of the masquerade, bringing a new, home-stitched mask and pair of gloves which allowed Delys to dance her dual swan role.

Neither Bauer nor Paquette had returned to question anyone at either Café Violette or *l'Opéra Blanche* regarding the murder of Teresa Dorleac. Their seeming lack of interest scared me more than if they'd popped in on an hourly basis to grill every person associated with either venue. Rosemarie had called them "games for the mind," but to me the physical stress was just as wrenching. We were in the middle of the proverbial cat-toying-with-mouse scenario and the German felines were simply waiting for an unexpected moment when the mice were feeling complacent and content. They'd have to wait quite a while. As one of the mice, I shared the tension and wariness and was not really up to teasing the cats with acts of sabotage.

The big news was that twenty-four hours ago Paquette arrested William Gale, the clarinet player for both Café Violette and *l'Opéra Blanche*, charging him with the murder of Teresa Dorleac.

Bauer had informed Papa Pierre, taking pleasure in telling him Café Violette was out one very fine musician. Supposedly, William confessed to being Teresa's lover and killing her in a jealous rage when he realized she was involved with her friend Frederick Müller from Alsace-Lorraine. Bauer also again claimed Teresa was collaborating with "his office" and William added collusion to the list of offenses committed by his girlfriend, which supposedly caused him to decide murdering her was patriotic.

I called total B.S. on this one. William might have been jealous, "might" being the operative word, but he was no killer, and I refused to buy this garbage about Teresa passing info off to the Nazis. It was another game.

We were all worried about the arrest. Clearly, the confession was a crock. William was innocent and we were all in big trouble. The clarinetist had been part of the activities taking place at Café Violette. He knew about signals and codes to help the pilots who'd been given shelter. He knew someone important was on the way tonight. Bauer had to have already known more pertinent facts, but he had needed William to clarify and verify and wasn't above torturing the man to obtain what he wanted.

There was something surreal about the whole scenario, and my Cassandra warnings were telling me the drama and danger were just beginning.

I shivered. As of this evening, approximately seven people at Café Violette were in on the fact that *L'Audace* was due to arrive at the club sometime tonight. Any other musicians, waiters, or performers who might have previously aided in rescues of downed pilots had been told to stick to whatever passed for a normal evening, but that another R.A.F. pilot was expected. Basically true. *L'Audace* had assumed the identity of Squadron Leader Rob Tigger, which was the name we were keeping.

I finished my set—three Cole Porter tunes signifying nothing but fine music—drew back from the curtain, and began to quietly make my way through the maze of props and fly-rigging equipment, intending to change clothes and join Delys and Paulette. *L'Opéra Blanche* was holding a special late night showing of the *Swan Lake* selections, so I was needed as Delys's dresser. Some kind of fancy gala party was planned for the dancers at Hauptmann's residence, which meant making sure Paulette not only took over during final bows but had a gorgeous dress to wear for the party.

Someone grabbed my wrist and whispered, "Cori, *attendez!* Wait. Do not leave. *Ici*, there is trouble!"

I turned and looked into the worried eyes of Papa Pierre.

"What's wrong?" I asked.

"Cori, Squadron Leader Rob Tigger is to be coming to Paris this night." Pierre managed a brief smile. "We did not tell you this before, but the pilot you helped rescue, Seymour, was working for Tigger. When you helped him, you were helping the Squadron Leader."

"Oh, wow! Pretty awesome to hear that particular escape was kind of a double coup."

"It was indeed." The smile dimmed. "But, Cori, there is indeed wrong…tonight…because it is what Bauer has been waiting for. We tried to send the word for the Squadron Leader to wait at the chapel until, as you Americans say, the coast, she is clear, but, as we fear, he never received the message. So, he did not stay at the chapel."

"Wait. Oh, *Mon Dieu!* Are you saying Tigger is *here*? Now?"

"*Oui*. He is currently in your dressing room, Cori, as you are the only female performer tonight. I thought this to be the safest place for the moment."

"With Bauer and his boys out in the audience in full force. Ouch."

Papa Pierre grimly stated, "This is not the coincidence. Of course they have known of our activities, although not dates and times. After Val's escape they discovered the existence of the tunnels, which now have a steel enforcement upon the doors. It is very suspicious. After Val's escape they close us and now we suddenly are open? Someone other than Monsieur William has provided information. William knew only the possibility of an officer in the Royal Air Force arriving. Not where or when or who. But, Cori, Monsieur Gaspard also is aware this officer to be more than what seems. It is quite possible Gaspard was tortured into giving Bauer this news. Bauer has waited for this chance."

"Cat and mouse," I mumbled.

"*Précisément.* The cats in the shapes of Major Bauer, Kessler, and Webber inform me they will be having the examination of the papers of every individual here, including the waiters and kitchen staff and all our performers and members of the band at the close of the show. It is the understanding if anyone leaves before then, he has men stationed at every door to make certain no one slips by who, Bauer tells me, 'does not belong.' If we could demolish the doors to the tunnels they would still be waiting for him. They are not sure, of course, Squadron Leader Tigger is truly *L'Audace,* but they take no chances. It is the big score. It is the 'why' for not closing us down for these last months. Bauer has the obsession over capturing this man. It means the destruction of so many in France and other parts of Europe if *L'Audace* is caught. Mademoiselle Cori, I rattle on, and I apologize, but I am at a loss about what to do."

I glanced around the backstage area. Donald Joseph was currently on stage, but we didn't need to take the chance of being overheard. "Let's go down to my dressing room now. Maybe we can figure out a plan. And Noel needs to be here."

We took the stairs leading down to the small green room where performers could smoke or drink a beverage before going on stage. No one was inside, but we hurried past, almost running down the hallway, in case a comic or singer suddenly appeared and began asking questions.

We paused outside my room.

"Let me go inside and tell him I 'ave bring with me the lady who belongs in here."

I nodded. "I'll stand guard." I grinned at him. "Maybe I should 'lie down' guard? Put my feet up on the wall? Anyone who happens by will understand a performer's need to relax."

Pierre raised an eyebrow. "In your gown?"

"Oh. Yeah. Dumb idea. Okay. I'll just drop into this lovely old chair then and tell anyone who asks I'm getting claustrophobic and wanted out of my room. Considering the influx of Germans keeping everyone inside, who could blame me?"

Pierre smiled at me, then knocked four times on the door before opening and entering my dressing room.

About two minutes later, the door opened and Pierre motioned for me to enter. At first glance, the room appeared empty.

I heard rustling, glanced down at my drape-covered makeup table, and stayed silent, watching, as a man in his early forties, wearing the gray-blue uniform of the Royal Air Force with a leather flying jacket atop, crawled out from behind the makeup table, dusted himself off, and tried to smooth down curly reddish hair from springing into what had to be a perpetual cowlick. An inch or two taller than I, he smiled the cocky, impudent, confident smile only pilots seemed able to pull off and immediately endear themselves to anyone not German. I was standing in front of the leader of much of the *Résistance* in Europe.

His face was very familiar. It should be. I saw the feminine version of it every time I looked in the mirror.

My eyes filled with tears as both of us reached our hands out to each other. He enveloped me in a tight hug as I whispered, "Daddy?"

Chapter 31

Papa Pierre beamed at my father and me as if his entire mission in life had been to bring us together. "I give you two a few moments alone, *non*? Then we must plan."

"Did you know before?" I asked Pierre.

"*Non*. Not until I saw the Squadron Leader, up close. I did not want to say anything until you saw him. But the resemblance is remarkable. Now, quickly, make your reuniting. I will be outside the door."

He left and I faced my father, Robin Christopher aka Squadron Leader Rob Tigger, aka *L'Audace*. I had far too many questions to ask, but the one most pressing was personal. "Why did you leave me? I was ten. Ten! And Granny and Gramps were gone. Mom died trying to get us to safety. Now Ajay is dead too."

His eyes were moist. "I'm so sorry, Cori. But, like your grandmother, I was about to be picked up by the Delegates. The Committee wasn't bothering with a trial, I knew my execution was already set, and I wanted to live. I also wanted to do anything I could to stop the Committee's destruction of freedom in New York City. I holed up at Jericho for a day or two, trying to find a way to get out of the city without jeopardizing your life or your mom's if I was caught. The second day at the house, I hear a knock on the door. I open it and there stands this absurdly short, odd, possibly deranged, woman dressed like a carnival fortune teller."

"Fiona Belle," I said, then smiled. "She does love her costumes. Her Arabian Nights harem ensemble is the best."

He chuckled. "She truly excels in creating over-the-top outfits. Anyway, the first time I met her she told me a wacky tale of fantasy about time travel, yet I somehow believed her. Being desperate and seeing no feasible alternative possibly helped with the belief. I decided to go back to nineteen-thirty-one and use my skills in planning rebellious activities and my knowledge of history to try to help those wishing to escape the tyranny of the Nazis, who, thankfully, aren't quite as technologically savvy as the Committee. I knew I couldn't change Hitler's plans for invasions or destroy those horrible camps or do anything to keep his rise to power from happening, but I could start building a network that would be in place once France was occupied. Perhaps be able to save a few lives."

"This is why Mom wouldn't go or let me go with you?"

He nodded. "She'd had enough of the activities with Ostinato and said she couldn't deal with more intrigue and didn't want you anywhere near anything that could get you killed. She wanted to take you back to the late eighteen-hundreds…in Canada."

"Well, I just remember hearing you and Mom arguing about *Anne of Green Gables*. Didn't make any sense, of course. Until now."

"You heard right."

"But why couldn't you have *told* me you were going? Why couldn't I have just gone with you? Heck, when I was ten I was probably better equipped to deal with early *Résistance* activities than half of France."

"I needed everyone, including you, to assume I'd died in the storm while helping to shore up the wall downtown. You're a terrific actress, but I couldn't dump a secret on a ten-year-old and expect you to keep it from the Delegates. And your mom was insistent she would get you to safety. I agreed. There was a traitor in Ostinato, and he or she wouldn't hesitate to throw you to the wolves. Delegate wolves with sharp teeth. So I 'died.' I gather from what Fiona Belle told me they quit searching for me, thanks to descriptions of others at the wall who claimed they'd seen me washed out into the ocean. Which they did. They just didn't see me holding very soggy sheet music and disappearing into whatever tunnel of time Fiona Belle provides."

I couldn't help but smile. "I would have given my entire store of New Manhattan wealth tokens to have seen you pull off your own drowning."

"I have to admit, it was one of my better efforts." He paused before adding, "It never occurred to me your mother would be killed in an accident. I thought she'd taken you to safety in Canada circa late eighteen-hundreds. Then a few months ago I had a surprise visit by Fiona Belle telling me she was going to try to steer you to the Café Violette if you were ever in trouble. I was already planning for 'Squadron Leader Tigger' to come to Paris for a few meetings. I just waited until I got word you were here. I had to see you."

I nodded, letting my own tears fall. "I've missed you so much."

His voice grew hoarse. "Cori, I can't tell you how gut-wrenching it's been for ten years not to be able to see you grow up. And Fiona Belle would only say you were fine, although you were stirring up trouble in New Manhattan, and now of course at Café Violette. Which is what the French would call *totalement fou* and *très* dangerous, young lady. Frying pan into fire."

I tilted my chin up proudly. "I *am* my father's daughter."

He laughed, "And you are your grandparents' granddaughter and your great-uncle's niece. Enough rebellious DNA in both families to last several centuries."

A soft knock sounded at the door. It swung open and Pierre entered.

He quietly said, "I wish there is more time for you being to talk alone. But the situation is growing of the urgency. I have not heard why our communications did not go through and became so muddled and wrong, although Noel and I have belief there has been a traitor in our family for some time. We are trying to come up with a solution for the Squadron Leader. We cannot let you be taken. We must find a way to hide for you. And a change of clothing."

Robin Christopher shook his head. "Perhaps it's best if I stay as is. I'm in the uniform of a British pilot, Monsieur Simon. If I give myself up I would be sent to a prisoner-of-war camp. It would not be pleasant, but if it would keep all of us from being shot as spies then I will do it. The word could go out. *L'Audace never arrived here...just Squadron Leader Rob Tigger.*"

My voice shook. "I hate to sound distrusting of those justice-loving, righteous Nazis, but I'm not convinced they wouldn't shoot you regardless of your current status as a British officer. There's a rage that's been building for weeks, with Bauer especially. He ordered the execution of Pierre's nephew…and I'm sure he's behind my roommate's murder as well. They're not stupid. Especially Bauer. They've heard rumors, they've been given information, they're ready for this night." I shook my head. "And it's weird. I've been sensing a strange, almost maniacally obsessive reason Bauer is determined to capture *L'Audace*."

The three of us lapsed into silence. Pierre finally said, "There must be *something* we can do. We are creative people, *non*? This is a theater. We are performers. Not only singers but actors. We adhere to the idea of the suspension of disbelief for the audience. We simply need to find a way to allow a big helping of disbelief for our enemies." He paused. "Excuse my bad language, Mademoiselle Cori, but damn these Nazi bastards! *Merde!* I am desolate they found our tunnels and have barred the way for so many. They stop at nothing."

I smiled. "I've heard worse and I agree." I glanced at my dad, then into the mirror reflecting both of us, pursed my lips and let out a low whistle. "I have an idea."

Both men immediately turned to me. "Yes?"

"Look at, um, Squadron Leader Tigger. He's a bit over my height. Most of the time people here at the club see me in heels so they assume I'm taller than five-ten. He has a slight build… No offense, Daddy, but you need to try and eat now and then! He is also red-haired and freckle-faced—like me. Currently clean-shaven. The Nazis haven't seen him. There are no photographs. Have any of the rumors regarding *L'Audace* included descriptions?"

Pierre shook his head. "Non."

"Finally, a break for us. Look, we have costumes

used by Val and by me. They're hanging on racks somewhere back in wardrobe. And not just slinky gowns but normal dresses any girl in France could wear to, say, see a show."

My dad raised an eyebrow. "Beg your pardon? Val?"

"Val was Café Violette's female impersonator. He escaped two weeks ago through the tunnels, just before the Nazis boarded them up. But he left costumes and everyday wear."

Pierre exclaimed, "Excellent! We dress and wig our pilot and make him up to look more like you and send him outside at the end of the show. But, Cori, there is *le grande* problem with this. More than one. If he goes now he will need *your* papers and he will be scrutinized by the Boche standing guard. There is him being older than you. And the last problem, if they do not notice the age difference, and he passes for you, you yourself will need those papers when you leave, and if you do not have them, you could be arrested."

"I'm willing to risk it. He's a lot more important than I am."

My dad shook his head. "No. I won't do anything that could harm you, Cori."

A new voice was suddenly heard. "It can work. But, as has been stated on more than one occasion, what is needed is a diversion."

We'd been so intent studying my dad to determine if it was really possible to pull off the substitution we hadn't noticed the door quietly opening.

I whirled around. "Noel? Thank God!" I could hear the relief—along with what must be evident to everyone, the love—in my three brief words the moment he stepped into the room.

"In the flesh. I started getting concerned when you did not join me at intermission, so I decided to come and find you. The ladies are preparing to leave to get to *l'Opéra Blanche* to dance the special performance and attend General Hauptmann's party."

Noel glanced at me, then at my dad. His eyebrows rose and the corners of his mouth twitched in an effort to suppress a very large Cheshire-cat-style grin. "Ah, what an…extraordinary resemblance." He extended his hand to shake that of the supposed Squadron Leader Rob Tigger. "I am very pleased to meet you…sir."

Chapter 32

My dad stared at Noel for a long moment, then smiled as they shook hands.

"Nice to meet you as well, Monsieur Matheson. Pierre told me you are a man of integrity and quite a formidable opponent when it comes to protecting those entrusted to your care. A very talented man as well. I heard you sing the last set while I was hiding in Cori's dressing room. For the record, as both a music lover and someone who is interested in the safety of Mademoiselle Cori, I approve."

Noel bowed as the double meanings swirled between the two of them. "*Merci.* And let me say now, the respect and admiration is much returned. But…we do have an immediate problem tonight. I overheard Cori's solution for your escape, and while I agree with most of these ideas, especially considering the almost uncanny resemblance between the two of you"—at this point Noel tried to stifle a laugh and ended up emitting a sound somewhere between a snort and a chuckle as I bit my lower lip and gazed up at the ceiling—"I have to say there are some large holes in this plan and if we are not changing them things could end badly for all concerned."

Noel turned to Pierre. "I worry. Not just for Cori or the Squadron Leader but for many of the people here at the club."

Pierre nodded. "We are aware, *aussi.*"

I grabbed Noel's hand. "You have a better idea." It wasn't a question. Noel was here to take charge. It was going to be okay. The knot in my stomach unclenched a bit.

Noel squeezed my hand back and stated, "Perhaps. Much like your original idea but with what you call an added twist? I must admit I spend a lot of time dreaming up new ways to escape, should the time come when the Nazis either find proof I am part of a group engaging in rebellious activities or learning my mother to be a Romanian gypsy. There are days I wait to see which sin becomes worse and sends me to Drancy." A twinkle appeared in those mesmerizing dark eyes. "I have become quite creative with escape scenarios."

"Seems I heard the word 'diversion' as you were coming through the door. Anything in mind?" my dad asked, then added, "I simply haven't been here long enough to get the layout of this place and be able to come up with something. So...specifics?"

"Specific, *oui*. Although possibly *vraiment fou*. As Pierre has said, we are theater people. We are in an old theater. They once performed operas and have many original properties stashed away. A theater providing us with equipment to create interesting illusions. Such as ways to stage a fire in the kitchen of this fine establishment which will be more of the greasy thick smoke than flames. I do not want to burn the place down or injure anyone, although if a few Germans officers are singed, I cannot say I would spend much time crying."

My dad brightened. "I can create such illusions. I've designed more than a few sets and included what could be termed special effects using everyday cleaning items. Just show me what's available and I can rustle up a smoky blaze to scare the livin' daylights out of everyone."

"*Bon!*" Pierre clapped his hands.

Noel continued to lay out the plan. "Once the kitchen is in flames—or appears to be—we begin moving out patrons, staff, and performers in the confusion. People at the café will listen to me. I should be able to engage the services of Bauer and his goons to aid in the safe exit of about one hundred people." Noel turned to me. "Your roommates can join us. I can keep them safe and the Boche will not know they're engaged in anything apart from helping others escape a possible inferno."

Pierre was right with him. "*Excellente.* Perhaps we enlist the aid of the roommates by bringing them backstage to help with their friend Cori, who has been doing a second job as dresser at *l'Opéra Blanche*? They are here to accompany her back to the theater for the gala. Once we have made up our Squadron Leader in Cori's clothes, we start up the smoke. All three 'ladies' escape, and then, along with the other performers, everyone goes outside."

Noel smiled. "Mother Nature is with us tonight. She has sent a strange snow ten minutes ago. So even if the guards outside want to stop every running performer or three women escaping a fire, huddled in their coats and ducking their heads in their scarves to avoid icy rain or snowflakes falling, they won't want to be out in the cold any more than we do and they might glance at the papers but not do any sort of thorough check."

"It's brilliant!" I exclaimed. Softly. Noel had shut the door firmly behind him when he entered, but voices can carry and this needed to stay hush-hush.

Papa Pierre suddenly looked worried. "It is a fine plan, Noel, but what about Cori? How does *she* leave?"

I shook my head. "I don't. Not for a while. I'll just hide in the dressing room for the night. I doubt anyone would come back here to look for me once they've seen me leave with my roommates, and no one would imagine I'd be staying in a smoke-filled theater following a fire. Maybe we could send Fiona Belle to help with Delys's quick change for the ballet, and she could come back here later with my papers?"

Then it hit me. "Or…what about Charles?"

"Who?" my dad asked.

"Charles Souverain. One of the other primary members of the Café Violette lovers of freedom." I grinned. "He looks like a thin Santa Claus and has the generosity of the saint as well. He's the band leader and totally trustworthy. Perhaps Charles could accompany the girls and, uh, Squadron Leader Tigger, dressed like me. That would seem natural. After all, he's escorted me home more than once when I performed—and, well, he could then bring my papers back here and tell whatever Germans are around he left in such a hurry he forgot something important. He could give me the papers and I could wait until the Germans have gone before leaving, but hopefully not have to spend the night."

"It's a big risk," my dad stated, frowning. "If Souverain is caught with you here after you've supposedly gone with your roommates, the Germans are going to suspect you're both part of the scheme to help me escape."

"It's *all* a big risk," I replied. "Which about sums up life in Occupied Paris, right? Anyway, unless someone has a better plan, I say let's go with the fire, the impersonation, and Charles Souverain as escort and messenger service. Burn this mother down!" I blushed. "Uh, not literally. Sorry. My less than polite American phrases occasionally slip out when I'm excited or nervous. Blame it on my Great-Uncle Ajay's love of old movies."

Noel bowed. "*Mademoiselle* Cori Christopher, I salute you and your brilliance."

The freckles I'd inherited from my father must have blended with my sudden blush until my entire face was undoubtedly red. "*Merci.* I think. But we might save the salutes until we've managed to pull this off. It's all a crapshoot. Iffy."

Noel shook his head. "It is iffy, as you say, so I am thinking we should be adding one more change to the plan. After I see patrons safely to the exit and perhaps hurry along any identification process to include three young 'ladies' and Fiona Belle and Charles, *I* shall be the one to return to the Café Violette. Not Charles. He will go as planned and help see to the safety of Delys and Paulette. I also need to get the Squadron Leader to the people he originally came to meet and not put Cori's roommates or our band leader or wardrobe mistress into further danger. It will make sense, for any Germans questioning why I return to the theater, for me to explain I wanted to be certain a fire did not break out again. Once here, I sneak backstage and wait with Cori in Donald's or Jacques' dressing room. *Not* in hers."

"Echoing Papa Pierre, *excellente*. Again, *merci*." I smiled at him. Noel. The man I loved. "So, Mr. Matheson, half-American, half-French citizen, with the wild creative blood of a Romany, I assume you're familiar with the story of Chicago and Mrs. O'Leary's cow?"

He winked at me, raised his hand like a band conductor, and we softly sang in unison, *"There'll be a hot time in the old town tonight!"*

Chapter 33

Less than six minutes later I was blinking in awe and admiration at my doppelganger. Papa Pierre and I had transformed Squadron Leader Robin Tigger into a version of me so identical it was spooky. I'd always loved the fact I'd taken after my father in looks—and in diving into dangerous situations—but it never once occurred to me such a strong resemblance could end up saving his life. Or mine. Or a group of people I'd come to call my friends and family.

Delys, Paulette, and Charles had joined us only seconds after the transformation. They now stared in amazement at the "Squadron Leader," unaware they were about to help a phenomenal *Résistance* leader. Or how he and I were related.

"If I hadn't shared rehearsal time, long nights of conversation, and more than one decanter of brandy over these last weeks, I'd swear I was looking right at my flat mate Miss Cori Christopher," Paulette said in amazement. She laughed. "Only our *new* Cori has much bigger feet. Thank heaven for boots and galoshes and falling snow. No one will notice."

Noel critically eyed the metamorphosis of Robin-to-Cori after bringing Paulette and Delys down to the dressing room supposedly to encourage me to hurry it up so they could get to *l'Opéra Blanche* in time to warm up before the late-night show. He took off the fedora he'd clapped back on his head as he left my dressing room, and used it to great effect in a theatrically sweeping bow.

"I literally take my hat off to all of you. With all the deference to the Squadron Leader's masculinity…" Noel chuckled. "You could be twins. As long as no one notices Cori has aged a few years in one night."

My dad grinned and assumed his fake British accent for the benefit of my roommates. "Thanks, mate. If I do make it out, I plan to keep this particular operation a secret from my squadron. I'd receive more than a bit of razzing if they knew I'd spent a night running around France in women's clothing and a great lot of cosmetics."

He stopped. Delys, Paulette, and Charles knew nothing about Tigger's true identity. To them he was a British R.A.F. pilot who'd been shot down and was trying to get home, just like the others we'd helped. They didn't know he was my adored father whom I hadn't seen in ten years. They didn't know if he escaped tonight and made it to his next contact, he'd be meeting with leaders of *Résistance* pockets to discuss ways to help free Parisians from the grip of the Nazis, as well as to plan a big 'to-do' resulting in German soldiers scurrying throughout France while citizens created havoc and made it out of the city. And none of us might ever learn whether whatever scheme he'd cooked up was a success or a failure.

Noel eyed him carefully. "Is your raincoat similar enough to what Cori was wearing earlier so as not to arouse suspicion?"

I answered him. "It is. We made certain. And the dress is the same color and basic style as mine. The shoes work, too. Thankfully, Val left a few pairs and the

Squadron Leader happens to wear Val's size, plus they'll be covered by galoshes. Hopefully, we just need to fool the Germans for a moment," I added. "I mean, in the ice and rain, panicked people scurrying around trying to get as far from a burning building, I really can't imagine the Nazi guards taking more than a second or two to check identification of three girls and a man escorting them who's carrying a trumpet case and nothing more sinister." I paused. "But, Noel, you're the one who might have to really sell this whole thing with your reaction to walking with the fake Cori Christopher."

"He can do it. It is our hope and our prayer we can all of us be playing this charade. Too many lives, they are dependent," came from Papa Pierre. "*Très bon.* The young ladies are now being downstairs for four minutes. It is time for your O'Leary cow to work her magic."

All of us spared a moment of Papa Pierre's hope and the prayer in shared silence, then everyone hugged everyone else as though we might never see one another again. An outcome all too possible and too horrific to contemplate.

Noel crept down the hall, back to the house of the theater. My dad, Delys, and Paulette checked one more time to make certain the papers for "Cori Christopher" were all there, then bundled up in the coats they'd brought when Noel asked them to come downstairs. Charles kept an eye out for anyone who might choose this moment to come wandering backstage.

They'd just started to exit the dressing room toward the backstage exit door to wait for the signal to run, but I grabbed Delys's arm and spun her back around to face me.

Chapter 34

"Cori, is something more being wrong?"

"Delys, you need to flee. Get out of the country. Tonight is the best time to do so."

Delys shot me a look of mixed surprise and fear. "Why now?"

I hesitated for a moment. My dad, Paulette, and Charles rejoined us.

"What's going on? Why aren't we leaving?" asked Paulette.

"Do you all believe in…I guess you'd call them premonitions?"

Delys nodded. "My family is saying for the years there is to be more than one voodoo princess among my ancestry. Many of their beliefs are of more, uh, *outré* than having a gift of seeing what is to come."

I smiled at her. "I like your family. Anyway, you're willing to listen. Well, I get them. Premonitions. My family used to call them Cassandra warnings. We don't have enough time to dive into all this, but I have a very strong sense Delys is in danger if she doesn't escape Paris. Oddly, with one scheme already going to get the Squadron Leader to safety, this could be the perfect time."

Bless my friends. There was no argument, just a question.

"What are we to be doing?" asked Delys.

"After you meet up with Noel, tell him this is the night you need to get out of Paris. It's asking a lot, with everything else and the whole switched identities bit, but he'll be able to steer you to a contact who can get you to safety." I turned to Paulette. "Can you perform Odette/Odile tonight if you have to? You can trust Fiona Belle to help you in any way she can. It could give Delys more time to escape."

She nodded. "Of course, I'll do it, and while my dancing will never be as marvelous as hers, I should be able to copy her style enough to fool Hauptmann and everyone else watching."

My dad added, "There's no need for more than one escape plan, Cori. We'll tell Noel Delys is coming with me. That should simplify the whole process. I'll stay at *l'Opéra Blanche* long enough to establish the presence of Cori Christopher, which could also allow Delys the opportunity to perform, then figure out a way to get us out. I'll keep her safe. I promise."

After hearing my dad's words, Charles Souverain nodded, then gave me an extra hug before following them. "I will send Noel back with your papers in a few hours, *chérie*. Take heart and stay courageous."

"*Merci. Tu, aussi,*" I told him. I watched the quartet slowly walk down the hall, waited to be certain no one else was downstairs, then made my way to hide inside Donald's dressing room, wearing the outfit I'd worn to the café earlier in the evening, which was a close match for the one my dad now had on.

I barely made it inside before I heard the shouts of *"Feu! Feu! Tout le monde dehors! Vite! Vite!"* followed by screams and the sound of crashing tables and chairs. For a brief moment, I felt terror. Was there actually a blaze destroying the kitchen, possibly harming someone on staff? Then I grew calm. Papa Pierre and Noel knew their stuff and my dad had provided great tips on how to make a fake fire seem very scary without the possibility of it turning real.

Pierre employed people who were intensely loyal to him. I refused to accept that William had provided information about activities…not unless he'd been forced to do so through means I'd prefer not to dwell on. At any rate, if Pierre quietly announced to his people at the club he needed their cooperation and wanted them all to leave seconds before a fire was detected, they would oblige without question. He would make certain no one was hurt.

By now Noel would be taking care of the customers, aided, ironically, by Bauer and his men who would efficiently guide everyone outside to safety. I'd noticed several high-ranking German officials in the audience tonight. Bauer would not allow one teensy iota of panic. He was the type of man who needed to prove he was in charge of every situation. Even if he instinctively mistrusted having a fire breaking out and blazing in the one place and on the one night he was certain scurrilous events were in full swing, he now was experiencing the dilemma of a lifetime.

William had been clueless about escape plans for "bigger fish"—namely, about *L'Audace* arriving soon, probably tonight. Bauer knew this, thanks to the still unidentified traitor. A fire was the perfect cover for escape, and Bauer would doubtless be suspicious. Yet General Hauptmann himself was in the audience for his "pre-show with drinks" before he headed over to *l'Opéra Blanche* for the late-night performance of the swans. If the fire proved to be real and Hauptmann's boots were coated with the tiniest bit of ash, it was Bauer's butt on the line. Hence the dilemma: Save his superior or catch a legendary *Résistance* leader without being a hundred percent certain he was anywhere near the club.

We were counting on Bauer to deliver Hauptmann safely to his limo, clean, unburnt, and possibly without a drop of icy rain to mar his pristine leather coat. Once his duty was done, Bauer would take advantage of what he saw as the opportunity to grab *L'Audace* somewhere in the nightclub after the hue-and-cry and sturm-und-drang had subsided and the theater was a soggy mess but no longer blazing. With any luck, *l'Opéra Blanche* would be welcoming a couple of ballerinas, their tall redheaded dresser, a dang short wardrobe mistress, and two escorts.

There was a small window in Donald's dressing room. I rushed over and opened it to keep my nose and lungs near clean air in case the smoke fumes sifted downstairs. I pressed close to the window but didn't stick my head outside. Cori Christopher couldn't afford to be seen inside a smoke-filled building. Cori Christopher was too busy cheerfully exiting with her friends, showing papers to any German officers not engaged in helping patrons leave or putting out the fire. Pierre had said he would stay by the kitchen door to forestall any heroics on the part of those officers to head downstairs.

I could hear the loud, piercing sirens of the Paris fire trucks. The fire brigade was generally efficient, which meant we had very little time before the firemen discovered the greasy smoke was no big threat apart from sore throats and some nausea.

I needed more air and risked poking my head out the window for a second. I saw my friends, joined by Fiona

Belle wearing a trench coat so long it dragged on the ground, and my dad in the guise of fake Cori, all running down the cobblestoned path behind Café Violette. That one small glimpse was enough to lift my spirits.

The ruse must have worked or they would not have been allowed to leave the site. If the Nazis doubted the veracity of their story—they were in a rush to be away from the dense smoke and get to *l'Opéra Blanche* in time to calm down and change into costume—two petite dancers, one band leader, a male singer, a wardrobe mistress, and one female "impersonator" would have been marched back to the building. Or just shot in the street.

There was nothing left to do now but wait. In the dark. I took the opportunity to change into my black cat burglar ensemble, found a moderately comfortable spot on the floor, and stretched out. Scenes of the horrors that could happen paraded through my mind. It was going to be a long night.

Chapter 35

I paced around the dressing room a few times, then thought I'd try and take a short nap, but it didn't happen, thanks to my inner sirens screaming at me to get up and get out. I wasn't in danger from the smoke. This was a warning...a premonition...about something ...*someone*...dangerous. I stood up and stretched for a second, then watched as the door to the dressing room burst open. The man in the doorway wasn't anyone I expected to see, yet his appearance made a sad and complete sense. I'd had a big Cassandra "itch"—the nagging suspicion I'd missed something—for weeks. Now I knew.

My answer came in the sudden recall of the night I'd sung "Johnny Has Gone for a Soldier" when anxious folks on all sides had been waiting backstage. I clearly remembered Major Bauer addressing Monsieur Gaspard Bassett as Gaspard, not as Herr Bassett. Bauer had never been familiar or casual with anyone at Café Violette. It was a tiny slip, so small I hadn't caught it then, just had that itch. I felt sick as I realized which side he was really on. And it was now improvisation time if I were to get through the next moments unharmed.

"Monsieur Gaspard? What are you doing here? We thought you were dead! Or halfway dead or sent to one of the camps. Did they let you go? Did you manage to escape somehow? Thank God you're okay!" I rose, about to fling myself at the emcee with the ready smile and quick wit and hug him until he begged for breath even though the idea disgusted me.

But there was no ready smile lighting up his face. Instead, his handsome features wore a combined expression of disdain and satisfaction.

"*Mademoiselle* Cori. *Quelle surprise.* I had supposed the notorious *L'Audace* to be in one of the dressing rooms, waiting for his chance to flee after the *faux* fire had been extinguished. I did not see him leave with the patrons and performers. Where is he hiding?"

I tilted my chin up. No point in faking anymore. I dropped my attitude of friendliness and responded, "Well, wow. Can I say, you've kind of dumped your charm? And *quelle surprise* on my part, *aussi*. It didn't hit me until now you were the one betraying your friends from Café Violette. Tell me. Was arranging for Teresa's murder also part of some game?"

He frowned at me. "Betraying? Of the rodent Jewish overseer of this club? Or the degenerate slut dancer who overheard me telling Bauer *L'Audace* was to arrive this night? Forcing me to dispose of her and blame her stupid lover, William. There is no betrayal of *my* beliefs. I fully support the German effort to rid our society of the vermin like Pierre and Teresa. And Michel and Val Valentin and their ilk. The Nazis will ensure France comes back to economic vitality and cleans out the garbage, and I will help ensure the Nazis are not, how you say, impeded in the doing."

I couldn't hold back my disgust or my honest confusion. I'd kept my temper as long as I could, but now it was rising because every word he said made me sick. So I spat out, "I don't get it. I really don't."

"What do you not 'get'?"

"You. The Nazis. Anyone who bases their behavior toward other people on race or religion or background. Who hates others for being different. Why in hell does it matter? Is *your* life—is *Bauer's* life—somehow worsened because Papa Pierre is Jewish? Because Val and Michel love each other? Because Teresa enjoyed dating more than one man? Because Delys is black?"

"You are very young, Cori."

"Are you trying to push the whole 'with age comes wisdom' thing? Sounds plausible. But what's wise about a bunch of clowns claiming you're somehow superior and consequently finding it okay to become bigoted killers? And, for argument's sake, assuming I was sick enough to buy into this whole B.S. notion of white guys being somehow superior...more intelligent ...whatever... Again, why should it *matter* about someone else and who they are and how they live their life? I repeat, where's the harm to you?"

Gaspard started to respond, but I was on a rant and not about to stop. "I sort of understand this desire for power. I don't agree with it, but it makes sense certain people are determined to have control. What makes no sense is why their control has to be at the expense of another human being. And while I'm at it, all you supposed Christians out there slaughtering Jews— When did the fifth commandment become disposable? Do you just need a refresher on all ten of the biggies, but most especially 'Thou shalt not kill'?"

I lost control and began screaming, "What in *hell* is wrong with you and the Nazis and the Committee and Delegates and everyone who hates!"

He glared at me. "You are silly, Cori. You ramble

on about things of which you have only a child's understanding."

I closed my eyes for a moment. "I'm young. Yes. Which doesn't make me wrong, and you still haven't answered. Because you *can't*. There is no answer. Just stupidity and hatred." I barreled on. "One thing you *can* respond to—are you the one who actually murdered Teresa Dorleac?"

He paused, then admitted, "*Oui.* I did. Then, as I said, I am being sure William gets the blame. Of course, Bauer and Paquette help with this plan. My, how you say, so-called capture was a ruse to allow me to work with Bauer to ensnare the annoyance of *L'Audace* this night." He paused before continuing. "*Je regrette*, Mademoiselle, you are caught in the middle. Poor American chanteuse so thrilled with parts she plays in resisting what is, um, inevitable. Who will be gone soon. Along with the club. Once I uncover the hiding place of the Englishman, there will be nothing left of Café Violette."

He took a step toward me, which was when I saw the rather large knife he held in his right hand.

"Wait! What do you mean, nothing left of the club?"

"I have used this time of chaos to…what is the word? Place? Plant. *Oui*, I have planted devices around the club to send it tumbling into the earth once they become alive."

"Remote detonator." I stated in a dead monotone. Dead being the operative adjective.

"*Exactement!*" I witnessed the hypocritical travesty of the beautiful smile I'd seen nightly, announcing the appearance of each performer with what had seemed like pride to be a part of this community of artists, as it suddenly flashed in my direction. "But, Cori, you will not feel the blasts. You will be past caring in a moment or two. And I promise, I am swift with the blade. You will not feel pain. I must admit, I did love your singing. It is *triste*—sad—the rest of the world will never hear you."

He took two more steps toward me. My back was against the wall of the dressing room and there was nowhere to run. If I could just reach my bag and find my sheet music I could escape through time, but the bag was behind him. I'd never realized before exactly how tall and muscular the club's emcee was.

But I refused to just stand there like a bunny facing a hawk. I kicked out at the knife, then his shins, then dropped to the floor as I quickly stomped on his foot. He shouted curse words at me in French, then reached down as I made an attempt to scurry on all fours toward the door. Amazingly, I'd managed to knock the knife out of his hand.

I'm tall but, as noted, Gaspard was taller. He was also stronger and definitely meaner. He grabbed my shoulders and forced me back toward the wall, then encircled my neck with his two hands and began to squeeze.

Done for. Kaput. I'd soon be seeing the faces of Teresa and Gabriel and— Would Ajay and Arthur and my mom be waiting for me?

But suddenly a weight fell on me as the hands dropped from my neck. I opened my eyes as I tried to shift Gaspard's body. The face now about six inches from mine was Noel's. He held what was left of a broken lamp in his hand.

"Cori."

"Noel."

"Are you hurt?"

I shook my head. "My throat is bruised and I'm not sure I'll be hitting high notes in the next few days, but I'm okay."

He reached down and pushed Gaspard to the floor, then helped me to stand. He put his arms around me and kissed me. It was a fast kiss, as this was no time for a romantic interlude, but it was enough to convince me I was safe…and I was loved.

"We must leave. I could hear you and Gaspard shouting at each other when I was down the hall. Cori, there are guards outside the window. It is possible they could be hearing, too."

"Is he alive?" I asked.

Noel leaned over Gaspard's body and checked for a pulse. "He is. But he should be unconscious for enough time for us to make our escape."

I nodded. "Noel. We have to get to *l'Opéra Blanche*. Gaspard knew about *L'Audace's* arrival and I guess whatever the original plan was to help get him to the *Résistance* cell. He probably found out about the masquerade and switching identities at the ballet. If I'm right, tonight is also when Delys is to be taken into custody." I paused for a moment as Cassandra warnings began ringing in my head. "Rosemarie. She's in danger, too. Then again, I'll bet a certain wardrobe mistress is taking care of her." Another pause before I asked, "Noel, what happened on your end? Did the girls and my…*L'Audace* get to *l'Opéra Blanche*?"

He flashed a brief smile. "We had a delightful but short trip. *L'Audace* cemented a firm friendship with Charles Souverain. I heard many references to New

Orleans jazz music." The smile dimmed. "But there has been more than one close call tonight. The guard posted at *l'Opéra Blanche* seemed confused about the arrival of so many people from Café Violette and at first was hesitant about allowing us in. Paulette proved herself a persuasive lady and even showed him a few ballet steps to convince him she was the swan. He stared at Delys overly long and Paulette told him she was her dresser. Then he asks why Charles and 'you' and I were there. Charles claims he is subbing for one of the musicians and I say I am a stagehand and you are my assistant. I am only twenty-four, but my heart is racing like a man in his eighties who has seen the angel of death at his door."

"Uh-oh."

"*Oui*. Uh-oh. Fortunately, we did get inside and I retrieved your papers without anyone to see me. But Cori, we have more trouble."

My own heart suddenly was one in rhythm with that of Noel's fictitious elderly man. "As though Gaspard the Murderous Traitor showing up hasn't been enough of a disaster. What else?"

"This guard told us he was on duty until Kessler and Webber were to arrive to guard *l'Opéra Blanche*. Orders of Major Bauer. Bauer is not stupid and he can smell the collusion of forces working against him. Of course, when Bauer remembers Delys is being the swan in the dual role, he will know where to find her. Once Kessler or Webber are at the theater, how can we get *L'Audace* and Delys away to a safe place? They are, in essence, trapped inside the theater now. When I left, Delys was preparing to go on, as she is certain this is the last time she will ever dance."

"Dammit! I knew it. I've felt it all night. Oh, my

God, what time is it? Can we stop any of this from happening?"

"The performance is in forty minutes. Midnight."

My eyes popped open wide. "Wow. I thought it was much later. Okay. Thankfully, *l'Opéra Blanche* is close by. Um, you said got my papers?"

"Yes. Your…father gave them to me before he and the others entered the theater."

"My father?" I asked innocently.

Noel reached into his coat pocket to produce the false IDs, which I then tucked into my bag. "Yes. Your father. Do not bother to pretend. To me it was obvious the instant I saw the two of you together." A wry smile crossed Noel's face. "It will be *très interessant* to see what happens when we arrive at *l'Opéra Blanche* and there are two Mademoiselle Christophers."

I grinned. "That's the only thing I'm *not* concerned about. By now my dad has tossed the Cori dress and wig and found something else to wear. Probably a fluffy white tutu and mask stolen from one of the ballerinas."

"If your papa improvises like his daughter, I would have no doubts he would bring an audience to its feet with applause for a very tall swan."

We smiled at each other. Then Noel said, "We must be quick now. Herr Bauer has been haunting the front doorway and barking orders to his men after the smoke and fire started. We must go the back way into the alley. Gaspard left another goon to guard the exit while he searched for your father."

I shivered. "And found his daughter instead."

"Do not be dwelling on it. Come, we must be on our way."

I donned my boots and threw on my coat, crammed

Ajay's hat on my head, then once more slung my bag over my shoulder. Noel quietly led me into the dark hallway, which remained foggy from the smoke. We could see enough from a street lamp shining through the exit door window to avoid crashing into any tables or chairs or props spilled in haste by performers running to leave the café during the fire.

Chapter 36

Bauer wasn't at the entrance to Café Violette. He was waiting for us at the end of the hall, lounging against the backstage door, smoking a cigarette and enjoying the night air.

"Herr Matheson. And Fräulein Christopher. What a surprise to see you here, especially so soon after you left during the…fire." His tone was as slick as the Paris streets after ice, snow and light rain have turned cobblestone into a dangerous mess. He added, "But why are you in the dark? You could stumble and be hurt."

Noel quickly answered, "Is the electricity back on? I must admit I did not try to find out. I assumed with fire knocking the power out, it would be dark for days and we would have only the moonlight and the street lamps making do as our guide."

Bauer was standing beside a light switch. He flicked it and the hallway became far too bright. "As you can see, the smoke did not damage any of the wiring." He paused. "Neither did the fire, which was so feeble one is amazed it caused so much smoke throughout the kitchen. They are very efficient, these French firefighters, when it comes to dousing a blaze."

I quickly asked if anyone had been injured and tossed in what I hoped was more cause to absolve Noel and me from any skullduggery. "My friends and I were already on our way out to get to *l'Opéra Blanche* when

271

we heard the commotion, and we saw smoke but had to keep going to be on time for tonight's performance."

Bauer smiled. It was incredibly charming, and my body lost circulation and became as cold as the night. "No one was injured here. And how fortuitous you and your friends just happened to be leaving at the same time the fire started."

"Well, they were already set to go to *l'Opéra Blanche* so they could warm up. We were very lucky." I sighed. "But I forgot my bag. And I needed it, which is why I braved the big nasty disaster down near the dressing rooms. Can we get out of here now? I can still smell smoke and it's making me sick."

The three of us had reached the exit door. Bauer politely opened it, and then stepped back to allow Noel and me to go through first. We turned to say good night and found ourselves staring at his right hand and the gun aimed in our direction.

"*Que Diable!*" Noel exclaimed. "What is wrong with you, Bauer? Have you inhaled too much smoke? *Devenir fou*? What is it the Americans say? Flipped your lid?"

"*Major* Bauer, if you please. Had I been so foolish as to inhale some greasy smoke, nothing more than a cough would have resulted." He paused and smiled again. I really did not like seeing this smile, especially after seeing a similar false expression on Gaspard's face only moments ago. My throat tightened.

Bauer continued, "There have been many strange occurrences tonight. Too many involve Fräulein Christopher and Monsieur Matheson to be considered mere coincidence. I would like some answers..." He lifted the gun slightly. "And if it takes the threat of lethal force to get those answers, so be it. Starting with the truth as to why you both returned to Café Violette. Assuming you ever really left. Were you supposed to meet up with someone often described as a 'bold' character?"

Slight digression here: When I was about six years old, first my grandfather, then my dad, and then Ajay taught me techniques of marksmanship. It was part of training for all Ostinato members, or those who'd grow up to be Ostinato members. The group aimed for nonviolence, but there were times it was agreed weapons were needed and necessary. I would learn how to shoot. I'd slaughtered clay plates in a private shooting range up in the Bronx and admittedly had fun hitting the targets.

This was not fun. The targets facing one large weapon weren't inanimate objects. The targets were the man I loved and me. Running was not an option. I couldn't help but hear echoes of the shot that had murdered Pierre's nephew, Gabriel, only two weeks ago. Who would hear those echoes in the next few minutes if Bauer chose to end our lives?

I felt Noel twitch beside me. I sensed he was about to attempt some wild heroic move to disarm the German and turn the tables. Great, if you're a stunt man and the script calls for the bad guy to go down in one punch. Not so great if the other actor hasn't read the script and refuses to cooperate. I had to do something to stop him before anyone got hurt—or worse. We'd been lucky because Gaspard only carried a knife (and his bare hands) and Noel had grabbed the lamp in time to whap Gaspard over the head.

I held my hand up in a pause-it-now gesture. "Wait. Please. Listen. Just ask your questions, Major Bauer. You don't need the gun. We have nothing to hide. It has been a very confusing and frantic night. We're all on edge." I sounded astonishingly calm and reasonable. Inwardly, my pulse was racing, my skin was shifting from cold to feverishly hot, and my churning stomach was grateful I hadn't eaten since the croissant and coffee at yesterday morning's breakfast.

Bauer turned and trained the weapon directly at me for another minute. A minute so frozen in time I could literally hear the snowflakes melting and dripping from the trees in the alley. A minute instilling such fear in me I was certain if it continued another second I'd throw myself to the ground at Bauer's feet and beg for a quick death. I kept thinking, *Noel must be saved. My dad can't be discovered. Delys can't be taken.* And again, *Noel must be saved.*

Finally, a lifetime later, Bauer lowered his gun. It did not find its way to his holster, remaining instead in his hand but by his side. "We will see what intriguing and, no doubt, entertaining responses you would like to share."

He addressed me first. "Fräulein Christopher, supposedly you left the club an hour ago, accompanied by Herr Matheson, two dancers, the band leader Charles, and the very odd wardrobe mistress. Yet here I find you and Herr Matheson, at the *Café Violette* once again. And I ask myself, 'Has something peculiar been happening this night?' Certainly, smoke accompanied by nothing more than a wisp of fire is a strange event, and when more than one strange event occurs on the same night at a café that seems to experience *many* such strange events, I am determined to discover the truth."

Would Bauer spot a lie before one left my lips? Would Noel and I be able to bluff our way out of being killed?

Bauer smiled. "Before you begin to invent stories, I would like to say one word to you. Drancy."

Chapter 37

Noel and I were in sync. No need to look at each other or clasp hands to exchange a silent communication screaming, "We're in trouble!"

Bauer wasn't an idiot. Doubtless he'd been informed by Gaspard—aka collaborator, traitor, and murderer—about all the various activities sponsored by Café Violette, particularly those dealing with arrival times for legendary leaders of the *Résistance*. Their close association probably began the day of the Occupation of Paris when Gaspard made the choice to cozy up to Nazis. Bauer had been unsuccessful in catching *L'Audace*, thanks to Noel's diversionary tactics and the masquerade of the dual Cori Christophers. Bauer had a large ego and larger ambitions. If General Hauptmann discovered his top man in investigations of clandestine activities had allowed a legendary *Résistance* leader to escape and not instigated immediate reprisals against those responsible, Bauer's career was in the toilet and his next assignment would be closer to Siberia than Berlin.

Bauer cleared his throat before stating, "Before we continue, I have to admit you are a...beautiful woman, Fräulein Christopher, and you have a voice to match."

He paused. I was about to say, *Well, thanks. That being said, can you put the big gun away now?* when he continued with, "However, since your arrival as a singer at Café Violette, you have put yourself into situations best described as questionable. You seem to be in the wrong place at the wrong time, and your explanations for your actions range from the dubious to the ludicrous. It is an American expression, but it is apropos—as a 'shining example' of this idiocy, let us return to what has happened tonight. In summary, you leave what appears to be a burning building, you reach *l'Opéra Blanche*, yet barely an hour later I find you here, with Herr Matheson, who also possesses a talent for being discovered where suspicious activities are—what is the ridiculous idiom? 'Afoot'?"

There hadn't really been a question posed during these statements apart from musing about slang words. I stayed silent. It didn't help the situation.

Bauer's tone turned menacing. "Fräulein, exactly why did you come back to Café Violette tonight? What is planned here?" He raised his weapon again without giving me time to answer, then sighed. "I am tired of this. Who is hiding inside?"

Thankfully, Noel had kept his wits about him. "No one." (True.) "Major Bauer, as has been said, Mademoiselle Christopher was accompanying her friends to *l'Opéra Blanche*. There is to be a midnight performance of the *Selections from Swan Lake* and because Cori has been acting as the dresser for the quick costume changes, especially for the ballerina playing the dual role of Odette/Odile, she was needed to continue to help. She brought the wrong bag with her and was not dressed appropriately for her task. She decided to return to Café Violette to don the black sweater and trousers to not be seen behind the stage in the theater when she assists. I accompanied her as a gentleman should do."

I chimed in with, "Stupid of me, really. But this is

the *only* midnight showing Luc Hebert's company has had up to now, and I'd forgotten it was tonight because I was focused on singing a new number and changed into the wrong clothes. I mean, I thought I'd be up in the audience at Café Violette once I finished my set because Donald was going to do his Cole Porter medley and I wanted to see it from the patrons' point of view instead of in the wings." I gestured to my outfit. "As you can see, I was finally able to get into my dressing room and change my clothes, although the fabric is somewhat of a damp mess. It's like, wow, all of Café Violette is just a big puddle, not just my dressing room, and I'm tellin' ya, no one is hiding in there other than a few scared mice. Um, Noel and I really should be getting back to *l'Opéra Blanche* because there's only about twenty minutes before they start the performance and I'm not sure about the lineup of the dances. But I need to be there to make certain the swans turn into perfect princesses with all the feathers on the tutus intact."

I smiled. Bauer did not smile back. Instead, he pointed the gun directly at Noel.

"Enough! My patience is at an end. Again, Fräulein, you have told a silly tale. The truth is Fräulein Christopher never left Café Violette. And you, Herr Matheson, returned to the club to help with the escape of Squadron Leader Robin Tigger of the Royal Air Force, who was unable to get out earlier during the stupid diversional tactics you tried so hard to achieve. I hear there occurred what Americans call a 'glitch' in the communication, a planned glitch on the part of my men, and Tigger arrived at Café Violette at the wrong time. You are going to tell me where the Squadron Leader is now hiding."

I was mesmerized by the gun, but Noel caught what I didn't.

"Exactly *who* are you hearing such imaginative stories from, Major Bauer?" he asked.

At first Bauer said nothing. I could almost read his thoughts. Should he reveal the name of his source of information? As in Gaspard, the man I already knew to have betrayed everyone at Café Violette? The man who now lay unconscious in a dressing room? The man who had known about the original plans made weeks ago for getting Robin Tigger from the chapel to Café Violette and from there to the next *Résistance* cell. Would Bauer buy it if I said his informant had switched sides again and come to the club to tell us what Bauer was up to?

Nah.

We'd gone from trouble to catastrophic doom.

Noel, being braver than I, jumped in with both feet. "Exactly what is it you want?"

Bauer's eyebrows rose. "You are suddenly very direct. *Gut.* I tire of the games. What I want is the current whereabouts of Squadron Leader Robin Tigger. Who answers to the name of *L'Audace* and, it seems clear, is a very close relation to Fräulein Cori Christopher."

Visions of Ajay's body, of Jimmy Pinder's house, of Pierre's face after hearing the shot that murdered his nephew Gabriel, of Gaspard's expression as he prepared to take a knife to my throat…they all merged into one as I stared up into Bauer's blue eyes.

My voice came from somewhere a century away, "What if we have no idea what you're talking about?"

Bauer turned to me. "Then you will find yourself in a small cell facing interrogators who do not share my admiration for your music and will not hesitate to ensure neither of you ever sings a note again. Or I simply end your lives in this moment."

No amount of tap dancing was going to get us out of this situation. And no matter what, we were not giving up my dad's location.

Bauer shook his head. "You seem confused. Perhaps I should tell *you* a story for a change. A story of how, from the moment I met you, Fräulein, I began struggling to recall where I might have seen or heard you. Nothing made sense. Until tonight when I saw someone who appeared to be you leave this theater, only to encounter you here less than an hour later. And, as you Americans say, 'everything clicked into place.' My memory returned."

Chapter 38

It was almost comical. Despite the anxiety and terror of being in a life-or-death situation—Bauer's choice—and staring down the barrel of one nasty-looking weapon, I found myself intrigued. It appeared my dad had run into Bauer at some point in the last ten years here in Europe. And whatever had happened had turned a chance encounter into a Valjean/Javert feud so intense Bauer recognized the face of his enemy even dressed in women's clothes and fleeing from a "burning" nightclub.

Bauer inhaled. "In the year nineteen-thirty-seven I was visiting in Munich and reuniting with friends from the *Hitlerjugend*, which I have heard the English refer to as the Hitler Youth. We were visiting the gallery of Degenerate Art, which the Führer had created to show the German people the depravity of modern painters. I was fascinated by art and considered myself quite an authority on artists. I sadly did not possess enough talent to become a working artist who painted in a classical style, but I studied art history in the university. I paused in front of a disreputable painting I was telling my friends was *Femme aux Bras Croises,* an early work by Pablo Picasso."

Oh, hell. I instinctively knew what was coming. I was right.

"Out of nowhere, a red-haired, bearded man, dressed in a suit, hat, and scarf almost obscuring his features, joins our group. He tells me I am mistaken. This is not *Femme aux Bras Croises* by Picasso but it is called *La Juive* and was painted by Modigliani. An Italian Jew. A Jew making a portrait of another Jew! I knew French. I knew the translation of this portrait to be *The Jewess*. It should have been clearly identified as a Jew painting! I was infuriated, hearing an English man correcting me in front of my companions."

I interjected. "Well, it's an easy mistake. There are art historians who can't tell the difference. I've heard that Modigliani's works have more than once been confused with paintings from Picasso's Blue period. Especially the nudes, which I guess were somewhere else in the degenerate gallery?"

Bauer inhaled sharply, then shouted, "Do not interrupt me!"

I lapsed into silence.

He continued. "As I said, this man corrected me in front of my old comrades-in-arms from *Hitlerjugend*. Then he turned and walked out of the museum before I had a chance to find out who he was. I wished to confront him. And then, fortune favored me. Barely six months later, in Hamburg. I am now a strong member of the *Abwehr*, recruited directly from my university. Along with a troop of *Hitlerjugend* from Hamburg, several members of the *Abwehr* are one night surrounding a club set up for dancing. Nothing but a vile den of American Negro and Jew swing music. We are arresting the people there. And I see this same red-haired man leading a group of young dancers through an exit none of us knew existed. It became a mob scene and they escaped because we were unable to push through in time. They were well organized on the outside. I was told this man is called

L'Audace. But what I saw of his features stayed with me." He turned to me. "The eyes, the nose, the hair. They are yours. I see you always with your stage makeup, which changes features. Tonight, the pieces came together because I had been informed *L'Audace* would be arriving at Café Violette."

My first thought was, *Arresting swing dancers? Come on. Talk about total crap. You guys were beating the hell out of kids who only wanted to listen to American music and dance their dances.* My second thought was, *This has nothing to do with the Third Reich, with Nazi ideals, or obtaining a higher rank by capturing a Résistance leader. This is personal. Bauer felt humiliated by L'Audace and wants payback. At any cost.*

"There is no more use denying you do not know who this man is…or *where* he is. I have no more patience or desire to play stupid games." Bauer shrugged, then flashed a smile. "Perhaps now my greatest satisfaction will be when *L'Audace* learns his actions caused your deaths. He will feel much pain. Oh, yes. I will shoot you, Cori Christopher. I will shoot Noel Matheson in front of you. And I will feel nothing as each of you falls."

I watched, then, as it died. It was quick and it was final. Not a trace, not a wisp remained of the sweet boy from Munich who once loved art and music and medicine and dreamed of bringing beauty into an ugly world.

I tamped down a burning desire to sing "Johnny Has Gone for a Soldier" and forced myself to focus. Was there a chance I could surreptitiously remove the sheet music to "Joshua Fit the Battle of Jericho" from my bag, grab Noel's hand, start singing, and whisk us through time back to 2061 New Manhattan? At least the

Delegates hadn't been on the doorstep of the house at Staff Street when I left, so Noel and I might have some time to strategize how to wriggle out of danger once we arrived. Walking miles to Tarrytown and hiding in bushes or whatever to avoid Delegates sounded almost pleasant compared to dealing with a man harboring a grudge larger than Paris itself. Hitting Jericho assumed I'd grabbed the correct sheet music for the song, but at this point if "The New York Glide" came out, instead, I'd be happy to land in a Manhattan speakeasy circa 1921. Then again, the way things were going, the tune was jazzy and could also lead me to a swing dance venue in Hamburg in the middle of a raid late in 1937, one led by Johann Bauer, and the swinging would be done by wooden bats.

Was it irony or just fate being a bitch? I'd traveled to Paris to save Noel, believing my dad to be dead, and now found myself in a situation where I'd helped save my dad but Noel and I were headed for the next train to hell.

I reached inside my bag and felt around for paper. I'd started to pull the music out when I heard a *Boom!* and the ground around my feet shook as if a 7.2 earthquake had hit this section of Montmartre.

But this was no act of nature. It was Café Violette exploding and sending flames—for real this time—and debris into the night sky.

Chapter 39

Bauer shouted something in German and ran across the street toward the entrance of Café Violette. Perhaps he was hoping the explosion would flush out a certain R.A.F. squadron leader he believed might be hiding inside.

Noel grabbed me by the hand and we took off in the opposite direction. Destination: *l'Opéra Blanche*. We didn't look back. We didn't talk. We ran. We didn't stop until we saw the door leading to the backstage area of the theater. A door guarded by a man wearing a German uniform. The man was holding an even bigger weapon than Bauer had been flashing.

Noel slung me behind a clump of trees and tree stumps lining the front of what had once been a *patisserie* across the street from the theater.

"Down!"

I hit the ground and stayed low. Noel immediately joined me.

"Is it the same guard?" I whispered. "Will he remember you?"

Noel nodded. "Yes. Sergeant Dietrich Manheim. He was here when I arrived earlier with our friends. He checked everyone's papers twice and then let us through into *l'Opéra Blanche*. He saw *L'Audace* dressed in your clothes and stared at each of us. He asked to see my papers again when I left to go back to Café Violette. I told him one of the dancers had forgotten something because we were fleeing the fire. He did not seem to care. He let me go on my way to the club.

I swallowed. "Café Violette. My God, Noel. What happened back there?"

"Something unimaginable and tragic."

"Could our teensy fake fire have suddenly gotten out of control?"

Noel shook his head. "It was never a danger. Impossible for an explosion to happen."

"Okay. So do you think Gaspard regained consciousness and finished placing his bombs…and then just…detonated them?"

"What! He had explosives?"

"Yeah. I guess you didn't hear everything he said. When he and I were having our tense but informative chat before he pulled the knife, he claimed he'd been setting devices. Maybe he figured he didn't have time to continue searching for my dad and he'd just go with blowing up Café Violette in the hopes *L'Audace* might be hiding in another dressing room and it'd be easier to kill rather than capture."

I grabbed Noel's arm. "Oh God! Pierre? Was he inside? We have to go back! We have to see if he's okay!"

"*Non! Non!* It is all right. Pierre was leaving as I was coming into the club to find you. He was on his way to warn our friends in another part of the city and say *L'Audace* would not be able to meet with anyone tonight. Pierre was also angry because he couldn't continue to help your father. Any attempt to contact his friends would put them both in more danger. But Pierre was not inside the club. I promise. Do not worry about him. He will find his way to Spain or Switzerland as soon as he has delivered his message. We agreed it was best for all concerned if he was not seen tonight."

"Do you suppose Gaspard made it out of the club? Or did he choose to blow himself up? He failed in his mission, although he did manage to kill a few people in his quest to present to the Nazis the famed leader of the *Résistance*. Including Teresa."

Noel shook his head. "I may sound heartless, but I cannot forget Gaspard tried to kill you, and I cannot spare concern over his death. We go on, Cori. We must now make certain your father and Delys can find their way to safety. We take the next step."

I took a few deep breaths, trying to calm my mind and erase images of Café Violette burning and of a man we'd all thought to be a friend now lying dead in the ruin of his own making. "I agree. I'm just not sure what the next step is."

Noel stared into my eyes and then smiled. "I am also unsure of steps. What I *do* know is I want...I need to take advantage of this very brief time of a breathing space."

He leaned down and kissed me, tasting of soot and smoke and fierce longing. The first two could be washed away. I knew the last would remain forever.

I could have stayed in his arms the rest of the night...the rest of the war, the rest of my life...but we had an escape to complete, and a rescue as well. Bauer would now be headed for *l'Opéra Blanche* and he was beyond angry. The ante had been upped—another Ajay-ism learned from the game of poker.

I pulled away, shivered, and looked up into Noel's eyes. "Noel?"

He nodded. "*Oui.* You are wise. Sadly, our respite is

over. We must try to get inside the theater before Bauer recovers from the shock of seeing Café Violette blown to bits and realizes the second act of this drama includes not only female impersonators but graceful swans in masks."

"Agree. What do you say to taking a page from *L'Audace*'s book and going bold?"

"What do you have in mind?"

"Can you distract that whatever-the-heck-rank-he-is Manheim long enough for me to sneak in behind him right at the door?"

Noel got it. "Ah. You are to be seen as coming *back* to the outside rather than entering when you were never supposed to have left?"

"Exactly. Total fake-out. Um. Here. Take my bag."

He didn't ask. We didn't waste time. Noel gave me one more quick kiss, then managed to crawl to the corner of the *patisserie* before standing and shouting at the guard in front of the theater.

"*Attendez!*" he called.

The guard immediately turned his direction. "*Was ist los*? What is it?"

Noel, in English, asked him if he'd seen the explosion a few blocks away.

Manheim understood and replied, "Yes," adding he assumed it was the same nightclub seen on fire earlier and perhaps a boiler had ignited and blown the place up?

Noel agreed, then told him he'd been at the club getting what he'd forgotten earlier but fortunately was not inside at the time of the explosion. He told the guard he'd been about a block away and turned as he heard the blast. "Should you go and check on the safety of Major Bauer? I saw him near Café Violette not long before everything went into flames."

The guard joined him for this discussion, but insisted he could not leave his post and Bauer had troops with him near the theater. They would ensure his safety.

This sweet, albeit short, conversation, gave me barely enough time to run to the doorway and open it, then call out to Noel, "Noel! Did you bring the bags? We need the extra lambswool now for the pointe shoes, before the Odette/Odile sequence."

The guard turned. "Who are you?"

"Cori Christopher. You met me earlier, remember?" I assumed my dad had made this soldier's acquaintance on the way into *l'Opéra Blanche*. "I was in a dress when I got here because we left Café Violette so fast. But I changed to black trousers and a sweater so I could help backstage to change costumes." I added a sense of urgency to my tone. "Noel, could you please hurry with the bag? We don't need bleeding toes from our delicate swans."

Manheim looked at me, then grabbed my bag from Noel and opened it. I hadn't lied. I had extra lambswool I'd been carrying around from the days when I'd taken class with the dancers from Luc's company. The guard pulled out sheet music, my papers—thank God Noel had brought them back with him—the lambswool, extra ballet slippers, and a bag filled with stage makeup.

He walked back to the entranceway, handed me the bag, and told me to go. "*Gehen Sie.*"

Then he turned to Noel. "You go as well. I do not want you out here acting as a distraction for my duty. You both stay inside now until the performances are over. No more of this entering and exiting tonight."

We smiled at him, nodded in agreement, then turned and went inside *le Théâtre de l'Opéra Blanche*.

Chapter 40

Early training, courtesy of Ajay and my dad, to explore every inch of a space I'd be in (whenever possible) was about to come in handy. I hurried into *l'Opéra Blanche* without needing to stop to find my way in the dark to the wings where Delys was waiting to make her entrance and Paulette was waiting to become Delys once the dance was over.

A crowd had gathered around Delys. A small crowd but definitely quality as opposed to quantity—Paulette, ready to go on as one of the background dancers, and a dancer about my height oddly dressed as the Mouse King from *The Nutcracker*. I say odd because Luc's program hadn't included any dances from that particular ballet.

Which meant... I tapped him on the shoulder. The Mouse King turned and became Robin Christopher. He hugged me. "Cori. Thank God! Are you all right? Did Noel get your papers to you? We heard an explosion, but no one will tell us anything."

"Noel did bring the papers. Long story, but we had to escape from Café Violette after the traitor who knew about your arrival popped in backstage, tried to kill me, and then blew the place up."

I'd kept my volume at whisper level, but everyone was close enough to hear. The gasps were kept to a minimum. I held up my hand. "More later when there's time. Important thing is we have to find a way to get

Delys and the Squadron Leader out of here as soon as she finishes the dance. Bauer is onto everything, including secret identities. Having the club blow up probably wasn't Bauer's intention, but it actually helps us. Gives us a bit of wiggle room to figure out what we can do."

Another person joined us. Rosemarie Ducote.

"Rosemarie? What are you doing here?"

"I was at home when Fiona Belle arrived and told me to bring a gown to Paulette Reeve for a party." Rosemarie whispered back, "It appears Herr Hauptmann is hosting a gala party at his residence following tonight's performance. Of course, he wants his swan there. There is a car waiting to take her from the theater. I did bring with me a gown, but I am afraid. There are too many things happening tonight, and I am afraid for all of you. I had to stay to see if I can somehow help." She stared at the Mouse King. "I am sorry, but who are you?"

"Oh! Rosemarie, this is my, uh, this is Squadron Leader Rob Tigger." I grinned. "Not normally part of the *Luc Hebert Danse* troupe, but he's taking on many disguises tonight in order to help Delys escape, and…himself as well. Squadron Leader, this is Rosemarie Ducote, who owns the house where my roommates and I live and is very talented at not only being a friend but showing up at the right place and the right time."

Rosemarie smiled at my dad. "If I understand Cori, you have already been in disguises and are ready to continue to help, *non*?"

"*Oui*," was his response. "Whatever is needed." He turned to me. "Cori? What exactly is this about a party?"

"Something I should have mentioned as soon as I got here. Rosemarie is right. General Hauptmann is hosting a big bash at his place. I spotted what must be Hauptmann's car when Noel and I got here. There's a soldier dressed up very prettily as a chauffeur but with Nazi written all over him. He's parked on the other side of the theater. Last I saw, he was lounging on the car door smoking a cigarette."

Paulette held up her hand. "I can go to the party in costume, if it helps. Which leaves Delys at the theater. The guard who greeted us when we first arrived was quite clear she was to be taken to the camps after the show. What are we going to do?"

Silence.

My dad spoke. "It appears, chums, another diversion is called for."

"What?" I asked.

"Nothing solid in mind yet, but ideas are percolating. Cori, the first step is for you and Noel to get to the lighting booth. If you can trust whoever is in charge, we need to plunge the theater into total darkness as soon as Delys finishes her dance. It will be easier to create chaos and confusion if no one can see."

I looked at the Mouse King's head and suddenly laughed. Quietly.

"What?"

"A thought, here. Squadron Leader, perhaps you can make use of your costume to surprise the chauffeur of Hauptmann's car?"

My dad nodded. I could envision the grin hidden behind the goofy mouse head. "Yes. Even a dancing rodent is entitled to some air. And I'm definitely up for a spot of car theft, especially a slick limo belonging to a

German general. But what about the second guard? The one who met us earlier this evening?"

Noel quickly said, "Manheim. I shall take care of him. You must have the time needed to get everyone into the car and away."

"I'll help Noel," I added. "We'll hurry down from the booth as soon as we've arranged the blackout."

The music for Delys's entrance began.

"Cori, Noel, go ahead. We'll get this in motion as soon as the lights go out after our swan performs."

I hugged my dad one more time as the others, apart from Noel, stared, curious about this sudden close connection. "If Noel and I don't have time to get to the car, you go anyway. Understood?"

"Yes." He paused then softly began to sing. I recognized the tune—"House of the Rising Sun" with the original lyrics from the nineteenth century. And I knew my dad's mind, although I hadn't seen him for ten years. This was a clue as to where we could meet up again. I stored it away for later, when hopefully there'd be time to figure it out.

Noel and I quickly moved to the ladder leading to the catwalk and made our way to the lighting booth. We were in luck. The crew member in charge, Jerome, adored Delys and was amenable to dowsing the lights once we told him she was in danger.

We watched from above as Delys went through the movements of the black swan, finishing with perfectly executed *fouettes*. It took no time…it took forever. Out of a series of stellar performances, this was her best. She knew it would also be her last, at least in Paris during this war.

We left Jerome to deal with the lights. He started by

skillfully shifting to a spot as Paulette, in Delys's costume, hurried onstage to bow and gracefully acknowledge the applause. Noel and I headed back down the ladder to the wings, and the instant we reached the floor, we saw Paulette leave the stage.

The theater then plunged into darkness, accompanied by screams and curses from the patrons, who panicked at not being able to see two feet in front of them. We could hear shouts of "Stay seated! There is no danger!" in both German and French.

We reached the exit door and hurried outside. Sergeant Manheim seemed a bit confused about where to go after hearing the noise from inside. There was more light out here, thanks to a full moon, and I watched as Delys, Paulette, and Rosemarie climbed into a limo bearing some kind of fancy German crest. My dad, now with a German helmet covering his head and the German chauffeur's jacket covering the rest of the costume, climbed into the vehicle and started the motor. The stunned driver was on the ground, wearing a mouse head.

But Sergeant Manheim, stationed at the exit door, was seconds away from putting an end to the escape. He'd realized there was mischief afoot, both in and out of the theater, and was ready to do his duty by stopping the group now safely ensconced and ready to leave in General Hauptmann's car. Noel and I reached Manheim just as he was pulling his gun out. Noel executed a tackle I'd only seen on old films of football, and he brought him down. The gun went flying.

I grabbed it and tossed it as far as I could, while Noel smashed his fist into the guard's jaw. He was tough. Still awake and now angry.

Noel hit him again. We heard sirens and spotted

German cars surrounding the theater. Major Bauer jumped out of the lead vehicle and began to run toward the theater, followed by two of his men. He hadn't yet seen us. He was too busy staring at Hauptmann's car with Robin Christopher at the wheel and three women, two in ballet costumes, huddled in the passenger seats.

As I watched the car driving away, I was overcome with such panic my heart seemed squeezed inside my chest. Would I ever see my dad again? At least I knew he was alive in this era. I needed to find Fiona Belle and ask if there was some way to ensure seeing him in whatever timeline I landed in. I also worried about what would happen to my dad, to Rosemarie, to Delys, and Paulette.

I waved at my dad. He waved back, shouting, "Fat Tuesday!"

L'Audace didn't hesitate. He shifted the car into a higher gear, pressed the accelerator, and was gone into the night.

Chapter 41

Noel and I crouched near the conscious but woozy Sergeant Manheim for a second and watched Hauptmann's car disappear down the street at a speed perhaps not quite appropriate for driving guests to a swank party.

We then jumped up, joined hands, and ran toward the *patisserie* where we'd sought shelter less than forty minutes earlier. The shop's broken windows seemed to suggest to passersby they'd be best served by moving on to someplace actually open with products to sell. The inside was filled with cabinets which had once held pastries and breads and now provided a hiding place, albeit for a very short time, before the pursuit continued.

We looked outside and down the street. Bauer had spotted the two guards on the ground, one wearing the head of the Mouse King. Curse words in German flew from his mouth. I didn't ask Noel to translate.

"We did it." Noel hugged me.

"We did." I grinned at him. "My heroes. Both you and my dad."

"Much as I love what you say, we are in horrible danger the more we hide here. Yet where we can go? I wish you could have made it to the car and gone with them. They will make it safely away long before dawn."

"You think I would leave you, now that you're one of the most hunted men in Paris?"

"And you, the most hunted woman." His tone turned grim. "Bauer hates us both. Any ideas about what we do now? We have no car. We cannot go to Rosemarie's. I have been making *Café Violette* my home for weeks now, but because of Gaspard, it is not longer in this existence."

I stayed silent for a long moment. "Do you trust me?"

"With my life. With my love. Yes."

He put his arms around me and we kissed. Danger, for the moment, was forgotten.

Before things escalated, the door to the bakery was flung wide open. Fiona Belle Donovan Winthrop ducked inside. Noel and I broke apart and stared at the short, chubby, aging ballerina garbed in a pink tutu, pink toe shoes, and a tiara encircled with pink stones. Her costume was topped by a sweatshirt bearing the image of the king of rock n' roll holding a guitar and posing atop a stack of vinyl records. She was clearly in a hurry, but not a bit out of breath. Noel and I both took a long moment to absorb the impact of the pink fairy.

She allowed the moment, then stated, "Quit the canoodlin', kids. Save it for a private place later. Now listen. Hell, Hades, and Ifreann are breakin' loose everywhere. Cori, it's time."

"Yeah, yeah. Got it. I was just about to tell Noel." I paused then meekly asked, "What's Ifreann?"

"Celtic hell. Just as bad, but colder and with better music."

There was no response to this. I simply said, "Ah. Got it. Okay. So…uh, do *you* want to explain to Noel?"

"Nope. You need to do it. He's your *one*…your job." She turned to Noel. "What she's afta tellin' ya is unbelievable, but you'd best believe if you're going to escape Paris tonight."

She handed him a flask produced from a belly bag draped around her torso, covered in pink tulle. "It's brandy. Drink it down. It helps with the believin' and the travel. Cori, ya need to do it fast. The troops are multiplyin' in the streets and you'd best be gone soon."

She turned and ran back down the avenue in the direction of what was now the burnt-out shell of Café Violette, her pink tulle flapping in the breeze.

The comic relief of Fiona Belle's presence was cut short by the sound of Bauer yelling something at Kessler and Webber. In German.

I looked at Noel.

The color had drained from his face. "*Mon Dieu!* No! He can't!"

"What? I didn't understand what he said."

"Cori, he is ordering his men to…"

There was no need to finish. We peered out and watched in horror from inside the *patisserie* as Kessler aimed a very large revolver at Sergeant Manheim, and Webber mirrored his actions toward Hauptmann's chauffeur. Two shots, neatly and expertly fired, felled the two young German soldiers. Executed.

Noel whispered, "*C'est le diable.*"

I sank to the floor and stuck my fist into my mouth to keep from screaming before moaning, "It's too much. Ajay and Jimmy and Teresa and Gabriel. Now two Germans—kids, really, who probably had no desire to come to France and become the puppets of men like Bauer. I'm going to be sick."

"No. You are not. You are the bravest woman I have ever met, Cori Christopher, and you must tell me now the story Fiona Belle wants me to hear and we must leave this madness if we can."

He wrapped his arms around me and held me for a long moment. "Please. Tell me."

I swallowed, then motioned toward the flask of brandy Fiona Belle had given him. "Take a swig. You'll need it."

Noel shook his head. "Perhaps. But so do you."

We each took a large sip, then Noel put the flask into his coat pocket. "Cori? Time."

"Time. That's the word, all right." I shook my head. "Not enough, yet too much. But…okay. Noel, you've been puzzled about my sudden appearance at Café Violette and some of the strange references I've made to things you've never heard of, not to mention songs not exactly available on sheet music."

He nodded. "The night I met you when you helped save Sam Seymour. You sang part of a song with odd references to gravity and refusing to be held down. The movie *Casablanca*. And 'DVD' was an oddity you never really explained. Tonight, when you were fighting with Gaspard, I heard mention of Delegates and a Committee, which also made no sense."

Nothing to do but jump and hope. "Take another swig and a big breath. Look, a few months ago I needed to escape a different tyrannical regime. And in the middle of trying to figure out what to do or where to go, I watched a hologram starring my grandmother and Fiona Belle Donovan Winthorp, oops, just make it Donovan…she seems to really have it in for Winthorp, whoever he was. Okay."

Noel grinned. "I am sorry, but what is a hologram?"

"Oh, hell. They haven't been invented yet. Um, like

a movie but projected anywhere in the room, not just on a screen. Not important right now."

"Go on."

"Noel, I…traveled here through time from the year twenty-sixty-one."

Noel started to say something but I held my hand up. "I was part of a *Résistance* group called Ostinato and we were being hunted by a Fascist-style regime called the Committee. They don't have Gestapo or the SS, they have Delegates. I took refuge at my grandparents' old house in what is now called New Manhattan, and while I was there Fiona Belle appeared on this hologram, dressed like a belly dancer in a Bollywood musical, and—this is a tangent, but she was baking cranberry-orange scones. You've tasted them when she's had the ingredients here, but I swear I could smell them coming over the durn screen. Anyway, Fiona Belle told me I had a way out, via time travel, hinting very broadly that here and now in Paris was where I needed to be. So I came, although now I can't see where I've really accomplished much."

Noel, naturally, was stunned.

I tried to smile. "Take another swig of brandy. It helps."

He did. "But how? I don't understand. Fiona Belle? How does this work?"

"Truthfully, I don't understand it either. Is our friend a witch, a catalyst, a guide, a space alien, a goddess, a guardian angel? A classic theatrical *deus ex machina*? Honestly, I decided not to waste time trying to figure out the science, logistics, or miraculous means of transporting through time. Maybe there was a whopping big hallucinogen in the brandy and this is all one big dream. A very realistic dream. Thank you for very realistic kisses! Anyway, I just did what was required to make the travel happen."

"Which was?"

I reached into my bag and brought out sheet music to "Joshua Fit the Battle of Jericho" as I explained, "We have to start singing a few measures of a song on sheet music while envisioning the date and place we want to travel to. I used the song "Toujours" and I thought about March nineteen-forty-one to get to Paris and Café Violette after I heard the recording you and others made." I pointed to the sheets in my hand. "Noel, this music represents my grandparents' home, and I wrote the date on each page. I hadn't really planned to use it to return. I was so stupid. I thought I'd be able to help rescue you and save Café Violette and we'd just take off for England. After that? Not a clue. I'm not kidding about the danger in New Manhattan, but we should be safe on Staff Street long enough to figure out where we need to go from there."

I could see Noel was struggling with all this news, as well he should be, but he was also smart enough to realize, as weird as it was, it helped explain the odd pieces missing from the life of Cori Christopher.

But first he smiled. "You really came to Café Violette because of music?"

"No. I came because of you. I heard your voice and fell in love."

He lapsed into silence, then softly said, "I fell in love with you the moment I saw you backstage at the club the night you arrived. It seems we both have taken the huge leap of faith in our feelings. Even with everything falling apart here, I am glad we found each other."

I gently added, "Noel, we can try and make it to one of the cells Pierre set up here in Paris if you can't wrap your head around the whole time-travel thing. I'd understand. We can hide here until we get the chance to sneak out. Like I said, the world I left is also dangerous, and we'll need to make another trip to another time once we get there, to be sure we're safe. But I need different sheet music to get us to the next place. Anyway, we just have to decide…now."

He nodded. "I hear him, too. Bauer. Shouting our names. This *patisserie* will not hide us much longer." He suddenly flashed a huge grin at me. "As you Americans say, 'What the hell!' Let us do it! We shall travel through time and take what comes at the end of this particular journey and try to find some peace and safety…whenever. As long as we are together."

We each took a last dose of brandy. I handed him one of the sheets of music.

"Oh…it's kind of pointless to say this, but you might not remember much when you hit the future. It took me about three hours before I knew I was Cori Christopher. Although, with luck, Fiona Belle will be waiting for us in New Manhattan and help with the whole transition. If not, supposedly on the second trip there's total recall, so I can explain things to you. Are you ready?"

"*Oui.*"

"Okay. Sing a few measures and concentrate on the date. We're going for the same time I left. March tenth, twenty-sixty-one." I paused. "You're handling this remarkably well. Much calmer and more accepting than I was."

"Ah. Well, it is as Papa Pierre has said when talking

about a diversion for an escape. We are performers in the theater. We trust in the willing suspension of disbelief. If ever there was a time for this suspension, well, tonight seems to be it." He leaned forward and kissed me. "In case we get separated, or worse, this I promise I will remember. I love you, Cori."

Chapter 42

March 2061, New Manhattan

Fiona Belle's assurance the second trip would be easier than the first turned out to be correct. I was back at Jericho, standing in the library and staring at a table where a record album titled *Café Violette* sat beside an ancient turntable. My memory was intact.

The actual *when* of my arrival, as in day and time, was not quite so clear. My first trip through time had started with a firm destination and an iffy date…Paris, Spring,1941. But now in the hurry for us to escape I'd barely considered anything beyond getting away from Bauer and Paris during a rain-and-snow-filled April night in 1941. I'd written March 10, 2061 on the sheet music, but there was nothing in sight in the house to tell me what the actual day was and whether any inquisitive Delegates might come knocking at the door in the next few minutes, hours, or days.

That was the *least* troubling aspect of this journey. I didn't see Noel anywhere in the library. I called out his name but received no answer. This was his first experience traveling through time. He had been trusting and believing me when I told him this was possible and our best way out, and he had somehow gotten lost. Disaster! If his trip had been anything like my arrival in Paris at Café Violette, he wouldn't remember details.

Like his name. Or where exactly he was, especially since this was nothing like the New York City of his childhood.

My bones and my heart were telling me we shared this same time and place. March whatever, 2061, New Manhattan. I just needed to find out what had gone haywire and why he'd ended up somewhere other than the house on Staff Street.

Were we supposed to have held hands or to have harmonized a duet? Fiona Belle hadn't exactly gone into specifics about the ways and means of traveling as a pair. But Noel *had* to be close by. He'd had the music in his hand, and the date. He should have landed right here in the library with me, or at least somewhere in the house. I'd heard him start the song, so I knew he'd been on his way.

Then it hit me. Like a hammer to my heart.

The song.

I glanced down at the sheet of paper I held in my hand and felt as sick as I had upon seeing the two German officers murdered by Major Bauer's two thugs while Noel and I hid behind cabinets and shelves in a French bakery. Stupid, stupid, stupid!

When I'd been in this house on Staff Street the first time, prepping for my journey back home in case things didn't go as planned in 1941, I'd written out the music for "Joshua" on the other side of sheet music for "Wayfaring Stranger." I'd been in such a hurry to get us the hell out of Paris I'd thrust the pages at Noel without bothering to check details. He must have been singing the notes to "Wayfaring Stranger" instead of singing about battles and Jericho. Same date, wrong song, which meant wrong place.

I stood still, frozen with fear. I finally found a computer with the correct date, turned it on and discovered it was only a day later in 2061 than when I'd left. I had a very clear memory of singing "Wayfaring Stranger" in front of Jimmy's Pinder's house, or what was left of it, on Payson Avenue. The house where now sharp-eyed Delegates could, no, make that *would*, be watching for anyone coming to visit Jimmy or take shelter with him, unaware they'd be facing nothing but a shell, crumbling like Café Violette had done when Gaspard destroyed it. This was the spot where rash, sassy, idiotically bold Cori Christopher had opened her big mouth and provided a very nice, clear, clean, pitch-perfect version of Jimmy's favorite song.

Time to leave. I would have enjoyed just one small respite from the horrors of this night, but Noel was in as much danger if he was found wandering around the streets in New Manhattan as we'd both been only moments ago…a century ago…from Bauer.

Time to leave, yes, but for once, I curbed my impulse to go rushing out the door without a plan or a place of refuge. Leaping before looking wasn't going to aid in the rescue of Noel Matheson. I repeat, my organizational skills before the first trip through time had not been what one might call stellar. I'd had zero backup plan, apart from sheet music, to send me on a return trip to March 10, 2061. It was familiar, and therefore seemed easier to deal with than spending an extra hour or two to search out a better place in time to come back to. I admit it. I was nuts enough to assume I'd be staying in 1941, a happy *Résistance* worker freeing French singers from their German occupiers and then settling down with Noel Matheson in Paris once we'd made it through the war.

I sank down in the same chair in the library where I'd sipped brandy and watched the hologram of Granny Aubrey and Fiona Belle. Fiona Belle. The pushy time traveler with the bizarre wardrobe who offered options with no answers.

Or had she?

As noted, there was a computer running. The hologram device was gone (and I didn't care to speculate as to how or where) but the record player with the turntable was also on, its blinking red light signifying power. I was sure I'd turned it off before I went sailing into time. Was it possible Fiona Belle had made a pit stop during her last travels and kindly provided a clue for the future?

I hoisted myself up out of the chair and crossed over to the table. There was a vinyl album I hadn't remembered seeing before at any time: *Ballads: New Orleans Style, with the Charles Souverain Band.* I stared at the cover, which featured a great photo of Charles— the same Charles who, this very night, had helped all of us escape the Nazis. He looked a bit older, although with his white Santa beard, Charles always seemed as ageless as St. Nicholas himself.

I turned the album cover over and glanced through the liner notes. The record had been recorded live at Club LaSalle in January of 1948 in New Orleans. I scanned the songs. Number four on the list was "House of the Rising Sun" but with no info on who was doing the vocals or which of the numerous versions of the song they'd recorded.

I had no idea how Fiona Belle worked her magic or what went into the decision as to who or when to help someone, assuming she was the one making those choices, although I figured another Divine Presence had to be involved, but it appeared she'd snuck into Jericho and left the record album for me to find. My supposition grew stronger when I discovered the sheet music to "Rising Sun…New Orleans" copyright February 10, 1948, neatly placed on the music stand closest to the piano.

I snatched it up, checking to see if any other music, dates, or places had ended up on the backs of the sheets. I scrawled the date February 10, 1948 into the corner of the sheet music, then tucked it into my bag. I risked taking another minute or two to change into a dry outfit almost identical to my well-worn cat burglar apparel. Black sweater and black trousers, but this time I added black boots. Ballet slippers weren't conducive for wandering the streets of either Paris or New Manhattan, and mine were a soggy mess.

Noel. He'd need new clothes as well. He'd be as damp as I, thanks to chasing through Paris in the mix of snow, ice, and rain. Noel was just a bit taller than my dad, and if Robin had left anything behind years ago before he started his own journey to Europe, I should be able to find some things that fit. I began scrounging through the closets in the bedrooms of Jericho.

Again, thanks to luck and/or some nice planning by Fiona Belle, I found black trousers and a black turtleneck sweater, along with a nifty black jacket I recalled Ajay saying he'd worn in a production of *Grease* back when he was in his teens and theater had been thriving in Manhattan. There was a pair of men's boots, black, in the closet and a pair of black socks in one of the drawers in my grandparents' bedroom. I figured as long as the boots weren't tight they'd be a welcome change from Noel's own damp and soot-covered shoes. I tossed in a few extra pairs of heavy socks as well.

I spared one last long moment to take in my surroundings of the refuge of Joshua's Jericho. No matter what happened this night, I knew I wouldn't see it again.

But it wasn't my home. That was yet to be found in an uncertain future.

Chapter 43

I slung my bag over my shoulder and headed out onto Staff Street. A lone street lamp was on, barely illuminating the dark night. Bells rang out from the Church of the Good Shepherd north of me over on Isham Street. The Committee had never bothered to destroy some of the historical churches in the Inwood area. Not worth their time or explosives when there was so much to be "corrected" in Center Town. I was amazingly cheered upon hearing the sound.

The rain had stopped. Either the forecasters had been wrong about how bad Hurricane Thora would get or we were in the middle of a lull, like the one which provided such a false sense of security ten years ago during Hurricane Madison.

I'd left my rain gear at the house. I'd also left Ajay's fedora. For a moment, I considered going back to get the coat and hat—mainly the hat. I didn't care about getting wet, I just wanted to feel Ajay's presence through the fabric. There simply wasn't enough time. I'd already been forced to delay leaving until I was sure I had everything in order for the next trip. Noel needed rescuing. A hat was a hat. I continued my journey toward Payson Avenue.

The church bells had rung once. Which meant it was now one in the morning. I took a deep breath. With luck, all the beastly Delegates would be snugly asleep in their beds with the firm mattresses and clean pillows, getting much needed rest before starting a day hunting down various degenerates such as Cori Christopher and her friends.

I'd planned to use the Empire State Trail to reach Jimmy's house, but stopped just as I reached the corner of Payson Avenue. The whole area was too open and exposed. Thanks to the Committee's determination to grab anyone from Ostinato who might be tempted to pay a visit as a memorial to Jimmy, one in the morning might not be such a deterrent after all. My Cassandra warnings were on high alert. Noel and I were in as much trouble as we'd been, oh, gee, a couple of hours ago, more than a century ago.

I sensed it. Knew it. Betrayal. I'd pushed the feeling away the last time I'd been on Payson Avenue, telling myself I was wrong, but I now had to face it. Jane Warwick had been talking on a banned cell phone while I was singing "Wayfaring Stranger." I'd seen the look on her face when she surmised I'd put the pieces together and realized that she, doubtless with her husband Richard, was the one who'd been informing on all of us. It wouldn't surprise me if she was keeping watch over the ruins in case the overly sentimental Cori came back. So I snuck into Inwood Hill Park and made my way down the block, staying low and behind trees and bushes and what had once been benches.

Then it hit. I could smell the now soggy ashes of what had been Jimmy's house. I felt the same punch to the heart as when I'd seen the destruction months ago…hours ago. I damned the Committee for its ruthless, pointless grab at power. Ironic. Hitler and his boys had gone that route and, while they achieved the goal for a few years and let loose a reign of terror and genocide and admittedly changed the world, once the war was over…they were nothing. Ajay had told me that back when non-Committee-sanctioned schools were operating in Manhattan the Nazis had become almost like a footnote to history. Horrible to read about, but the real horror was it had happened so far back in the past there was no one alive who remembered the Holocaust and World War Two, and consequently the emotion was gone. Which also meant those years the Third Reich ruled Germany and parts of Europe didn't get the kind of attention they deserved. It should have served as a cautionary tale to anyone seeking world domination, but the aftermath was ignored.

Clearly, the Committee had not learned the lesson. They truly believed they were the exception to every power-hungry dictatorial regime to rise and they wouldn't fall spectacularly into dust like all the others. All of them. Killers like Bauer and Kessler and Webber were now dead and forgotten, apart from any access granted to their lives by time-travelers from the future.

All my waxing philosophic while trying not to breathe in too hard had brought me to a clump of bushes about twenty yards away from Jimmy Pinder's house. Where I received another punch in the gut.

I could see him. Noel Matheson. Standing in front of the same bench where Ajay and I had had our last conversation before my great-uncle had gone off to watch the destruction of the Chanson Theater and been murdered. Noel was flanked on one side by Delegates Lang, the nastier of the pair, and Becker, a *bit* less intense, and on the other side by Jane Warwick. Former friend.

I derived no pleasure from identifying Jane as the traitor. Richard, in the business of betrayal as well, wasn't with Jane at the moment. Fine by me. The less enemies to deal with the better.

Jane and Delegate Lang were chatting like old friends, not bothering to lower the volume of their voices. The subject of their conversation was me.

"She'll be here. He was singing 'Wayfaring Stranger' and staring around the street like a lost puppy. When I asked if he was friends with Cori Christopher, he looked relieved. Said yes. Claims he doesn't remember how he got here or his name, but he knows Cori."

"Perfect," said Lang. "We wait. And catch two birds with one stone when she comes to find him. Then march both of them directly to Camp Virtue for some solid interrogation." His cell phone was in his hand and I heard him asking for more Delegates to come to the area. I spotted two more men in black about a block away. They'd probably been hanging out on Payson thanks to Jane's phone call to them following the Cori-led chorus in front of Jimmy's ruined house.

Wow. "Two birds, one stone." Bloody un-original. And bloody scary. My emotions swung from fear to anger to disgust at myself. My haste in fleeing New Manhattan the first time had caused this carelessness in not checking the music properly. I'd put Noel in as much, if not more, peril than he'd faced back in 1941. At least then he knew who he was and was aware of the reality of his situation.

I shook off the self-blame. It wasn't helpful. Action, not reflection, was needed, although I wasn't sure what would be the best action to take to save Noel from being hauled off by the Delegates, thrown into prison, and tortured for information he would never be able to provide.

Chapter 44

Typically, I needed a diversion. The last one, executed about three hours earlier in Paris outside *l'Opéra Blanche*, had featured a *Résistance* leader wearing a Mouse King head, which had surprised a German soldier long enough to allow my dad, Delys, Paulette, and Rosemarie to escape, although I was clueless as to where. But I couldn't worry about them now.

Diversion. There wasn't exactly a closetful of clothes hidden in the bushes in Inwood Hill Park, so switching identities was out. There'd also been a fake-out with a fake fire before the identity switch with my dad, but how I could manage to start one, with only a pack of Noel's cigarettes and a book of matches in my bag, would be difficult, given everything in the area was soaked by the rain.

I silently sent up a prayer for a clue, an idea, a plan. And suddenly my prayers were answered, because I got one. Admittedly, not one I was expecting.

Down the street, close to where I'd entered the park from Empire State Trail, a plump, aging, fierce Irish gamin wearing a costumed medieval suit of armor was taking a page from the Cori Christopher Book of Brash Behavior and belting out the chorus of the opening number from the musical *Man of La Mancha.*

Lights began flashing on from inside apartments the

entire length of Payson Avenue. Residents were rushing outside to see what was causing the one a.m. disturbance. Most were applauding, which made me smile, at least for a brief moment.

Lang and Becker both immediately turned and headed down the street. Jane stared at the madwoman in armor but stayed where she was. I didn't hesitate. I vaulted over a bench, ran to Noel's side, and demanded, with urgency, "Time to go!"

Jane's jaw dropped. She appeared a bit stunned. Whether over Fiona Belle's incredible attire, her less than melodic rendition of a song from an award-winning Broadway musical, my spectacular leap over a bench, or the fact I was risking capture by arriving on the scene, I honestly didn't care.

I faced her, spat out, "Traitor!" then hauled off and landed a fabulous—and gratifying—punch on her open jaw. She dropped like Lang's proverbial stone. Knockout by Cori Christopher in one.

Noel grabbed my hands. "Cori? *Mon Dieu!* I do not know where I am! And I do not know *who* I am!"

At least he knew who *I* was. The whole recall thing following a time trip was weird in who remembered what and for how long. I pulled at him. "We need to go. Yes, it's me, and I'll explain once we get to someplace safe, but for now, *run.*"

We ducked back into the trees lining Payson Avenue. I heard shouting from Lang, who'd made it back to the bench and found Jane stretched out beneath it. Lang, being smart as well as nasty, ordered Becker and another black-clad Delegate to follow him and plunged into the park. I could hear one or both on their cell phones calling for their fellow hunters to join them in catching their easy prey.

I had a destination in mind, if only we could reach it before Lang caught up with us. Fiona Belle had provided more than a brief diversion. She had given me a clue based on the clunky suit of armor. I had to admire her ability to come up with hints I could easily understand.

We ran. Feeling my bag bump against my back and hip was a bit of a nuisance, but I'd deal with bruises if we made it to safety. I couldn't lose it. The sheet music inside was our only way out.

For several minutes, Noel didn't speak, but as we dared to leave the park, headed for the ruins of what had once been a storage facility just off the Empire State Trail, he asked, "Where are we going?"

"The Cloisters."

"Ah! I have heard of this. A medieval museum, *non*?"

"*Oui*. With many places for us hide until I can explain some things to you and we can get away from goons and killers for more than five minutes."

Once we hit the storage facility just off the Empire State Trail, I seriously considered just ducking inside one of the lockers and pulling out the music and getting on with the next leg of the journey. Then I heard Lang yell something about "storage" and knew there wasn't time to sneak inside, grab sheet music, and get Noel to sing along, focusing on New Orleans, circa 1948. Lang was simply too close.

We ran to the back of the warehouse and then spent a few minutes weaving around ancient dumpsters in vacant lots. I blessed the Mormon community who'd long ago built a church not far from a long-abandoned playground. An outsized billboard announcing services had withstood the elements for years and served as a brief place to hide behind. Unfortunately, the street lamps were also intact. They beamed brightly down on us, and I heard Lang shout, "I see them!" as we darted out across the lawn of the church. His shout was accompanied by what sounded like a gun being fired. Great. Open season on Cori and Noel.

We didn't waste time turning around to see how close Lang and Becker were behind us. We sprinted around bushes and benches and various debris. And five minutes later, we were in one of the botanical gardens around the exterior of The Cloisters. Ajay had once told me they were the most incredibly beautiful, superbly kept gardens up until the Committee decided all of Upper Manhattan was a waste of space, so what Noel and I now entered resembled a jungle. But it also made for excellent cover as we hunted for whatever entrance to the actual museum was closest and open.

Chapter 45

The Cloisters officially closed its doors the year I was born, 2041, along with all the theaters, opera houses, every building making up Lincoln Center, the Metropolitan Museum, The Museum of Natural History …the list goes on. If there was a place that provided culture and made people think or feel something other than blind obedience, it was banned by the Committee.

But bans weren't for the Christophers, Colliers, and Kapoors. The entire family was all in favor of culture, thinking, and feeling. Consequently, I haunted The Cloisters before the age of ten, visiting whenever my dad, Ajay with or without Arthur, or granddad Yash was in the mood for peace, quiet, and a glimpse into what the world might have been like many centuries ago.

For some reason, the only females in my family (my mom Celeste and Granny Aubrey) weren't as enamored with The Cloisters and instead kept sneaking me into the old Apollo Theater in Harlem. Granny Aubrey once told me The Cloisters had beautiful things but seeing sarcophagi and statues of dogs looking more like dragons gave her the creeps. I wasn't sure I bought this excuse. What was undeniable was that Aubrey loved the Apollo because of the memories of seeing some awesome musical performances after the theater was restored in the 1980s, and she was determined to share those with me in hopes I could experience a portion of what had touched her heart and soul forty-odd years earlier. Celeste was more prosaic. She found The Cloisters to be too bloody cold and wanted to hang out in places with better heating.

But, admittedly, as usual I digress. Noel and I were in the Cloisters Museum, and much as I'd have loved giving Noel a tour, we needed to head for the nearest area that would keep Delegates from finding us long enough for me to try and explain what had happened over the last few hours. And once Noel recovered from hearing he'd traveled over a hundred years into the future, I would have to hit him with the second whammy—we were about to travel *back* into the past again, although to an era and a place safe for us both. Heck, my own brain was spinning from all this traveling, and I actually was aware of the what, why, where, and how—well, in a general way—and, of course…the when.

Another, smaller, digression here but important for the narrative: Most of the paintings and sculptures and small items such as chess pieces and board games and manuscripts had been taken by the Committee not long after they'd come to power. They didn't want to deal with the upkeep of this museum, but the greedy bastards knew the value of its offerings and had no intention of letting them rot. They'd taken the unicorn tapestries and most of the armor and removed the stained-glass windows.

I quickly took Noel into the chapel, hoping we could hide in the archway. My eyes stung with tears, seeing the empty space where the painted, wooden hanging statue of Jesus on the Cross used to be. I hoped the Committee had at least seen the value in the art of the piece, given what the work represented was distasteful to their no-religion philosophy, apart from everyone having the Morality One frame of mind, with morality being defined by a few men in the Committee who, for example, considered being born anything but white to be immoral. I'm sure being born female wasn't high on the Morality List either, but they did recognize the importance of women in terms of providing those white males with the next generation.

Sadly, there wasn't a great place to take shelter anywhere in the chapel itself. Everything was too open. And for comic relief, I had to push down the desire to sing a few bars of the cheery "Once in a Blue Moon" under the archway—the acoustics were much better there than they'd been at Café Violette.

"Late Gothic," I muttered.

"What?"

"Sorry. Musing aloud. Thinking we might have a chance in the Late Gothic Gallery. I'm hoping some of the stands and cabinets that held artwork are still there and could provide a place for us to take a breather and better, keep us safe long enough to get to where we're ultimately headed."

"Which is where?"

"Oh, boy. Memory not returned, right?"

"Bits and pieces."

We hurried through the rooms that had once held the tapestries and down the hall into the Late Gothic Gallery.

To my complete astonishment and delight, on many levels, I discovered the Committee had left the Merode Altarpiece intact and in place. It's a truly inspirational piece, made up of three panels, done in oil over oak. One panel depicts the patrons who commissioned the work sometime in the fifteenth century, the right panel shows

Joseph, father of Jesus, with carpentry tools, and the middle panel, the largest of the three, represents the Annunciation to Mary of the coming birth of Jesus. I felt I'd been given another sign all would ultimately work out when I remembered the name of the angel who'd delivered the message—Gabriel. The same name as the thirteen-year-old nephew of Pierre Simon who'd given his life for someone else to be free.

This was it. My Cassandra visions were telling me this was our jumping-off place. Now I had to explain to Noel (again) that we had no choice but to time travel, which meant belting out a certain song and focusing on time and place while staring at sheet music.

I sank down to the floor in front of the Merode Altarpiece and motioned for Noel to join me. He did.

"What do you remember?"

"You." He smiled. "It is impossible to forget my only love. I knew you would find me. I remember this is New York because we are in the Cloisters Museum and I visited here once when I was a child. But other things? Such as how I arrived in New York?" He shook his head. "I have blanks in my memory, although I do recall trying to run from someone and ending up in a *patisserie* in Paris, which seems like a stupid place to be hiding. I remember holding you and staring at sheet music and singing and then suddenly I was sitting on a bench in front of a ruined house."

I grinned at him. "I'm amazed. You're *almost* up to speed."

"Well, clearly I experienced something traumatic. Um. Cori? Before we try to regain my memory, who am I?"

"Noel. Noel Matheson. Cabaret singer, member of

323

the French *Résistance*, all around amazing person, and the love of my life."

He exhaled with relief. "*Oui!* Thank you for the name and the, uh, character traits. It has been bothersome not having a name. The last thing I have the clear recall was holding you and being afraid we were going to be caught by someone named Bauer. We were in Paris. It was raining."

He glanced at his damp clothes. "This is obvious to me." He groaned. "Why do I not remember anything else?"

"It'll come back. I promise. Unfortunately, we don't have a lot of time to wait for your memories all to return, or for me to provide a lot of explanations. We need to escape again, like in the next few minutes, tops. What happened when you were back on the bench before I arrived?"

"I was singing 'Wayfaring Stranger.' " He smiled. "I love this song, although we did not sing it at the Café Violette, since it is not a jazz piece." He stopped. "Café Violette. I am visualizing the place. This is good. It is very familiar."

"We'll get to it. Go on with what happened at the bench."

"A man and a woman saw me. Or perhaps they heard me singing? Either way they came over and asked me who I was. I said I did not remember, and then they asked why I sing this song. I said I was not sure, but I had been given the sheet music and told to start singing."

"You told them Cori Christopher gave you the music?"

"I did. And they told me to wait at the bench and they would help find you. The woman said she is sure you are coming back soon to help me because I obviously had some memory loss. They left, but in a few minutes the woman returned with another man. And then there was madness, with a short woman wearing what appeared to be a suit of armor and singing down the street. I saw you and you punched the woman who had spoken to me at the bench…and here we are."

"Nice. Your most recent memories are spot on."

"Who was the woman who said she would help me? Why did you hit her?" Noel asked.

"She was a traitor. The same way Gaspard was at Café Violette. I am so stinking sick of traitors. Oh, sorry. I know that means nothing to you."

He brightened. "No! It *does*. Café Violette. I sang there. I met you in the club the night a pilot came to escape." He inhaled. "Cori, it is coming back. All of it. Including the *fou* story you have been telling me of travel through time."

"And I hate to tell you, because I bet you'd like to just sit back and do a rehash of your life, but we have to go again. But you should remember everything at the end of this next trip."

There are many reasons I love Noel Matheson. One of them is his willingness to jump in and do whatever is needed at the moment, even if it's cuckoo and he's just been through one bizarre experience. He nodded. "I am ready. Give me music and a date and a place."

I pulled music out of my bag and handed one sheet to Noel. "Focus on February 10, New Orleans, nineteen-forty-eight. You sight-sing, so we should be fine. I just hope this is what my dad was trying to tell me. If not, well, New Orleans in the late forties is a lot safer than New Manhattan in the present."

We held hands—I wasn't taking the chance of losing him again—and shivered, hearing the stomps and shouts of Delegates barreling through the museum trying to find us. We sang. I couldn't help noticing the acoustics in the Late Gothic Gallery compared quite favorably to those in the chapel. I couldn't help grinning, convinced the angel Gabriel depicted in the Merode piece was smiling…at both of us.

Chapter 46

February 10, 1948, New Orleans

The sign over the doorway read:
Club LaSalle
Established 1933
Noel and I had arrived in the middle of some kind of wild celebration. People in masks and costumes were roaming the streets singing and dancing and shouting. Many appeared to be inebriated. I wished I'd thought to tuck a bottle of brandy from Jericho into my bag, but it probably wouldn't have survived the race to The Cloisters.

We stayed in the shelter of the doorway of Club LaSalle for a few minutes and watched the revelers while we attempted to get our bearings. There were pirates, fairies, witches, skeletons, clowns, and a couple of Vikings, dressed in armor similar to what I'd last seen gracing the body of Fiona Belle Donovan, but with giant horns on their heads. Everyone who passed by waved at us and hollered, "Join us!"

I glanced at Noel and at our matching black ensembles. "We're under dressed."

He grinned. "If anyone asks what we are costumed in for this carnival, we can tell them we are portraying stagehands who are also travelers through time."

"They're probably too drunk to notice. You'll be

happy to hear I did bring a change of clothes for us both. Stuffed black sweaters and trousers into my bag. Same look and style, but dry and clean. Now we just need to find a place to change, although it's obvious no one cares what anyone else is wearing."

Noel pointed to the Vikings, who were doing a rather nice jitterbug as one of the marching bands played "When the Saints Go Marching In." "Talk of costumes…I hope Fiona Belle is safe. I feel badly we had to leave her, as she helped us escape."

"I do too, although she's the one person who always comes through anything and everything unscathed," I responded. "I wouldn't put it past her to have stayed on Payson Avenue, having a lovely time entertaining all the neighbors with the entire score of *Man of La Mancha*."

"Of what?"

"Ah. *Man of La Mancha*. Broadway musical. Inspired by the book *Don Quixote* by Miguel Cervantes. Takes place in a dungeon. Gorgeous music. My great-uncle, Ajay, got to play Quixote's sidekick, Sancho, back in New York City before theater got banned. He taught me the entire score. It was all I could do not to join Fiona Belle and take Sancho's part back there. I'm not sure how much you got to hear when she was singing, but the music is awesome. The musical came out in the mid-nineteen-sixties, so we might actually get to see it in about seventeen years or so."

Noel shot me a look of amusement. "Much as I would love to hear this, I am glad you did *not* sing. We could have ended up with both of us in a different dungeon, if my memory is correct with what you told me about these Delegates and Committees back in Paris. Popular music is not allowed, *non*?"

I sighed with relief. "You *do* remember everything. And yes, if we hadn't managed to escape, we'd be in one ungodly place called Camp Virtue by now, and those jerks hate music as much as they hate anyone who is less than thrilled with a government ruled by force and tyranny." I paused. "We could have also ended up dead." I shuddered.

"Cori, this is amazing. Not only do I remember how we escaped those men in New York moments ago but how we escaped from Bauer and his pigs in Paris. The best is I recall both of *our* names and I love you very much." He leaned down and kissed me. I didn't mind the grime at all. "So, Mademoiselle Christopher, what do we do now? You have taken this time journey twice…"

I interrupted him. "Actually, it's been three times. First to Paris, where I blessedly got to meet you, then back to New York, which, in the time we were there a few hours ago but also when I was growing up, was called New Manhattan. I'm sure it will be New York again. Just not in my lifetime. Or the lifetime I had. Although if I'm right and we've landed in nineteen-forty-eight, New York is still New York. Wow. Sorry. If all that doesn't give you a headache, nothing will."

Noel started laughing. "It is very confusing."

"Oh, yeah. Anyway, the third and hopefully last trip is the one we just took to get here to New Orleans. This is the first time and place where I've felt safe upon arriving from another era. But we do need to find someplace to rest, preferably away from all these crowds, and to figure out what comes next. Not to mention getting some food. I'm hungry, and I imagine you are too."

Noel glanced down at the sheet music he held in his

hand. "Hmm… Do you suppose we might be able to locate Charles Souverain somewhere here in the city? He would help us. And we know he is safe because he is pictured on the sheet music we used." He thought for a moment before adding, "It is seven years since we saw him in Paris, yes? But for us it has only been one night. Which, as I have said before, is very confusing."

I shook my head. "Don't bother trying to make sense of any of this. It doesn't help. I decided to ignore anything logical about time travel if I wanted to maintain my sanity. That was about two minutes after I realized I'd zapped into a whole different century. And, yes! Brilliant thought—track down Charles. He played at Club LaSalle. He did a record album there. Someone inside might have an idea where to find him."

Our hopes were squelched when we discovered the doors to Club LaSalle were locked. I glanced up at Noel. "At least we're dry. A big plus. And the people here, while wearing freaky costumes, seem friendly. Bigger plus. Nobody will be hauling us off to a jail, or a prison camp, or worse."

Noel grinned. "And whatever is happening here, the music is delightful. We are hearing from all the different bands marching down the street." He paused as a parade float came into sight. "Cori, of course—it is Mardi Gras here! Finally, something that makes sense."

"Fat Tuesday. Of course. That's what my dad shouted as he drove away. This is great! I've never had the chance to experience a Mardi Gras celebration," I replied. "I'm excited to see all the floats and bands and people, although I really am getting faint from hunger, and we need to find somewhere to just rest for a while and figure out what's next."

Noel laughed. "What is coming next is Charles." He pointed to our friend, who was dressed in black trousers and a white shirt with a fancy red vest over the shirt and wearing a funny-looking bowler hat. He was playing trumpet and marching along with four other musicians, all similarly dressed. Everyone appeared surprisingly sober.

As his band came closer, Charles lowered the trumpet, and that's when he spotted us. He immediately left the parade and joined us in the nightclub's doorway. The logistics were a bit tricky, what with giant carryall bags and a trumpet, but within seconds I was being hugged and hugged again. Charles then turned to Noel for another round of hugs.

"A miracle! This is indeed a miracle. Seven years with no word as to whether the two of you survived the night Café Violette was destroyed, and here you are, alive, well, looking remarkably the same. I am so happy to see you!" Charles exclaimed. "How did you come to be here?"

"It is so totally wonderful seeing you, too," I responded. "I was thrilled to discover you were in New Orleans, and when Noel and I were trying to track people down and saw your band was working here, well, it made a huge impact on our decision to come. We never got the chance to thank you for helping us. You were a huge reason we were able to escape."

"But how did you manage to get away from Bauer?" Charles asked.

Noel and I exchanged glances. I hadn't thought through an explanation either for Paris or getting to New Orleans, and the last time I'd been in this situation my lies had been lousy.

Charles caught the looks. "Never mind. Many, many of us who left France and made it to America have stories we can't share. And it doesn't matter. You're here. Can you at least tell me when you arrived?"

Noel smiled at him. "Just now. Literally."

"Charles!" A clarinet player yelled at our friend from his spot marking time marching with the parade-goers. "Come on!"

Charles waved at him, then turned back to us. "Where are you staying?"

I shrugged. "No idea. We're kind of lost. And hungry. Any suggestions you can give us in two seconds before you join your band again?"

"If you'll follow the band and the parade for a few blocks, I'll signal when you should split off from the crowd, which will be on Freret Street. Once there, you'll find the right place. I'll meet up with you later. I guarantee you'll be pleasantly surprised."

Chapter 47

We followed Charles and his band for a few blocks as they marched down streets with names like Calliope and St. Peter's and St. Charles Street. We were having a fabulous time, singing and dancing alongside other parade-goers, although hunger was starting to be an overriding concern.

Finally, as we passed a street with the unusual name of Freret, Charles lowered his trumpet for a moment, used it to point to the right, and shouted, "Halfway down," then raised the instrument to his lips and began another round of the spiritual "Rock My Soul" but with a distinctly New Orleans-style jazz tempo.

Noel and I broke away from the celebration and headed down Freret, looking right and left for any indication of a café or nightclub. It didn't take long.

I grabbed Noel's arm. "Look."

I pointed to a large building resembling a typical French café, with the sidewalk tables and checkered cloths. There was a poster on the window: *Join Us for Mardi Gras Night with Charles Souverain and his Regal Five!* Above the entrance to the café was a brightly lit sign with the logo of an angel blowing a trumpet. The sign read *Gabriel's Horn.*

Noel nodded at my unspoken question. "*Oui.* This is it. I am certain."

His certainty was rewarded when the door to the

club was opened by a smiling Rosemarie Ducote. We stood in silence, stunned, until she waved and shouted, "Cori! Noel! Come in! Come in!"

I ran to her side and hugged her and cried and hugged her again. Noel waited his turn, then continued the hugs—without as many tears, although his eyes appeared suspiciously moist. The three of us entered the club. It was like being back at Café Violette, with its tiered tables and the large stage promising patrons that, within minutes, great entertainment would be one's reward for stepping through the doorway.

Rosemarie motioned for us to sit, and we sank onto chairs around a medium-sized table, close to the stage…and the kitchen. I could smell what might be some kind of spicy soup, but I forced myself to ignore the hunger and get to the question and answers.

"Rosemarie. Wow! I thought I'd never see you again. This is amazing and fantastic. When did you leave France? What are you doing here?" I hesitated but had to ask, "Do you know what happened to Squadron Leader Robin Tigger? And Delys? Did you all get away the night of the ballet gala? I guess you must have, because you're here. Noel and I kind of had to leave in a hurry after Bauer turned into a lunatic, shooting people, including his own soldiers."

A hint of a smile crossed her features. "You did more than simply leave, Cori."

I swallowed. "What?"

The hint turned into a huge grin. "You had help from a certain wardrobe mistress, n'est-ce pas?"

Not really a question. I just wasn't sure how much she knew about that kind of help, and I couldn't ask.

"I, uh, how…yeah, Fiona Belle created more than

one diversion."

"One of her specialties. But much later she sailed on the ship to America with us. She did not say much, but she did mention mysterious forces were at work in the universe and not to be surprised if we ran into Cori Christopher in the future, and to be less surprised if Cori Christopher hadn't aged a single day. Or anyone who might be with her." She winked at Noel. "She also hinted New Orleans would be a wonderful place to start life again for more than one person who had been at Café Violette or *l'Opéra Blanche*."

I didn't ask what secrets Fiona Belle had revealed regarding time travel, but it appeared she'd done some major bending and stretching of rules by materializing onboard a ship somewhere crossing the Atlantic Ocean, just to have a chat.

"When did you come to live in New Orleans?" I asked.

"A few weeks after the ship arrived in Galveston. That was in nineteen-forty-five. There was a lot of paperwork, but I hear it was easier than Ellis Island, which was rumored to be *très fou*. Many, many refugees. I knew I had to be here in this beautiful Crescent City. Papa Pierre and Charles Souverain often talked about it, and Delys's mother had lived here for years. It was home before I ever stepped foot onto Bourbon Street. I love it. It is a city unlike any other."

"There *is* a special feeling. We noticed it immediately."

Rosemarie motioned for Noel and me to sit at one of the tables close to the stage. "There is much more to tell, Cori."

I tensed. "Good or bad?"

"Ah. Both. But mainly good. Let me start with the bad and get through it. Papa Pierre's nieces, who were captured when Gabriel was murdered…they did not survive the camps."

"I am so sorry," I said, closing my eyes for a moment and sending up a prayer for all those lost. "It's just so horrible, so senseless, so…"

"Evil," Noel finished for me.

Rosemarie nodded. "Of this I agree. There are other bad things, but blessedly they are not so tragic. After all, a building is only a building. But Café Violette, the real building, burned to the ground the night everyone was escaping."

Noel and I exchanged glances.

Rosemarie was quick to notice. "You knew this?"

"We saw it happen," Noel told her. "Gaspard, who was the one who betrayed everyone at the club, set the devices and blew it up. We never learned if he was inside or not. He was determined to kill Squadron Leader, uh, Tigger, if he couldn't help capture him. He must have assumed Papa Pierre was in the club and could be easily captured. Pierre was next on the list of people the Nazis were rounding up to send to Drancy or, very possibly, to Auschwitz."

Rosemarie nodded. "This makes sense, yes. We honestly had not heard the result of what happened, apart from the club being destroyed."

"But go on," I urged her. "First, did Papa Pierre make it out of Paris that night? We saw him outside the club, but not after we headed to the opera house. And clearly *you* escaped, but what about the Squadron Leader and Delys and Paulette? What happened after you all went tearing off in Hauptmann's limo?"

Rosemarie smiled. "There are many stories. But would you like to hear them from a better source?" She turned and called out to someone in the kitchen, "Bring gumbo for two tired refugees!"

"What? Who?"

The doors leading from the kitchen to the house were flung open. In strode Robin Christopher, followed by Papa Pierre Simon. Fortunately, they'd ignored the suggestion to bring gumbo, because my actions quickly became a repeat of the reunion moments ago with Rosemarie—lots of hugging and crying and hugging again.

"How did you—? What—? Where—? And how did—?" I was so excited I kept interrupting myself.

My dad grinned at me. "All shall be revealed. Sit. You'll enjoy this particular tale."

Before he had a chance to say anything else, Rosemarie interrupted. "I have lived this story, so I will go get more food. But, first, I must be telling you of wonderful news I have just received." She held out her hand and for the first time I realized she was holding a letter—crumpled now from all the hugging, but intact.

"Who's it from?"

"Paulette. Who proved herself to be a true friend and very brave."

"I worried about her so much," I said. "Heck, I just worried about all of you. I had no idea whether you'd make it out of Paris, which was maddening and frustrating. But Paulette is okay? Where is she?"

"Paulette is in England. And a blessing…her fiancé from the Royal Air Force survived the war. They have been married several years. And this letter says she is going to have a baby."

"I am so, so very happy!" I exclaimed.

Rosemarie lifted the letter. "Her first baby is now about two years old. They name him Luc after Monsieur Hebert. But Paulette tells me if the new baby is a girl, she is naming her Cori."

Tears again welled in my eyes. "This is the best news ever."

Rosemarie smiled. "We shall drink a toast to Paulette. Wait and let me get glasses and champagne. And of course, the gumbo and sourdough bread."

Noel started to rise. "Let me help you carry everything."

Rosemarie put her hand up. "*Non, non.* There is no need. You are anxious to hear how we all escaped, so stay and listen." She rose and headed toward the kitchen. "I will call out if I need help bringing your food...and the champagne."

Chapter 48

I looked at my dad and at Pierre. I was in shock and so happy. My head was spinning, and it wasn't only from shifting my gaze from one man to the other. "All right, gentlemen, what's the story?"

Robin nodded toward Pierre. "You first."

"Mine is *très simple*. I watched Café Violette blow up. I spared a few seconds to mourn the loss. I saw Bauer racing toward the club shouting, and I knew it was time to go."

I opened my mouth to ask, but Pierre knew what the question was. "Gaspard died in the blast. I saw his body. Whether this was his intention or if he, how you say, miscalculated the time he needed to set off the devices…who is to tell? But I ran to hide with the companions I knew who had helped save so many of the British pilots." He flashed a wry smile. "We did not know until after the war we were called the *Résistance*. We only knew we were providing assistance with what the Germans said were 'clandestine activities.' *Mes amis* sheltered me for the rest of the night and then, through the usual route, I left Paris and headed to my cousin's farm. This is where I send also Michel and Val." He paused. "And you will be pleased to hear both of them survived the war and they moved back to Paris. Val is entertaining again at a club not far from where Café Violette stood, and Michel is sommelier."

I smiled with relief. "I'm so glad. I was terrified they'd be caught. Two great people who didn't deserve the garbage the Nazis were trying to throw at them. I want to hear all about them later. For now, go on with your story, please?"

Pierre continued. "I stayed for a day and a night and then was joined by your father. The rest is his story."

I turned to my dad. "Out with it. I went nuts worrying about what happened after we saw you take off in the car with the girls. We couldn't really see anything from where we were hiding, which was a wrecked and abandoned *patisserie* down the block from *l'Opéra Blanche*. And then of course, we, uh, escaped."

He winked at me. He knew what "escaped" actually represented.

"Well, Cori, I hate to say it was fun, but in a way it was, because I had the opportunity to drive one amazing car while being terrified I'd be shot the moment I stopped and parked. Anyway, we're in the limo, the Nazi chauffeur is on the ground with the Mouse King head on top of him, and I start to drive like I'm in Indianapolis at a racetrack. We arrive outside Hauptmann's residence. It was nuts, but I figured we had a better chance if all seemed 'normal' with the car, and we could leave from Hauptmann's. So we get to Hauptmann's place, and some German officer holds up his hand and we are forced to stop. There was a bunch of cars there and we couldn't just plow our way through."

"Oh, man. I'm tense just imagining this scene," I said.

"Hey, I'm tense just remembering. I freely admit I was scared this would be the end. But, to continue, I brake the car and the soldier comes over and I lean out the window and pray the officer can't see the bottom of what should be a uniform is really the bottom of a Mouse King costume…and bloody to boot."

"Bloody?"

My dad nodded. "As we were struggling with the Mouse Head, the guard got off a shot. Grazed my leg. Thankfully, not an artery."

"Dad!"

"I'm okay, Sweetie. Like I said, not life-threatening. Just painful, especially when shifting gears. But Rosemarie managed to bind it up while we were driving. Used a scarf. Amazing woman. Not to mention, smart as a whip. Anyway, I tell the guard at Hauptmann's residence I'm driving everyone to the party he's hosting for the swans from the ballet and we are late. He stares daggers at us all."

"*Attendez*. In the car is you, Rosemarie, Delys, and Paulette?" asked Noel.

"Yes." My dad laughed. "And, bless her, this is when Paulette, the sweet English rose, shows her thorny side. She'd been wearing the swan mask, but she tears it off and announces in her snootiest voice that she is the prima ballerina and special invited guest of Herr Hauptmann and if this low-rank soldier continues to delay us, he will answer to the *Oberkapitän* himself. I had no clue what a brilliant actress she could be. And the courage it took? Incredible."

"Well, I always knew she was brave," I told him.

"Definitely. Wish I could have given her a medal on the spot. Anyway, the guard tells us to drive to the back entrance and park under the awning so we'll be dry and the ladies won't ruin their gowns. Very fortuitous, that rain. We drive to the back, but from there I floored it. We went zooming down the road before anyone had a clue what was really happening. Pierre had already arranged to have his friends meet us all in a patch of wooded area outside Paris, no matter *when* we arrived.

"I will spare you the boredom of the details because it really was just a matter of getting on a plane from there and heading to England. Paulette stayed. Delys, Rosemarie, and I decided to come to America, but we had to stay in England for the next couple of years. The best thing was when we were finally able to take the boat to the States, we were joined by Pierre. And, of course, by Fiona Belle. She knew I'd planned to come to New Orleans after the war…but I was very much a wanted man following the escape in Paris…and the bullet wound did more damage to my leg than I thought at the time. Result being I couldn't enlist for combat.

"America hadn't yet entered the war, and I was working for the Brits, who knew I was handy breaking codes. No one would suspect a theatrical designer in New Orleans of being able to knock the socks off of cyphers." He grinned at me. "The end. Sorry. Long story."

I reached across the table and grabbed his hand. "You tell it well and better…there's a happy ending."

Pierre smiled. "More than one."

"Which leads me to…where is Delys now? You said she was able to escape. Is she also here in New Orleans?"

Pierre nodded. "Yes. She is out now with the parade. But she did not come with us to America at first. She escaped with everyone to England, and then she discovered where her Maman was, with a certain black dancer with the *Résistance*. She was able to join them, and she helped with their activities as well."

Rosemarie came back in, bearing a tray with a bucket and a bottle of champagne and five stemmed glasses, and overheard him. "Cori, after the war was over, Delys came to America and we got to reunite. And she has asked all the time if you were safe and to tell her if you ever arrived here because she will…how did she say? Hug you until you were all squeezed out."

My dad added, "We want her to start a dance school here. There are too many black kids unable to have the benefit of learning arts because of white-only studios."

"She'd be amazing. It's a great idea. She's so badly needed. Maybe I can join her and teach some music."

He and I exchanged a quick look. Bigotry wouldn't dissipate with the end of a war, but if anyone could help lead the battle, it would be Delys. He rose and helped Rosemarie with the tray with champagne and glasses. "So much to celebrate!"

Rosemarie smiled at him. "Have you told her?"

"I was just about to. I wanted you here first."

"Told me what?" I asked.

"About six months after arriving in England, Rosemarie and I got married." He grinned, then took Rosemarie's hand in his. "I used my real name at the church, so let me proudly introduce Mrs. Robin Christopher!"

I couldn't help it. I squealed with delight. Rosemarie, and my own sense when I first met her, had been right about us sharing a future. My stepmom and good friend. More hugging ensued, with no tears now.

Robin turned to Noel. "So enough about me. Monsieur Matheson, exactly what are your plans?"

Noel laughed. "If you're asking about work, I have yet to make a plan. If you are asking about my intentions toward your wonderful daughter—yes, I have been aware of your relationship—the answer is, um, now there is a beautiful lady in the Christopher family to use your name, I would like Cori to become part of the Matheson family and bear my name." He reached out and grabbed both my hands. "This is not how I planned to ask you. We are dirty and tired and hungry and in shock over all things that happened over these past...weeks. But there is already champagne arriving and I have learned time is a very precious thing and I do not want to waste any moments given me, and so now I ask, will you marry me?"

As proposals go, it wasn't traditional. And I didn't care. I wasn't into tradition. I was into love.

"Of course I'll marry you! Yes! Yes! *Oui!*"

A kiss passionate enough to curl my toes but with enough modesty not to embarrass anyone around us sealed the deal.

Pierre tapped Noel on the shoulder. "You mention work. As it so happens, the club you are now in belongs to me and to Monsieur Christopher. We are in need of singers as well as persons who are able to run things backstage and supervise kitchen activities. As you see, this is not a small New Orleans saloon. I wanted to give Americans a taste of the Paris we knew before the Occupation."

"Offering me a job, Papa Pierre?" Noel inquired.

"*Oui.*"

"I accept, as long as Cori Christopher, soon to be Matheson, agrees to be onstage singing as often as she likes. My partner in life and in music."

"Cori likes," I stated. "But, and I hesitate because I don't want to bring up sad memories, I'm curious. The name of this club—Gabriel's Horn—is it…?"

There was a brief silence before Pierre quietly said, "It is. We named it in honor of my nephew."

My eyes misted again. "I never knew him, but I'm sure it's a tribute he would love. People from everywhere coming to the café for nights to enjoy music with their friends and loved ones. It's brilliant, Papa."

We all lifted our glasses and toasted to marriages—one going into a sixth year and one yet to come—and to friendship, to loyalty and bravery, and to the success of Gabriel's Horn.

"This is silly, because I'm starving and I do want to eat," I said, "but I have this odd feeling I just need to tour the club first. Wander around by myself for a bit and soak in everything, if you guys don't mind?"

Papa Pierre beamed at me. "Of course. We will have the food ready for you when you come back. Cori, as yet, the ladies' dressing room is empty. We have not found any female singers to match your talent. I kept hoping we would someday be joined by Mademoiselle Cori Christopher. So…please, become acquainted with what will be your new venue to sing. The dressing room for the ladies will need your touch."

My dad gave me another wink. "And for once, you can take in the whole space without worrying about escape routes."

I spent the next few minutes just peering into the kitchen, gazing up at the catwalk leading to the lighting booth, and wandering through the very tiny "green room" used as the actors' lounge.

As I headed down the hall from the green room, pausing for a quick peek into the men's dressing room, I caught a whiff of fresh pastries. The scent apparently came from the bakery I'd noticed when Noel and I were about two buildings away from the club, and I hoped Gabriel's Horn had worked out an arrangement with the owner for sweet treats for its patrons.

I opened the door to the women's dressing room conveniently located next to a non-gender-specific restroom.

It was small but not nearly as tiny as the broom closet I'd inhabited for the months I'd worked at Café Violette. A wardrobe rack took up space against the wall, facing two tables with lights and mirrors. It would be nice not to have to use a restroom for applying makeup and fastening buttons on a dress. Yet, oddly, I knew I would miss escaping to my sheltered dressing room after singing for the mixed crowd at Café Violette. I would not miss wondering if Herr Bauer was standing just outside, waiting for his chance to destroy me, to destroy my friends.

The moment I entered the room, I spotted a hat stand on a table under the window. I drew closer. Resting on top was the black fedora I'd last seen at Jericho when I'd neglected to cram it into my bag. Ajay's fedora. The same hat I hadn't had time to go back and get if I wanted to save Noel. Next to the hat rack lay the sheet music for "Johnny Has Gone for a Soldier," the song I'd been inspired to sing, thanks to an enigmatic, fierce lady with a penchant for creative costumes, one big heart, and the talent to push people to do courageous deeds.

"Cori?"

I turned. Noel joined me in the small dressing room. "I followed a wonderful scent down the hall. There must be a *pâtisserie* nearby." He glanced at the hat stand. "*Intéressant.* Just how is it you could get your fedora here? I thought you lost it in New York. *Pardon.* I meant to say New Manhattan."

"Forget New Manhattan. No one in this time needs to hear anything but Manhattan or New York City. Well, except my dad. But it's wicked-cool finding the hat. Do you suppose Fiona Belle knows we're now safe and free to live our lives together? I'm guessing she figured we'd try to make our way to New Orleans and Gabriel's Horn, and she dropped off Ajay's hat for me? You're right, by the way. I left it behind when I was rushing to find you."

Noel put his arm around me, dropped a light kiss on my forehead, and smiled. "And you did, in perfect timing. For which I am very grateful and happy. But, Cori, you were asking about Fiona Belle? Something tells me she visited very recently. Look."

I'd been so excited to be reunited with Ajay's hat, I hadn't yet noticed. I glanced down at the table. We'd both been wrong about the scent of pastries coming from some establishment outside and down the street. Resting on top of the sheet music was a large plate of freshly baked, still warm from the oven, cranberry-orange scones.

A word about the author...

Flo Fitzpatrick was born in Washington, D.C. and spent her first years living in a chateau in France (as an Army brat). Flo received a B.F.A. in Dance from Southern Methodist University and an M.A. in Theater from Baylor University.

She is multi-published in romance and mystery, with a great deal of genre overlap and often adding paranormal elements and/or humor. Her second novel, *Hot Stuff*, was nominated as Best Romantic Suspense (2005) by RT Book Reviews and optioned for film.

Flo is now living in Alabama with her ancestrally-challenged mutt Juniper where (before Covid) she used her performing chops to sing with a jazz band called The Usual Suspects.

www.flofitzpatrick.com

~*~

Watch for more romantic time travel adventures featuring tall, smart, and sassy redheads sent by the enigmatic Fiona Belle Donovan into eras where strong heroines can change history.

Thank you for purchasing
this publication of The Wild Rose Press, Inc.

For questions or more information
contact us at
info@thewildrosepress.com.

The Wild Rose Press, Inc.
www.thewildrosepress.com

www.ingramcontent.com/pod-product-compliance
Ingram Content Group UK Ltd.
Pitfield, Milton Keynes, MK11 3LW, UK
UKHW020959030325
455781UK00011B/470